Rosie Hendry lives by the sea in Norfolk with her husband and two children. She is the author of the East End Angels series, uplifting and heart-warming sagas that follow the lives and loves of Winnie, Frankie and Bella, who all work for the London Auxiliary Ambulance Service (LAAS) during the Blitz. Listening to her father's tales of life during the Second World War sparked Rosie's interest in this period and she loves researching further, seeking out gems of real-life events which inspire her writing.

Keep up-to-date with Rosie by following her on Twitter, becoming her friend on Facebook or visiting her website:

@hendry_rosie
rosie.hendry.94
www.rosiehendry.com

Rosie HENDRY

The Mother's Day Club

sphere

SPHERE

First published in Great Britain in 2021 by Sphere

1 3 5 7 9 10 8 6 4 2

A CIP catalogue record for this book
is available from the British Library.

ISBN 978-0-7515-7570-5

Typeset in Bembo by M Rules
Printed and bound in Great Britain by
Clays Ltd, Elcograf S.p.A.

Papers used by Sphere are from well-managed forests
and other responsible sources.

Sphere
An imprint of
Little, Brown Book Group
Carmelite House
50 Victoria Embankment
London EC4Y 0DZ

An Hachette UK Company
www.hachette.co.uk

www.littlebrown.co.uk

In memory of Maggie Jackson
1948–2020

The Mother's Day Club

Chapter 1

East End, London – 3 September 1939

It was a beautiful late-summer day with a blue sky soaring high above the East End streets and Marianne Archer was in a hurry, her gas mask box banging against her hip and her heavy suitcase making her slower than usual. Her step faltered as she spotted a newspaper billboard set out on the pavement ahead of her and read the bold message printed in stark black and white: 'Peace or War?' It made her catch her breath. Would it *really* come to war?

She'd listened to the wireless, read the newspapers and seen all the preparations going on around London, and she knew full well that the country was teetering on the brink of war, but deep down she'd held on to the hope that somehow, by some miracle, it wouldn't come to it, and that something would happen even now, at the last minute, to stop it.

Looking up at the sky, which looked so perfect today, without a single cloud to mar the blue, you'd never know what was going on, she thought, never know what chaos was probably about to be unleashed.

Pushing on past the billboard, she followed the stream of people heading to the local school where all evacuees had been instructed to gather. The sight of so many evacuees carrying their luggage through the streets had become a familiar one in the last few days. The children had been the first to go; now it was the turn of the expectant mothers, and Marianne was glad to be leaving, not just because of the threat of war and what it might bring here, but because London had turned sour for her. What had started out as an exciting adventure and blossoming career had gone badly wrong and she was eager for a new start.

Inside the school, she joined the end of the queue of people waiting to register their arrival, relieved to put down her suitcase at last. Looking around her, she saw that the hall was already busy – not just the expectant mothers and young children who were preparing to leave, but also their relatives and even some husbands too, who'd clearly come to see them off. The noise level was rising steadily among the swirl of cigarette smoke, people having to speak ever louder to make themselves heard above the din of chatter, grizzling children and even a few weeping women.

The queue shuffled forwards slowly. The woman ahead of Marianne had to heave her fractious toddler up on to her hip, her swollen stomach making it impossible for her to hold the child in her arms in front of her. Nudging her brown suitcase forward with her foot, Marianne looked down at her own growing belly – it was impossible now to do up more than the top three buttons on her thin summer coat; there was no hiding the fact that she was expecting any more.

'Next.' The mother in front of Marianne had been dealt with and moved off, heaving her toddler and string bag of belongings with her. The WVS woman sitting at the desk looked up at Marianne through her round glasses and smiled. 'Your name?'

'Marianne Archer.'

She ran her finger down the list, found Marianne's name and put a tick beside it. 'If you'd like to take a seat . . . ' She looked around the hall and shrugged: there wasn't an empty seat to be had. 'We weren't expecting *quite* so many family members to turn up. We'll be leaving shortly anyway, so you won't have long to wait.'

'All right, thank you.' Marianne picked up her suitcase and went to stand by the open door where the fresh air, or at least what passed for that around here, was blowing in on a welcome breeze, ruffling her dark brown, shoulder-length wavy hair. She could smell the distinctive tang of the East End – chimney smoke from the many homes and factories combined with a salty twist from the docks and the River Thames. Proper fresh, clean air that didn't irritate your nose was something she was looking forward to again, along with wide skies, space and greenery. She had lived in London for the past four years, coming to work here when she was sixteen, but the city had never truly felt like home. In fact, Marianne dearly missed the countryside, so now, being evacuated to a place that didn't have a shop on every corner, buses one after the other, or street after street of terraced houses, would be no hardship for her.

They set off walking through the streets towards Liverpool Street station a short while later, forming a raggle-taggle line behind a WVS evacuation officer in her smart green uniform, who, like a modern-day Pied Piper, was leading them to safety. Many of the evacuees carried luggage that looked inadequate for the journey ahead, their belongings stuffed into string or paper bags, sacks or cardboard boxes; not many of the expectant mothers had a suitcase like Marianne.

As they passed through the streets where some of them lived, the evacuees' neighbours stood in their front doorways watching them go and calling out tearful farewells.

'Look after yourself, ducks.'

'We'll keep the 'ome fires burning for yer.'

There was a real sense of loss in the air as part of their community was leaving, Marianne thought, looking at the women who were waving them off and wiping their eyes with their spotlessly clean handkerchiefs. The East Enders were a close-knit bunch, sharing their ups and downs, helping each other out, so to have mothers evacuated was like taking the beating heart out of their homes, and they'd be sorely missed by those they left behind.

She couldn't say the same about herself, though. Her departure was leaving nothing but an empty room behind, and her landlady probably had a new tenant lined up already. There was no one around here to be sad that she was going, but that was the way she'd wanted it. Moving to the East End to work in a clothing factory two months ago and live anonymously had been the best thing to do, but seeing the emotion and heartfelt tears of friends and family saying their goodbyes tugged at her heart and prodded at the loneliness she'd felt since then. Making the best of a situation wasn't always easy, her gran had often said, but that's what she'd had to do.

'Dad says to tell you, Chamberlain says it's war!' A boy hurtled out of one of the houses, broadcasting the news as he ran up to one mother just ahead of Marianne, grabbing at her hand. 'He just said so on the wireless.'

Surprisingly, no one stopped at the momentous news, the formation kept on moving, and although it wasn't unexpected, the certainty that they were now at war with Germany made Marianne's heart sink. It was little more than twenty years since the last time they'd been pitched against this enemy, and she'd grown up with the shadow of the last war blighting her life – her father had been killed in the last few months before she was born. She'd heard the stories of the muddy trenches and the huge death toll, seen the men with shattered lives and missing limbs. That had been the war to end all wars, and yet here it was, happening all over again.

The sudden sound of an air-raid siren began to wail out across the rooftops, its eerie cry rising and falling again and again, like some wounded animal. It changed the mood like the flick of a switch, and the formation faltered. People halted, looking up at the sky, their eyes wide in shock. Several mothers began to cry, and toddlers, picking up on the women's distress, added their own wails.

Marianne looked around her, uncertain what to do. Could the Germans be about to bomb them so soon? A passing red double-decker bus pulled over to the side of the road, the driver and passengers spilling out in panic and quickly disappearing down side streets. Should they do the same?

One of the evacuation officers clapped her hands and shouted, 'Keep moving!'

'Don't stop! We need to get to Liverpool Street,' another added, working her way down the column encouraging everyone to move off again. They did as they were told; no one questioned it or ran off, but they quickened their pace, adults picking up any toddlers who were too slow, everyone anxious to reach the station and get under cover.

'You'd best go back, Granddad,' a young woman near Marianne said to the old man who was accompanying her. 'If they comes, you can't run. I can't let the Nazis catch you.'

'Curse 'em. I ain't letting you go alone.' The old man shook his stick at the sky and kept on walking, doing his best to keep up.

There'd been no sound of aeroplanes approaching or bombs falling, but Marianne still felt hugely relieved when they finally arrived and had the domed roof of Liverpool Street station, with its ornate iron beams, between her and any enemy planes.

'This way,' the leading evacuation officer shouted in her loud plummy voice. She led them across the busy station

6

concourse where the air smelt of burning coal from the steam engines, parting the people hurrying to and fro, like Moses had the Red Sea.

As they reached the barrier at platform ten, the steady sound of the all-clear rang out and the atmosphere lightened. They were safe – for now, at least.

'Evacuees only on the platform,' another WVS woman called. 'There isn't room for everyone so you'll need to say your goodbyes here.'

Marianne side-stepped the families saying their tearful farewells, grateful now that she didn't have the emotional wrench of having to leave loved ones behind. Quite the opposite, in fact: she was glad to be going. From the way some of the expectant mothers were clinging to their husbands or relatives, tears streaming down their faces, they didn't share her feelings.

Walking past the railway guards who stood by the barrier to make sure that no other family members sneaked on to the platform, she headed to the far end of the train that stood ready to take them to safety and climbed aboard a carriage. She chose a compartment, slid open the door, stowed her case and settled herself by the window facing the engine, so she'd be able to enjoy the view as they travelled.

As Marianne waited for the train to fill up, her mind wandered over the possibilities of what lay ahead. She tried to calm the tingle of apprehension that had lodged itself in her chest, visualising what it might be like, who she would be billeted with. She hoped it was someone nice; she'd done her best to look presentable, wearing the new dress she'd designed and made herself with its pin-tuck detail on the bodice, in a beautiful deep green fabric that went well with her green eyes. It was important to make a good first impression – another of her gran's many sayings. She smiled as she pictured her saying it so many times as she'd grown up, though what she would say about the situation Marianne had got herself into she hardly dared think. Perhaps it was just as well that Gran had passed away a year ago now, because she'd have been bitterly disappointed in her, and that would have been nearly as hard to bear as her own anger at her stupidity and naivety.

'Excuse me, is that seat taken?'

Marianne was pulled out of her thoughts and looked up to see an auburn-haired young woman standing in the open doorway of the compartment and pointing at the empty seat opposite her. In fact, it was the only empty seat left – while Marianne had been absorbed in her own world, the other seats had filled up with another expectant mother and her two little girls and two other women who had pulled out their knitting and were already busy, their needles clicking.

She smiled at her. 'No.'

'Oh, thank Gawd.' She shuffled past the other occupants' legs and stuffed her bag of belongings in the overhead luggage rack then plopped herself down on the seat. 'I'd begun to think I'd 'ave to stand all the way to wherever we're goin'. The train's filled up so fast, but I 'ad to stay with my Arthur for as long as I could, and then the WVS woman was chivvyin' me to get a shift on or

8

the train would go without me.' She paused for breath and stuck out her hand with a friendly smile. 'I'm Sally Parker.'

Marianne shook her hand. 'Marianne Archer.' She smiled at the other woman, noticing her red-rimmed eyes and pink-tipped nose.

'Pleased to meet you, Marianne. Are you looking forward to this? Cos I ain't, but my Arthur said I 'ad to go for the sake of this one.' She stroked her stomach, which protruded from her slender frame like a football, pushing out the front of her floral dress. 'He's going to enlist for the Army right away, not wait to be called up, so he won't be around here anyway. Did your hubby want you to go too?'

Marianne nodded.

'He come and see you off?'

'No.'

'That's a shame.' Sally frowned. 'Couldn't he get time off work?'

'He's in the Navy, at sea.' The words tripped awkwardly off Marianne's tongue.

'Well, he'll be glad you're on your way to safety.'

Marianne nodded, relieved when they were distracted by a sudden loud blast from the guard's whistle outside. Soon the carriage began to move, the platform slipping past, as the steam engine at the head of the train belched out great chuffs of sooty smoke that swirled up to the ornate station roof.

'Where do yer think we're going?' Sally asked as they cleared the gloom of the station and slipped out into the beautiful sunshine.

Marianne looked at this young woman, who suddenly seemed very vulnerable and nervous in spite of all her chatter. 'I don't know, we haven't been told, but as we're leaving from Liverpool Street, I'd guess it must be somewhere in the east, not Devon or Wales.'

'Right out in the countryside, then?'

'Yes. And away from where they might drop bombs.'

Sally stared out of the window for a few moments. 'I ain't been out to the countryside much before, I've been 'op picking a couple of times down in Kent, but that's all.'

'It will be different from London, but I'm sure it'll be fine,' Marianne said. 'Better to be safe.'

Sally nodded, leaning against the back of her seat. 'That's what my Arthur said.' She rubbed her hand across her stomach. 'So, when's yours due? Mine should be 'ere by Christmas.'

'Late January for me.'

'Will your husband be home before then to see yer?' Sally asked. 'Arthur's promised to come and visit me when 'e can, though once he's in the Army it'll be up to them when he's allowed.'

'I'm not sure.' Marianne looked down at the still-shiny gold ring on the third finger of her left hand. She'd bought it herself.

'Well, yer can always write letters in the meantime, can't yer?' Sally said as they passed row upon row of tightly packed terrace houses.

'Of course.'

'My Arthur says he can't wait to get my first letter ... '

Marianne listened to Sally chattering on, the young

10

woman having enough to say for both of them, while the wheels of the train clickety-clacked beneath them. Through the window the streets gradually gave way to more greenery, space and light, and the sight made her heart lift. Wherever they were heading had to be better for her than London had turned out to be.

Chapter 2

Rookery House, Great Plumstead, Norfolk

Thea Thornton flicked her wrists, sending the clean white sheet billowing out to settle over the mattress of the single bed, and breathed in the smell of the lavender that she'd picked and dried this summer to scent the linen press. Tucking in the sides and corners, she worked quickly, adding another sheet on top, then a blanket, turning back the top end of the upper sheet over the thicker woollen cloth to make a neat finish, and finally spreading out the dusky-pink feather eiderdown over the top. Pulling the eiderdown straight and smoothing the satiny material with her hand, she smiled at the thought of who'd be sleeping in here tonight: their evacuee — a child who'd been whisked away from London because of the risk of war.

She was looking forward to a child living here with her at Rookery House, having the chance to give them a home away from home, one where they'd feel safe and be well looked after. It was both exciting and terrifying in equal measure. It would be a massive change in her life and for the evacuee too, who would not only have been forced to leave their family to come and live with strangers, but would be moving to the alien environment of the countryside. Life in Great Plumstead was a world away from the busy streets of London, and Thea knew from experience that such a change would take some adjusting to.

She'd made the move herself, although in reverse – from here to London; but she'd been an adult when she'd taken the plunge and already had some experience of living somewhere different as she'd gone to drive ambulances in France during the Great War. Still, going from village life to the city had been a huge shock; the noise and busyness had been overwhelming at first. She'd longed to be able to see further than the end of the road. The world seemed to have shrunk, closed in by the buildings that were packed in so close together that the views of the sky were limited to patches above the crowded streets. It had taken her a long time to adjust. Starting her business and growing it had absorbed her time and energy but it had eventually led her back here now, some seventeen years later, after she'd sold up and returned home just three months ago to buy this house. Now, with the country teetering on the verge of war, it was probably none too soon either.

Thea looked around the room, with its cast-iron fire-place, sash window overlooking the back garden, wooden wardrobe and chest of drawers that shone with elbow grease and beeswax polish. She still pinched herself some-times, hardly believing that she was actually living here, the owner of Rookery House, the house that she'd loved from as long ago as she could remember. As a child she had often stopped to admire the house, saying to herself that one day, if she could, she'd live here, and now ... here she was, forty-one years old and with her life-long dream come true.

Rookery House was a detached Victorian house, set back from the road, lying a quarter of a mile out of the village with a generous three and a half acres of land to go with it, which looked out over woods and fields. Its name came from the rookery in the stand of tall elm trees some fifty yards down the lane from the house, where the birds filled the air with their plaintive cawing in the spring, while they tended their chicks in their twiggy nests. Thea loved them, the sound of their calls instantly calming her, and their flying antics on a windy day making her smile, their sheer joy in riding the wind plain to see.

This house, with its five bedrooms, was far bigger than she needed just for herself, but Thea was intent on filling it up. She'd invited her friend Hettie to come and live with her, the older woman having recently retired from her job as cook up at Great Plumstead Hall. Reuben, Thea's older brother, had accepted her invitation too, although he refused to live in the house, preferring to set up home in an old railway carriage he'd bought and sited over by the orchard. He said he wanted peace and quiet, and it was probably a wise move with the way Hettie liked to talk, but he often joined them for meals. The loss of his wife the previous year had hit him hard, so a move to live nearby had been a compromise, one that suited them both: she could keep an eye on him, but he could go his own way without bothering anyone.

So for the five bedrooms, this one would soon be the evacuee's, she and Hettie had one each, and the other two would be ready for anyone who needed them. Thea liked having people around her and whoever might come to stay in those rooms in the future would be most welcome.

Going over to the window, she looked out over the back garden to where Reuben and her sister's two boys – her nephews, Jack and Edwin – were digging a hole for the Anderson shelter. It looked like it must surely be big enough soon, the pile of earth they'd dug out like a monstrous mole hill on the grass. Was it really necessary to have it? she wondered. Well, it was best to be prepared, and with the way things were heading most people were saying it was only a matter of *when*, not *if*, war would be declared; but ever the optimist, Thea refused to give up hope that peace would prevail and she'd hold on to that until proved wrong.

This morning the British Ambassador in Berlin handed the German Government a final note stating that, unless we heard from them by eleven o'clock that they were prepared at once to withdraw their troops from Poland, a state of war would exist between us. I have to tell you now that no such undertaking has been received, and that consequently this country is at war with Germany.

Thea let out the breath she'd been holding as the fate

15

of the country, which had been balancing so precariously on the edge of peace, finally crashed down on the side of war. She breathed in slowly, her heart heavy – although there'd been so much talk of war on the news broadcasts, in the newspapers, by people gossiping in the village shop, she'd still held on to the conviction that it wouldn't come to war again in her lifetime. Hadn't lessons been learned from last time? Apparently not.

Glancing around at everyone else as they listened to the Prime Minister's broadcast, she tried to gauge their reactions. Sixty-year-old Hettie's lips were pressed together, her blue eyes bright with tears behind her round glasses, red spots appearing on her plump cheeks as she fished a clean handkerchief out of her cardigan pocket.

Standing just outside the open half-glass doors that led out of the sitting room into the back garden, Reuben chewed on the stem of his unlit pipe, his forehead creased in a deep frown. Her nephew Edwin stood beside him, an identical expression on his face. Only her other nephew, Jack, who leaned on the door frame, looked as though he welcomed the news.

'Well, that's that, then!' Reuben sighed as the broadcast finished and Thea switched off the wireless. A widower at fifty, he'd served in the Great War, spending four years in the trenches and seeing their brother William killed in action in front of him. 'Hitler wouldn't back down; it was a lost cause appealing to his better nature.'

'I really hoped he would,' Thea said. 'He knew what would happen if he didn't.'

'Bloody Hitler!' Hettie muttered, pulling a face. 'He's

probably glad we're at war, he's a nasty blighter. Never did like the look of him, and now look what he's gone and caused.'

'We couldn't let him get away with invading Poland, though, could we?' Jack said, his eyes feverishly bright. 'We've got to stop him.'

Reuben looked at his nephews and shook his head, putting his unlit pipe back in the pocket of his old tweed jacket that had seen better days. 'Come on, you two, we'd better get the shelter finished; we might be needing it after all, if bombers come our way.' He turned to go but then stopped, nodding his head in the direction of Wykeham. 'Hear that?'

Bess, his devoted collie, started to whine, joining in with the rising and falling wail of the air-raid siren that they could just make out coming from the nearest market town four miles away.

Thea hurried over to the open doors to see what was happening.

'Are they here already?' Hettie followed her, craning her neck to peer up at the sky and search for enemy planes, her grey curly hair bobbing about.

'Doubt it,' Reuben said. 'Probably just testing it and putting the wind up everyone.' He shook his head and headed back to the site of the Anderson shelter, Bess following faithfully at his heels as always.

'It's hard to believe we're actually at war,' Jack said. 'It doesn't feel any different, though.'

'Not yet,' Thea said, 'but it will. Try to remember how it felt before the start of this war, and hold on to that inside, because if it's anything like the last one and it goes on and on, then it'll get harder and harder to remember a time when there was peace.'

'You were right to get a shelter, Aunt Thea. Best to be safe.' Jack smiled at her. 'I'd better get back to work.' He strode off to join Reuben, who was already back at work, thrusting his spade into the ground with more force than was necessary, stamping down on it hard, venting his feelings with his actions rather than words. She knew he'd be feeling this deeply and she would need to keep a close eye on him.

'Do you really forget what living in peace feels like in wartime?' Edwin asked.

Thea turned her attention to him. At twenty, and one year younger than his brother Jack, Edwin was the quieter and more sensitive of the two. 'Yes, and I fear this war will be worse; it won't just be going on out there in France and Belgium, it'll hit us at home more than ever before. The war will come to us this time.'

Edwin nodded, his blue eyes solemn.

'I'd like to see Hitler turn up in my kitchen, I'd give him what for,' Hettie said.

'I don't think he'd dare.' Thea smiled at the older woman. 'Seriously, though, things have moved on a lot since the Great War, aeroplanes go faster and further. Remember how the German Luftwaffe bombed that town in Spain? The Government must think it'll happen here too, or why else would they encourage us to put up Anderson shelters, have air-raid sirens and give us all gas masks?'

18

'I'm not frightened,' Edwin said. 'I'm just sad it's come to this.'

'So am I, but it is what it is, and we're going to have to live with it, there's nothing you or I can do to stop it, and things will change — they've already started to.' She looked to where Reuben and Jack were digging. 'We've got evacuees arriving in the village today. Life's already changing because of the war whether we like it or not.'

'My buns!' Hettie suddenly yelped. 'I nearly forgot! They'll be burning if I don't look out.' She rushed off to the kitchen.

'You'll be all right.' Thea touched her nephew's arm. 'Go on, go and help the others and I'll bring you all out a drink and one of Hettie's warm currant buns.'

Watching Edwin walk away, Thea blinked away the sudden tears that welled up in her eyes. Blasted war! Why couldn't everyone just live in peace with each other? Didn't they remember that last time had cost millions of lives — and for what? Had another generation, lads like Jack and Edwin, been born and grown up just to feed the guns of war?

Enough of that, she told herself, sniffing back her tears; maudlin thoughts weren't going to get her anywhere. She just had to get on with it; they all did. She closed the outside doors and headed to the kitchen where the currant buns were now out of the oven, piled up on the wire rack to cool and filling the room with a mouth-watering aroma.

'They smell delicious.' Thea picked up a still-warm bun, broke a bit off, blowing on it to cool it down, before popping it in her mouth, chewing slowly to savour the flavour and juicy sweetness of the currants. 'And taste good too. The evacuees are going to love them.'

'Good, the poor little mites will be hungry by the time they get here.' Hettie poured hot water into the teapot, then returned the kettle to the side of the hot plate on top of the range, which was lit, as always, to provide heat for cooking and hot water. 'There'll hopefully be a good spread for them.'

'Prue's persuaded a lot of people to contribute to the welcome tea, so I'm sure it will be a good one.' Thea's younger sister Prue was in charge of organising the tea, ably supported by other women from the village's Women's Institute.

'She's got it all planned to the last detail; you know what she's like, she's in her element with something like this to organise, and now war's actually been declared she'll be into everything, all in a good cause.'

Hettie took off her glasses, huffed her breath on them and cleaned them with the cloth of her wrap-around, blue paisley-print apron. 'Do you really think we'll have to go and sleep in that shelter?'

Thea swallowed her mouthful of bun. 'You don't like the idea?'

Hettie shrugged as she put her glasses back on. 'It's not natural, is it? I'd rather stay in here by the range; it's much more cosy in here.'

'I know,' Thea agreed, glancing around the kitchen. It was certainly warm and cosy, with its black range at one end sunk into the chimney breast, the large scrubbed wooden table around which they sat for their meals and which doubled up as a work space when they were cooking, the red quarry-tiled floor with its rag rugs. The large stone sink, with its hand pump to bring water up from the well, was by the window looking out over the back garden. The view was framed by pretty yellow curtains with blue flowers that gently stirred in the soft breeze coming in through the open window. Two dressers lined the walls, where the china was kept, Thea's favourite blue and white patterned cups and plates looking fresh and cheerful.

Leading off the kitchen was the sizeable pantry, its shelves lined with food, including jars of pickles and jam that they'd made, which would be added to over the coming months as more fruit was harvested and stored for the winter.

At the far end of the room, a doorway led into a single-storey annexe that now housed the scullery, with its copper for heating water for doing the laundry, another sink and the mangle for squeezing the water out of washed clothes. Beyond that, Thea had had a bathroom installed because after years of living in London where her flat had had an indoor bathroom, she didn't want to go back to the days of having to bathe in a tin bath in front of the fire. It had been worth spending money on putting in a bathtub, sink and indoor lavatory. Now she could have the luxury of a bath in a full-sized tub and not have to traipse outside on a cold night to use the lavatory. She'd decided to keep the old outdoor lavatory too, as it was handy if you were working outside. A bathroom upstairs would have been even better, but she'd had to make allowances because with no electricity or gas here, unlike in London, getting water upstairs was problematic. It was more practical to house the bathroom on the ground floor where water wouldn't have to be pumped upwards, and it was easy to heat it in the tank behind the bathroom stove.

The changes that Thea had made here since she'd arrived had made the house more comfortable and she felt very much at home here, with the kitchen being the place they spent a lot of their time – it was like the beating heart of their home – and she had to agree with Hettie: it was far more appealing than a hole in the ground with a metal shell, but if the bombers came ...

'If bombs are being dropped the shelter will be safer than the house.' Seeing the worried look on the older woman's face, she added, 'But it may never come to that, it's just there if we need it. I don't suppose Great Plumstead's on Hitler's list of prime targets, but I'll feel happier knowing we've got somewhere to go to if the bombers come. We'll just be going underground like the rabbits do when there's a fox about.' She reached out and touched Hettie's arm. 'We'll be fine. It's just a precaution, that's all.'

Thea didn't like seeing Hettie looking so worried; she was normally such an upbeat, feisty person, but the news that they were at war again had clearly hit home with her. She'd know Hettie all her life as she'd been a close friend of Thea's mother, and had spent her working life in the kitchens at the Hall, eventually rising to become the cook. It was where Thea had had her first job, working alongside Hettie in the kitchens after she'd left school and before she left to do her bit in the Great War. Hettie had taught her a lot about cooking and it was that knowledge that she'd put to good use in her business in London. So, to have Hettie come and live with her after she'd retired was a blessing, a chance to spend time with a woman who she'd come to love as much as any blood relative.

'We'll see.' Hettie pulled a face. 'Right, will you take out the tea and buns for Reuben and the boys, while I get on with making some sandwiches for the evacuees?' She poured tea out of the brown earthenware teapot into three mugs. 'Digging's thirsty work and they'll be parched.'

'Of course.'

Carrying out a tray with mugs of tea and a plate of still-warm buns, Thea saw that Reuben and Edwin were now measuring the hole they'd dug. 'Is it big enough yet?' she asked.

'Seven foot, six inches long,' Reuben read off the tape measure. 'That'll do, we'll start fitting the shelter after a tea break.'

Jack climbed out of the four-foot-deep hole and joined Reuben and Edwin as they each took a mug and a currant bun. 'That'll be the easy bit, better than the digging.'

Thea looked at the curved, corrugated sheets that lay on the grass nearby, like upturned shells, imagining how they'd look once they were bolted together and put into the hole, then covered with soil and turf. She hoped that they never actually had to run to it for shelter, that it would remain just a precaution rather than a necessity.

Chapter 3

Prue Wilson and her fifteen-year-old daughter Alice shifted the last table into place and stood back to survey the arrangements.

'What do you think?' Prue asked.

'It looks fine, Ma.' Alice smiled at her. 'I don't think the children will be that bothered about how we've set it out, they'll be more interested in what there is to eat.'

They'd set the tables up in a long row on one side of the village hall, from where the food and drink would be served. Chairs had been placed around the other sides, where the children would be able to sit and eat before going to their new homes. The banner Alice had made was pinned up on the far wall, opposite the door, and declared 'Welcome' in bold blue lettering. Everything was looking as it should and as she'd planned it.

'There's just the plates and cups to sort out and then

we're ready for the food to come in,' Vera, one of the other women from the village's Women's Institute, said.

'Can you stay and organise that while I pick up the food I've promised to collect?' Prue asked.

Vera nodded. 'Of course.'

'Excellent. I'll be back in a while and then we can get it all set out and ready.' Prue glanced at her watch; it was now almost two o'clock. 'They're supposed to be arriving on the quarter-to-four train, so I'll be back here by three at the latest. Alice, you can come and help me.'

Prue picked up the empty wicker basket that she'd brought her own donation of sandwiches and cakes in, and trusting the other WI members to finish the preparations, she headed outside to where she'd parked her Austin 7 car. *So far, so good*, she thought, climbing in and starting the engine.

Today had been weeks in the planning: first surveying potential homes for the evacuee children, then persuading people to take strangers in to live with them. Not everyone had been keen, she recalled, reversing her car and turning it towards the first of her calls, but with a little persuasion and a firm reminder that the law required those with spare rooms to provide a billet, she had enough homes promised for the number of children they were being sent, plus the adults accompanying them.

'Where are we going first?' Alice asked as they drove past the row of village shops, which were all closed with it being a Sunday.

'To Thea's.' Prue glanced at Alice and smiled. 'We can see how they're getting on with the Anderson shelter.'

Taking the road leading out of the village, Prue thought how it still felt a novelty to have Thea back here in Great Plumstead after so many years away living in London, and how glad she was that she'd come home again. Thea had surprised them all by selling up her business and returning to buy Rookery House, which she'd loved as a child, and had always claimed she'd buy one day when she had the money. Prue had thought it was just one of the childish things she'd said and hadn't expected, when she'd mentioned that the house was up for sale in a letter to Thea, what outcome it would have. She wasn't the only one glad to have her home again. Jack, Edwin and Alice were delighted to have their aunt close by, and Reuben, too, although he'd never say as much. The only person who'd been less than keen on Thea's return was Prue's husband Victor, but then he and her sister had never seen eye to eye.

Prue slowed and turned in through the gate of Rookery House and came to a stop, switching off the engine and collecting her basket from the leather seat behind her. Outside, she could hear the sound of laughter coming from the back garden, so she and Alice followed the path around the side of the house. There they found Thea, Reuben and her sons laughing at poor Hettie, who stood in the entrance of the Anderson shelter, peering out like a toddler with just her head and shoulders showing above ground.

'I might be able to get in – or fall in, more like – but I aren't going to be able to get out again!' Hettie said, her plump face breaking into a smile as she joined in the laughter.

Reuben's dog spotted Prue and Alice and came rushing over, wagging her tail and alerting the others to their arrival. Alice bent down and made a great fuss of Bess, as she rolled over on to her back for a tummy rub.

'Prue! Alice! You're just in time to try out the new shelter,' Thea called.

'Only get in if you think you can get out again, but you're taller than me so you probably can,' Hettie said.

'I'll go and get a box for you to step on, to help you get out,' Reuben said and he disappeared into one of the sheds to look for one.

'You've done a good job,' Prue said, admiring the shelter. She smiled at her two sons – although strictly speaking, Jack and Edwin were her *step*sons, but she never thought of them like that; as far as she was concerned, from the moment she'd married their father, she'd loved the two boys as if they were her own. At just one and two years of age, they'd been in desperate need of a mother to replace their own, who had died in childbirth when Edwin was born. They had taken to Prue as easily as she had to them. They might not be her flesh-and-blood sons, but they were as precious to her as if they were.

'We could put one up at home,' Edwin said.

Jack rolled his eyes. 'Good luck convincing Father to get one.'

'I've tried persuading him,' Alice said, 'but he said absolutely not!'

'He can afford it, it's not that much, and if it saves your lives it's worth every penny,' Thea said.

Prue frowned. 'According to him the cellar is all we

need, no point in spending money unnecessarily. You know what he's like if he thinks he can save money!' That was Victor all over. Despite having a thriving business, her husband liked to keep a tight hold on the purse strings and was averse to any spending that he considered unnecessary.

Thea pulled a face. 'There are no pockets in shrouds, he should remember that. Well, you're all welcome to come and shelter in here any time; leave Victor to his cellar.'

Jack, Edwin and Alice all laughed.

'We will. He might change his mind now war's been declared,' Jack said. 'Did you hear it on the wireless?'

'Yes, your father, Alice and I all listened together.'

'This should help.' Reuben had returned with a wooden crate, which he turned upside down and put in the bottom of the hole near the entrance to the Anderson, then held out his hand to help Hettie out.

'Thank you.' Hettie took his hand and with a lot of huffing and puffing, climbed on the box and then out on to the grass. 'You might have done a good job putting it together, but who wants to spend any time sheltering in there?'

'It's not finished yet,' Reuben said. 'I'll make some steps leading down to it, so you won't have a problem getting in and out.' He wriggled his eyebrows at Hettie, who pulled a face back at him. 'And I'll put some wooden boards down on the floor to keep your feet dry and build some benches along the side to sit on, and we can add a hook from the ceiling to hang a Tilley lamp.'

'And we'll bring in some blankets to keep warm,' Thea added. 'It'll be fine.'

'Will you shelter in here as well, Reuben?' Prue asked.

'Me? No.' He shook his head. 'If the bombers come, Bess and I'll go in the woods; we'll be all right in there.'

'I'm sure you will.' Prue knew her brother would be more comfortable out of doors than stuck in a tin box underground.

'If you give me your basket I'll go and get the buns and sandwiches I've made for the evacuees.' Hettie held out her hand to Prue. 'And I'll go back to the village hall to help you set it out, if you like?'

Prue passed her the basket, smiling at the older woman who she'd known since she was a girl. 'Thank you, the more the merrier.'

'You come and give me a hand,' Hettie said, putting her arm through Alice's. 'You can have one of the buns; the boys have already had one and I know how much you like them.'

Prue watched the pair of them heading off to the house. Hettie had become like a grandmother to her children since she'd retired and come to live here at Rookery House. It was lovely to see.

'Is everything ready for the evacuees?' Thea asked.

Prue turned her attention back to her sister. 'Yes, we just need to set out the food. I've got enough homes arranged for the number they're sending us.'

'Are you having an evacuee as well?' Reuben asked.

'Of course, but one of the teachers rather than one of the children.' She sighed. 'Victor wasn't keen on having a child in the house; he took some persuading even to agree to have an adult.' Victor had been adamant about not having a child and had only agreed to have an adult after she'd gently reminded him that it was his duty to obey the law and that they should set a good example. It really wouldn't look good if he, as a councillor, didn't offer a home, while his wife, as billeting officer, persuaded others to do just that. He had eventually given in, but not without a lot of bad grace and grumbling, and her reassuring him that the teacher wouldn't be a problem in their home.

Jack snorted. 'Bloody hypocrite!'

'Jack!' Prue snapped. 'You shouldn't speak about your father like that.'

'Sorry.' Jack sighed. 'But he is sometimes.'

Thea laughed. 'We all know that Victor only does something if there's something in it for him.'

Prue's cheeks grew warm; she knew her sister was no fan of Victor.

In fact, Thea had tried to persuade her not to marry him all those years ago, but she hadn't listened because her heart had been set on being a mother to those two dear little boys. She had hoped that marriage to the widowed Victor would be fine, and it hadn't been as if she was going to get any better offers, had it? So many women in their generation had lost the chance to marry and have a family because of the Great War; it had robbed the country of thousands of young men. Look at Thea: she'd never married, her own fiancé killed on the Somme. Prue had taken the chance that had come her way, marrying a man fifteen years her senior, who'd given her two stepsons and then a daughter, Alice, and they were more precious to her than anything. She'd grown used to Victor's ways over the years and they rubbed along together; they'd never been a great love match but she'd known that when she'd accepted his proposal.

'Prue?' Hettie's voice brought her back to the present. 'Here we are. I've made cheese sandwiches and some tomato as well, and there're currant buns.' She pointed to the basket Alice was carrying.

'Thank you.' Prue glanced at her watch. 'We'd better get going; we've got more food to pick up on the way back. I'll see you at the village hall at four then, Thea.'

'Are you all right?' Hettie asked as they made their way to Prue's car. 'Only you looked a bit pale when I came out.'

'Yes, I'm fine.' She smiled. 'It's been a busy day and it's not over yet. Still lots to do.'

Hettie frowned, her blue eyes meeting Prue's. 'You're always on the go; you should slow up sometimes and relax, you know.'

Prue laughed. 'Keeping busy keeps me out of mischief!'

Why did she keep herself so busy these days? she thought as she climbed into the car. The simple answer was that it helped to fill the gap left by her children not needing her the way they used to when they were small. With the boys now grown up and Alice almost, getting involved with things outside the home helped shape her days and made her feel useful.

Chapter 4

'Here it comes,' the stationmaster announced, as the train appeared around the corner of the line, puffs of smoke chuffing like billowy clouds into the air. 'All set?'

'Absolutely.' Prue smiled at him. 'Everything's ready, all we need are our evacuees.'

Alice grabbed Prue's arm. 'This is it, Ma! Do you think they'll like it here?'

Prue smiled at her daughter, who'd been such a big help today and was genuinely excited about having the evacuees arrive in the village. 'I hope so. I'll be keeping a close eye on things to make sure all of them are happy and being well looked after.'

Checking that her hat was straight, she smoothed down the front of her blue, fine wool jacket as the train drew alongside the platform and came to a halt. The first hint that something was wrong was when she saw the faces looking out of the carriage windows – they were mostly women's, with only a scattering of children, and young ones at that. There were no school-aged children – not a single one.

'Where are the schoolchildren?' Alice asked.

Before Prue could answer, a woman dressed in the green uniform of the WVS, stepped off the train and called out in a plummy voice, 'Mrs Wilson?'

Prue nodded and went to meet her. 'Yes, that's me.'

'Excellent. We have forty-five expectant mothers and their accompanying infants for you.' The WVS woman smiled at her. 'They're all very keen to get to their new homes; it's been a long journey and, of course, we had to change trains and stations in Norwich – I didn't know Norwich had two stations!'

Prue stared at the woman, her chest tightening. 'But there's been a mistake; we were told we were having schoolchildren and their teachers ... not mothers and infants.' She glanced at the women who were starting to get off the train, helped by the guards and porters. 'All the arrangements have been made for children, *not* adults.'

'I see.' The WVS woman frowned. 'But this is where they sent us from Norwich; it was enough of a palaver having to switch stations with so many people and their luggage.' She sighed. 'I'll telephone HQ and see what's to be done. Is there a telephone I can use?'

'In my office,' the stationmaster said. 'This way.'

Prue felt sick. This wasn't supposed to be happening; her careful planning was crumbling at the foundations.

'What are we going to do?' Alice asked, looking worried.

'Not panic.' Prue pasted a smile on her face. 'I'm sure it can be sorted out.'

33

Another WVS woman came up to her. 'What's going on?'

'We've been sent the wrong evacuees; we're expecting schoolchildren. Your colleague's gone to telephone HQ to find out what to do,' Prue explained.

The woman shook her head. 'They'd better be quick about it; these women are tired and hungry and need to get to their new homes.'

Prue looked along the platform, which was filling up with the evacuees, most of whom looked so unlike any of the local women that they would stand out like sore thumbs in the village. Each was dressed in a cross-over apron with their hair in curlers under a headscarf; another was teetering on high heels, her peroxide-blonde hair swept up in a fancy pompadour hairstyle and her tight-fitting purple dress displaying the swell of her pregnant belly.

'They won't be long, I hope,' Prue said, trying to sound positive.

'I'd better say something before we have a mutiny on our hands.' The WVS woman clapped her hands several times to quieten down the women, then she cleared her throat and explained the situation to them.

'What's going on?' Marianne asked, looking around the crowded platform. She and Sally were some of the last evacuees off the train and were greeted with the sight of many of the East End mothers looking furious.

'We've been sent to the wrong bleedin' place!' said a woman with a grizzling toddler on her hip. 'Seems as Great Plumstead,' she nodded at the black-and-white station sign, declaring the village's name in bold letters, 'was expecting evacuee children, not us.'

'Can't they take us back to where we should be, then?' Marianne asked.

'Gawd knows, but I've just about 'ad enough of being stuck on a train,' the woman said. 'My back's aching and I need the lavvie.'

'What will happen to us?' Sally's face was pale.

'I'm sure it'll be all right.' Marianne smiled at her. 'See, the WVS women are sorting it out.' She nodded to where one of the two women who had accompanied them from London was in serious discussion with a blonde-haired woman in a neat petrol-blue skirt and matching jacket, who looked like she'd come to meet them.

'Are we staying here or goin'?' another expectant mother shouted out across the crowded platform. 'We're tired and 'ungry and my daughter needs changin' again.'

'Ladies, if you'll bear with us for a moment.' The WVS woman held up her hands. 'My colleague is telephoning headquarters at this very moment to find out what we should do; we'll let you know as soon as possible.'

This news was accompanied by mutterings and grumblings from the evacuees, several of whom had decided they were going to get back on the train and had opened the carriage doors and were in the process of climbing in with their small children and luggage.

'You can't do that, missis,' the guard shouted, hurrying towards them. 'Not till we know what's happening.'

'Bleedin' 'ell, I wish I'd stayed at 'ome!' a woman shouted back at him as she climbed back on to the platform.

It must only have been a few minutes, but it felt like much longer before the older WVS woman returned from the stationmaster's office and clapped her hands, calling for their attention again. 'Ladies, we've been told by our headquarters that since we've been sent here, then *this* is where we must stay; this will be your new home. I'd like to introduce you to Mrs Wilson who's in charge of billeting you all.'

The woman in blue stepped forward, smiling at them. 'Welcome to Great Plumstead. We have tea waiting for you in the village hall, so you'll have a chance to have something to eat and rest before you go to your new homes. I hope you'll settle in and be happy here. If you'd like to follow me.'

'Thank Gawd for that,' the woman nearest Marianne said, picking up her string bag of belongings. 'A cuppa tea is just what I need.'

Prue was relieved to see that the expectant mothers quickly forgot their grumbles when they spotted the generous spread laid out for them on the trestle tables in the village hall. The members of the village's WI had done themselves proud: they'd provided a delicious assortment of generously filled sandwiches, sausage rolls, biscuits and huge slabs of homemade cake, alongside jugs of lemonade and big teapots ready with hot tea, bowls of sugar and jugs of milk. The evacuees happily piled their plates and with WI members and Alice serving them drinks and assisting them with their infants and luggage, the mothers were soon settled down on the chairs and tucking in.

'This is bleedin' lovely,' one mother said through a mouthful of cake, spattering crumbs down the front of her cross-over apron.

'Nothing beats a good cup of Rosie Lee,' the woman sitting next to her said, taking a gulp of her tea.

Feeding these women and their infants was the easy part, Prue thought as she watched a little girl of about two years old eat her way through a sausage roll with a look of pure pleasure on her face. It was making sure they had a billet to go to that might prove difficult. Being prepared to give a home to a schoolchild was one thing, but to have another woman come to live in your house and use your kitchen as her own was quite another. There would be some in the village who would undoubtedly be less willing to have an expectant mother rather than a child evacuee. Prue knew that word would already have spread around the village that the evacuees had arrived, and that they weren't what had been expected. Their walk from the station to the village hall had attracted quite a lot of attention.

Prue was doing her best to keep calm and not let the mess-up throw her any more than it already had; when the WVS woman had broken the news to her at the station that they'd have to live with the mistake, she'd just wanted to break down and cry in frustration and tiredness. All her careful planning, the cajoling of people to give an evacuee child a home, organising this reception here at the hall – all of that had been thrown off kilter and it wasn't a pleasant feeling. Now she would have to try to pick up the pieces and make sure every woman had a home to go to.

Added to that, these women would need to be registered with the local midwife and doctor for their antenatal care; that would be extra work to sort out. It was nothing that she wasn't capable of but if she'd known in advance they were having expectant mothers, she could have prepared.

'You look like you could do with this.' Hettie handed her a cup of tea. 'Drink it up, I've put plenty of sugar in it.'

'Thank you.' She took the cup. Lowering her voice, she said, 'It was such a shock seeing them get off the train.' Prue did her best to smile. 'We just need to deal with what they've sent us. The organisers wherever these mothers should have gone will have to do the same thing only in reverse.'

'Can't they just swap them over? Bring us the children and take the mothers to wherever?' Hettie asked.

'Apparently not. There have been so many evacuees on the move again today; we've been told we'll just have to manage with what we've got.' She sighed. 'But not everyone's going to like it. It was hard enough getting some people to agree to have children, they're not going to like billeting an adult; though on the plus side, we've been told their hosts won't be expected to provide meals for the mothers, just a bed and access to their kitchens to cook in, and sanitary arrangements of course. I can't see that going down well with some.'

Hettie sniffed. 'Well, they'll have to like it or lump it, won't they? The women will need to eat. You've got the law on your side, so they'll have to give a home to an evacuee if they have space, it's as simple as that.'

Prue nodded. 'I know, but I'll need to brace myself for a battle with some.'

Hettie touched her arm. 'You'll be fine, if there's one person here who can sort out this mess, it's you.'

'I hope so, I really do.' Prue took a sip of tea. 'I'd better go and drink this outside and wait for the hosts to arrive . . . Head them off at the pass, as they say. That way, I can explain what's going on before they come in. I don't want the evacuees to feel they're not welcome.'

'What do you mean, they've sent expectant mothers and their infant children?' one of the hosts asked, her mouth pinching into a hard line.

'Just as I said, so you'll have an adult and possibly her small child or children staying in your house instead of an unaccompanied child to care for. All you have to do is provide a bedroom and allow your evacuee mother to use your cooking and sanitary facilities.' Prue spoke calmly, keeping her expression pleasant in contrast with the frowns and pouts of the women gathered before her. 'There's actually less work involved for you this way: you don't need to provide meals, shop for the ingredients or wash their clothes. You'll be paid five shillings for the mother and three shillings for each child per week.'

'I'm not happy about having another woman using my kitchen,' another of the host women sniffed, folding her arms across her ample bosom. 'That's not what I agreed to have at all; they might not have my standards of cleanliness. I'm not sure I want an evacuee now.'

Several of the other women nodded in agreement, muttering among themselves.

'Look, I know it's not what you agreed to, but have

a heart; these women have been ripped away from their families, their homes and all they know. On top of that they're expecting; think how you'd have felt if the same had happened to you when you were having your babies?' Prue looked at the women, many of whom didn't meet her eye.

'That's all well and good, but I don't see why we should have to be put out by someone else's mistake sending them here and not where they should have gone!' another of the women said huffily.

Prue sighed. 'Well, the law clearly states that if you have a spare room then you are obliged to billet an evacuee, be it a child or an adult.' She paused for a moment before adding, 'It's your patriotic duty to help, or face being fined fifty pounds or given a three-month prison sentence.'

The woman's cheeks flushed and she spluttered, 'I'm sure it won't come to that.'

'I hope not.' Prue fixed her with a hard stare. 'We're at war now and all of us need to do our bit. Imagine if you'd been sent off to live miles from home with strangers when you were expecting a baby, how would you have felt? And added to that stress, that war had just been declared and the home and family you'd left behind were likely to be a target for bombers.' Prue met the eyes of several of the women, some of whom had the grace to look away, ashamed, although one looked her straight back in the eye, a look of defiance on her face.

'So, you'll be giving a home to one, then, will you?' the woman asked.

'Of course I will, and my sister will be, too.' Prue

beckoned to Thea who'd just arrived. 'There's a slight change of plan: we've been sent expectant mothers instead of children.'

'Oh.' Thea glanced at the other women, clearly picking up the hostility coming off them. 'That's all right, the room's ready, it really doesn't matter if we have a mother instead of a child, does it? Who's coming to stay with me?'

'Anyone. Just go in and introduce yourself to a mother, there's no list of who goes where.' Prue smiled gratefully at her sister. 'We need to get the billets sorted out quickly. The women will be anxious to get settled; they look exhausted after their long journey.'

'Will do.' Thea winked at her as she turned and then headed inside the village hall.

'So, ladies,' Prue turned her attention back to the group of gathered women, 'I hope you'll have the grace to do the same without me having to involve the constable.' Then, leaving them to stew and consider their options, she turned on the heels of her well-polished brogues and followed Thea into the hall where her sister was already talking to a young woman sitting not far from the door.

'Shall I take that?' Hettie came up to her and held out her hand to take her empty teacup. 'I take it the arrival of our unexpected evacuees hasn't gone down too well?'

Prue passed her cup. 'Let's just say they weren't thrilled at the change, but I've made it clear how things stand and now Thea's setting a good example and I must do the same.'

She approached an auburn-haired young woman sitting next to the evacuee who Thea was talking to and held out her hand. 'Hello, I'm Prue Wilson, I'd be very happy to have you come and live in my home.'

The young woman looked relieved and shook her offered hand. 'Thanks very much. I'm Sally Parker; pleased to meet yer. I was a bit worried no one would want us to go and live with them, what with us bein' sent to the wrong place and all. It must 'ave been a shock seeing us lot get off the train.'

Prue smiled at her. 'It was a surprise, certainly, but nothing we can't sort out. Don't worry, we have enough homes arranged for everyone.'

Out of the corner of her eye, she was relieved to see the other hosts had ventured in through the hall doors and were beginning to introduce themselves to the evacuees. Even the most ardent complainer had come in; the weight of a fine or prison sentence or perhaps, more likely, the shame of not being seen to be charitable was the lever they needed. Whatever it was, she was grateful as the most important thing now was to get these women settled into a home, with a roof over their heads and somewhere to sleep.

Chapter 5

'Let me take that for you.'

'Thank you.' Marianne gladly let Thea take her heavy suitcase as weariness after the long journey had crept up on her. She followed her out of the hall, grateful to have been offered a home by Thea, who looked far friendlier and kinder than some of the sour-faced women who were now introducing themselves to evacuees. The fact that Thea was dressed in slacks rather than a customary skirt or dress made her stand out. Her cheerful poppy-red cardigan complemented her dark brown curly hair which she wore in a bob, around which was tied a red and white spotted scarf with the bow on top of her head. Thea Thornton looked like someone who knew her own mind and wasn't afraid to do things her way. 'It must have been a bit of a shock having expectant mothers turning up when you thought you were having children.'

Thea looked at her and smiled; her eyes, which were the

colour of bluebells, were warm. 'I suppose so, but it really doesn't matter now; what's important is that everyone has a home to go to.'

'The lady who's in charge – Mrs Wilson, I think – she looked worried,' Marianne said as they reached a green Morris 8 that was parked just down the road from the hall.

'What, Prue?' Thea opened the boot and stowed the suitcase inside. 'Well, she's put a lot of effort into organising everything and wanted it to go well; she likes things to work out the way they're supposed to. I should know – she's my sister.'

'Your sister? Sally's going to live with her.'

'That's good; it'll make it easy for us to see each other. Have you been friends long?'

Marianne shook her head. 'No, I only met her on the train; we were in the same carriage and got talking.'

'Well, jump in and I'll take you home.'

Driving through the village, Marianne liked what she saw; they passed the village green, which had the school next to it, a row of shops, and then went out past the station and up and over the bridge across the railway line and out into open countryside. It was wonderful to see so much sky and greenery again and to have a feeling of space around her instead of being crowded in by buildings. Marianne sighed happily.

Thea shot her a glance. 'Are you all right?'

'Yes, I'm fine, I'm just so glad to be out of London again.'

'You like the countryside?' Thea asked.

'Yes, I was born and grew up in a village in Kent. I only went to work in London when I got a job there.'

'What did you do?'

'I worked as a dressmaker in the West End designing and making wedding dresses, ball gowns and other smart clothes. I loved the work but living in the city was a bit of a shock.'

'I know what you mean; I moved to London to work after the Great War, and only came back here three months ago. It took me a long time to get used to the noise and busyness.'

Marianne nodded. 'Oh, absolutely. So many people rushing around this way and that, I couldn't believe it at first.'

Thea glanced at her and smiled. 'It's a lot quieter around here. Right ... ' She slowed the car and turned off the narrow lane, driving through a gateway and pulling up in front of a house. 'Here we are; welcome to Rookery House. I hope you'll be very happy here.'

Marianne certainly liked what she saw. The house stood on its own, built of red brick with a bay window on either side of the front door and three windows on the floor above. She turned to Thea and smiled. 'Thank you. It looks lovely, a friendly-looking sort of house.'

Thea laughed. 'That's what I always think, its chimneys look like pricked-up ears and the windows like eyes. I always wanted to live here one day when I was a child and when I heard it was up for sale I bought it and came back to live here. I love it. Come on, let's get you inside.'

Taking Marianne's case, Thea led her around to the back of the house. 'We usually come and go through the back door.' Their arrival was quickly spotted by a black-and-white collie who came bounding over to them, wagging its tail. 'This is Bess, my brother's dog.' She put the case down outside the back door and ruffled the dog's ears, who, satisfied that she'd greeted Thea, turned her attention to Marianne, who held out her hand for her to sniff and then stroked the dog's soft head. 'Come on, I'll introduce you to my brother while we're out here. He lives in the converted railway carriage over there by the orchard.' Thea pointed to a structure about fifty yards away across the garden: it still had the basic look of a carriage but had a veranda built around it and a chimney coming out of the top. 'He's close enough to join in with what he wants, but still has his own space the way he likes it,' she explained as they made their way off towards an Anderson shelter which had the sound of someone hammering coming from inside it. 'Reuben and Prue's two sons put this up today; it looks like a giant mole's taken up residence in the garden. I'll have to plant something on it – some flowers or something – to make it look nice. Reuben?' Thea called as they reached the shelter. 'Our evacuee's here. We were sent expectant mothers instead of children.'

The hammering stopped and a man emerged with grey-streaked dark brown hair, dressed in worn, brown corduroy trousers with string tied around the waist and a checked shirt; he shielded his eyes from the brighter sunlight for a moment.

'Blimey, I bet that put the cat among the pigeons!'

Thea laughed. 'Just a bit, but nothing Prue couldn't cope

with. Anyway, this is Marianne, our evacuee. Marianne, this is my brother, Reuben,' Thea introduced them.

'Hello.' Reuben held his hand up to Marianne and then looked at it and withdrew it quickly. 'My hand's all mucky, best not to shake it.' He smiled warmly at her instead, creases fanning out at the sides of his eyes, which she noticed were the same shade of blue as Thea's. 'Welcome to Rookery House, hope you'll be happy here.'

'Thank you, I'm sure I will.' Marianne returned his smile. 'I'm glad to be here.'

'How are you getting on?' Thea asked, peering into the opening of the shelter.

'Just putting the boards down for the floor then I'll get started on some steps so Hettie can get in and out more easily.'

'She'll be pleased to hear that. Will you come in to have your tea with us?'

Reuben nodded. 'All right, I will, thank you.'

'Good, we'll see you later.' Thea linked her arm through Marianne's. 'Let's go and get you settled in.'

Inside the house, Marianne loved the homely kitchen which they passed through on the way to a hallway where the afternoon light streamed in through the stained glass of the front door, splotching the black-and-white tiled floor with colour.

'That's the sitting room,' Thea pointed to the nearest door leading off the hall, 'and the dining room is down there.' She indicated a door on the opposite side of the hall beyond the staircase at the front of the house. 'We don't use it very often as it's much cosier eating in the kitchen,

47

and easier too!' She led the way up the stairs, which were painted white and had a dark red carpet runner secured with brass stair rods running down the centre.

'That's my room,' Thea pointed to a door at the front of the house, 'and Hettie's, opposite. She's still helping out at the village hall so you'll meet her properly later. And you're in here.' Thea opened the door of a bedroom at the back of the house and stood aside to let Marianne in. 'I hope you'll be comfortable.'

Marianne stepped inside and loved what she saw. The single iron bedstead looked comfy, the pillow plump and the dusky-pink eiderdown warm. The scent of lavender mixed with beeswax polish reminded her of her childhood home with her gran in Kent. It felt like a good omen.

She turned to smile at Thea. 'Thank you, it really is lovely.'

Thea looked pleased. 'Well, I'll leave you to settle in; come down when you're ready and I'll show you where the bathroom is.' She put Marianne's case on the bed for her to unpack. 'It's downstairs. We've no electricity, so I'm afraid it's oil or Tilley lamps and candles after dark.'

Marianne smiled at Thea. 'It will be fine, that's how I grew up.'

'Good. I'll see you in a bit, then.' Thea went out and closed the door quietly behind her.

Marianne sat down on the bed and stroked the soft eiderdown cover, a huge sense of relief washing over her: she was very lucky to be billeted here with such a nice person and in such a lovely place.

Chapter 6

Thea leaned on the gate to her meadow watching the barn owl flying on silent wings as it quartered back and forth above the grass in the dusk light, tilting its head as it listened for the rustle of potential prey in the grass. Suddenly it stalled in flight and plunged, talons first, to the ground, then moments later rose up with a vole in its claws.

'Did it get it?' Reuben's voice was soft as he came up behind her and leaned against the gate.

'Yes.' Bess, Reuben's dog, nudged at her hand and she stroked her black-and-white head. 'It's gone to perch in the oak tree and enjoy its meal.' She turned and looked at her brother, who was gazing out over the meadow where bats were starting to flit about searching for insects. 'You all right?'

'I've had better days but . . .' He took off his flat cap and ran his hand through his dark, grey-streaked hair. 'The thought of us being at war again . . .' He shrugged.

Thea put her hand on his arm. 'I know. I keep thinking of William, what he'd have thought.'

'Bloody fools, that's what.' Reuben sighed. 'Did he and all of those other men die for nothing, only to have us fighting all over again twenty odd years later?'

'I'm worried about Jack and Edwin; they'll be called up.'

'Or volunteer, like William and I did.' He shook his head. 'We had no idea . . . '

'It'll be different this time, though, won't it?'

Reuben nodded. 'Yes, but people will still get killed or injured; it will still change and ruin lives.'

'I've been thinking what I can do,' Thea said. 'I was desperate to do something last time and I'm not going to be able to sit back and do nothing now.'

Reuben frowned. 'You thinking of running off to drive ambulances behind the front line again? You've only just come back here.'

Thea stroked Bess's silky-soft ears, and remembered how she'd felt about going to France: she'd been thrilled at the sense of adventure and the fact that she'd been allowed to go off and do her bit. Not many girls like her got to drive ambulances, but she'd been taught how to drive by the young chauffeur at Great Plumstead Hall where she'd been working in the kitchen. He'd taken a fancy to her and, risking his job, had given her lessons, the pair of them sneaking off to practise on quiet roads away from the Hall. Luckily, she'd picked it up quickly before he'd been called up, and she'd volunteered, ending up driving ambulances in France ferrying wounded men to hospital. It was a crazy, scary and exhilarating time, and one that she wouldn't have missed for the world.

'I'm tempted but I've got responsibilities here now, what with buying this place and taking in my first evacuee. I'll find something else that I can do to help.'

'Prue will find you something. You could join the WI and get busy knitting and sewing for the war effort or whatever they get involved with.'

Thea laughed. 'She's been trying to get me to join ever since I got back here, but I'm not so sure it's my sort of thing. I'm more tempted by the WVS – they might have something I can do that suits me better. I could drive an ambulance for them!'

'You'll find something, you're not the sort to sit and do nothing.' Reuben looked across the meadow: the barn owl was hunting again. 'How's Marianne settling in?'

'Fine, she's gone to bed: tired out after the long journey. I think she'll fit in well here; she grew up in the country-side so won't be bothered by the change from London. It'll be nice to have a baby in the house.' She smiled. 'Though we'll have to find a cot from somewhere before it's born, and a pram. Hettie's delighted; she's already got her knitting needles out and started on some bootees.'

Chapter 7

'What do you mean we've got an expectant mother billeted with us?' Victor's face started to grow blotchy as it
always did when something had riled him.

It was a little past nine o'clock that evening, and he'd
just returned from Norwich where he'd gone for a meeting of some sort, something that had turned into a regular
occurrence over the past few months.

Prue put her hand on the back of the kitchen chair
to steady herself. She didn't need this, not now, she was
exhausted. After all the preparations today and then
dealing with the evacuees – she'd even had to take some
mothers around to homes whose hosts hadn't turned up
at the school to collect them, no doubt having heard
who'd arrived instead of the schoolchildren. She'd had to
lean heavily on some with threats of fines or prison and
it hadn't been pleasant. That, combined with having to
remain upbeat for the poor expectant mothers who were

tired out and aware that their arrival was less welcome than she'd wanted it to be – it had been a strain. A home had eventually been found for each woman, but it hadn't been the way Prue had planned for it to happen and now, to top it all, Victor was making a fuss.

Prue sighed. 'There was a mistake: the schoolchildren we were supposed to have were sent elsewhere, and we got the expectant mothers and infants instead.'

'Then they should have been sent back again. Couldn't you have sorted it out, you're supposed to be in charge, aren't you, Prudence?' Victor narrowed his ice-blue eyes and glared at her. 'Or did you just let them get away with it?'

'Of course not, I tried to sort it out.' She did her best to keep her voice calm, while her stomach knotted inside her. 'A telephone call was made to the headquarters and they decided that it was best if the mothers stayed here; there have been so many people on the move and they were tired and had had enough travelling, it's not good in their condition.'

Victor banged his hand down on the kitchen table sending ripples juddering across the surface of the tea in Prue's cup and dislodging a strand of his shiny brilliantined, dark hair. 'Well, I'm not having one in my house. I don't want a screaming baby waking me up all night long; I've got a business to run.'

'Other people in the village have given a home to the evacuees. Thea took one home with her and so did the vicar's wife.'

Victor sneered. 'Trust your sister to get in on the act.

53

You don't have to do the same as Dorothea.' He always insisted on calling the sisters by their full names, no matter how many times they'd told him not to. 'Well, you'll have to get rid of her in the morning.'

'No, I'm sorry I can't do that.' Prue squeezed her hand into a tight fist behind her back, the nails digging into her palm. She had to stand up for what was right here. 'The young woman is perfectly nice and she needs a home; it's our duty to provide one since we have space ... and she won't be any bother to you, I'll look after her.' She hesitated for a moment, feeling her heart pounding as she watched Victor's temper rising, his cold, pale eyes boring into her face and his lips pinched into a thin line beneath his brown moustache. 'It wouldn't look good if we threw her out, with me being billeting officer and you a local councillor. There's a fifty-pound fine or three-month prison sentence for refusing to have evacuees – do you want to go to prison because I don't.'

'It wouldn't come to that!' Victor spat. 'I know people, Prudence, *I* have connections.'

'Do you want to chance it?' Prue pushed home her trump card, knowing how much he cared about his role in the community. 'You're a respectable business owner and member of the local council; people might take their custom elsewhere if you refuse to comply with the rules like everyone else.'

Her words hit home, she could see it in Victor's face: a muscle in his clenched jaw twitched as he grappled with the thought of losing face and, more importantly, losing custom in his beloved hardware shop and the accompanying seed and agricultural merchant business that he ran in the nearby market town of Wykeham.

'All right, she can stay,' he said grudgingly. 'But don't expect me to do anything for her. Understand?'

'I don't expect you to, Victor. All you need to do is agree to her staying – and her name is Sally, by the way – other than that you'll see her at some mealtimes, you'll hardly know she's here.'

'And if the baby starts squawking in the middle of the night?'

'All babies cry; Jack, Edwin and Alice did. You can stuff something in your ears if you're being woken up.' *Though your loud snoring disturbs other people every single night*, Prue thought; she could hear it from her bedroom, which was at the opposite end of the landing from his. She had the good sense not to mention that, though: she'd got what she wanted and it wouldn't be wise to rile him further, it would be like poking a stick into a wasp's nest and she wasn't foolish enough to do that. Over the years she'd had to learn to monitor Victor and gauge his moods carefully, choosing when and when not to challenge him, often seeding in suggestions of something she wanted to do or get, so that when the time came he thought it was his idea and was happy for her to go ahead. Of course, in this case the evacuee mix-up had made that impossible. It helped having the weight of the law behind her and his innate desire to make money, plus his overblown sense of how important his image was to other people – if only they knew the real Victor behind closed doors.

He opened his mouth to speak but was silenced by a gentle tapping on the kitchen door.

'Come in,' Prue called.

The door opened and Sally's head popped around it. 'I'm sorry to disturb you, only I wondered if I could get a drink of water, please.' She darted a glance at Victor and looked worried.

She must have heard his raised voice, Prue thought, feeling sorry for the poor young woman. What must she be thinking? 'Of course, come in, I'll get you one.' Prue smiled at her and hurried over to the dresser, took down a clean glass and filled it at the sink. 'There you are. This is my husband, Victor. Victor, this is Sally, our evacuee.'

Sally looked at him warily. 'How do yer do?' Her Cockney accent sounded more pronounced than ever.

Victor swallowed hard, and Prue could see him fighting the urge to be rude as he glanced down at the young woman's swollen belly, which pushed out the front of her dress. After a few seconds he nodded and managed to speak. 'Good evening. If you'll excuse me, I have some business to attend to.' He gave a curt nod and left the room.

Sally looked at Prue, her blue eyes wide. 'I'm sorry.'

'What for?'

Sally shrugged. 'I couldn't 'elp 'earing as I came down the stairs, his voice was loud. I don't mind movin' somewhere else – it's not like I've got used to being here yet.'

Prue smiled, reaching out to touch the young woman's shoulder. 'Absolutely not, you are welcome here and I want you to stay.' She lowered her voice. 'Victor can be ... Well, he's rather set in his ways and not used to having strangers come to live with us but he'll get used to having you here, and besides, you won't see that much of him. He works long hours, even going to meetings in Norwich most Sundays.' She smiled. 'How about a nice cup of cocoa?'

'If you're sure about me stayin'? I don't want to cause no trouble for you. You've been so kind to me.'

'I am sure. Now I'm going to have some cocoa, will you join me?'

Sally nodded. 'Go on then, yes, please.'

Settled at the kitchen table, Prue warmed her hands around her mug of cocoa, glad of the warmth it gave her. She still felt upset by Victor's response although she shouldn't have expected otherwise really, but there were times when she wished he could at least try to be more sympathetic to other people's problems.

Pasting a smile on her face she looked at Sally, who was blowing on the surface of her cocoa to cool it. 'Where did you live in London?'

'In Whitechapel. It ain't nowhere like here. I live ... *lived* wiv my husband, Arthur, and his ma. I used to work in the corner shop servin' behind the counter.'

'Tell me about Arthur.'

A dreamy looked passed over Sally's face. 'Oh, you'd love 'im, he's the nicest man I've ever known, loves me to bits.' She giggled. 'And I love him right back. It was 'im that made me come 'ere; I didn't want to leave but he was that concerned about me and the baby in case there was bombin'. He said it would be safer for us out of London and he's goin' to be joining up and leavin' too.' She sighed. 'I wish he'd wait to be called up, but he wants to defend the country. Will your sons join up?'

Sally had met Jack and Edwin at teatime when they'd all gathered in the kitchen to eat the meal Prue had prepared for them.

'I expect they will, although I'd rather they wait to be called up, but knowing Jack, I think he won't.' Prue sighed. 'I don't think he fully appreciates what he'll be letting himself in for, war's not a game, but then my brothers couldn't wait to join up last time either – they went off full of excitement and bravado.'

'Did they come back?' Sally asked.

'One did: Reuben. William was killed on the Somme.' A dart of pain at the memory of his loss sliced through her – even years later it still had the power to hurt – and the thought of her sons going off and facing possible death would keep her awake at night. She took a sip of cocoa. 'Reuben lives here in Great Plumstead, close to my sister Thea – your friend's gone to live with her, so no doubt you'll get to meet him sometime. I can take you there tomorrow to see your friend if you'd like?'

Sally nodded. 'Yes, I'd like that. Marianne's 'er name, we got on well and it'd be nice to see her again. To be honest, I don't know what I'm going to do 'ere, I'm used to bein' busy havin' a job to do.'

Prue smiled. 'I'm sure we can find you something to do; now there's a war on there's bound to be things to help with. Perhaps you can help me with the evacuee mothers;

I think it might be hard for some of them coming to live here so far away from what they're used to.'

Sally laughed. 'They'll be feelin' like fishes out of water – most of them 'ave never seen so much greenery and space in their lives!'

Chapter 8

Marianne woke with a start and for several moments didn't know where she was, then she remembered, and relaxed back into her soft feather pillow with a sigh. She was out of London and away from anyone who might know her, away from the constant worry that she might be spotted. Even when she'd moved to the East End, the worry hadn't left her and she'd always been looking over her shoulder, fearful that someone from her previous life would see her and expose her lies. Tears filled her eyes as she looked down at her belly pushing out the front of her nightgown. It wasn't as if she'd committed a crime – stolen something, murdered someone even – but to be an unmarried mother was regarded by many as morally lacking. Marianne had grown up with the stigma of being an illegitimate child herself, and she was determined to do everything she could to protect her child from suffering the same fate.

Inside her belly, her baby somersaulted in its watery world and she laid a hand on her skin to feel it, marvelling at the new life growing inside her and loving it. From the first moment she'd felt that butterfly-wing flutter inside her, her fierce love and sense of protectiveness had kicked in. Like a lioness protecting her cub, she'd do anything to look after her child. She would even lie and deceive if need be – she didn't like it, knew it was wrong, but she was doing what was necessary to protect her child. She didn't want what she'd done to blight her child's life, for the child to pay for its mother's mistake, to grow up being called names because she was unmarried. There simply was no choice. Marianne had been the one to believe and let herself be misled, she'd been foolishly naive and should have known better. It was up to her now to make good on her mistake and to shield her innocent child, even if it meant fabricating a marriage that didn't exist, although she'd once believed and hoped it might happen. The hardest bit was lying to good, decent people like Thea, but it would only be for a little while, she consoled herself. Once the baby was born and she was back on her feet and earning enough then she'd move on, find somewhere to rent on her own, and it wouldn't matter if she was pretending to be something she wasn't. Till then she'd have to carry on with her pretence for the baby's sake.

She'd been so lucky to be billeted here with Thea and Hettie in this lovely house, Marianne thought, rolling on to her side and swinging her legs out of bed, her feet landing on the soft rag rug on the wooden floor.

Crossing over to the window, she opened the curtains

and removed the blackout blind, the Lighting Order that had come into force on 1 September now requiring that all windows and doors be blacked out at night. Glorious September sunlight streamed into the room: it was another beautiful day, the blue sky clear of cloud. Removing the blackout must have caught Thea's eye as she walked past the Anderson shelter down in the garden, heading towards the house, because she waved up at Marianne with a warm smile on her face.

Marianne returned her wave, a heart-warming glow of being welcome here flooding through her. She was so very lucky to have been invited to come and live here by Thea; some of the other women who had followed Thea into the hall had had such a sour look about them. She couldn't imagine them striding about with a basket of freshly picked mushrooms, wearing slacks and gum boots with a red polka-dot scarf tied around their hair like Thea. But then from what she'd seen of her so far, Thea wasn't like most people, there was a definite spark about her – she was someone who wasn't frightened to go her own way, the sort of person who was good to have on your side. Marianne sighed, that made not being totally honest with Thea all the harder, but she had to do what was necessary to protect her child and perhaps that's something that Thea would understand, although she wasn't going to risk it by telling her – or anyone else, for that matter.

A gentle tapping on Marianne's door a few minutes later drew her away from the window where she'd been watching the swallows' acrobatics as they dived through the open doorway of a shed where they must have had young in a nest.

'Come in,' she called.

'Good morning.' Thea came in carrying a jug. 'I've brought you some hot water for a wash.' She put it down on the wash-stand next to the jug of cold water already there and the bowl. 'How did you sleep?'

'Very well, I was exhausted after the journey.' She smiled at Thea. 'Thank you for the water.'

'You're welcome.' Thea walked over to stand by the window next to her. 'It's another lovely day. I've picked mushrooms for breakfast and Hettie's getting busy with the frying pan if you're hungry.'

'I am, thank you.'

Thea pointed to the framed photograph that Marianne had put on top of the chest of drawers near the window. 'Is this your husband?'

Marianne nodded. 'That's Alex.'

'He's a handsome chap.'

Marianne stared at the studio portrait that Alex had given her. He was handsome. And funny. And kind. And honest . . . or so she'd thought. 'Yes.'

'Well, he'll be glad that you're safely out of London.' Thea smiled. 'Come down as soon as you're ready. Hettie cooks a fine breakfast.'

Left on her own, Marianne looked at Alex's image, tears filling her eyes. It hurt her to have to look at it, but if she was going to be convincing, she needed to have a photo on display, it's what a wife would have. She could have used a photograph of any man but had thought it was more realistic if at least part of the image she portrayed was true. Alex was the father of her baby and she had loved him dearly – still loved him deep down – but their relationship had been doomed from the start, if only she'd had the sense to see it.

Marianne could smell the mouth-watering scent of frying bacon as she went down the stairs, her stomach grumbling in response.

'Ah, here she comes,' Hettie said, turning from where she stood by the range to smile at Marianne as she came into the kitchen. 'Did you sleep well?'

'Very well, thank you,' Marianne said. 'It's so quiet here after London; all I could hear were owls hooting. It was lovely.'

'Right, sit yourself down and I'll dish you up some breakfast. There's tea in the pot if you want to pour yourself a cup and you can do one for me while you're at it, please.'

Marianne did as she was told and was pouring out a second cup of tea from the brown teapot with its delightful tea cosy that was knitted in a rainbow of colours and decorated with delicate crocheted flowers, when Thea came in from outside. This time she was carrying a basket full of cut wood to feed the range.

'You're just in time, Thea.' Hettie put a full plate down on the table in front of Marianne.

'Thank you.' Marianne looked at the plate with everything cooked to perfection: a gloriously orange-yolked fried egg, crispy bacon, mushrooms and tomatoes.

'Tuck in,' Thea said, as she and Hettie joined her at the table with their own plates of food.

Marianne wasn't used to having a breakfast like this,

usually it was a bowl of the porridge her landlady provided or bread and marge with some jam on top if she was lucky. She picked up her knife and fork and began to eat, the flavour of the foods bursting on her tongue like fireworks. The egg was so rich and the mushrooms the freshest she'd ever tasted with a deep earthy flavour.

'This is delicious, Hettie, thank you,' she said.

Hettie smiled at her. 'I'm glad you like it; I've had years of practice cooking so I should hope it's good. We don't have a breakfast like this every day, mind you, so it's a treat to make one. I thought it would be nice for you on your first day; you look like you could do with some feeding up, it'll help put some colour into your cheeks. Probably that London air gives people's skin a pallor.' She turned and looked at Thea. 'Your skin's perked up since you came back here to live, lost the city look it had, and you've got roses in your cheeks again.'

'I'm glad to hear it, Hettie.' Thea's eyes met Marianne's and she winked at her. 'Must be all the fresh country air after smoky old London.'

'I could smell the difference as soon as I got off the train yesterday,' Marianne said. 'It's lovely.'

'I thought I'd show you around the village this morning if you'd like, Marianne, I need to do some shopping,' Thea said, cutting one of her mushrooms in half and spearing a piece on her fork.

'Yes, I'd like that. I need to look for a job and thought I'd ask at the shops to see if they need anyone to help.'

Hettie frowned. 'Isn't your husband going to send you any money?'

65

Not if he doesn't exist, Marianne thought. That's why she needed to work, but she couldn't say that. 'Yes, but I'm used to working and I'd like to earn money for my keep while I can. I need to do some shopping for my food as well.'

'I've been thinking about that,' Thea said. 'I know Prue said that hosts are only supposed to provide accommodation and not food, but it seems silly to have two lots of cooking going on in here, so I wondered if you'd be happy to add a bit on to your billeting payment to cover food and we can all just eat together?'

Marianne looked at Hettie, who nodded her agreement as she chewed a mouthful of bacon. 'It sounds like a good idea, thank you. I can help with the cooking, too.'

Thea smiled at her. 'Good, that's settled then.'

'Did you always want to work as a designer and dressmaker?' Thea asked as they set off to walk into the centre of Great Plumstead later that morning.

'My grandmother was a dressmaker and I learned my love of sewing and creating from her; it was all I ever wanted to do, it makes my heart sing.' A warm glow filled her at the thought of her love of dressmaking. 'When the chance came up to train further in London, I had to take it, my grandmother insisted I did, even though it meant moving to the city.'

'How did you get the London job?'

'Quite by chance: Dorothy Abrahams, who I went to work for, came to stay with a friend in our village and saw one of the dresses I'd designed and made – her friend was wearing it – and asked who'd made it. She came to see me and my grandmother and offered to take me on as an apprentice.'

Thea smiled at her. 'She must have recognised your talent and wanted to nurture it.'

Marianne shrugged. 'I suppose so. She taught me a lot. What about you? What job did you do in London?'

'I got a very boring job in an office to start with. I just needed something to earn my living the same as a lot of other young women. I shared a flat with three others.' Thea frowned. 'But it was hard to make ends meet sometimes, what with paying the rent and having enough money to buy something affordable to eat at midday. I wasn't the only one struggling to get by until payday.' She sighed. 'Anyway, that gave me the idea for my business: I set up as a mobile lunch provider, started with making sandwiches and taking them into work in a basket to sell to the other girls at a cheaper price than if they had to go into a tea room to eat. It grew from there: I baked cakes and sold them in slices. After a bit I was able to give up my office job and concentrate on being a caterer, bringing food into the city to feed the many women working there. It grew into a good business, and I had several vans going out each day, selling meals to people in offices and on the street. I ended up employing people to work for me – the business worked because people have to eat.'

'I might have bought some lunch from one of your vans – I did that sometimes, it was cheaper than going in a restaurant or café, and the food was good.' She smiled at Thea. 'So why did you come back here?' Her cheeks grew warm. 'If you don't mind me asking.'

'Not at all.' Thea linked her arm through Marianne's. 'It was the right time to come back. I'd achieved more than I ever thought possible, I heard Rookery House was up for sale and I've always wanted to live there, and I'd had an offer for the business, so I took it. I'm enjoying living back here and being out in the countryside again, I missed it very much.'

Marianne nodded. 'I understand that completely. I loved my work but wasn't so keen on living in a city.' She glanced at Thea and smiled. 'I'm pleased to have been evacuated here, it's like a breath of fresh air.'

Marianne could feel all eyes on her as she went into Barker's grocery shop with Thea. The other two ladies who were talking to the woman behind the counter fell silent and looked at her without any attempt to hide their curiosity as they clutched their handbags tightly in their hands along with their empty baskets.

'Good morning, Thea,' the woman behind the counter said cheerfully. 'And who have you got here? This your evacuee?'

'Morning, Grace. Yes, this is Marianne, who's billeted with me.' Thea nodded at the other two customers, who stood silently watching. 'Morning, Rosalind, Sylvia.'

'Good morning, Thea,' the two women chorused back.

Marianne was sure she'd seen the women at the hall yesterday.

'Welcome to Great Plumstead, Marianne.' Grace gave

her a friendly smile. 'I hope you'll settle in well and enjoy living here.'

She smiled back at the older woman. 'Thank you.'

'Rosalind and Sylvia here were just telling me about their own evacuees,' Grace said, raising her eyebrows.

'They not with you?' Thea asked.

'No.' Rosalind's lips pinched into a thin line. 'She wasn't up when I came out.' She paused for a moment, her face pulled into a sour look of disapproval. 'She went to the Half Moon last night with a few of the other evacuees. That is *not* what we expect; I shall be having words with Prue, women simply do not behave like that around here.'

Sylvia nodded in agreement, the pheasant feather of her felt hat bobbing up and down comically.

'But they do in London where they come from,' Thea said. 'Women go in pubs just as much as men there, they probably just wanted to get together – it's not easy going to live in a strange place.'

'Well, really!' Rosalind snapped.

Thea glanced at Marianne, her lips twitching, before turning her attention to Grace. 'Right, I've got a list of things we need. Should I leave it with you and come back in a bit, Grace, so you can serve Rosalind and Sylvia first?'

'No, you go ahead, we're happy to wait.' Sylvia spoke for both of them.

'All right, if you're sure, thank you.' Thea handed the list to Grace, who quickly scanned it. 'And are you looking to employ anyone at the moment, Grace, only Marianne's looking for a job?'

'No, not right now, with me and Jim we're managing

fine between us.' Grace put a blue bag of sugar down on the counter. 'Sorry, dear. You should try the butcher's or baker's; they might be looking for staff. I hope you find something.'

'Thank you.' Marianne smiled at the older woman who did look genuinely pleasant, unlike Rosalind and Sylvia, who seemed to be watching her every move.

'And if I hear of anything, I'll let you know. Did you work in a shop in London?' Grace asked, adding a bag of flour to the growing pile of groceries on the counter.

'No, I'm a seamstress,' Marianne said.

'Worked in London's West End designing and making gowns for the upper class,' Thea added. 'She's a talented young woman; that dress is one of your designs, isn't it?'

Marianne nodded, her cheeks growing warm as the three women scrutinised her dress, taking in every detail.

'It's beautiful,' Grace said. 'You've got a good eye for detail and it's very well made, looks a picture on you, dear. She's clearly a very talented young woman, isn't she, Rosalind?'

'Indeed,' Rosalind grudgingly agreed.

Sylvia nodded in agreement, her features softening slightly as she cast her eyes over Marianne's dress.

'That's everything.' Grace placed the last item on the counter and she added up the cost while Thea packed them into her basket.

Outside in the bright sunshine again, Thea tucked her arm through Marianne's. 'I'm sorry about that. I wouldn't have gone in there yet if I'd known those two were in there – they gave you a good looking-over, didn't they?'

Marianne nodded. 'Don't worry, us evacuees must seem like a terrible intrusion on village life, especially the ones who are getting up to things women don't usually do around here.'

Thea pulled a face. 'I hope you didn't mind about me saying where you worked, only I could see the way Rosalind and Sylvia were looking at you and knew what they were thinking, they're sour pusses the pair of them.' She shook her head. 'I feel sorry for the evacuees billeted with them; no wonder they escaped to the pub.'

'Life in the East End is a lot different from here,' Marianne said as they walked along the street towards the other grocer's shop.

'Exactly, and Rosalind and Sylvia need to become more broad-minded and tolerant, and appreciate that not everyone has lived a sheltered life in a Norfolk village like they have. We don't want to turn the arrival of evacuees here into a clash of cultures.'

'Marianne!' a loud voice shouted from further down the street. Marianne and Thea had just stepped out of the baker's after once again failing to find anyone who was looking for staff.

'Sally!' She smiled at the young woman who was hurrying towards her with Prue by her side, the pair of them out doing the shopping like her and Thea.

'Good morning.' Prue looked pleased to see them. 'How are you getting on?' She directed her question to both of them.

'Absolutely fine, aren't we, Marianne?' Thea said.

'Good, I wish everyone was.' She paused for a moment. 'I had a telephone call at eight o'clock this morning complaining about evacuees and their behaviour.' She sighed. 'They haven't even been here twenty-four hours yet and some people are moaning.'

'Rosalind?' Thea asked.

Prue nodded. 'She'd find something to complain about even if she had a saint go and live with her.'

'Watch out, she was holding court in Barker's,' Thea warned.

'Right, well, I'll go and see her there.' Prue turned to Sally. 'Why don't you go and sit on the seat under the beech tree and wait for me? Perhaps you and Marianne can have a chat while you wait.'

'Shall we?' Sally asked.

Marianne looked at Thea. 'Do you need me to come back with you straight away?'

'No, you go and talk to Sally and I'll see you back at home later,' Thea said. 'We'll have dinner at half past twelve.'

'I'll be back by then.'

Sally and Marianne headed over to the metal seat that circled the girth of the large beech tree on the edge of the village green.

'What have you been up to, then?' Sally asked, plonking herself down on the seat.

Marianne sat beside her. 'Looking for a job.'

'A job? What sort of job?'

'Anything they might have going in the shops here. We've asked in all of them – the two grocers, the

72

baker's, the post office, even the butcher's – but none of them needed anyone.' She sighed. 'I'll have to look further afield.'

Sally frowned. 'Ain't your 'usband giving you any money, then?'

'I like to work, to keep busy; it's what I'm used to.' Marianne avoided telling her the whole truth: if she didn't work, there'd be no money coming in from anywhere else and certainly not from her fictitious husband.

'Well, I'm glad to 'ave finished work.' Sally sighed, leaning against the back of the seat. 'I'll be busy soon enough with the baby so I'm makin' the most of it.'

'How are you settling in?' Marianne asked. 'Do you like it here?'

'The house is lovely, Prue's kind and her sons, Edwin and Jack, and daughter, Alice, 'ave all been very nice to me but her 'usband, Victor . . .' Sally pulled a face. 'Well, I 'eard 'em arguing last night – he didn't want me billeted there and she 'ad to remind 'im about the fifty-pound fine or prison sentence.'

'What's he like?'

'If he made his moustache any narrower then he'd have a definite look of Hitler about him – he slicks his dark hair down like him.' Sally giggled. 'It ain't for me to say but he ain't the sort of man I would've thought Prue would be married to, she's a bit bossy but in a nice way and she's kind-hearted. They sleep in separate rooms not like proper married couples.' She paused. 'Mind you, if I was married to 'im, I'd want my own bedroom.'

'Shhh!' Marianne looked around to check they hadn't

been overheard. 'You oughtn't go telling people that; Prue might not appreciate others knowing their sleeping arrangements, even if her husband is horrible.'

Sally's cheeks flushed. 'I don't want to upset her; she's been really nice to me. Don't worry, I ain't going to tell anyone else.'

'And you'd better just keep out of her husband's way.'

'Oh, I intend to and I don't think he'll want to spend any time around me either, so between the two of us we should 'ardly know the other's there.' Sally stroked her swollen belly. 'So, what's it like where you are?'

'I like it, Thea's house is out in the countryside and her and Prue's brother live there too, only in an old railway carriage next to the orchard. You should come over and visit, I'm sure Thea wouldn't mind.'

'Yeah, I'd like that. Look!' Sally grabbed Marianne's arm, nodding over to a group of expectant mothers who were wandering along the row of shops. 'They were on the train with us yesterday, weren't they?'

Marianne recognised the woman with the peroxide-blonde hair arranged into a pompadour style. 'Yes, they look out of place here, like they're lost.'

'It ain't like Whitechapel around 'ere, that's for sure. I've been writin' about it in my letter to Arthur, must get it in the post before I go back to Prue's.' She pulled an envelope out of her pocket and stroked her husband's name, which she'd written neatly on the front. 'Have you written to your husband yet?'

'No, not yet.' Marianne watched as the group of evac-uee women walked along, several of them with infants in tow, their presence attracting attention from local women who'd come to the shops. 'There was a woman in the grocer's complaining that her evacuee had gone to the pub last night, she wasn't happy about it at all.'

'What's wrong with that? Perhaps they should have invited her to go with them.' Sally giggled.

'I don't think she'd go even if they asked, she looked a bit sour.' Marianne smiled. 'I got the feeling that whatever her evacuees do it won't be right with her. We've been very lucky who we've been billeted with, Sally.'

'It's a pity no one wants any more help in their shops,' Hettie said, washing up a plate from their dinner.

'I know; I'll have to look further afield.' Marianne picked up another clean plate from the draining board and dried it with the teacloth. 'Where's a good place to start?'

'Well, there are a lot more shops in Wykeham and a seamstress as well. I think you should try offering your services there first; you're more likely to get a job doing something you've got experience in. It's market day on Thursday so we'll be going in, you can come with us.'

'How far away is it?'

'Only four miles, the train runs there on the way to Norwich so it's easy enough to get to,' Hettie explained. 'I'm going blackberrying this afternoon, see if there's enough ripe to make a pie; do you want to come with me?'

Marianne smiled at the older woman. 'Thank you, I'd like that. I used to go with my grandmother when I was little. Is Thea coming?'

Hettie put the last of the clean plates to drain. 'No, she's seeing to her beehives this afternoon down in the orchard, so we'll steer clear of them, don't want to get stung.'

Slowly making their way along a hedgerow bordering Rookery House land a short while later, their fingers staining purple from the blackberries that were starting to ripen nicely – and with plenty more still green, there promised to be a good crop this year – Marianne told Hettie about the unwelcoming attitude of the women she'd seen in the grocer's shop.

'You don't want to take any notice of them; they'll find something to moan about with anything. I feel sorry for the evacuees living with them, though, it's not a nice feeling not to be wanted.'

'Prue's husband didn't want one either. Sally heard him complaining to Prue.'

Hettie pulled a face. 'I'm not surprised, he's not one for putting himself out for other people unless there's something in it for himself. I feel sorry for Prue, being married to him, I really do. Why she lumbered herself with him I don't know ... well, I do, it's because of them boys: she wanted to be their mother.'

Marianne added another handful of berries to the basket. 'Sally said she was surprised Prue was married to someone like him.'

Hettie shrugged. 'We – me, Thea and Reuben and Lizzie, she's Thea's youngest sister and lives in Norwich – we all thought she was doing the wrong thing marrying him ...' Hettie sighed. 'But she knew her own mind and wouldn't be persuaded otherwise ... Still, she's done a good job bringing up the boys and her own Alice. I suppose she's got used to Victor over the years but it's not a loving marriage, I don't think. She hasn't said as much, but Victor's not a kind or generous man, and likes to be the king of his castle at work and at home. She's put up with him far longer than many women would, though most wouldn't have married him in the first place!' Hettie shook her head. 'I suspect she makes the best of things for the children's sake, though to me that's living a lie . . . but each to their own I suppose. You never know what someone's life is like unless you walk in their shoes, do you?'

Marianne nodded, thinking that Prue wasn't the only one who was living a lie: she and Prue were both doing it for the sake of their children. 'I hope Sally gets on all right there.'

'We'll see.' Hettie looked at the pile of blackberries in the basket. 'Let's pick as far as the gateway and then we'll have enough for a pie.'

Chapter 9

Reuben fitted the bench into place and stepped back as far as the narrow gap in front of the opposite bench would allow to check it looked straight. He'd been busy fitting out the Anderson shelter to make it more comfortable and now it had a bench along each side, with another shorter one at the back for people to either sit or lie down on, depending on how many were occupying it. He'd covered the floor with wooden boards and built a short flight of steps down to the shelter with bricks and cement, so it was easier to get in and out – Hettie wouldn't have a problem any more.

A warning bark from Bess, who was lying outside waiting for him, made Reuben look out of the doorway. He could see someone was patting the dog's head, but couldn't make out who it was as they were just a dark silhouette against the blue sky.

'You've been busy,' a voice called in to him.

Emerging into the sunlight, Reuben saw it was Jack. 'Thought I'd better get it ready for whatever happens. Come and have a look.'

He stepped to the side as his nephew went inside to look around.

'It's much better now.' Jack sat down on one of the benches and then lay down, tucking his hands behind his head. 'You could even have a sleep if you didn't roll around too much.'

Reuben sat down on the bench opposite him. 'You not at work today?'

Jack swung his legs round and sat up. 'I had the afternoon off. Father let me because I wanted to go and sign up.' He grinned, throwing his arms wide. 'You're looking at the Royal Engineers' newest recruit.'

Reuben stared at the young man; even in the dim light of the shelter, he could see that he was glowing with excitement. He knew exactly how that felt, he'd felt it himself when he and his brother William had gone rushing off to volunteer not long after war had been declared back in 1914, along with hundreds of others who'd wanted to defend their country's honour while having a lark and seeing the world at the same time. They had believed it would be easy to overpower the enemy and that they'd be home by Christmas. How wrong they'd been.

'Well . . . what do you think?' Jack asked. 'I want to get out there and do something to fight, not just sit back and wait to be called up.'

'I wish you well, lad, I really do.'

'You don't think I've done the wrong thing, do you?'

Reuben shrugged. 'I did the same thing. I wanted to fight, but I didn't know what I was letting myself in for – none of us did or we probably would have waited to be called up.'

'It'll be different this time, though,' Jack said. 'We won't be fighting in the trenches.'

'No, but war isn't a game. You've got to be careful, watch your back all the time and those of your mates, too.'

'I will.'

'What did your mother say?'

Jack rubbed the side of his forehead. 'I haven't told her yet. She didn't know I was going to sign up. Father did, of course, and he's pleased.'

'But your mother won't be.' Reuben knew Prue would feel quite the opposite.

'I'd have to go sooner or later because of the call-up,' Jack reasoned. 'At least this way I get to choose which regiment I'll be in and can do the sort of things I like – like building stuff. That's better than waiting and being told where to go and ending up doing something you don't like.'

Reuben nodded; the lad was talking sense, but it didn't make him feel any better. He completely understood why Jack wanted to go but did he really know what he was letting himself in for? There was only one certain thing: Reuben knew from his own experience that the young man who sat here with him now wouldn't be the same when he came back. *If* he came back. Going to war would change him.

Bess, who'd been lying looking into the doorway of the shelter, suddenly got up and trotted off and moments later returned walking at the side of someone. From the shape of her silhouette, with its broad-brimmed bee keeper's hat and veil, it couldn't be anyone else but Thea.

'Jack's here.' Reuben got up and went out into the sunshine.

'Jack?' Thea frowned, looking down into the shelter as her nephew emerged from the gloom and followed Reuben up the steps. 'Is everything all right? Shouldn't you be at work?'

'Normally yes, but I've had the afternoon off.' Jack stroked Bess's ears, the dog having come over to greet him again. 'I've been to join up.'

Reuben met his sister's eyes, the message in them clear to see: this wasn't something she wanted to hear.

Pulling herself together, Thea nodded. 'Army, Air Force or Navy?'

'Army – the Royal Engineers.' Jack smiled. 'Better than waiting to be called up and getting sent wherever they want to send me.'

Thea nodded. 'What did your mother say?'

Jack glanced at Reuben before answering. 'I'm telling her tonight with the others, except Father, he already knows because he gave me time off to go and sign up. He's pleased I'm volunteering and carrying on the family tradition in the Army like he did in the Great War.'

Thea snorted. 'There's a difference between working in the army stores like your father did and what you'll be doing. He went nowhere near a front line.'

Jack laughed. 'I know but at least he gave me time off. Anyway, I wanted to come and tell you.' He smiled at them both. 'I'd better get going.'

Thea touched his elbow. 'I'm glad you did. Thank you.'

'I'll see you soon. Bye, then.'

'Mind how you go.'

Reuben and Thea stood in silence, watching Jack go, and then Thea spoke. 'Prue's not going to like that. And as for Victor saying he's carrying on the family tradition, the man's a jumped-up fool.'

'Too right, but we knew Jack would go, it was only a question of when.'

'I know, let's just hope he comes home in one piece when it's all done.' Thea met her brother's eyes, and he knew she was thinking about their brother, William, who had never come home.

He nodded, not needing to say anything.

Chapter 10

Prue cut into her portion of steamed syrup sponge, pleased with how light and fluffy it had turned out. Sally had done a good job mixing the ingredients up, the pair of them working together earlier this afternoon as they'd prepared their evening meal of shepherd's pie and carrots followed by the sponge and custard.

Savouring the delicious sweetness of the dessert, with its top layer of golden stickiness, she looked around the table at everyone else tucking in: Jack and Edwin always had healthy appetites, but Alice and Sally seemed to be enjoying it too.

Sitting at the opposite end of the kitchen table, Victor poured another helping of custard into his bowl and Prue was relieved that despite his disagreeable attitude to Sally the night before, he now seemed in a much better mood. Granted he hadn't actually spoken to the young woman, but neither had he given her any unpleasant looks. In fact, he looked positively happy about something; he'd probably been counting his profits, Prue thought to herself.

'I've got something to tell you.' Jack broke the silence, making everyone look at him. 'I've joined up.' He beamed, the look of joy on his face leaving no doubt as to how excited he was.

Prue dropped her spoon into her bowl with a clatter. The sponge in her mouth, which only moments ago had tasted so sweet and delicious, now felt like sawdust, and it was all she could do not to choke on her mouthful. Swallowing hard she managed to get it down and took a sip of water, aware that Alice had asked her brother something but she'd tuned it out in her shock.

'... the Army, Royal Engineers,' Jack was saying in response to Alice's question.

It was as if her blood had been replaced with icy water, chilling her to the bone. Grabbing hold of the table, Prue glanced at Victor, who was smiling benevolently at his son. He knew. He knew about this, and that was why he was sitting there looking so full of himself. Why hadn't he warned her what was coming, instead of letting her find out like this?

'Ma?' Jack's voice made her look at him. 'Say something.'

She bit her bottom lip. 'When? How?' It was all she could manage.

'This afternoon; Father gave me time off work to go and join up. I didn't want to wait to be called up, and this way I could choose where I went,' Jack explained.

Prue glared at Victor. 'You knew he was going to enlist?'

'Of course. You should be proud of him being prepared to fight for his country, Prudence,' Victor said, scraping the last of his pudding and custard from his bowl.

'I've *always* been proud of him.' Prue looked at Jack, who smiled at her.

'It's what I want to do, Ma.'

She nodded. 'I know, but I didn't think it would be so soon ...'

'It'll be Edwin's turn to go next, then we'll have two sons doing their bit.' Victor stood up. 'I've got some work to do.'

He knew and yet he hadn't said a thing to her, hadn't warned her to help her and give her time to prepare herself. She squeezed her hands into fists below the tablecloth as she watched him leave the room. With a spark of fury igniting in her stomach she stood up.

'Can you see to the clearing up, Alice, please?' Without waiting for an answer, she followed Victor to his study. He was already behind his desk, smoking a cigarette, the smoke spiralling into the air in the ray of evening sunlight coming in through the window.

He looked up as she closed the door behind her. 'Prudence?'

'Why didn't you tell me he was going to join up?' she said, fighting to keep her voice calm when all she wanted to do was scream and yell, to take out on him the fury and hurt that weighed heavily in her chest.

Victor drew on his cigarette as he leaned back in his chair. He looked at her through cold blue eyes. 'Because I knew *you'd* make a fuss, Prudence. It was best if it was just done cleanly and swiftly, and you were told afterwards. The boy wanted to join up, and even if he didn't, he'd be called up soon enough.'

'It would have *helped* to know first . . . ' She paused, her mouth dry. 'I know he'd have to go eventually, but to find out like that,' she pointed back to the kitchen, 'when the deed was already done. I would have appreciated being warned.'

'You're far too attentive to the boys, always have been.' Victor knocked the ash off his cigarette into the glass ashtray on his desk. 'Now I've got work to do.' He opened one of the ledgers in front of him, picked up a pen and started totting up the rows of figures.

Prue stared at him for a few moments, her throat aching from the tears she was fighting to suppress – she knew from past experience that Victor loathed such displays of emotion, and the last thing she needed right now was any of his cutting remarks. He could have helped her to deal with this, given her a hint at what Jack was going to do, but instead he'd dismissed her feelings as fuss . . . It wasn't fuss, it was a mother's love for her child.

Turning on her heel she left the room, closing the door with more force than necessary, then she grabbed her cardigan from the coat stand in the hall and made for the door. She needed time to think and take in the news that Jack was going so soon.

Outside she turned and headed away from the centre of the village; she didn't want to run into anyone as they'd expect her to stop and chat or would want to complain to her about their evacuee. Walking fast, she headed down to where the river snaked its way across a water meadow – a place she loved as it was so peaceful and soothing. Close to the bank, a majestic weeping willow dipped its acid-green leaves into the slow-moving water, the green water weeds streaming out like hair. Dragonflies darted through the air, their gauzy wings catching the light, while swallows skimmed the surface of the water, hawking for insects. The whole scene was beautiful and tranquil. She closed her eyes and breathed slowly and deeply, the sounds of nature acting like a balm to her battered heart.

'Ma?'

Opening her eyes, she saw Edwin standing close by, a worried look on his face. She smiled at him and reached out her hand and he stepped forward and kissed her cheek.

'Are you all right?' he asked, his blue eyes anxious.

'Yes, I was just shocked by Jack's news.' She tucked her arm through his and looked across the river to the other side where some cows were grazing. 'I knew he'd want to go and do his bit, but not quite so soon. I hoped he'd at least wait to be called up.'

'Father knew,' Edwin said. 'He could have told you, warned you.'

Prue sighed. 'It would have helped.'

They fell into silence for a while until a flash of azure blue and orange caught her eye. 'Look, a kingfisher,' she whispered as the bird settled on a branch overhanging the river for a few moments before it took flight again and flew out of sight.

Edwin smiled at her. 'I love seeing them. Such beautiful

birds.' He looked at her, his face serious again. 'Will you be all right when Jack goes?'

'Of course I will. He's a grown man and as long as he writes now and again to tell me how he is, I shall be fine.' Though she would be worrying about him every single moment, she thought. 'I suppose you'll be next.' She did her best to smile.

'Ummm.' Edwin looked down.

'But hopefully not for a good while yet.' Prue knew her younger son didn't share his brother's enthusiasm for joining up. 'And you won't go springing it on me at tea-time like Jack.'

Edwin's blue eyes met hers. 'I promise I won't.'

'Good.' She patted his arm. 'Come on, let's walk for a bit, it's such a beautiful evening, far too nice to spend indoors, and,' she smiled, 'hopefully Alice will have cleared up the kitchen by the time we get back.'

Chapter 11

'This is it.' Hettie stopped outside the bow-fronted shop with a tailor's mannequin in the window clothed in a navy, flower-patterned dress.

Marianne looked up at the sign above the window which declared 'Iris Stokes – Seamstress' in gold lettering. This was where she had her best chance of finding a job that used her skills and experience. She was willing to work in a shop, but a job doing what she loved would be so much better.

'Do you want me to come in with you?' Hettie asked. 'I know Iris and it might help.'

Marianne shook her head. 'I think I'd like to do this on my own, if you don't mind, but thank you.'

Hettie patted her arm. 'I understand, I'm just going to nip to the ironmonger's and then I'll come back here and wait for you. Good luck.'

'Thank you.' Marianne waited a few moments, watching

Hettie cross the road to the ironmonger's shop, which had a fine display of goods outside, from tin baths hanging up to wheelbarrows, ropes and lamps. Turning her attention back to the seamstress's shop, she took a deep steadying breath and opened the door, making the bell above it ring out loudly.

Inside the shop the sight of dressmaking equipment – a sewing machine, another tailor's dummy, the large workbench with fabric laid out on it alongside pins, tailor's chalk and tape measures – made Marianne instantly feel at home. Before she'd had a chance to more than glance around the room, a tall, thin woman with her brown hair scraped back into a bun, making her thin face look more severe, appeared in the doorway that led to the back of the shop.

'Can I help you?'

'Are you Iris Stokes?' Marianne asked. The woman nodded. 'I'm Marianne Archer.' She held out her hand and the woman stared at it for a moment before shaking it briefly with a limp grip. 'I'm looking for a job and wondered if you're looking to take on anyone at the moment.'

'I haven't got time to train someone.' Iris frowned. 'I'm busy enough as it is.'

'I'm a fully qualified seamstress. I did my training in the West End of London with Dorothy Abrahams, learning how to design as well as make garments.' She smiled. 'So there'd be no need to train me. I've just been evacuated to Great Plumstead and would like to find work – preferably something that I'm skilled at and love doing.'

Iris's eyes fell on Marianne's swollen belly. 'Well, that's as maybe, but I'm not looking to employ anyone.'

Marianne nodded, forcing herself not to show how disappointed she was. 'Well, if you change your mind, I'm billeted at Rookery House in Great Plumstead.'

Iris opened her mouth to speak but the opening of the door and the jangle of the bell interrupted her and they both turned to see Hettie coming in.

'Good morning, Iris,' Hettie said. 'How's things with you?'

'Very well, thank you, Hettie,' Iris said. 'I hear you've retired from the Hall and now live with Thea Thornton who's come back from London.'

Hettie nodded. 'That's right, and now young Marianne here as well. We wondered if you could take her on, take advantage of having a West End-trained seamstress working for you.'

Iris folded her thin arms. 'I've just explained that I'm not looking for anyone right now.'

Hettie shrugged. 'Well, if you decide to take on anyone do get in touch.'

Iris nodded. 'I'd better get on, then.' She opened the door, making the bell jangle yet again, then stood to one side to let them pass.

'Thank you for your time,' Marianne said as they left.

Iris responded with a brief nod of her head and swiftly closed the door behind them.

'Well, that's a pity.' Hettie linked her arm through Marianne's as they headed towards the market square, which was full of stalls and busy with shoppers. 'Though

I can't help thinking the loss is more on Iris's side than yours. She's been running that business, taking over from her mother, for many years and a fresh pair of eyes and new designs would have brought it up to date. She should have snapped you up in the blink of an eye, if she had any sense.'

Marianne laughed. 'I may be wrong, but I got the impression that she's not the sort of person to do much snapping up of anything that comes her way without a lot of thought and consideration first.'

Hettie threw back her head and laughed, making several people nearby look at them. 'How right you are. I've known Iris for a long time, and it wouldn't surprise me if she has second thoughts about giving you a job.'

'Perhaps, but in the meantime, I still need to find something else to earn money. I'll ask around in the shops here.'

'All right, but don't go in Wilson's Hardware, will you? Only that's Prue's husband's business and it might help if Thea or I went in with you to ask. It might give you a better chance, but then again it might not, there's no telling with Victor. So, we'll leave that one to last if you don't have any luck anywhere else. I've got to do a stint on the WI's stall this morning, so that's where I'll be when you've finished. Good luck.' She squeezed Marianne's arm.

'Thank you.' She watched as Hettie made her way over to the WI's stall, which was busy with customers and where they'd delivered some cakes to be sold when they'd first arrived in Wykeham.

Looking around her she decided the best thing to

do was to systematically work her way around the shops. There were quite a lot of them facing on to the market square as well as some on the streets leading off. Hopefully one of them would be willing to give her a job because if none of them were, she wasn't quite sure what to do next.

'It's best if I do the talking unless he asks you something. I know Victor and how best to approach him, all right?' Thea said as they entered Wilson's Hardware, Seed and Agricultural Merchant.

Marianne's hunt for a job that morning had proved fruitless. She had visited every shop: some had taken her name and address, but most had just said they weren't looking for anyone right now. Although that was probably just a nice way of saying they didn't want to give a job to an expectant mother who'd been evacuated from London; at least nobody had been rude or unfriendly though.

She nodded and followed Thea to the counter at the back of the shop, her eyes drawn in so many directions by the shop's diverse stock – spades, mole traps, galvanised pails, mops, candles, nails, seeds and all manner of things involved with country life; you name it and they probably had it.

'Can I have a word with Victor?' Thea asked one of the men at the counter. 'Tell him it's Thea Thornton.'

'I'll go and see if he's available,' the man said before going through to the back of the building.

While they waited for him to return, Marianne tried not to get her hopes up that there might be a job here for her.

'Victor said to go right in,' the man said, returning from the back of the shop. 'First door on your left.'

'Thank you.' Thea led the way to Victor's office, pausing outside the closed door. 'Brace yourself,' she whispered. She tapped on the door and without waiting for an answer went in.

Marianne recognised Victor at once from Sally's description and her first thought was that her friend was absolutely right: if he had a narrower moustache he'd have a definite look of Hitler about him with his slicked-down dark hair.

'Dorothea!' Victor looked up from his desk, which was immaculately neat, with papers in precisely stacked piles, their edges even. 'To what do I owe this visit?' He took a draw on his cigarette and sat back in his chair, his cold blue eyes narrowing as they fell on Marianne, who stood slightly behind Thea.

'Good morning, Victor. Do you have any job vacancies at the moment?' Thea said.

Marianne hadn't known Thea long, but she could hear a different tone to her voice: she sounded as though she was having to force the words out.

Victor leaned forward in his chair and tapped the ash off his cigarette into the ashtray on his desk. 'Who's looking? Is it you? Run out of money already, have you?'

'It's for Marianne, my evacuee.' Thea nodded towards Marianne.

'You worked in hardware or agricultural merchants before, then?' Victor directed his question to Marianne.

She shook her head. 'I'm a dressmaker.' Victor snorted

and leaned back in his chair again, his attitude annoying her. 'But I'm a quick learner and a hard worker.'

'That's as may be, but I don't have any jobs going.' Victor returned his gaze to Thea. 'Is there anything else? Only I've got a business to run.'

'No, nothing else.' Thea gave him a curt nod and left the office, Marianne following close behind.

'Horrible, slimy . . . ' Thea muttered as they went out through the shop and out into the bright day outside.

Marianne put a hand on Thea's arm. 'It's all right; I'll find a job somewhere, don't worry.'

'It's not that, the man just . . . he makes me want to slap his smarmy face every time I see him. Why my sister ever thought it was a good idea to marry him . . . ' Thea shook her head. 'I'm sorry. Victor and I have never seen eye to eye. To be honest, it was a very long shot that he'd give you a job because of me, even if he had one going.'

'I wouldn't have wanted to work for him anyway,' Marianne said. 'He didn't seem very nice.'

'He's not.' Thea sighed. 'And I don't like him, and he doesn't like me either! The only thing we have in common is my sister and their children. It pains me to see them having to live with a man like that.'

'Prue seems all right.'

Thea looked at Marianne, her blue eyes weary. '*Seems* is the right word, but underneath I dread to think what she's really thinking and feeling. She doesn't let on to me, but I get the feeling that all's not right.'

Marianne nodded, remembering what Sally had told her about Prue and Victor sleeping in separate rooms and the man's attitude to her being evacuated there, but it wasn't her place to say anything, not now, she'd only recently come here and didn't know these people well or fully understand the situation yet. 'You could always ask her.'

Thea smiled. 'Oh, I have, many times, but my sister always says everything's fine. I don't believe her. I'm there for her when she wants to tell me.'

'I'm sure she knows that.'

'I hope so.' Thea linked her arm through Marianne's. 'Come on, let's go and find Hettie.'

'Any luck?' Hettie asked. She'd finished her shift on the WI stall and was waiting for them on a bench overlooking the busy marketplace.

Marianne shook her head as she and Thea sat down too. 'No.'

'Didn't Victor offer anything?' Hettie directed her question to Thea.

Thea shook her head. 'Of course not. I didn't really expect him to but I had to ask since Marianne's had no luck elsewhere. You know Victor.'

'Couldn't Prue have a word with him?' Hettie suggested.

'It wouldn't make any difference, and, besides, do we really want Marianne working for him?' Thea asked.

'No,' she and Hettie both chorused and then laughed.

'Don't worry, if I can't find work here then I'll just have to try in Norwich,' Marianne said. 'There must be something I can do in the city, even if I have to travel back and forth each day.'

'In your condition?' Hettie frowned. 'That's a daft idea, Marianne.'

But needs must, Marianne thought. Her savings would only last so long and she had to find a way of earning money. Of course, she couldn't tell Hettie or Thea that without telling them the truth about her being an unmarried mother-to-be, and that couldn't happen.

'I'll employ you,' Hettie suddenly announced.

'You?'

Hettie nodded. 'Yes, me.'

'Do you want me to cook or something?'

'No, I can do that perfectly well myself, but the thing I can't do very well and that you *can* is dressmaking. I'm going to employ you to make me a new dress.' Hettie beamed at her. 'We'll go and get some material from the haberdashery and you can start this afternoon if you like.'

'Thank you, Hettie, I appreciate that, but to be honest, me making you new dress isn't going to be a very long job, I need something more than that to bring in regular money.'

'I know that, but I have a plan.' Hettie looked at Thea who nodded encouragingly. 'Come on, I'll explain on the way.' The older woman stood up. 'We'll meet you back at the car in half an hour, all right, Thea?'

Thea smiled. 'I'll be there.'

Marianne shot Thea a glance as she got up and hurried after Hettie, who was already bustling her way across the busy marketplace towards the haberdashery.

'So, what's your plan?' Marianne asked as Hettie stopped to allow a woman pushing a pram to pass through the gap between the market stalls.

'You're a talented dressmaker, right? So you need to let people around here know that and the best way to go about it is to advertise your skills. I thought that if I go around wearing something you've made, it'll be showing off what you can do. If I know anything about some of the women in our village, it's that they like to dress nicely and having someone design and make something *especially* for them . . .' She smiled, as they set off again. 'They'll be thinking they're the bee's knees. Thea told me about Rosalind and Sylvia giving your frock a good looking-over in the shop the other day. They know good workmanship when they see it, and to have someone who designed and worked in the West End of London available in our village . . . Well, it's only a matter of time before you have enough customers wanting your services, trust me.'

Marianne laughed. 'You make me sound far grander than I am.'

'Most women in our village who don't sew their own clothes have them made by the dressmaker that just turned you down, so to have you, with London experience, will be far better than anything Iris Stokes can offer them. She really should have had the sense to take you on; your skills would have brought a lot more business to her. Still,' Hettie stopped as they reached the other side of the marketplace where the haberdashery stood, 'she'll rue the day she didn't snap you up. Come on, I need you to help me choose a good material.'

'Thank you, Hettie, I won't let you down.' Following the older woman inside the shop, Marianne felt her spirits rise for the first time today.

*

Back at Rookery House, Marianne followed Thea up the stairs.

'You can use the back bedroom next to yours as a sewing room,' Thea suggested as they reached the landing. 'There's already something in there that will be useful for you.' She opened the bedroom door and stepped to the side, ushering Marianne in ahead of her.

Marianne gasped when she saw what was standing under the window – it was a treadle Singer sewing machine. Walking over to it she stroked the black shiny paintwork, her fingers itching to get to work. She turned back and smiled at Thea, who stood watching her.

'Is this yours?'

'It was my mother's. Prue's kept it all these years but gave it to me when I moved back here as she never used it.' She smiled. 'Nor have I, but I couldn't part with it as I have happy memories of watching my mother working at it making clothes for us children.' She came over and ran her hand over the wooden base that the machine rested on. 'It just needs a drop of oil so it'll run smoothly and then you can put it to good use.'

'Oh, I will.' Smiling happily, Marianne touched Thea's arm. 'Thank you. I can't tell you how much this means to me. If I get designing and sewing again, and if Hettie's plan works, then I can earn a living from what I love doing best.'

Thea nodded, smiling at her. 'Good, that's what we want for you, too.'

Chapter 12

Marianne checked the measurement from Hettie's neck edge to her shoulder bone on her tape measure and wrote it down.

'If you hold your arms out to the side like this.' She demonstrated what to do and Hettie obliged, holding her arms out parallel to the floor like a child playing aeroplanes.

She wrapped the tape measure around Hettie's upper arm and again noted down the figure.

'You're very thorough, I must say,' Hettie said.

Marianne smiled at the older woman who stood before her in her petticoat and undergarments. 'If you want a garment to fit well then you need to be. Can you turn around please, so I can measure your back?'

'Did you do this where you worked in London?' Hettie asked as she turned around.

'Of course.' Marianne measured the width of Hettie's

upper back. 'My boss was strict about taking careful measurements, and they had to be double checked. Her reputation was built on providing her customers with a perfect fit and workmanship and she wouldn't tolerate any corners being cut.'

'She sounds like a hard taskmaster.'

'I suppose she was, but only because she expected the tailoring and fit to be perfect.' She wrote down another measurement. 'It was excellent training.'

'What were your customers like?'

'Rich!' Marianne smiled up at Hettie from where she was now crouched on the floor taking the older woman's waist-to-knee measurement. 'They'd think nothing of spending more money on a dress than some people earn in a year. The fabrics we used were beautiful – sumptuous silks and rich velvets, taffetas for ball gowns – all of the very best quality.'

'A bit different from my cotton, then?' Hettie said.

Marianne stood up. 'Yes, but you will appreciate and value your dress far more than some of the women I've made things for.'

Hettie nodded. 'I know the sort; I came across plenty of them in my time at the Hall.'

'How long did you work there?' Marianne asked as she added the final measurement to her notebook.

'I started in the kitchen when I was fourteen, straight after I left school, and worked my way up to being the cook. I liked the job, but not always the people I cooked for, not that I saw much of the visitors being down in the kitchen, though I heard about them and their ways from the other servants ...' She raised her eyebrows. 'They were born with silver spoons in their mouths and went through life not appreciating what they had and how lucky they were.'

Marianne nodded in agreement. 'Well, let's make you a dress you'll love and wear with much joy. Now I've got your measurements we need to work out a design.'

They sat down, side by side, on Hettie's bed and Marianne began to sketch the basic outline of a dress in her notebook. 'What sort of neckline would you like: round, V-neck or something else?'

'V-neck, with buttons opening down the front, if that's possible,' Hettie said.

'Absolutely, anything you like.' Marianne added a V-neck to the design she'd drawn, adding the button detail to the front. 'What sort of sleeves? Short, long, puffed at the shoulder, three-quarter or full length, with a cuff or without?'

Hettie laughed, her blue eyes twinkling behind her round glasses. 'I'm spoilt for choice; never had to think about such details before. When I was little my mother just made me a dress and I wore it – no questions were asked about what I'd like, and when I was getting my own clothes it was what I could afford.' She paused for a moment, considering, and then smiled at Marianne. 'Three-quarter-length sleeves ... now that sounds fancy, let's go for that, but not tight ones, mind.'

They spent the next few minutes perfecting the design, altering little details here and there until it was exactly as Hettie wanted.

'There, how's that?' Marianne said. 'It will work well on your body shape as well.'

'What, plump and short?' Hettie rolled her eyes. 'I've never been the shape of a Hollywood starlet so a dress that will make me look good is much appreciated. It's going to be wonderful, thank you, dear.'

'It's about making the most of what we have and wearing clothes that are a good fit and style for each of us. A woman should be proud of her body because it's a marvellous thing and where would we be without it? Most clothes bought off the peg aren't a good fit for the wearer, but this dress will fit you perfectly, Hettie.' Marianne paused and then laughed. 'Sorry, it's just a passion of mine and I like to see people wearing clothes that look good on them. I'll get the pattern drafted and get to work on it; I'm going to enjoy making this, Hettie, thank you.'

'And I'll be paying you for it,' Hettie reminded her.

Marianne frowned. 'It won't feel right taking money from you.'

'Nonsense, this is your job and I wouldn't expect you to do it for free. I insist, and I'll be proudly wearing it around the village at various dos, displaying your talent for all to see – like bait to catch a fish.'

'All right, thank you, but I'll owe you a free design and make it for you if it brings me customers. Deal?'

Hettie laughed and held out her hand to shake Marianne's. 'Very well, it's a deal.'

Chapter 13

Prue put her hat on and stared at her reflection in the dressing-table mirror. She looked smart: her honey-blonde hair was neatly coiled at the nape of her neck, a string of pearls at her throat, and she was wearing one of her favourite dresses, a blue one made of silk that made the skirt swish nicely as she walked. Wearing it always made her feel good – but not this morning. Nothing was going to lift the hollow aching that had settled in her stomach over the last few days and which had grown deeper and heavier if that were possible, and yet she had to carry on putting on a good face, pretending that she wasn't feeling this way. No, she had to present a strong front, keep her feelings firmly under control – there'd be time enough to let them go when she was alone in her room tonight. Then, and only then, would she cry because Jack was leaving, mourn that her son was gone and let herself recognise the fear for him that was bubbling away below the surface like lava in a volcano.

'Ma? Are you ready?' Edwin's voice called from the landing. 'We need to get going.'

'I'll be right there.' With a final look at herself she took a deep breath. *You can do this*, she told herself. *You must do this for Jack's sake — send him off with a smile. No tears allowed. Not yet.*

It would have been easier to say goodbye to him here, but she didn't want him to go to the station alone. Victor wouldn't be there, of course, he'd said goodbye to Jack with a shake of the hand after breakfast; he wasn't prepared to take any time away from his precious job. Alice had tearfully said goodbye to Jack before going off to get the bus to school, so it was up to her and Edwin to go with him, Victor having grudgingly consented to Edwin having an hour off work to see his brother off.

Downstairs in the hallway, Jack stood waiting with Edwin, his suitcase ready by his side. He smiled at Prue as she walked down the stairs, that beautiful, charming smile of his that had made her love him from the moment she'd first met him when he was just two years old.

'Come on, Ma, I mustn't miss the train,' Jack said.

Prue pasted a smile on her face. 'I was just making sure I looked respectable; don't want to send you off looking a mess.'

'You never look a mess.' Edwin put his arm through hers and she smiled at him, their eyes meeting, and she could see her feelings reflected in his own. He was going to find it hard to see his brother go.

*

The station platform was busy with people waiting to get the Norwich train. To Prue's shock, she spotted amongst the crowd three of the London evacuees, who from the look of the luggage piled on the ground beside them – string bags and paper parcels – were leaving. Two of them had young children who clung to their mother's legs, thumbs stuck in mouths as they looked around with their wide-eyed gaze.

'Oh no!' This was all she needed. She didn't want to waste a single precious moment of the time she had left with Jack, but she couldn't ignore the evacuees.

'What's the matter?' Edwin asked.

Prue nodded to the women. 'I'm going to have to speak to them.'

'The train will be here soon,' Edwin warned her. 'You mustn't miss Jack going.'

'I know, you keep him company for a moment, I won't be long, but I really do have to try to stop them.'

Leaving her sons, she marched along the platform to the women, trying to recall who they'd been billeted with. Was that their problem? If so, she could always move them somewhere else.

'Ladies, is everything all right? Where are you going?'

The three women turned to her, a look of recognition passing over their faces.

'Home, where we belong,' the tallest one said.

'But why?' Prue asked, looking at each of them. 'If there's a problem I'll sort it out, move you to a different billet. Please don't leave, you really are safer here.'

'*You've* always been kind to us, Mrs Wilson, but this

place ain't our 'ome and I keep wondering what my fella's gettin' up to without me there to keep an eye on him,' another woman said.

'And there ain't nothin' much to do around here – no pictures and they ain't keen on us goin' in the pub,' the tallest one added. 'We appreciate what you've done for us but we're better in our own 'omes.'

Prue sighed. She didn't have the mental energy to fight this right now. 'Isn't there anything I can do to persuade you to at least wait a bit longer and see if you get to like it more?'

'No,' the three women chorused as the sound of chuffing announced the arrival of the train.

Prue glanced further along the platform to where Jack and Edwin were waiting, this was rotten timing. 'I have to go. I'm sorry you're leaving, I really am. If you change your mind you can always come back.'

'It's all right, ducks, we'll be fine,' the tallest woman said, smiling at her. 'You go and see your lad off.'

Prue nodded and hurried to her sons as the train pulled into the station, cursing the bad timing, her conscience and sense of responsibility pulling her in two when there was only one place she'd wanted to be and that was with Jack, while they still could be together.

'Are they going home?' Jack asked.

She nodded. 'Won't be persuaded otherwise.' She smiled at her son, brushing imaginary fluff off his shoulders. 'Are you sure you've got everything?'

'It's a bit late now if I haven't.' Jack smiled back at her. 'I'm not going to need much, I'll be wearing uniform once I get there, but if I do need anything sent to me I'll let you know.'

She nodded. 'Look after yourself and write. Definitely write to us as often as you can.'

'I will, I promise.' Jack leaned forward and kissed her cheek. 'You look after yourself, Ma.'

She nodded, unable to speak, and threw her arms around him, resting her head on his chest for a few seconds before releasing him and stepping back.

'Goodbye, Edwin.' Jack held out his hand to shake his brother's. 'It'll be your turn soon.'

Edwin shook his hand. 'I'm not in such a rush as you.'

'All aboard!' the guard shouted.

Jack picked up his suitcase and grinned at them before climbing into the nearest carriage and slamming the door shut behind him. He pulled the window down and leaned out. 'Next time you see me I'll be in uniform.'

Prue swallowed hard. 'And very smart you'll look, I'm sure.' She wanted to say more, to tell him to be careful, look after himself, come home safe, but she dared not because it might release the hard knot of distress that was aching in her chest. She'd already told him these things, he didn't need reminding now, he needed sending off with a smile and good cheer.

A blast from the guard's whistle at the far end of the platform was followed by great chuffs of smoke as the train driver made ready to leave.

'Bye, then.' Jack reached out his hand and Prue grabbed it, squeezing it in hers.

She walked along, still holding his hand as the train

began to slide forwards along the platform and then she had to let go. Jack waved, his head sticking out of the window, a wide smile on his face. Prue waved back, conscious of Edwin coming to stand beside her, watching until Jack's face became a blur and then finally disappeared as the train went around the curve in the line and was gone, leaving just the tang of sooty smoke in the air.

'You all right?' Edwin asked.

Prue nodded, not meeting his eyes. 'Come on, let's go home.'

Chapter 14

Taking care not to stand on the pair of wasps that were feasting hungrily on the juice of an overripe, split plum that had fallen into the grass, Thea reached up and picked more of the ripe ones still hanging on the tree and added them to her basket. There was a fine crop of Victoria plums this year; the firm, dark purple fruits with their delicate dusting of white bloom on their skins hung like decorations in the tree, standing out against the green of the leaves. She'd been picking them regularly for the past few days and Hettie was busy turning them into jam or bottling them to use during the coming months. There was such a lot that she'd take some to sell at the market this week in Wykeham.

Several of the apple trees were just as heavily laden with fruit, their boughs drooping down with the weight of the apples as they gradually ripened, the skins of some varieties developing a reddish blush. They'd all need picking and storing away. The next few weeks were going to be busy.

'Thea.'

She turned around and saw Prue making her way towards her. She'd had a feeling she might appear today.

'Watch out for wasps on the ground, they're feeding themselves silly,' she warned her sister. 'You come to help pick?'

'Hettie told me you were out here,' Prue said, not answering her question.

Thea put her heavy basket down. 'Did Jack get off on time?' He'd dropped by last night to say goodbye to her, Hettie and Reuben.

Prue nodded, reached up to pick a plum and then took a bite. 'Umm.' She licked a dribble of juice that started to snake down her chin. 'Delicious.'

'You're welcome to take some home if you like.'

Prue nodded. 'Thank you. The boys love plums . . .' She was about to take another bite but stopped, her eyes filling with tears.

'You all right?' Thea asked gently.

'Yes . . . no!' Her voice came out hoarse.

Thea put her hand on Prue's arm. 'It's hard to send your son off but, knowing Jack, he'll be just fine.'

Prue sniffed. 'I hope so.'

'Did you all go to the station with him?'

'Just me and Edwin. Alice wanted to be there but with her doing her School Certificate this year Victor wouldn't hear of her taking time off school and, of course, he wouldn't take time off work either.'

111

Thea frowned. 'But he's the boss! He can take time off whenever he wants, and it wouldn't have been for long!'

Thea, Reuben and Hettie had all asked Jack if he'd like them to go to the station with him when they'd seen him last night, but he'd said no, he didn't want a fuss, which was fair enough, but for Victor to use his work as an excuse for not seeing his son off to war was feeble and to her mind showed where his priorities lay.

'I know, but you know what he's like, he said his good-bye before he left for work.'

Thea shook her head. 'I still sometimes can't believe that you married him.'

'Don't! Not now, Thea.' Prue sighed. 'I know you and Victor have never got on, but it was my decision, not yours, and it's not as if I had a lot of choice after so many men got killed in the Great War, is it? Look at you, for instance, you've never found another man to marry ...' She put a hand to her mouth. 'Thea ... I'm sorry, I shouldn't have said that.'

'No, you shouldn't.' Thea bit her lip, giving herself a moment to quell the anger starting to fizz inside her. Prue was upset at Jack leaving and was hurting inside and lashing out. 'But you know, I would rather have stayed unmarried than settle for a man like Victor.' She sighed. 'I'm going to say what I think, Prue: he doesn't deserve *you* or his wonderful children.'

Thea still remembered the shock she'd felt when she'd heard that Prue was getting married to Victor – she was living in London by then and had come back to try to persuade her sister to pull out of the wedding, but Prue had been adamant that it was the right thing for her to do. It had been a bitter day watching her sister tie herself to a man they both knew Prue would never seriously have considered marrying if the Great War hadn't happened and so many decent men hadn't been lost. Since then it had been a bone of contention between them, Thea finding it impossible to hide her dislike of the man. Perhaps it was just as well she'd lived in London for most of her sister's married life and not seen much of them, otherwise she and Prue may have had an irrevocable falling-out and never spoken to one another again. As it was, part of her reason for returning to live here, apart from buying her dream home, was to keep an eye on Prue, sensing that her sister was hiding a growing unhappiness.

'You don't need to worry about me; I'm used to Victor and his ways. If he chose not to come this morning, then he's the one that missed out, that's the way I see it.' Prue shrugged. 'Let's not argue about this, I really don't have the energy or the patience, it's been difficult enough this morning as it is with Jack going and then the evacuees leaving—' She stopped, her voice betraying the tears that threatened.

'Evacuees leaving? What's going on?' Thea asked.

Prue explained what had happened at the station. 'They were adamant about going back and I couldn't persuade them to stay longer or give it a try in another billet.' She frowned. 'They've only been here just over a week, that's not long enough to give it a fair chance. And what if the bombers arrive over London? Their infants and unborn babies will be in danger.'

Thea picked up the basket of plums. 'Come on, let's go in and have a cup of tea; I think we could both do with one.'

The sweet, rich smell of plum jam met them at the kitchen door. Inside, a flushed-faced Hettie stood watching over the large preserving pan on top of the range, a wooden spoon in her hand as she gently stirred.

'Oh, that smells good.' Thea went over to peer into the pan, its contents roiling and boiling, the bubbling mixture rising and rolling like inside a volcano. It was hypnotic to watch. 'Is it nearly ready?'

'Won't be long.' Hettie glanced at Prue. 'You look like you need a cup of sweet tea.'

'That's what we've come in for.' Thea reached for the kettle at the back of the range and moved it on to the hot plate. 'Do you want a cup?'

Hettie nodded. 'I'd love one; it's thirsty work making jam.'

'Can you put the tea in the pot, Prue, while I see if Marianne wants to join us?' Thea asked.

'Sally's up there with her,' Hettie said.

'I forgot to say, she came with me,' Prue said. 'She went up to the sewing room.'

'I'm sure they'll both want one, then, so put enough tea leaves in the pot for all of us,' Thea said.

Sitting around the large kitchen table, with cups of steaming tea in front of them a few minutes later, Prue told Marianne, Sally and Hettie about the evacuees leaving.

'I ain't surprised, to be 'onest,' Sally said. 'It ain't just because they've got to keep an eye on their 'usbands, although that might be true for some, but being 'ere . . . well, it's so different from where we come from, and if they were staying somewhere where they didn't feel welcome then that would 'ave tipped the balance to make them decide to go 'ome.'

'I appreciate that, but they just refused even to consider giving it another go in a different billet,' Prue said. 'They'd made up their minds and there was no shifting them, but they could be putting themselves and their children in great danger.'

'There haven't been any bombs yet,' Marianne said, 'but there's a good chance there will be.'

'Exactly.' Prue took a sip of tea.

'You'll need to keep an eye out for more leaving, Prue,' Hettie said, getting up to check on the jam.

'I know, that's what worries me: once a few start going, it might open the floodgates and before we know it they'll be leaving in droves.'

'I ain't planning on goin'.' Sally smiled at Prue.

'Me neither,' added Marianne.

Prue smiled at them both. 'I'm glad to hear that, but what can I do to help the other evacuees feel more at home here?'

'You can't do anything about what women's husbands might be getting up to back in London,' Thea said, 'but perhaps there's something that can be done to help keep the evacuees occupied here.'

'Idle hands make work for the devil,' Hettie chimed in. 'Give them something to do, get them involved with the goings-on in the village. You of all people are in the thick of that, Prue, what with the WI.'

'When's the next meeting?' Thea asked. 'Perhaps some of them could be persuaded to go along.'

'It's this Wednesday,' Prue said. 'Do you think the evacuees would want to go?'

'I will,' said Marianne, 'will you?' She directed her question to Sally.

Sally nodded. 'Course I will, and so might others if they know about it. It's a night out for them, perhaps not what they're used to at the pub, but it'll be something to do.'

'You need to spread the word, Prue,' Thea said. 'If they don't know about it, they won't come.'

'I'll help you go around and tell them if you like?' Sally offered.

'Will you come to the meeting, Thea?' Prue asked, looking her in the eye.

Thea shrugged, her sister had been badgering her to join the WI since she'd moved back here, and so far she'd resisted, saying it wasn't her sort of thing. 'I'll see.'

Prue opened her mouth to speak but was cut off by Hettie.

'Marianne and I will be there, for sure,' Hettie said, spooning some jam on to a cold plate to see if it had reached its setting point. 'I'll be wearing the new frock Marianne's making me.'

'Well, you've got until tomorrow night to spread the word among the evacuee mothers,' Thea said.

'I'd better get started before any more leave.' Prue drank the last of her tea and stood up. 'All right then, Sally, are you ready to go?'

'I am.' The young woman got up too. 'The WI won't know what's 'it 'em when all the evacuees turn up tomorrow night.'

Thea laughed. 'It might do some of them the world of good.' She caught Prue's eye and grinned. 'I may well come along after all, that's something that would be worth seeing!'

Chapter 15

'Don't look so worried.' Hettie said to Marianne as the women from Rookery House approached the village hall on Wednesday evening. 'You've done the most beautiful job on my dress – I've never felt so comfortable or looked so good in a dress before in my whole life, even if I say so myself. I'm going to stand out tonight and it's all down to you and your talent.'

Marianne smiled at the older woman. She'd only finished the dress that afternoon. 'It suits you well and is a good fit.'

'Exactly.' Hettie nodded towards some other women approaching the hall from the other direction. 'Look out, here they come.'

Marianne recognised two of the women from the shop on her first morning in the village.

'Good evening, Hettie, Thea,' one of them said, her eyes giving away a look of surprise as she took in Hettie's new dress. 'You're looking very smart tonight, Hettie. You usually—'

'Why, thank you, Rosalind. It must be my new dress.' Hettie swished her skirt. 'I had it specially designed for me and made to measure by a West End designer and it makes such a difference . . .' She moved forward to usher Rosalind in. 'Let me tell you about these three-quarter-length sleeves . . .' Hettie winked at Marianne as she put her hand on Rosalind's elbow and shepherded her inside the hall.

'There she goes!' Thea said. 'Her first fish well and truly hooked. Did you see their faces?'

'They did look very surprised,' Marianne said.

'Hettie's never been known for being stylish – just practical and wears what she can afford – so you've truly made her stand out and . . .' Thea smiled. 'Well, she's loving it.'

More women were arriving, including some of the other London evacuees, who smiled and said hello as they went inside.

'Come on, we need to go in,' Thea said. 'I don't want to miss the shaking up of Great Plumstead's WI with some new members.'

Inside the hall, there was a table at the back where teacups and saucers were set out, alongside several large brown teapots and plates of biscuits. Chairs were laid out in rows facing a table at the front where Marianne could see Prue was talking to an older woman.

'Prue's talking to the WI's president,' Thea whispered to Marianne. 'She's the boss but leaves the work to Prue to do as her vice-president.'

'Marianne – over 'ere!' Sally jumped up from her seat

119

on the front row and beckoned them to join her. 'I saved you a seat.'

'Are you sitting with us?' Marianne asked Thea.

She shook her head. 'Oh, no, I'll stay near the back, if you don't mind. I'm only here to observe, really. And to spread the word about your dressmaking services along with Hettie. You go and join Sally and I'll see you later.'

'All right, thank you.' She glanced over to where Hettie was holding court with a group of village women and when they looked over at her, she knew they were talking about her. Feeling her cheeks grow warm, she headed over to Sally and gratefully sat down beside her.

'Are you all right, ducks?' Sally asked.

'I'm fine.' She lowered her voice. 'Hettie's on a mission to get me some dressmaking work – she's over there showing off the dress I made her.'

Sally craned her neck around so she could see. 'Well, she looks lovely in it; you've done an excellent job.'

'I really enjoyed making it; it was so good to be doing what I love again. I just hope I get some more work now.' She looked around and saw that more of the London evacuees had arrived and were gathered just inside the door, clearly a bit unsure about being here.

Prue must have spotted them too because she hurried over to them. From where she sat, Marianne couldn't hear what Prue was saying above the general hubbub of women chattering, but her movements were very welcoming as she ushered them to sit down.

'I'm glad they've come,' Sally said. 'When we went around inviting them, some weren't sure.'

'Going to the WI isn't something they're used to, me neither.'

'Nor me, but since we're living 'ere now we should join in and give it a try.' Sally shifted her attention to the front of the hall as more and more people were taking their seats and the table at the front was filling up with other committee members, one of them with a notepad and pen who was probably the secretary.

A hush fell over the women as the President stood up and regarded them all for a moment before speaking in a plummy voice. 'Good evening, ladies, and a warm welcome to our visitors tonight. I do hope that you enjoy our meeting and will join our organisation. For those of you who are new, I am Mrs Baden, the President; this is my Vice-President, Mrs Wilson.' She motioned towards Prue with her arm.

Prue stood up briefly. 'Good evening.'

The President went on to introduce the other members of the committee, each of whom stood up and greeted the audience.

'Tonight's business is one of great importance and I will hand over to Mrs Wilson, who will tell you all about it and our plan of action.' The President sat down again, her work clearly done for now.

'Do you know what it's about?' Marianne whispered to Sally.

Her friend shook her head.

Prue stood up, looking very smart in a suit of moss-green, fine wool with a cream silk blouse underneath her jacket. 'Ladies, autumn is upon us and with it our hedgerows are laden with blackberries – fruit that is ideal for jam making. If we don't do something about it, it will all go to waste. Why should that worry us?' Prue paused for a moment, her eyes scanning the audience. 'Well, because if this war is going to be anything like the last one, ships bringing foodstuff to us will be sunk, men's lives will be lost, so we need to do all we can to provide as much food here for ourselves as we can rather than having men risk their lives to bring it to us. So, we need to harvest those blackberries before they go to waste, and turn them into jam.'

A hand shot up from the front row.

'Yes, Mrs Talbot,' Prue said, smiling at the woman.

'It's all very well saying that, but we need sugar to turn them into jam,' Mrs Talbot said.

Prue nodded. 'You're quite right, but our national headquarters are ahead of the game and have contacted the Ministry of Food and secured four hundred and thirty tons of sugar for the Women's Institute to preserve fruit with.' A gasp at the amount was let out by many members.

'That's more than a bag or two,' a woman behind Marianne said, making others laugh.

'We are able to buy one hundredweight for twenty-seven shillings and six pence and we can have as much as we want at the moment. So, ladies, with all that fruit waiting to be picked and turned into jam, who's willing to help? We'll need pickers, and people willing to peel apples, wash jars and make the jam.'

A show of hands went up with most of the women volunteering, including many of the London evacuees.

'Should we do it?' Sally asked.

Marianne nodded, and the pair of them put up their hands.

'Excellent.' Prue smiled broadly. 'Now the question is: how much sugar shall we order? Think about what you could realistically make in your kitchens and come and tell our secretary when we have our tea break. Also, if you know of any good places for picking blackberries around the village tell me so we can work out a plan of action for this weekend; that will give us time to collect enough empty jars, sort out our big pans to make the jam in, or borrow them from neighbours and friends if necessary, and receive our sugar. Thank you.'

'What will we do with all the jam we make?' Mrs Talbot called out. 'My Stan likes jam on a bit of toast but there's a limit to what even he can eat.'

'We'll sell it,' Prue said. 'We can have a stall here at our meetings, through the village grocery shops or on our weekly WI stall at Wykeham market. Monies earned will go into the institute funds and be used to make more jam, buy materials to make comforts for the troops, or other fundraising activities.' She paused for a moment, looking around at the audience before going on. 'Now it is time for our member, Mrs Williams, to speak; she is going to talk to us about setting up sewing and knitting parties.'

Prue sat down and the hall erupted into chatter as the women discussed what had just been announced, only becoming silent again when Mrs Williams was ready to start.

*

123

'Looks like there's going to be plenty of jam making going on in Great Plumstead.' Thea nodded towards the queue of members waiting to speak to the secretary at tea break. She took a sip of her tea. 'Are you up for making some, Hettie?'

'Of course I am. I love making jam, any excuse.' Hettie smiled. 'I'll have my tea and biscuit first and then go and tell the secretary how much sugar I'll want.'

'I'll help you make it if you'd like,' Marianne said. 'I've never made jam before, but I can peel apples and do what's needed.'

'I'll 'elp too,' Sally offered. 'Unless Prue's making some of her own.'

'I'll ask her to come and make it at Rookery House with us,' Hettie said, 'then we can all work together – many hands make light work.'

'We've got plenty of apples in the orchard,' Thea said. 'Members can have some for their jam; I'll go and tell Prue.' She went off to talk to her sister, who was surrounded by a group of women.

Marianne took a sip of tea and nearly spluttered it out again when Hettie suddenly poked her in the ankle with the toe of her shoe, indicating with raised eyebrows and the slightest of nods that someone was coming up behind her.

'Mrs Archer,' a voice said just behind her, making Marianne turn to see Rosalind and her friend, who'd admired Hettie's dress when they'd arrived. 'I wonder if you could spare me a moment?'

Marianne nodded. 'Yes, certainly.'

'Come on, Sally, let's go and put in my order for sugar.' Hettie put her arm through the young woman's and steered her off in the direction of the secretary.

'Hettie tells me that you designed and made her new dress?'

'Yes, that's right.'

'It's rather good.' Rosalind glanced over to where Hettie was now in the queue waiting for the secretary. 'I understand you trained and worked in the West End of London?'

Marianne nodded. 'Yes, I've designed and made all sorts of outfits, from day dresses like Hettie's to evening gowns and wedding dresses.'

'Would you consider undertaking some work for me? I understand you're quite busy, but if you could possibly fit me in, I would appreciate it, and pay the correct fee, of course.' Rosalind looked hopeful, her haughty exterior slipping.

Marianne was about to say that she wasn't busy at all but glanced at Hettie who was looking back at her, smiling. Her sales pitch of Marianne's work had been a clever one, implying that she was far busier than she was in reality, playing on the idea that women like Rosalind here would want something even more if it was in demand.

'What were you thinking of having made?'

'*Designed* and made,' Rosalind said. 'I thought a new suit for winter and a blouse to begin with.'

'That sounds doable. I'm sure I could squeeze you in.' She paused for a moment as if she were mentally working out when was best. 'How about next week? Monday

125

afternoon for a first meeting to take your measurements and discuss possible designs with you. Then you'll need to get some fabric from Wykeham.'

'Oh, I'll be buying the fabric in Norwich: so much more choice there.' Rosalind smiled. 'Monday afternoon sounds perfect, thank you. Shall we say two o'clock at The Grange?'

'I'll be there.' Marianne smiled at her.

'Excellent.' Rosalind nodded her head and, with her friend trailing after her, turned and made her way over to another group of women; she looked like the cat that had got the cream.

'You've just hooked a big influential fish there,' Thea said in a low voice as she joined her. 'Where she goes, others will follow.'

Marianne shrugged. 'I hope so.'

As the women sat back in their places once more, Prue stood at the front and announced, 'I'm delighted to tell you that we will be putting in an order for two hundredweight of sugar.' She paused while the murmurs of amazement ran around the members.

'That's a lot of sugar,' Hettie said.

Prue went on. 'As soon as it arrives, we'll weigh it out into your required amounts and it's up to you to turn it into jam, and only jam. It can only be used for preserving fruit and nothing else – not making cakes!' Again, she paused while members laughed. 'Finally, with your help, we've a plan of where to pick our blackberries and will meet at the end of Hubbard's Lane on Saturday morning at ten o'clock. Bring your baskets with you. Thank you.' She smiled and sat down.

'Saturday's going to be a busy day,' Hettie said. 'It'll be the first time this village has had a mass blackberry-picking and jam-making session.' She smiled at Marianne and Sally. 'Bet you never thought you'd be involved with something like this when you agreed to be evacuated.'

'No, but it'll be fun,' Sally said. 'I 'ope.'

Hettie laughed. 'Oh, it will be.'

Chapter 16

Saturday morning was bright and sunny, but with a mellow warmth rather than the harsh heat of summer. It was a perfect autumn day for blackberrying, Marianne thought, as she, Thea and Hettie headed towards the meeting point at Hubbard's Lane with empty baskets in their hands.

'Looks like a good turnout, and plenty of our evacuees as well,' Hettie said as they drew near the group of women waiting for the off.

Marianne saw Sally was already there, standing beside a blonde-haired girl who she recognised from the village hall on the day they arrived.

Her friend spotted them and waved. 'Hello. Marianne, this is Alice; I don't think you've met.'

Marianne could see the resemblance between Alice and Prue: they both had the same honey-blonde hair, which in Alice's case was worn in a long plait.

'Hello, it's nice to meet you.' Alice smiled at her.

'And you.' Marianne returned her smile.

'I think Prue's been a bit enthusiastic giving me these to fill up.' Sally held up her two empty baskets, speaking in a low voice. 'I ain't ever goin' to be able to fill both, blackberries are only small.'

'You'll be surprised how they mount up,' Hettie said. 'There's a bumper crop this year.'

'I—' Sally began but stopped as Prue called out for everyone's attention.

'Good morning, everyone! Thank you all for coming along on this glorious morning.' Prue smiled, looking around at the gathered group. 'We'll be starting our harvesting here on Hubbard's Lane and then working our way around other laden hedgerows. For those of you who are new to blackberrying, watch out for the thorns and wasps. Happy picking!'

'They taste lovely, all fruity and sort of mellow, not sharp like a blackcurrant,' Sally said a short while later, popping another blackberry into her mouth.

'At the rate you're going, you'll never fill one basket let alone two!' Marianne put another handful of berries in her own basket. 'You eat most of them.'

'And they'll upset your stomach if you have too many,' Hettie added, from where she and Alice were working just along the hedgerow. 'You'll be rushing to the lavatory all day tomorrow if you don't look out.'

Sally pulled a face. 'All right, just this last one and I'll stop.' She reached up and picked a large blackberry and ate it, a look of pleasure on her face.

Marianne laughed. 'Now just pick for the jam.'

They fell into silence and Marianne thought how much she was enjoying herself, taking in the sounds around her, the buzzing of bees, birds singing and the gentle sound of women chatting as they worked, along with the giggles and singing of the small children who had come with their evacuee mothers. It was a perfect picture of country life, where women from the city were joining in on something they'd probably never done before.

'I 'ad a letter from my Arthur this morning.' Sally pulled an envelope out of her dress pocket and kissed it. 'He's got to report to the army barracks on Monday ... and he's that 'appy about it.' She smiled but it didn't reach her eyes.

'Are you?' Marianne asked.

Sally shrugged. 'I worry about 'im, but he'd 'ave had to go anyway sooner or later when he was called up; he's probably only going a few months early by enlisting 'imself.'

Marianne touched her friend's arm. 'Try not to worry. He'll be all right.'

Sally sniffed back a tear and nodded. 'He worries about me! I told him I'm all right, and about seeing the midwife the other day and 'ow she said the baby's growing just fine. I'll be able to tell 'im about today in tonight's letter.' She fell silent and picked some berries, putting them into her mouth absentmindedly. 'Prue had a letter from Jack this mornin', that made her 'appy.'

'How's he getting on?' Hettie asked.

'Fine; loves it, apparently,' Sally said. 'You 'eard from your husband yet, Marianne? I hope you told 'im the midwife was 'appy with you too?'

Marianne shook her head. 'Letters can take a while at sea. I keep him up to date with how things are.' Marianne put her hand on her belly; she'd been reassured by the midwife's examination earlier in the week that the baby was growing well and its heartbeat was good and strong. Prue had arranged for all the expectant evacuee mothers to be seen by the local midwife and was looking into arrangements for their babies to be born at the nearest maternity home when their time came.

'I wouldn't like that, being married to a Navy man, off in a ship for months on end.' Sally sighed. 'I should be grateful my Arthur can get to a post box easily and get my letters back in return. If I can't see 'im, then getting a letter from him is the next best thing.'

Further down the lane some of the women had started to sing 'Jerusalem' and it rippled along as more and more joined in, including Hettie and Sally. Marianne was glad of the distraction as talk of absent husbands and letters made her feel guilty; she'd rather avoid the subject than lie to people who'd become such good friends.

Chapter 17

'Here, let me help.' Thea hooked the old walking stick around the stem and pulled the end heavily laden with blackberries downwards, so they were within reach. 'The best ones are always that bit too high, but with this we can get to them.'

'Ta, ducks.' The evacuee smiled at her and reached up to pick them with her purple-stained fingers.

'You're welcome. I'm Thea.' She'd noticed that most of the London women were keeping apart from the local women. A few were mixing but the majority were keeping together, not far away, but separate enough to see there was still very clearly a division. It was to be expected, really, with people like Rosalind and her cronies part of the WI. Although surprisingly they had actually turned out to harvest the blackberries, they were working as a group and not with the evacuees, not even those who lived in with them.

'I'm Gloria.' The woman held out her stained hand to

shake Thea's. 'Gloria by name and glorious by nature, so my 'usband says!' She laughed a deep, throaty chuckle that made her ample bosom shake.

Thea laughed. 'You're certainly brightening things up around here, your hair and your clothes are lovely.' She was like a peacock among the dowdy village women, with her peroxide-blonde hair arranged in a pompadour style and her vibrant emerald-green dress.

Gloria's big, brown eyes opened wide. 'You think so?' She pulled a face and leaned closer and whispered. 'To be 'onest wiv yer, I get the impression some of them,' she nodded to where the likes of Rosalind were picking further down the lane, 'ain't so keen on how I dress, but I like to look bright and cheerful. That Mrs Wilson, she insisted I put this apron on to protect my dress from getting all mucky.' She plucked at the paisley-print, cross-over apron that she was wearing, which strained across her swollen belly, while the sleeves of her dress stuck out in marked contrast.

'Blackberries stain, so it's best.' Thea looked down at her own apron. She, like most of the women, had covered up her clothes to protect them, and Prue had brought along spare aprons for the evacuee women.

'Me shoes ain't ideal for picking, though,' Gloria added, lifting up one of her white, peep-toed shoes, which were looking scuffed and stained. 'But I ain't got anything more sensible.' She giggled.

'Mind the nettles, or you'll know about it,' Thea warned her.

'Which ones are they?'

'These.' Thea pointed to some tall nettles that had grown up in the hedge through the bramble stems, thinking how every child growing up around here knew what a nettle was from an early age, learning quickly that they stung. How different was a childhood growing up in the East End of London where the world was filled with houses, the ground was paved streets and unless a home had a garden there might be very little contact with plants. These women certainly had been sent out to what was like another world to them. 'If you brush against them, they'll sting your skin.'

Gloria pulled a face. 'Let's 'ave a go then.' She brushed the back of her hand against a nettle leaf and pulled it back sharply. 'Ow! See what you mean.' She examined the white lumps that were starting to rise up on her skin. 'I'll keep my distance from them. Just be careful to only touch the blackberries; mind you, you 'ave to look out for the thorns on them.'

They started to pick again, side by side. 'What do you think of living in Great Plumstead?' Thea asked. 'Do you like it here?'

'Yes and no.' Gloria popped a blackberry in her mouth and chewed.

'Are you thinking of going back to London to be with your husband, as some of the evacuees have done?' Thea asked.

'No point, he ain't there most of the time, he's in the Merchant Navy, so he spends more time away than at 'ome with me. If I go back I'd only be livin' with his mother and that ain't much fun, especially with my older children

134

evacuated down in Devon – I'd have to put up with 'er on my own.' Gloria rolled her eyes. 'We don't exactly see eye to eye, she thought I weren't good enough for her son. No, being 'ere's better than living with her, only there ain't much to do, that's the problem.'

Thea stopped picking and looked at Gloria. 'What do you mean?'

'Well, today's all right, doing this is fun, but most days I ain't got much to do once I've done any shoppin' for me food. And in the evening there ain't no pictures to go to or dance halls. I'm used to being busy with work and 'aving places to go to when I ain't workin'. It's drivin' me up the wall, to be 'onest, and that's what'll drive me back to London.' She shrugged. 'I don't want to sound ungrateful, but I'm bored 'ere.'

'Do other women feel like that?'

Gloria nodded. 'Yes, and some of them ain't very welcome in their billets either, so they feel like they want to get out of there in the day but don't know where to go or what to do.'

Thea nodded. She'd seen groups of the evacuees wandering around the village. She considered for a moment. 'Would it help if you all had somewhere you could go in the day and be together and perhaps do something . . . ? I don't know what, but at least get out of the house for a while and meet up?'

'Yes! Have you got an idea?' Gloria's brown eyes held hers, looking full of hope.

'Possibly, I'll need to talk to Prue about it – Mrs Wilson – she's my sister, first. But if it did work it might help you all feel more at home and stop any more of you deciding to go back.' She reached out and touched Gloria's arm. 'Listen, don't say anything to anyone yet, please, but I'll do my best to help.'

Gloria's pillar-box-red lips pulled into a wide smile. 'Thanks. Cos it is lovely countryside round 'ere. If we could just have somewhere to go and somethin' to do, it would be smashing.'

Carrying on with their picking, Thea thought about what Gloria had told her, understanding how difficult it must be for the evacuee women to be uprooted from their homes, jobs and communities and transplanted into an alien environment. Without a place where they felt welcome and having nothing to do, it left them drifting and was a breeding ground for discontentment that would drive more and more of them home and into potential danger. People who felt they belonged and had something to do were more likely to be happy and stay put.

Hooking another high stem down to pluck the glossy black fruits, she considered where the evacuees could go in the day. It would need to be somewhere central in the village with space for them to gather, facilities for them to make drinks and food, and a lavatory. The obvious place was the village hall. It was empty most days, the clubs and societies it was used by tending to take place in the evenings. Then there was the problem of what they could do there. Just being together, chatting, letting the children play together would be something, but perhaps they could do more, have a sewing or knitting bee to make comforts for the troops or clothes for their children.

As the idea grew in her mind, Thea was more convinced that she was on to something that could really work; the only sticking point might be access to the village hall and that was out of her hands, but Prue could influence those who had control over it.

'Well, what do you think?' Thea asked Prue a little while later, after she'd explained what she'd found out from Gloria and the idea she'd come up with.

Prue thought for a moment, pushing a strand of her hair that had come loose from her scarf out of her face, her purple-stained fingers adding another streak of blackberry juice to her cheek.

'It actually sounds like an excellent idea. We really don't want any more going home.' She paused and looked at the group of women who were stretched out along the hedgerow busy picking the fruit, their voices and laughter filling the air. 'They look like they're having a good time this afternoon.'

'They are, but this is just one afternoon; what about all the other days when they're wandering around the village with nothing to do? And what happens when the winter sets in and it's too cold for them to be out with nowhere to go and not much to do all day? If they had a club of some sort to go to during the daytime it would help.'

Prue nodded. 'And the village hall is the perfect place; all we'd need is to get permission and the rest should be easy enough to sort out.'

'Well, you know who to ask. If I asked him, the answer would be no, just because it was me. You're billeting officer and should have some leverage.'

'I'll ask him this weekend, then.' Prue lowered her voice, and added, 'Put a little pressure on him to do his civic duty like I did before when he objected to Sally staying with us.'

'You're one of the few people who can get anything out of Victor.'

Prue sighed. 'I've had to learn over the years, but nothing is guaranteed with him. I just know his weak spots, that's all. So, leave it with me and I'll do my best. Thank you for thinking of it – you might just have saved these women's lives, you know.'

Thea waved the idea away with her hand.

'No, I'm serious, if we can get this club up and running and it stops the women from going home where they might be bombed, your idea will have kept them out of harm's way, Thea, so credit where credit is due. Don't say anything to anyone until we have somewhere to hold it – no point in raising hopes unless we can fulfil them.'

Chapter 18

'That's the last one.' Marianne sliced the apple she'd just finished peeling into pieces and added it to the bowl. She, Sally and Thea had worked their way through the pile of apples that had been picked from the orchard by Reuben earlier, and now the curls of apple peel lay in a heap on a sheet of newspaper in the middle of the table and a large bowl of apple was ready to be combined with the blackberries and turned into jam.

'I've never peeled so many apples in me life!' Sally said. 'I'll be seeing them in my sleep tonight.' She giggled. 'And blackberries waiting to be picked. It's been quite a day.'

'And it's not over yet,' Prue said, from over by the sink where she was washing the glass jars for the jam to go in and Alice was drying them before they went in the slow oven to sterilise.

'Are you ready for the apple, Hettie?' Thea asked.

'Yes, bring it over,' Hettie said, gently stirring the contents of a large pan.

Taking the bowl of apple pieces over to the range, Marianne breathed in the mellow, fruity scent of the blackberries gently warming in the pan.

'Oh, that smells lovely.'

Hettie smiled at her. 'That's the smell of autumn hedgerows, nothing like blackberry and apple jam on toast in the winter to take you right back to September days. Right, let's get the apple in.'

Marianne tipped the apple pieces in, using her hand to guide them so they fell gently. Instantly the dark purple juice from the blackberries began to stain the crisp, greeny-white of the apple a rich pink. It was beautiful to watch and as Hettie stirred the mixture, the colours swirled and combined even more, the apples turning completely pink and all the while the aroma filling the kitchen with fruity deliciousness.

Once Hettie was satisfied the fruit was mixed well enough, she tipped in the sugar, which had been warming in a bowl at the back of the range. Again, Marianne watched as a transformation took place: the sugar crystals becoming coloured with the rich pink colour until the white vanished as Hettie stirred the mixture.

'We need to bring it to the boil now and let the magic happen. Can you watch it for a minute or two while I get a drink? Jam making's thirsty work.' Hettie held out the wooden spoon for Marianne to take. 'Stir it every now and then; we don't want the sugar burning.'

Marianne watched over the pan, enjoying the swirl of

colours and the roiling, boiling motion as the fruit and sugar mixture became hotter.

'It's lovely to watch, ain't it?' Sally said, coming to stand beside her friend as Prue and Alice put the clean jars in the oven to warm. 'Can I have a stir? I ain't ever made jam before, we always got it from the shop.'

Sally had a thorough stir, staring into the pan as she moved the mixture around and then offered the spoon to Alice. 'You have a go, too.'

'Thanks.' Alice took the spoon from her and like Sally was mesmerised by the dark purple jam.

'This jam will be better than any shop-bought stuff,' Hettie said, coming over to check on the jam's progress. 'That's doing nicely.'

'It's lovely to think jam making's going on all over the village this afternoon,' Prue said, joining the little group at the range.

Later, when the jam had satisfied Hettie's setting-point test and had been poured into the warmed, clean jars, tops put on and labels added, everyone sat around the kitchen table drinking a well-earned cup of tea and eating a slice of fresh bread and butter, topped off with a generous spreading of blackberry and apple jam from what was left over at the bottom of the pan.

'This is so nice,' Sally said, her mouth full.

It was delicious, Marianne thought, savouring the fruity, mellow taste, which was quite unlike strawberry or raspberry jam.

Hettie beamed at her. 'Told you you'd like it.'

'We've done very well,' Prue said, gazing at the jars full

of glistening dark purple jam lined up on the table. 'The WI will have plenty of jam to sell, and every single jar will save space on ships coming in.'

'We can make more still: there's a good crop of damsons this year as well; it would be a pity to waste them,' Thea said. 'Damson jam is lovely, too.'

Prue smiled at her sister. 'It would be a pity indeed. I'm sure other members of the WI and our lovely evacuees – who I hope will become members too – will be willing to make more jam.'

'I'm joining,' Sally said. She looked at Marianne. 'Are you?'

Marianne nodded. 'Yes, I'd like to.'

'Excellent.' Prue smiled at them both.

'And I'm up for more jam making,' Sally added.

'And me,' Alice added.

'Looks like we're going to be busy, then.' Hettie met Marianne's eye and winked at her.

Chapter 19

Prue's mind was whirling with ideas as she sat nursing a cup of tea at the kitchen table on Sunday afternoon after the dinner things had been cleared away. The house was quiet – Sally, Edwin and Alice had gone out for a walk – and Prue was poised and ready to ask Victor about using the village hall.

He'd gone upstairs to his room to get ready to go out – he'd told her he had another meeting in Norwich this afternoon, something that had become a regular occurrence over the past few months and was, so he reminded her, part of his duty as a business owner and councillor. With the country at war it was even more necessary, so he said. To be honest, she rather liked it – better for him to be out than at home and her having to tiptoe around him if he was in a grumpy mood. He was at work six days a week and with his regular Sunday trips to Norwich he spent more time out of the house than here, but she really didn't mind that at all.

Hearing his footsteps on the stairs, she hurried out to the hall to catch him.

'Victor, I need to ask you something.' He was looking smart in his best suit, she noticed, and he'd even trimmed his moustache.

'What's that? I'm in a hurry.' He took his hat down from the coat stand and put it on. 'Can't it wait?'

'No, it's important. As billeting officer for the evacuee women, I want to start a day club for them to attend – it would give them somewhere to go and something to do.'

'Yes, very good.' He started towards the door.

'Wait! The thing is we need somewhere to hold it and the village hall is the perfect place, only we need permission from the committee and as you are their chairman and members always follow your lead ... you'd be a fine example of doing your duty to help others in wartime.' She left the suggestion floating in the air.

Victor glanced at his watch. 'I don't have time for this now, Prudence.' A muscle twitched in his cheek.

'All you need to say is yes, nothing more. The goodwill to the committee – and particularly to you for being so forward thinking and community minded – will be noticed by the village, I'm sure.'

He considered for a moment. 'Very well, but you will be responsible for it being kept clean, tidy and in good order. I don't want any East End mothers and their brats causing damage.'

Prue smiled at him, biting back the retort that they were hardly likely to go on a rampage and destroy the village hall. 'Of course, thank you. I'll see you later; I hope the meeting goes well.'

Victor nodded. 'I may not be back until late, these meetings often over-run.'

As the front door closed behind him, Prue smiled to herself. With Victor's go-ahead she could get busy, put the ideas they'd had into action. If the day club plan worked it would make a big difference to the evacuee mothers' happiness here in the village, hopefully enough to stop any more from leaving.

Fixing problems like this was so satisfying, she loved immersing herself in worthwhile projects; she positively thrived on it. Keeping busy, helping people, was what she loved to do – had always loved. She'd known it ever since she used to help at the Auxiliary hospital that had been set up during the Great War. She'd been too young to go off to France as Thea had done, so she had found a role for herself helping out there, writing letters for the men who were unable to do it for themselves because of their injuries. It was a simple task but made a difference to the men and she'd enjoyed it and it had sown the seed of her love of helping, organising, doing worthwhile things.

Back to now: step one was completed; with the committee's permission she could now get on with organising the day club and would start by going to see Thea later, taking Sally with her when she got back, so she and Marianne could give the evacuees' points of view on what would be needed. But first she wanted to write to Jack, replying to his first letter, which had arrived yesterday. In it, he'd sounded like he was loving every minute but reading between the lines and with her mother's radar closely tuned to her children's well-being, she sensed he was missing home. She'd write and tell him all that had been going on in the village – the WI meeting, the blackberry picking and jam making – and she'd be sure to save some jars so he could have some on toast the next time he came home.

Chapter 20

Thea stretched out her legs and closed her eyes, sighing happily, as she relaxed in the Sunday-afternoon sunshine. It was good to sit down after a busy week.

'You sound contented,' Hettie said.

Thea opened her eyes, shielding them from the sun, and smiled at the older woman and Lizzie, her youngest sister, who'd come over from Norwich for the day, who were sitting out in deckchairs with her in the garden behind Rookery House.

'I am … and full of your roast pork and all the trimmings and enjoying just sitting down doing nothing for once, and it's lovely to have Lizzie here, too.'

'I'm so stuffed it feels like I won't need to eat for a week!' Lizzie said, rubbing her stomach. 'You're such a good cook, Hettie.'

'I'm glad you enjoyed it, you know I love feeding people.' Hettie reached out and squeezed Lizzie's arm.

'It's good to have a sit-down and rest in the sun, though. It's been a busy week, but I've enjoyed myself immensely, what with jam making and having this smart new dress designed and made specially for me.' Hettie smoothed down the skirt of her new dress, which she'd put on for her Sunday best. 'The look on certain ladies' faces when they saw me in it at the WI, it was priceless.' She chuckled. 'I won't forget that in a hurry.'

'It's a beautiful dress; Marianne's very talented,' Lizzie said, admiring it. 'It suits you so well, the style, fit and colour, everything about it is perfect! I think I might have a look for some nice material and then ask her to make a dress for me.'

Thea laughed. 'See, you've set a new standard, Hettie. You need to watch out, soon women will be wearing Marianne's designs all over the village.'

'Oh, I do hope so. Where Rosalind goes, others will follow.' Hettie frowned. 'Only we mustn't let Marianne take on too much, she needs to rest as well as work.'

Thea nodded in agreement. She'd told Marianne to go and have a lie-down and rest this afternoon for a bit. The young woman was looking tired after the busy day yesterday, and working hard to get Hettie's dress finished in time for the WI meeting earlier in the week. She'd said this morning that she hadn't slept well as the baby had been so active in the night.

'I do think she'd be better off not worrying about work, though, let that husband of hers support her.'

'She's been used to working, Hettie, and enjoys what she does,' Thea said. 'Let her work while she can if she wants to; she'll have her hands full with a baby to take care of soon enough and won't be able to work much then.'

Hettie rolled her eyes. 'Independent women! You two are just the same.'

Thea and Lizzie both laughed.

'I had to work, Hettie,' Thea said. 'Apart from enjoying what I did, I didn't have a husband to look after me.'

'And I like being in charge of myself, my money and doing what I want.' Lizzie narrowed her eyes at Hettie, pressing her lipsticked pillar-box-red lips together. 'You haven't had a husband either, Hettie; you worked all your life.'

'I know . . . but it feels different somehow. I worked at the Hall; it gave me a job and a place to live. Besides, I never met anyone I liked enough to marry, but if I had, I'd have been happy to let my husband earn the money while I looked after the home.' She sighed. 'Do you mind that you never married?'

Lizzie shook her head. 'Not so far. I'm not saying I might not ever – I enjoy the company of some gentlemen, but I've never found anyone who I liked enough to marry, not yet. And even if I did, I'd still not want to give up work and be wholly dependent on him.'

'What about you, Thea?' Hettie asked.

Thea shrugged. 'Of course I wish that my lovely Tom hadn't been killed before we could get married.' She touched the ring on the third finger of her left hand – the engagement ring that he'd bought her in France on a leave they'd had together when he'd asked her to marry him and she'd said yes immediately. They'd planned to marry on their next leave, but that had never happened as he'd been killed a month later, leaving her heartbroken like so many other young women who lost their loves to the fighting over the French mud. No man had ever come close to Tom. She'd had a few relationships over the years while she was in London but nothing as deep or lasting.

Hettie reached across the gap between their deckchairs and patted Thea's arm. 'You've never forgotten him, have you?'

Thea shook her head, blinking back sudden tears that stung her eyes. 'No, and I never will. I'd rather not marry than settle for someone who is a poor imitation of him or who makes me unhappy . . . ' She was going to say 'like Prue' but instinct told her not to and when someone called out 'Hello' she looked towards the house and saw her sister, Sally and Alice walking towards them.

'Hello! You're not wanting more jam made today, are you, Prue? Only you'll have to wait, because I need a rest this afternoon.' Hettie chuckled.

'No, not at all,' Prue said. 'Hello, Lizzie. I didn't know you'd be here.'

Thea could see the uncertainty on Prue's face: she and Lizzie didn't get on well. They definitely looked like sisters with their honey-blonde hair and blue eyes, but in temperament they were like oil and water.

'I came on the spur of the moment, you know me.' Lizzie laughed, jumping to her feet. 'It's nice to see you, Prue, and you, Alice.' She flung her arms around her niece and hugged her, then stepped back to look at her, still holding on to her arms. 'You're looking lovely, Alice, growing into a beautiful young woman.'

Alice flushed. 'It's lovely to see you, Aunt Lizzie. This is Sally, our evacuee from London.'

'Oh, like Marianne,' Lizzie said, smiling and holding out her hand. 'Nice to meet you, Sally.'

'And you.' Sally shook Lizzie's hand.

'I've come to talk through some ideas with you all . . . ' Prue said, recovering from the surprise of finding Lizzie here. 'And Marianne, too, as this will concern her.'

'She's having a rest in her room,' Thea said.

'I'll go and see if she's awake,' Sally offered. 'She won't want to miss this, I'm sure.'

Thea smiled. 'You know where to go.'

Sally nodded and headed back to the house.

'Lizzie, can you and Alice get some more deckchairs out of the shed,' Thea said, standing up, 'and I'll go and make us all a cool drink.'

Once Sally and Marianne had joined them and they were each settled in a chair with a glass of homemade elderflower cordial that Thea had made, Prue began. 'After talking to one of the mothers when we were black-berrying yesterday, Thea had the brilliant idea of starting a sort of day club for the evacuees to go to each day.' She smiled at Thea. 'I think one of the problems that's likely to drive them back to London is having nothing to do here, day after day, and we could potentially solve that by giving them a place to go and something to do . . . ' She took a sip of her cordial. 'The obvious place to hold a day club is the village hall, for which we would need permission from the committee ... so ... being married to the chairman of the village hall committee, I asked him,' she paused for breath and then smiling broadly added, 'and with some gentle persuasive pressure, reminding him of his duty especially in wartime ... he said yes!'

He must have been in a good mood then, thought Thea, glancing at Lizzie, who winked back at her, probably thinking the same thing – both of them shared the same opinion of Victor.

'That's marvellous, Prue, well done.' Thea smiled at her sister, who was bubbling over with enthusiasm for her latest cause.

'So, the reason I've come here is, I ... we ... need to think of how this day club should be run, what equipment we need, what the evacuee mothers and their infants will do there, and so on.' She looked round at them all. 'I thought between us we could work it out.'

'How much money have you got to spend on it?' Hettie asked.

Prue frowned. 'Precisely *nothing* at the moment. I was hoping we could rely on donations of equipment and volunteering time. I'll ask the WI to be involved, of course, but I want to get the club up and running as soon as possible before any other mothers go home to London.' She reached down and took a notepad and pen out of her handbag. 'What do we need?'

'Well, there's plenty of crockery and cutlery in the village hall kitchen already, so the mothers will be able to make themselves drinks and have somewhere to prepare some food,' Hettie said. 'We don't need to worry about that, for a start. Although you might want a kitty to provide tea, milk and sugar – the mothers could pay a weekly sum to cover that.'

'Good idea.' Prue wrote it down.

'Some toys would be useful for the children to play with, perhaps there might be some around in the village that people's children 'ave grown out of and would donate,' Sally suggested.

'They could have some of our old toys, couldn't they, Ma?' Alice said at once. 'They're just up in a box in the attic now.'

Prue smiled at her daughter. 'Of course, good idea. And I'm sure there's more around the village. We could store them in the cupboards at the hall, there's room in there.'

'How about some books and magazines – a gramophone and records, even?' Thea added. 'You never know, someone might have one they don't use.'

'I've got some magazines you could have,' Lizzie said. 'I'll bring them with me next time I visit.'

'Sewing and knitting materials,' Marianne said. 'They could make clothes for their children and babies.'

'And swap them as babies grow so fast.' Prue added the ideas to her list. 'All excellent suggestions which I'm sure would be enjoyed and appreciated by our evacuee mothers. So . . . the next step is to source all these things – we'll need to ask villagers for donations.'

'I've got some spare wool and knitting needles,' Hettie said.

Prue nodded. 'Thank you, that gets us off to a good start.'

'And I'll look out some books for you,' Thea said.

'I appreciate that, thank you. I really think we can do this, if most households in the village give a little something it will really mount up. And if we want to get the club up and running as soon as possible ... ' She paused, clearly thinking about the best strategy. 'There isn't another WI meeting until next month and we can't wait until then, so we're going to have to spread the word. I'll draw up some posters to put up around the village – outside the village hall, in the shops, at the station – and I'll go round and visit every house that has an evacuee billeted with them and ask, and others that don't as well. If you can do the same, tell anyone you meet. Any donations can be collected by me or left at my house.'

'Well,' Hettie stretched out her legs, 'it sounds like a marvellous thing to do, and knowing you, Prue, I'm sure you'll get it up and running by the end of the week.'

Prue shrugged. 'With plenty of help and donations from many others; it would be impossible on my own.'

'Ah, but you're so good at organising us, leading us in the right direction.' Thea caught her sister's eye and smiled at her.

Prue brushed away the compliment with her hand. 'I just like to keep busy, you know me. Nothing I like better than a problem to fix.'

Thea bit back the comment that was resting on the tip of her tongue. Dear Prue, she was so good at solving other people's problems, but seemingly blind to the one that was staring her in the face – the unhappiness of her

154

marriage. But there was nothing Thea could do about that if her sister wouldn't openly acknowledge it and face it . . . Perhaps one day she might and Thea would be there waiting to help her. There was always room for Prue to come and live with her at Rookery House – Alice, Edwin and Jack, too, even if they had to share rooms and needed to turn the dining room into a bedroom!

Chapter 21

The Grange was on the far side of the village from Rookery House, an area that Marianne hadn't been to before. Walking up the drive to the front door, she was glad that Hettie had offered to come with her to show her the way, as the house itself was quite imposing. Painted white, it was the size of three Rookery Houses put together. Rosalind was clearly a wealthy woman.

'Brace yourself,' Hettie whispered as they reached the front door and she rapped the lion's head door-knocker. 'I won't stay for long as I promised I'd go and help Prue spread the word about donations for the day club. Are you all right?'

Marianne nodded. 'A bit nervous.'

Hettie smiled and patted her arm. 'You'll be fine, just remember you're the professional with years of London experience. Don't let her walk all over you, and remember what we said about your fees?'

'Yes.' They'd had a discussion last night about how much she should charge, deciding it was best to do so by the hour rather than having a fixed fee because some garments were more time consuming than others to make. 'I can't afford not to be paid properly for the work, I . . .' Marianne paused as she heard footsteps coming towards them from inside and whispered, 'Here she comes.' She took a deep breath to steady her nerves.

'Don't worry, it won't be Rosalind answering her own front door!' Hettie hissed. 'She's too grand in her opinion to do that.'

The door opened and a woman who Marianne recognised from the WI stood there wearing an apron. 'Good morning. Mrs Platten is expecting you,' she said in a louder voice than necessary before leaning closer and whispering, 'Nice to see you both.' She indicated behind her with her eyes. 'She's looking forward to this.'

'Morning, Joan.' Hettie stepped inside and Marianne followed her into a wide hall with a polished floor of black-and-white tiles and a lovely wooden staircase sweeping up to the next floor.

'Mrs Platten is in the drawing room.' Joan led the way, paused at the door, then knocked gently before opening it. 'Your visitors are here, Mrs Platten.' She stepped to the side and ushered them to go in, raising her eyebrows at them before leaving and closing the door behind them.

'Ah, Mrs Archer.' Rosalind frowned. 'And Hettie – I wasn't expecting you.'

'Oh, I'm not staying; I just came to show Marianne the way,' Hettie explained.

'Right.' Rosalind reached for the bell on the small table near her armchair.

'No need to call Joan, I can show myself out,' Hettie said. Then, turning to Marianne, 'I'll see you back at home later then.'

Marianne nodded. 'Thanks for bringing me.'

Hettie smiled at her, nodded at Rosalind and then left.

'Do sit down, Marianne, if I may call you that.' Rosalind gestured to the armchair opposite her. 'Since I spoke to you last week, I have received an invitation to a dinner party at Great Plumstead Hall and I am desperately in need of a new dress for the occasion, so my plans for a new suit will have to wait. You do have experience of designing and making evening gowns?'

'Yes, although such a garment will take a lot longer to make than a suit, and since I charge by the hour it will be more expensive.'

Rosalind narrowed her eyes. 'I was thinking more of a set fee.'

This was what Hettie had warned her about. Rosalind may be wealthy, but she had a reputation for driving a hard bargain. 'I'm afraid that's not possible. If you want a unique design made exclusively for you and of excellent workmanship, then I will not cut corners to save time and spoil my good reputation for making quality garments. If that's unacceptable to you then you'll need to look elsewhere for a dressmaker.' Marianne stood up, aware that she was taking a risk here. 'Other clients are willing to pay by the hour.' Well, Hettie was and at a much reduced rate to what she would have charged Rosalind.

'Wait!' Rosalind held up her hand. 'Very well. Please sit down. I want quality work and am prepared to pay for it, on the condition that you work solely on my gown until it is finished. The dinner is on Saturday and I must have it by then.'

Marianne pretended to consider for a moment; it would take a lot of work and time but that wouldn't be a problem since she didn't have any other clients. 'Very well.' She smiled at the older woman, who looked satisfied with the deal. 'This morning I'll need to measure you carefully so the garment is made to fit you well, and we need to discuss what sort of design you'd like. Perhaps if you would show me some dresses that you already have with particular details that you like and try them on, we can see what style suits you best. The design phase is very important and worth spending time on.'

'Did you do that in London?'

'Absolutely.'

'Then that's what we must do, too.'

Upstairs in Rosalind's bedroom, with the measurements taken and noted down in Marianne's little book, she had to hide her initial reaction when the older woman opened the doors of one of the two large wardrobes – she already had plenty of dresses suitable for the dinner party. She might *want* a new one made for her, but she certainly didn't *need* one. But like so many of the women she'd made clothes for in the past, Rosalind didn't know the difference between wanting and needing, compared with what so many people in the country had to live by.

'Which are your particular favourites?' Marianne asked. 'What do you feel good wearing?'

Rosalind looked at her and frowned. 'I'm not sure.' She pulled out a dark blue silk dress. At a glance Marianne knew it wasn't the sort of dress she should be wearing: it wasn't suited to her figure at all. 'I've worn this the most.'

'Can you try it on for me?'

'Of course.'

It looked terrible to Marianne's trained eye, fitting badly and making Rosalind's heavy shelf of a bust the focal point as the front of the dress strained across it.

'Tell me what you like about this dress?' she asked.

Rosalind walked to the window and back. 'The swish of the skirt as I move.'

Marianne made a note of that. 'What else?'

'The colour and the fabric.' Rosalind looked down at the dress for a moment. 'That's it, I suppose.'

'All right, let's try on some others and see what you like about them.'

By the end of the morning, they'd worked their way through more than a dozen dresses and Marianne had built up a good picture of what Rosalind liked and didn't like. None of the many dresses Rosalind owned either fitted with her preferences for colour and fabric or were a good match for her figure. Designing and making a well-fitting dress that met with the older woman's likes was going to be a challenge, but one that she would enjoy immensely.

'My next step is to come up with some possible designs based on all you've told me and your measurements,'

Marianne explained as they went back downstairs. 'I'll go home and start designing this afternoon and come back and show you them later, if that's all right?'

'Why don't you stay here and have something to eat? I can get Joan to make you a sandwich and that way I can see the designs more quickly.' Rosalind smiled at her. 'I'm rather enjoying myself.'

Marianne nodded. 'All right, thank you. As soon as you're happy with the design you can get the fabric and I'll start making a toile.'

Rosalind frowned. 'What's that?'

'A toile's an early version of the garment that I'll make from calico fabric to test the design and pattern to check everything is right. It's best to do one for more complicated garments first. So if you can buy some calico too, please.'

'Of course, I can go to Norwich tomorrow to get it.'

'Which one do you prefer?' Marianne asked later that afternoon after she'd presented Rosalind with several designs to choose from, all of which would be more flattering to her figure than anything the older woman already had in her wardrobe.

'It has to be this one.' Rosalind put her finger on her chosen design. 'Although ... do keep the rest of them because I might want them made up too!' She laughed almost girlishly. 'It's been such a delightful process so far, nothing like I've ever experienced before when I've bought clothes.'

Marianne smiled at her. 'This dress will be uniquely designed and fitted to suit your figure.'

Rosalind nodded. 'Precisely.' She smiled. 'I can't wait to show it off on Saturday. I just need to find the perfect material now. I'll ask for the type of silk you recommended.'

Chapter 22

Prue arranged the toys so that they looked attractive and inviting, then kneeled back on her heels to survey what would be the children's play area of the new day club. There were cushions to make it more comfortable for the children to sit on the floor, and a variety of toys that had been generously donated by the people in the village who'd answered her plea for anything that would provide the evacuee mothers and their infants with something to do while they were here. She propped up a rag doll that had fallen forwards, then stood up, smoothing down her skirt.

'The tea things are all set out,' Sally said, coming to stand beside her. 'Oh, don't that look nice? I'm tempted to get down there and play with the toys myself.'

Prue smiled at the younger woman. 'It brought back good memories setting out the toy cars. I remember how much Jack and Edwin loved playing with them.' She wished she could go back and have that time with them all over again. She'd loved mothering those young boys and had spent many happy hours playing with them, but now they were both grown up, with Jack away in the army and it was only a matter of time before Edwin would be called up to follow. At least their toys would be put to good use by the evacuee children.

Prue glanced at her watch. 'It's almost nine o'clock; we should go and wait by the door ready to welcome our first mothers. I do hope they'll come.' As usual with worth-while projects, she'd put a lot of energy and time into getting the day club ready in just a matter of days, but all that would be for nothing if the mothers failed to use it.

Sally tucked her arm through Prue's as they walked the length of the village hall to the front door, passing Thea who was unpacking the small library of books and magazines that they'd amassed and arranging it invitingly on a table at the side of the hall. 'Don't worry, of course they'll come, everyone I spoke to was keen, and any that weren't so sure will soon change their minds when they 'ear what's on offer 'ere. There's plenty to keep them occupied all day, what with the sewin', knittin', and readin', and no doubt as time goes on we'll think of other things they can do, as well. The main thing is they can get together, talk and laugh and 'ave somewhere to go that's theirs every day.'

Prue nodded. 'I hope so. I don't want any more of them going home.'

'Ready for action?' Thea asked as she joined them by the door.

Prue looked at her sister and Sally and nodded, then opened the doors and smiled at the sight that met her. Standing outside were five expectant mothers, three of whom had infant children with them.

'Can we come in?' Gloria asked eagerly.

Prue smiled at her and stepped to the side ushering the women and children inside. 'Welcome to Great Plumstead Day Club! Coats can be hung up on the pegs and make yourselves at home, there's plenty to do.'

The women hurried inside and to Prue's delight seemed very happy with what they saw around the hall.

'There's a gramophone!' one woman exclaimed when she spotted the gramophone that had been donated by the owner of Great Plumstead Hall, along with a pile of records.

The toy corner had drawn the infants like a magnet, and they were soon happily sitting on the cushions and playing with the toys.

'I'll put the kettle on, shall I?' Thea asked as more mothers appeared in the doorway.

Prue nodded and went over to welcome the new arrivals, feeling relieved that the women had come and all she had to do now was make sure that they enjoyed themselves and wanted to come back again.

By mid-morning twenty mothers and their accompanying infants had arrived and the village hall was a hive of activity, with much chatter and laughter as the women made the most of having somewhere to go and something to do.

As Prue went around collecting used teacups on a

tray she dipped in and out of different conversations that were going on.

'You put the wool around here between the needles like this,' Gloria demonstrated to one of the other mothers, teaching her to knit, 'then slide your right-hand needle like so and slip it off to make a new stitch. See.' Several of the mothers had made use of the needles, wool and patterns that had been donated, and were busy at work making booties or mittens for their babies.

An impromptu dance lesson was going on in the corner by the gramophone where one heavily pregnant mother was doing her best to teach another some dance steps while the music played softly in the background.

'Do you want to join in?' one of them asked as Prue passed by on her way to the kitchen.

'Come on, do, the washing-up can wait,' Sally said, coming up alongside her.

Prue hesitated for a moment and then nodded, putting the tray safely out of the way on the table behind them. 'But I should warn you I haven't danced for years, I've probably forgotten how to!'

The woman giving instructions laughed. 'There ain't no need to worry about that, as long as you enjoy yourself, that's all that matters. Ready, follow me . . . Feet together and step to the side and forward and to the side, wriggle your 'ips . . .'

Prue followed her instructions as best she could, bumping into Sally when she went the wrong way, the pair of them dissolving into giggles as they did their best to keep up, Sally linking her arm through Prue's to steady them.

By the time the record finished, Prue was gradually getting the hang of it and was thoroughly enjoying herself, and to her amazement the hall erupted into a round of applause, led she noticed by her sister who'd been playing with the infants over in the toy corner.

'A right twinkletoes you are, Mrs Wilson,' one of the mothers shouted.

Prue laughed, her cheeks growing warm. 'There's room for you to come and join in too,' she called back, enjoying the banter, thrilled that the day club already had such a warm and inviting atmosphere, everybody looking like they were enjoying themselves. This was what she wanted to achieve and with the help of many people, it looked like she'd done it.

'Right, I really must get these teacups washed up.' Prue retrieved the tray and headed to the kitchen where she mentally worked through the next steps of the day club as she filled the sink with water. She had drawn up a rota of WI members who were willing to take a turn running the club, either setting up the equipment at the start of the day or packing it away at the end. Hettie was due on duty to help her this afternoon and Sally said Marianne would be coming along with her later as she was fitting the toile on Rosalind this morning. Perhaps Marianne would be willing to share her sewing skills with the other women the way that Gloria was helping them learn to knit, Prue suddenly thought, her mind starting to spark more ideas about what they could do at the day club. Today had got off to an excellent start but it was just the beginning.

Chapter 23

Thea set down the cup of tea that she'd just brought for Marianne, putting it safely out of the way of where the young woman was working. Then she went over and gently ran her fingers over the teal-blue silk that Rosalind had bought for her new evening gown. 'This is such lovely material.'

Marianne nodded. 'Cost a lot too, but she clearly doesn't skimp on clothes for herself by the amount she's got in her wardrobe. At least this will fit her well and suit her, unlike most of the other dresses she's got.'

Thea watched as Marianne carefully pinned the pattern she'd designed and made on to the material that was spread out on the large table in front of her. Marianne was working in the dining room, which was the perfect place when she needed a larger space than she had in the small bedroom that housed the sewing machine.

'Was she happy with everything this morning?'

'Yes, I just needed to make a few adjustments to get the perfect fit and now it's good to be working on the real thing.'

'I can see that you enjoy what you do,' Thea said.

Marianne stopped working and looked at her, smiling warmly. 'I love it, and that's why I need to carry on doing it, it's what I do best.'

'You will mind you don't overdo it, though, won't you?'

'Of course, but dressmaking isn't like doing hard physical labour – I can do most of it sitting down.'

Thea laughed. 'All right, I'll stop fussing! You're sensible enough not to overdo it, I'm sure your husband wouldn't want you to either.'

'No, I'm sure he wouldn't,' Marianne said, returning to her work, smoothing the pattern so the piece of paper was completely flat before she pinned it in place on the material.

Marianne had been living at Rookery House for almost three weeks now and Thea didn't know any more about the young woman's husband than she had that first morning when she'd seen his picture in her bedroom. She didn't talk about him much, Thea thought, which was in sharp contrast to Sally, who often chatted about her Arthur. But then Sally was a lot more talkative than Marianne altogether, so perhaps it was just a case of different personalities saying more or less. If Thea wanted to know more, then perhaps she should just ask.

'How did you meet him?'

'Through my work: I made a dress for his sister and he came along to one of the fittings.'

169

'His sister must like having you for a sister-in-law, then; a talented dressmaker in the family must go down well.'

Marianne shrugged but didn't say anything.

'Where does his family live?'

'In London.'

That explained why Marianne hadn't gone to stay with them rather than being evacuated out here.

'Perhaps they could come and visit you here, especially after the baby is born. Do tell them that they're welcome when you write to them.'

Marianne nodded and smiled. 'Thank you.'

'What did you think of the day club?'

'I liked it very much and so did the other mothers, I think, they all seemed to be enjoying themselves,' Marianne said. 'Some of them were doing some sewing and I helped someone who'd got in a muddle with a buttonhole.'

'Gloria was teaching someone to knit this morning,' Thea said. 'It's a good place to share skills. Perhaps in time we can do more things. I know Prue wants to set up knitting comforts for the troops, and the mothers could do that while they chatted. Some of them were even teaching Prue some crazy dance.'

Marianne smiled. 'Sally told me about that, she was delighted to get Prue dancing, thinks she ought to do more of that sort of thing . . . ' She suddenly put her hand over her mouth, her cheeks flushing. 'I'm sorry, I shouldn't have said that, Prue's your sister!'

Thea laughed. 'She is indeed, but I completely agree with you and Sally: it would do Prue a lot of good to do more things like dancing and enjoying herself. Sadly I think she's not had a lot of that in her life since she got married . . . She used to love dancing, though, was on the dancefloor all the time at village dances, a real belle of the ball she was.'

'Well, the East End mothers aren't shy about dancing and letting their hair down, they'll get her moving again if she'll let them.'

'The evacuees have been like a breath of fresh air to Prue and many others in this village, shaking them up a bit – and they *really* needed shaking up, believe you me. After living in London so long I could see the difference in a small village when I came back.' Thea frowned. 'There are good and bad points about both city and village life, and this war is stirring them both up and bringing them together in ways that have never happened before and,' she nodded, 'that's a very good thing, in my opinion.'

Chapter 24

'Roll up, roll up, get your fresh blackberry jam 'ere!' Sally shouted, immediately attracting the attention of nearby market goers who turned to see who was making all the noise.

Prue, who was manning the WI's weekly stall on Wykeham's market day, looked in astonishment at the young woman who was clearly in her element. 'My goodness, Sally, I had no idea you could shout so loudly, and you've got the patter off perfectly.'

Sally beamed at her. 'My granddad was a market trader with a fruit and veg stall, I used to go and 'elp him on Saturdays before I left school.' She paused, took a deep breath and bellowed out, 'Come and try, before you buy, you won't be disappointed.'

The stall, with its colourful striped awning, always did well and was popular with its customers, items on sale varying with the seasons. Today, they had a selection of cakes, pies and biscuits, all home-made and tasty looking, alongside surplus produce from gardens including fresh eggs, some fine-looking marrows, and orchard fruits such as apples, plums and pears. In prime position, displayed in a pyramid of stacked jam jars was some of the blackberry jam that members had made the previous weekend. To encourage their customers to buy the jam, they'd opened one jar and provided teaspoons so customers could try it before they hopefully went on to buy some.

'What you think? It's tasty, ain't it?' Sally asked a woman who was sampling some of the jam. 'And you won't get fresher, the berries were only picked last weekend and swiftly cooked into jam before they lost their goodness – you won't get any bulk, factory-made goods 'ere, and you can taste the difference.'

The woman nodded and smiled. 'It certainly is tasty; it'll be lovely on a slice of toast for breakfast. Can I have two jars, please?'

Sally handed her two jars. 'We should have some in next week, if you want to get some more then, but there's a limited number so I can't guarantee we won't sell out.'

The woman frowned. 'In that case, I'll have two more now.'

Prue watched as Sally obliged, giving the woman two more jars and charging her the correct amount for them. She was a natural at this selling and a great asset to the stall, Prue thought.

'You did well there,' she said in a low voice, as the shopper disappeared into the crowd with her four jars of jam safely stowed in her basket. 'She's quite a difficult customer and not known for buying extravagantly.'

Sally laughed. 'My granddad always said if you tell people they might not be able to 'ave something, that makes them want it more, especially if they think something's sold out because other people have bought it cos it is so good, and our jam is *excellent*, so much better than the stuff I used to sell in the shop where I worked.'

'It certainly is.' Prue smiled at her and then turned her attention to another customer who was after one of the sponge cakes that Hettie had made for the stall, while Sally set about selling more jam.

Chapter 25

Marianne watched, her stomach knotting, as Rosalind stared at her reflection in the long cheval mirror. To her eyes the dress was as perfect as it could be: the fit was impeccable and the design accentuated the positives of Rosalind's figure. But would the older woman think so? Marianne had seen how picky and particular Rosalind was, but if she was going to see more orders coming in as a result of this commission, she needed her approval.

'It's marvellous, completely and utterly marvellous!' Rosalind's voice was husky and Marianne could see that her eyes were bright with tears. 'Thank you so much, I've never looked or felt so good in any dress or clothes I've worn before.' She held out her hand and rather than shaking Marianne's she squeezed it gently before letting it go.

'I'm so glad that you like it and you do look wonderful in it; it really suits you, I knew it would.'

Rosalind ran her hand down the material of her

three-quarter-length sleeve. 'I can't wait to wear it tonight; this dress is going to be much admired.' She smiled at Marianne. 'Prepare yourself, my dear, for many more commissions, although I hope you'll make me a new suit and blouse before you do work for anyone else.'

'Of course, when would you like me to start?' Marianne asked.

'How about Monday morning? If you come and see me, we can discuss the type of suit I'd like, and I can tell you about tonight.'

Marianne nodded. 'I'll be there.'

Rosalind went over to her dressing table and took an envelope out of the top drawer. 'This is your fee, payment by the number of hours you spent and an extra bonus for such good work.'

'Thank you.' Marianne took the envelope.

'Now, if you could help me get out of this, I'll hang it up so it's ready for tonight.' Rosalind turned so that her back was facing her, and as Marianne undid the small buttons at the back of the dress she felt a huge sense of relief. Not only had she earned a bonus on top of her fee, but she already had some more work lined up for next week. Her determination to find work had paid off and to be doing what she loved and was good at made it all so much easier.

Chapter 26

The Sunday-morning service at the village church of St Andrew's was almost over, the vicar drawing it to a close after saying the final prayer and blessing. Marianne let her gaze wander around the old building, taking in the beautiful stained-glass windows through which the autumn sunlight filtered making the jewel-like colours glow, while the stone pillars stood solidly upright, holding up the tall ceiling with its carved wooden beams. The whole place had stood here for centuries, watching over as people of the parish were christened, married and buried, their lives coming and going over the generations, witnessing history in the times of different kings or queens or wars.

She and Hettie had been a little late in getting here this morning so they were sitting in a pew towards the back, which gave her a good view of the other members of the congregation.

She could see Sally was there with Prue and her family,

including the horrible Victor. To look at him now he seemed an upstanding member of the community, smart and clearly well regarded, someone others wanted to know. People were always seeking him out to shake his hand after the Sunday services, but Marianne knew from Sally that he had another side to him, a side that was never on public display. She felt sorry for Prue; to look at her sitting in the pew beside her husband, smart in a blue wool suit with a jaunty hat on her head, no one would suspect that her husband wasn't a kind, loving man. It didn't seem to stop her from getting out and about and doing things, though, but perhaps that was her way of coping: distracting herself by being busy. Marianne knew about that herself, preferring to bury herself in her work to escape unhappiness. Even when she'd lost her job and gone to live in the East End, she'd been glad to throw herself into a new job, grateful for the long hours because they'd helped her to stop thinking too much about what a fool she'd been and how naive. It had been a hard lesson to learn but then, coming here, she'd had the chance to make a fresh start and she was grateful for it.

The movement of people around her brought Marianne's thoughts back to the present: the vicar had gone to wait by the church door and members of the congregation were slowly filing out into the sunny late-September morning.

'That was a nice service,' Hettie said. 'It always is when we sing "All things bright and beautiful", it's my favourite hymn; and it's the harvest festival next week so that will be good, too.' She smiled and nodded at one of the women whom Marianne recognised from the WI, as she walked past down the aisle. 'I'll try to get Thea to come along to that, she's more open to coming to church on high days and holidays than on ordinary days.' She sighed. 'I have tried to persuade her to come along more often but she's not keen, the same as she is with the WI.'

'Why doesn't she belong to the WI?' Marianne asked.

'Oh, several reasons, I think; she's not one for putting up with what some people think should be the hierarchy in the village.' She lowered her voice, leaning closer to Marianne before continuing, 'There's some that think they should be in charge because of who they are rather than what they're capable of doing. Thea doesn't want any part of it after being in London and being her own boss, and of course being in France in the Great War. It all changed her and made her see things differently.' Hettie shrugged, smiling at her. 'Thea always goes her own way and that's not such a bad thing.'

'There you are!' Sally's loud Cockney voice made Marianne look up to see her friend coming towards her alongside Prue. 'I thought you weren't comin' this morning.'

'We were running a bit late.' Hettie got to her feet and stepped out into the flow of people filtering out of the church.

'We had our first evacuee baby born last night,' Prue said, looking pleased. 'A little boy born to Gracie at the maternity home. The host she's billeted with rang me in a panic and I managed to drive her there in time. I telephoned the home this morning and both mother and baby are doing well.'

'That's lovely,' Hettie said. 'And there'll be more babies in the village over the next few months.' She put a hand

179

on Marianne's arm and squeezed it gently. 'I'm looking forward to having a baby in the house.'

Marianne smiled at her, glad that her child would be so welcome.

They slowly made their way out of the church, briefly stopping to shake hands with the vicar. Some of the congregation were lingering in the churchyard, chatting in small groups; nobody seemed in any hurry to get home, perhaps because it was such a nice day.

'Do you realise you're the centre of attention this morning?' Hettie whispered as they stopped by the lichgate while Prue answered some questions about the day club from one of the evacuee hosts.

'What do you mean?' Marianne asked, keeping her voice low.

With her back to the church, Hettie gave a gentle jerk of her head and motioned with her eyes for Marianne to look behind her. Marianne could see Rosalind was talking to a rather grand-looking woman and several others, who were all looking her way.

'You're being watched,' Sally said, thankfully keeping her voice low too. 'Hang on a minute, they're comin' our way.'

Marianne had the strongest urge to leave; she wasn't comfortable with any sort of attention.

Hettie must have sensed her reaction and put a steadying hand on her arm. 'Wait,' she hissed quietly. 'You're about to reel in a much bigger fish, keep your nerve.'

Marianne didn't have a chance to ask Hettie what on earth she meant before Rosalind arrived at her side.

'Good morning, Marianne. I'd like to introduce you to

Lady Campbell-Gryce, whose dinner party I attended last night wearing the splendid gown that you designed and made especially for me.'

'Delighted to meet you.' Lady Campbell-Gryce held out her hand.

Marianne shook it. 'Good to meet you.'

'And good morning, Hettie,' Her Ladyship said, turning her attention to her former cook. 'I do hope you're well and enjoying your retirement. We do so miss your cooking up at the Hall.'

Hettie smiled at her. 'Good morning, madam. I'm very well, thank you.'

Rosalind put her arm through Marianne's and gently steered her slightly away from the little group. 'Lady Campbell-Gryce wonders if you'd have time to design and make some garments for her.'

'Of course, but I couldn't until I've finished the work for you,' Marianne said.

Rosalind smiled benevolently. 'I appreciate your loyalty, Marianne, but I'm prepared to wait a bit longer if it means that you can do the work for Her Ladyship. She's an important member of local society and far be it from me to cause a delay for her.' She laid an immaculately white-gloved hand on Marianne's arm. 'Come to see me tomorrow to discuss ideas and some new designs for me, and perhaps you'd come to Norwich with me later in the week to help me choose fabrics – at my expense, of course. Once we've sorted out designs and material then you can make them as you see fit, working around whatever Her Ladyship would like you to do for her.'

Marianne nodded. 'All right, I'm happy to do that.'

'Excellent.' Rosalind smiled at her. 'I'll pass that on to Her Ladyship and she'll be in touch to arrange a convenient time for you to call on her at the Hall. And I'll see you tomorrow morning at ten o'clock.'

'Well ...' Hettie beamed as they left the churchyard and headed home a few minutes later. 'It worked a treat, didn't it? I was the little fish that was bait for the bigger fish and you've just gone and hooked the biggest fish in the area as a customer. Rosalind's social-climbing ways might be galling, but in this case they've worked very well to your advantage.'

'She's asked me to go to Norwich with her later in the week, at her expense,' Marianne told Hettie. 'Wants me to help her choose the fabric.'

Hettie laughed. 'You are honoured indeed! Go and enjoy yourself; it will do you good to get out and about and see the city, it's a fine place.'

Chapter 27

It felt strange to be in a city again, Marianne thought, looking out of the taxi window that Rosalind had insisted they get from Norwich's City station, into the centre where they could begin their search for the perfect fabric. She'd quickly become reaccustomed to country life, enjoying having so much space and greenery around her, the song of birds and far less hustle and bustle. Norwich was nowhere near as large and busy as London, but after life in Great Plumstead, it was still a shock to her senses. She noticed the signs of a country at war were very much in evidence here, with buildings sandbagged to protect them and windows crisscrossed with tape in case of bomb blasts.

'Here we are, missus,' the taxi driver said, pulling up outside a shop with 'Gordon Thoday's' written on the sign above the door and large window display. Rosalind had insisted that this was *the* place in Norwich to buy fine fabric.

Rosalind paid the driver and they got out and headed into the shop, the noise from the street fading as the doors closed behind them. Marianne felt a great sense of joy and excitement at the sight of so many bolts of beautiful fabric, her eyes darting this way and that, taking in the various colours and patterns, the textures that caught the light in different ways. This indeed was so much bigger and better than the haberdashery shop in Wykeham. It was no wonder that Rosalind preferred to come here to choose her fabrics, and Marianne was glad that she'd been asked to accompany her; it really would be a pleasure to spend time choosing fabrics from such a wide selection.

She reached out and gently ran her fingertips over a particularly fine pearly-grey silk that seemed to shimmer like water on a summer's day as it reflected the light.

'We need silk for a day dress and a blouse.' Rosalind's voice pulled Marianne's attention back to the job she'd come here to do. 'What do you suggest? Which fabrics would work best for me?'

'How about if I pick some I think would work well and then you can make a final choice from them?'

Rosalind nodded. 'Absolutely.' She wandered off, leaving Marianne the enjoyable task of selecting bolts of silk from the wide choice available.

Working her way slowly round the shop, she gently felt the texture and thickness of potential choices, unwinding some fabric from bolts to see how they fell and draped. Ones that passed muster in colour, pattern, texture and drape, she pulled out and took over to the wide counter where Rosalind was talking to one of the assistants, her loud voice ringing out across the shop as she explained that she'd commissioned Marianne, a designer from London's West End, to make her new garments, clearly revelling in having someone of her experience working for her.

The sales assistant caught Marianne's eye and smiled at her as she placed another two bolts of silk on the counter for Rosalind's approval.

Finally, when Marianne was satisfied that she'd found all the options that would work for Rosalind's colouring and the designs that she'd drawn up, the older woman had to make her choices from the bolts of silk lined up on the counter.

'These will work well for the day dress,' Marianne said, pointing out the bolts on the left-hand side, 'while these finer silks are ideal for the blouse.' She pointed to the others.

'You've got a good eye for colour and pattern; any of them would suit you, madam.' The sales assistant smiled at Rosalind. 'Often people end up buying fabric that really doesn't do them any justice, but honestly any of these will look splendid on you.'

Rosalind smiled graciously at her. 'It makes such a difference to have an experienced designer and dressmaker who knows what she is doing. The evening gown that Marianne made me has attracted a great deal of attention and admiration.'

Surprisingly it didn't take Rosalind long to choose which fabrics she'd like, although she was unable to settle on just one choice for either the dress or the blouse.

'I can't make up my mind between them,' Rosalind said with a sigh. 'Could you possibly make me two dresses and three blouses? I simply adore these two fabrics for dresses,' she pointed to the ones she wanted, 'and these three for blouses.'

'Of course I can make them for you.' Marianne smiled at her. 'You'll just have to tell me which ones you want first, though.' She was going to be busy, but she was glad of the work.

'Excellent, thank you, Marianne. If you can tell the sales assistant here how much we need of each then I think we'll go and have some tea.'

Marianne obliged, and a short while later they left the shop with carefully wrapped parcels of silk fabric and headed into nearby Curls, a fine department store, where Rosalind bought them both tea and a selection of delicious cakes.

'I'm so glad you came with me.' Rosalind poured them each a cup of tea. 'I would never have chosen some of those fabrics on my own, thinking they wouldn't have suited me or been the right sort of thickness or drape. It's been quite a revelation coming fabric shopping with one as experienced as you. And after our refreshment we can look in Curls haberdashery for some woollen fabric to make my suit.'

'Thank you.' Marianne took her cup of tea and added some milk to it from the little jug that had been provided. 'It can be quite overwhelming with so many choices of fabric; I enjoyed choosing for you.'

'Do have some cake.' Rosalind nodded towards the cake

stand with its dainty cakes so prettily set out. 'We need to make the most of such things – it's sure to become harder to find decent cake once rationing kicks in, as it's bound to sooner or later.'

Marianne took a slice of Victoria sponge and bit into it, enjoying the soft, airy sweetness, with its filling of jam.

'It's National Registration Day today. Has your form been delivered?' Rosalind asked, helping herself to a slice of Bakewell tart.

Marianne nodded, her mouth full of sponge. Thea had shown her the form that had been delivered to Rookery House by the enumerator earlier in the week. Tonight they would fill in all the details of every person sleeping in the house: name, date of birth, gender, occupation, that sort of thing. The enumerator would be calling back to collect it the weekend and issue everyone with their identity card. 'It's the next step with the country at war, I suppose.'

'Yes, well, I suppose the government needs to know who lives where and how old they are, so they know how many young men they've got to call up to fight.' Rosalind took a sip of tea, replacing the china teacup carefully on its matching saucer. 'And who to issue ration books to. It will be just myself and my housekeeper at home tonight – my husband's away on business and my evacuee has gone back to London. I wasn't sad to see her go because the woman had no morals.' She lowered her voice and leaned towards Marianne. 'I discovered to my horror that she wasn't even married to the father of her children and she didn't seem to think it mattered. That sort of thing might not matter where she comes from, but it certainly does here.' She pressed her lips into a thin line.

Marianne's cheeks grew warm and she took a sip of tea to try to cover up the look of guilt she feared must be written across her face. She was an unmarried mother as well, the sort of woman whom Rosalind regarded as having no morals. If she knew the truth, it was very unlikely that she would want Marianne to work for her, even if she had trained as a designer and dressmaker in the West End of London.

'Are you all right, my dear, you're looking rather flushed?'

Marianne nodded and placed her hand on her protruding belly. 'This is rather like having a permanent hot-water bottle with me: I don't feel the cold now and on the contrary am sometimes rather too hot, especially if I'm having a cup of tea.'

'Would you like a glass of water?' Rosalind looked around for the waitress.

'No, thank you.' Marianne pasted a smile on her face. 'I'm fine.'

She only half listened for the rest of the time they spent over their tea and cake. As Rosalind discussed where they would go next and the merits of different types of woollen fabrics for her suit, Marianne's mind churned over the worry that her secret might leak out and the consequences of that – the loss of her job working for Rosalind and no doubt the potential job for Lady Campbell-Gryce, too. She had to maintain the façade of a respectable married woman whose husband was away serving in the Royal Navy, far from home and unable to get back to see her. Living a lie didn't suit her, she felt guilty and didn't like deceiving people, but she had to do it for her unborn child, she owed it to her baby.

Chapter 28

Prue prodded at the potatoes boiling in the pan – they'd need another five minutes. Glancing at the clock, she saw it was nearly half past five: Victor and Edwin would be home from work very soon and they would be expecting their tea. Victor didn't like to be kept waiting; he was very particular about having his meals at certain times and was sure to take umbrage if he had to wait. She sighed, it couldn't be helped tonight. She'd had a busy day: on duty at the day club all morning, and then there'd been the shopping to do and a WI committee meeting this afternoon that had run on much longer than expected, with more paperwork and ideas coming through from those in charge at both county and national level, because of the war. Even with Sally's help peeling the potatoes and chopping onions to go in the frying-pan gravy alongside the sausages she'd got from the butchers, there was nothing she could do to shorten the length of cooking time to make the mashed potatoes.

As she heard the front door open and close, Prue braced herself for Victor's complaints but when he came into the kitchen and saw that the meal wasn't ready to be served, he strangely didn't say anything.

'It won't be long,' Prue said. 'These potatoes seem to be taking longer to boil than usual.'

Victor ignored her remark and held up the newspaper he'd brought home with him. 'Have you heard what was signed by the King at the Privy Council meeting last night?'

'No, it's been a busy day; I haven't had time to listen to the wireless.'

'Read this, then.' He held out the newspaper to her and prodded at an article on the front page, a smug look on his face.

Instinct told her that it wasn't going to be good news from her point of view, and as she took the paper and read what it said, the blood in her veins chilled. The article described how men between the ages of twenty and twenty-one were now liable to be called up under the National Service Act, and that 21 October, in just under three weeks' time, was the date fixed for their registration. Edwin would be included in that number as he was now twenty years old. First Jack and now Edwin. She'd thought there would be more time before he'd have to go, but as luck would have it he was going to be in the first wave.

'Good news, eh? I shall soon have two sons doing their

duty.' Victor took the newspaper back from her, puffing out his chest like a pigeon. 'Following in their father's footsteps. I did my bit in the last shout and now it's their turn to do theirs.'

'What did Edwin say?' Prue asked, fighting to keep her voice steady and not betray how much she wanted to cry.

Victor narrowed his eyes as he looked at her. 'It's his duty to go, it's come a bit earlier than he thought, that's all. The boy's got to get on with it, it'll do him good.'

How little he knew his youngest son, Prue thought, turning away and stirring the sausages and gravy mixture in the frying pan. She couldn't bear to look at the smug expression on Victor's face.

'I'll go and get washed and then be ready for my tea.' She heard Victor leave the kitchen and bit back a sob that bubbled up in her throat. She was only just getting used to Jack being away and to have Edwin go as well . . . it was too much and far, far too soon.

Prue pushed her meal around her plate. She had tried her best to eat it but her appetite from earlier had gone, wiped out by the news that Victor had so joyously brought home with him. Edwin looked as though he was doing the same, his face strained and pale, so different from how it had looked at breakfast this morning.

'It'll soon be just you at home, Alice.' Victor speared a piece of sausage with his fork. 'It'll be something to tell your friends at school having two brothers off doing their bit for the country.'

Alice glanced at Edwin, clearly picking up on her

brother's unhappiness much more than their father did. She just nodded rather than replying.

'I've been wondering which service would be best – Army, Navy or Royal Air Force ...' Victor mixed some of his mash into the gravy and scooped it up on his fork. 'Course, if you'd volunteered like Jack did, then you'd have been more likely to be able to choose for yourself.'

Edwin kept his eyes on his plate and Prue desperately wanted to put her arms around him and comfort him like she'd done so often when he was a young boy. She knew what Victor would say about that; he always complained that she'd mollycoddled the children but to her mind she hadn't, she'd given them love and security.

Sally, who'd sat silently eating her meal next to her, gently nudged her elbow into Prue's as if to say she knew how she was feeling. She turned and smiled at her, glad of the small show of support, knowing that the young woman had seen plenty of Victor's opinionated proclamations at their mealtimes in the few weeks that she'd been living with them.

Eventually the meal was over. After apple pie and custard had been served, Victor had disappeared off to his study to do whatever he did in there, leaving the rest of them sitting around the table.

'Are you all right, Edwin?' It was the first chance Prue had had to ask her son, as he'd gone straight up to his room when they'd got back from work and had only come down to the kitchen when they were ready to eat their tea.

His blue eyes met hers and he shrugged. 'I didn't expect

it to come so soon.' He swallowed hard. 'I thought there'd be more time.'

Prue reached across the table and patted his hand. 'You're not the only one, but it will be all right . . . ' She tried her best to sound positive but her voice didn't sound very convincing to her ears.

'You might like it,' Alice said. 'Jack loves it, but then he would.'

'Perhaps the Royal Air Force might be better for you than the Army,' Prue suggested. 'You could always ask to join them. Going in with the first wave might mean you have more choice because there's more spaces available than later on.'

Edwin nodded, but didn't look convinced. 'I'm going to go over and see Thea and Reuben.' He stood up. 'Thanks for the tea, Ma.'

Prue smiled. 'I'll see you later, then.' Perhaps that was a good idea, she thought. Talking to Reuben, who'd been in the Army himself, might help Edwin feel better. Her brother would be much more sympathetic than Victor, that was certain.

Chapter 29

Thea raked the fallen leaves into a pile, working her way across the grass at the front of the house, enjoying the task in the soft, early-evening sunlight that dappled the lawn as the sun dipped lower in the sky. They'd been lucky with the weather so far but there was a definite feel of autumn in the air now. She caught movement out of the corner of her eye and turned to see Edwin dismounting from his bicycle having just ridden in through the front gates.

'Edwin!' she called to him, smiling at her nephew; it was always a pleasure to see him but from the look on his face she knew that something was wrong.

'What's the matter?' she said as he walked over to her.

'Have you heard the news?' he asked, his hands in his pockets as he poked at a pile of leaves with his shoe.

She instantly knew what this was about – the proclamation calling up young men of Edwin's age. She nodded.

'We knew it would come but not quite so soon.' She

reached out and touched his arm. 'I know you're not as keen on going as your brother, but it might not be so bad, especially if you end up doing a job in the services that you like. They're not all fighting on the front line – there are plenty of support roles.'

Edwin shrugged, hanging his head low.

Thea tucked her arm through his. 'Come on, let's go in and have a cup of tea.'

He resisted her, shaking free of her arm and stepping back, and when his eyes met hers Thea could see they were bright with tears.

'I'm going to register as a conscientious objector . . . ' He paused, shaking his head. 'I can't bear the thought of being ordered to kill another person and that's what I'd have to be prepared to do . . . And I can't.' His voice broke and once more he hung his head, his shoulders hunched.

Without hesitating, Thea put her arms around him and hugged him tightly. 'It's all right, I understand. And if it's any help, I wouldn't expect anything else from you, Edwin.' She stepped back slightly and looked up at him, her eyes meeting his. 'I've known you since you were a little boy and you've always been gentle and caring and I don't think you have it in you to hurt anyone.'

'I'm not a coward!'

'I know. In fact, it takes great bravery to go against the flow and stand up for what you believe in; there'll be other men like you who feel the same way but who aren't brave enough to make a stand. I'll support you completely and help you in any way I can.' Taking this path wasn't going to be easy for him – she'd seen what happened to men who refused the call-up in the Great War, witnessed how some people had treated them and it hadn't been nice. 'Have you told anyone else? Your mother? Father?'

'No, you're the first.' He sighed. 'I think Ma will be all right about it but not Father ... He was making a big thing tonight at tea about me joining up and how he'd have two sons doing their bit for the war.' He swallowed hard and looked off towards the other side of the garden before returning his gaze to Thea. 'He'll be furious when I tell him, I know he will; he's always going on about how he served in the Great War.'

Thea tutted. 'You mean how he issued army uniforms and equipment from behind the safety of a counter in the stores. He didn't even go to France, let alone see any action. The only danger of injury he faced was from a falling box of army tunics. It's very easy to be all gung-ho for his sons to be fighting when he has no experience of it himself. Reuben will tell you a different story about the so-called glory of war.'

She linked her arm through Edwin's again. 'Come on, let's go and tell your uncle – and before you start worrying about what he'll say, don't, because I can promise you that Reuben will support you in your decision one hundred per cent.'

Reuben was sitting on the veranda that wound around three sides of his railway-carriage home, smoking his pipe, the sweet scent of tobacco drifting on the evening breeze. Bess, who'd been lying by his side, spotted their visitors and came bounding over, nudging at Edwin's hand as if recognising that he was out of sorts. After a swift stroking of her ears from the young man, the dog trotted close by his side back to the carriage.

'Evening, Reuben,' Thea said as they approached.

'It's a beautiful one.' He narrowed his eyes as he looked at Edwin. 'What's the matter, lad?'

As Edwin repeated what he'd told her, Thea watched her brother's face, reading it as if it were a book, and as she'd predicted there was no animosity towards his nephew's decision, quite the opposite.

Reuben drew on his pipe, making the tobacco glow orange in the bowl before he spoke. 'I don't blame you, lad. If you feel it's the right thing for you to do, then it is. I saw plenty of men suffer because of what they had to do, and I still get nightmares even after all these years ... Not everybody will like what you've decided, or understand, but it's *your* life and only yours. No matter what some people think or how they try to bully you to change your mind, you must stand by your belief.'

'Thank you.' Edwin looked so relieved and a great deal better than he had when he'd first arrived. 'I know my ma will be all right, it's just Father ...'

Reuben pulled a face, shaking his head as he drew on his pipe again. 'When are you going to tell him?'

'Not yet, not until I have to, I'll wait until the twenty-first when I have to go and register.' Edwin sighed. 'He's already told me he'll give me the afternoon off to go – and with full pay! I suspect I'll be out of a job after that and maybe even be thrown out of the house, knowing him.'

'Well, you can come and stay here if that happens,' Thea said. 'I've got room for you.'

'And so have I,' Reuben added.

Edwin smiled at them both. 'Thank you, I really appreciate that. I know Ma would never throw me out but Father's different . . .'

Thea met Reuben's eyes and he raised his eyebrows at her, clearly thinking the same thing about their brother-in-law, who really didn't deserve to have a son like Edwin. Whatever happened to Edwin in the future she knew that both of them would fully support him and he would have a home here with them for as long as he wanted or needed it.

'Please don't tell anyone else,' Edwin added. 'I'm not going to say anything to anyone, not even Ma, until I've registered as a CO and then they'll all have to know and the rocket will go up!'

'And a bed will be ready for you here in that case,' Thea said, putting her arm around her nephew and hugging him to her.

Chapter 30

As usual these days, the wireless was on after tea to catch up on all the latest news of the war. Thea was washing up as she listened, while Marianne dried the clean plates and cutlery and Hettie sat by the range, working on the sock that she was knitting.

Sir Reginald Dorman-Smith, the radio announcer introduced the Minister of Agriculture.

It is clearly our duty, just as it is a matter of elementary wisdom to try to make doubly and trebly sure that we will fight and win this war on full stomachs – and that we can only do if in fact we grow as much food as possible at home, the Minister said. *In normal times our own farms produce nearly half our food requirements and we had not nearly reached peak production. While we could rely on the Navy to keep trade routes open, and while we would still be able to draw on food supplies from overseas, those supplies might not always be unlimited.*

Half a million more allotments would provide potatoes and

vegetables to feed another million adults and one and a half million children eight months out of twelve.

I appeal to you all – dig, cultivate, plant and sow. He paused for a moment before giving his encouraging finale. *Let 'Dig for Victory' be the motto of everyone with a garden and of every able-bodied man and woman capable of digging an allotment in their spare time.*

Thea realised that she'd stopped washing up, the plate she'd been about to clean when the announcer had first introduced the Minister of Agriculture still in her hand, so she plunged it into the water and quickly washed it, her mind considering what she'd just heard. After what happened during the Great War, when food supplies coming into the country were affected by German U-boats, it wasn't a question of *if* the same would happen this time, it was a certainty and the Minister's appeal was timely: the country couldn't risk being brought to its knees by the lack of food. By 'Digging for Victory' everyone could help to feed themselves rather than rely on imports.

'Seems like there's something new every day,' Hettie said, 'with Registration Day last Friday, getting our identity cards on Saturday, the government announcing the date for the first registration call-up of young men like Edwin yesterday, and today they're telling us to "Dig for Victory". The government are getting very fond of telling us what to do. What will it be next?'

'They can tell us what to do because we're at war.' Thea put the last of the clean plates on to the wooden draining board. 'No doubt there'll be plenty more rules and regulations put into place before the end.'

'Will we be "Digging for Victory"?' Marianne asked, drying a handful of cutlery with a tea towel.

Hettie laughed. 'We already do, we've been getting the vegetable plot back into shape and we can always make it a bit bigger, I suppose. Most people in the countryside grow a lot of their own food anyway, so a Government Minister telling us to do it won't make much difference around here.'

'I think it might.' Thea dried her hands on a towel. 'I've been thinking that we'll probably have more people billeted with us as we've got room, and they'll need to be fed. It makes sense to grow more of our food as we've got the land. We could get some chickens for eggs – and sell on any we don't need – and maybe keep some pigs, a house cow even. The more we can provide for ourselves, the better.'

'They're bound to bring in food rationing soon like they did last time so it makes sense to grow as much as we can. I'll help, too,' Hettie said.

'If we couldn't do it alone, we could get some more help when we need it. I'm sure Reuben would help when he's not at work,' Thea said. 'We'd need to sort out the old greenhouse and get a coop for the chickens and if we had a pig then we'd need to make one of the sheds pig proof, and a byre for a cow.'

Hettie laughed. 'Watch out, Marianne, once Thea's got a bee in her bonnet there's no stopping her.'

'I'll help, too,' Marianne offered. 'I can't do much digging at the moment, but after the baby's born I'll be able to bend again properly.'

'Thank you.' Thea smiled at her. 'I'm going to speak to Reuben to see if he could lend a hand to get us going.'

She found Reuben in the woodshed chopping some split logs into thin kindling strips, with Bess lying nearby. As soon as the dog spotted Thea she leapt up and hurried over, her tail wagging.

'Did you hear the news?' Thea asked, stroking Bess's ears as she leaned against her legs. 'We've all got to "Dig for Victory" now.'

Reuben stopped chopping and nodded. 'Won't make much difference to people around here, though, they don't need to be told to dig to grow their own food because most already do.'

'I suppose not, but it could make a difference to us.'

Reuben frowned. 'What do you mean?'

'I've been thinking I should take in some more lodgers as I've got a spare bedroom and could turn the dining room into a bedroom if necessary. Their rent will come in useful, but they'd need to be fed. Hearing what the Minister said on the wireless made me think that I should be growing a lot more of our food here – get chickens and maybe some pigs for pork and bacon as well, a cow for milk, and we could make our own butter and cheese. What do you think?'

Her brother picked up handfuls of the chopped kindling and threw them into the basket. 'I'd say it was a good idea. They'll bring in rationing sooner or later.'

'That's what Hettie said. But there's a lot to sort out first: the greenhouse needs mending and if we wanted to keep a pig then we'd need one of the sheds made into a sty and I'd need a chicken coop.'

'And you're looking for some help from me.' He put the hook he'd used to chop the wood back in its place and came to stand in the doorway next to her.

'Could you? Please. I can do digging and planting. I'm not sure how to mend the greenhouse, but if you showed me how I could learn. What do you think?'

'The old greenhouse's seen better days but it won't be hard to repair it, then you could grow tomatoes in there and cucumbers, and it would be ideal for starting off seedlings.' He nodded, staring across the garden where the colours were becoming more muted as the dusk deepened and bats were starting to flit about in search of prey.

Thea looked at him. 'So yes or no?'

He grinned at her. 'All right.'

'Excellent, thank you.' She beamed at him.

'You'll have to come up with a plan so you're growing crops all year round – we don't just want a glut of tomatoes in the summer. Think about what you could grow and where. Perhaps we could have a walk around the place in the next day or two and come up with some ideas?' Reuben suggested. 'I'll look into getting some point-of-lay pullets who're nearly old enough to lay eggs and a cockerel for you.'

'And I'll send off for some seed catalogues,' Thea said, thinking she was going to enjoy getting Rookery House land into shape to provide them with food. It would be a challenge and just what she needed after getting the house in order.

Chapter 31

A note requesting Marianne to go and see Lady Campbell-Gryce at Great Plumstead Hall to discuss designing and making a dress for a forthcoming wedding had arrived yesterday, and now she was on her way there accompanied by Hettie, who'd once again offered to show her the way.

'I've walked along this road I don't know how many times over the years, on my way to and from the Hall,' Hettie said. 'I dare say I could find my way there in the pitch black if I had to. It still feels a bit odd not coming this way to go home. Not that I don't love living at Rookery House – it's been a joy living there with Thea and you.'

'Didn't you want to have your own house after you retired?' Marianne asked, glancing at Hettie, who was wearing the dress she'd made for her and her best hat.

'I thought about it, but after years of living with other people at the Hall, I thought I'd be lonely in a place on my own. Thea's like family to me, so when she bought Rookery House and asked if I'd like to go and live there when I retired, I couldn't turn it down.'

'Did you ever want to get married?'

'Oh, I never ruled it out, but I never met and fell in love with a man who I was prepared to give up my independence for, because I liked my job and where I lived. I saw what happened to friends of mine when they got married, some of them ended up unhappy, little more than servants to their husbands and dragged down by having one child after another.' She shrugged. 'I decided that wasn't for me, unless I happened to meet a man that I was willing to give up my freedom for – and I haven't yet.'

Marianne nodded. 'I understand. I think you did the right thing, it's better to be single than live in an unhappy marriage.'

They fell into silence as they walked along until they reached the end of a driveway with a gatehouse on either side of it.

'Here we are,' Hettie said. 'The entrance to Great Plumstead Hall.'

They walked in, passing between the gatehouses and along a drive lined with mature trees part of the way. When the trees petered out Marianne had her first clear view of the Hall, set in parkland, the honey-coloured stone glowing warmly in the autumn sunlight.

'It's an impressive place.' Marianne took in the well-proportioned house with its porticoed front door, sweeping gravel driveway, and wings extending off on each side. 'That's a grand place to have lived in,' she said.

'Well, the servants' quarters are the smallest rooms and up in the attic. When I became Cook I had my own rooms, which were bigger and better, but when I first arrived here and worked as a kitchen maid, I was up in the attic with the rest of the servants.'

Approaching the front of the house, Hettie pulled on Marianne's arm to halt her. 'I'm going to leave you to go to the front door on your own, while I go around the back to the kitchen entrance to see my friends there.'

'But . . .' Marianne began; she'd thought that Hettie would be coming in with her.

'Listen,' Hettie patted Marianne's arm, 'I wouldn't leave you to go in on your own if I didn't think it's for the best. You're arriving here as a professional young woman, a talented designer and dressmaker, and you don't need to be accompanied by someone who was a servant here once because it might taint the way you're treated. Not necessarily by Her Ladyship but by some of the staff, who are just as bad if not worse. Lady Campbell-Gryce is one of the nicer upper-class lot, but there's always a gap between how they see servants and themselves.'

Marianne nodded. She knew what Hettie said made sense, although it irked her that it might be true. She'd seen enough in her work in London to know how different classes treated others, with so many of her previous boss's customers looking down on those who did the work for them. 'All right, if you insist.'

'I do,' Hettie said firmly. 'Right, off you go, remember you are a professional designer from the West End of London and Lady Campbell-Gryce is very lucky to have you come to her house to create an original piece for her. So, chin up and good luck.' With a final smile, Hettie headed off around the side of the house to the kitchen where she'd spent so many years of her working life.

Taking a deep breath, Marianne strode up to the front door, pulled on the bell pull and waited. The moment the door opened, and a tall, imposing butler stood there looking down his long nose at her, she knew that Hettie had been right about her coming in on her own.

'Good afternoon,' Marianne said, smiling pleasantly at him. 'I have an appointment to see Lady Campbell-Gryce. I'm Mrs Archer.'

'Good afternoon.' The butler's voice was deep and had the forced vowels of someone who was trying to imitate the speech of his employers. 'Her Ladyship is expecting you. Do come in.'

Marianne followed him inside and was led to a door off the large black-and-white tiled hall, which had an impressive wooden staircase sweeping up to the upper level. The butler knocked politely and went in, with Marianne following him at a distance.

'Mrs Archer to see you, Your Ladyship,' he announced.

Lady Campbell-Gryce, who'd been reading a book in one of the brocade-covered sofas beside the fire, held out her hand as Marianne approached her. 'Thank you for coming to see me at such short notice; I do appreciate it as I know how busy you are.'

'My pleasure.' Marianne shook her hand.

'Can I offer you some tea while we discuss what I'd like you to do for me?' Lady Campbell-Gryce asked.

'Thank you, that would be nice.'

'Can you see to that, please, Stokes,' Lady Campbell-Gryce said, addressing the butler who was hovering around, clearly loath to leave.

'Of course, Your Ladyship.' Stokes bowed his head before leaving the room, closing the door quietly behind him.

'Do sit down.' The older woman waved at the sofa opposite hers.

Marianne did as she was bid and took out the notebook and pen from her bag, thinking it was best to get down to business, portraying her professional image. 'You mentioned in your letter that you'd like me to design and make a dress for you for to wear to a wedding. When is that taking place?'

'It's the eighteenth of November, six weeks on Saturday, but I know how busy you are with work for Rosalind and wanted to give you plenty of time, plus I'll be away for two weeks during that time visiting my mother. Rosalind has very graciously suggested that I have my dress made ahead of hers but one doesn't like to push in. I thought if I contacted you sooner rather than later, it would allow you to plan out your work accordingly. And of course, if I'm happy with what you make, then I hope that we can work together in the future, too.'

Marianne nodded at her, smiling. How social-climbing Rosalind must have enjoyed Lady Campbell-Gryce feeling that Rosalind was being gracious in offering to step aside so that Marianne could work on her Ladyship's dress ahead of any of hers. 'That sounds fine and I'm sure I will be able to fit everything in, with good time.'

'Excellent. I may need you to make a new coat to go with the dress; churches can be so cold in winter, can't they?'

Marianne made a note in her notebook. 'What I need to do today is take your measurements, and then we can discuss what sort of styles you'd like, and I can come up with some designs for you to choose from.'

'Rosalind told me that you had a look at the clothes she already had to see what particular styles suited her best. And I must say the dress you made her is simply the best thing I've ever seen her in; it suits her . . . figure far better than anything else she has. It truly was made for her and brings out the very best in her.' Lady Campbell–Gryce smiled at Marianne. 'And that's what I would like too. I want something that will look fabulous on me in terms of style, cut and colour.'

'Very well, we can look at what you already have and see what individual design points you particularly like or dislike and what suits you best.'

'Excellent. First we'll have our tea and then we'll go up to my dressing room and have a look at my wardrobe.'

As if on cue the door opened and Stokes arrived with a tray of tea things, which he put down on the table between the two sofas. 'Shall I pour for you, Your Ladyship?'

'No, thank you, we can manage. That will be all.'

'Very well.' Stokes bowed his head, and as he left the room, Marianne had the feeling that he would have loved to have stayed and listened to their conversation.

*

By the time Marianne was shown out of the front door nearly two hours later, she felt exhausted, having had a thorough look through Lady Campbell-Gryce's wardrobe, which was far bigger than Rosalind's. It contained many fine clothes, but also some that didn't suit her at all. After much trying on of different dresses and coats, looking at what worked well and what didn't for her colouring and her thin, angular figure, Marianne had come up with some designs that had delighted Her Ladyship, and they had set a date later in the week to go to Norwich together to buy the fabric, just as she had done with Rosalind.

Unsure whether to go around to the back door of the Hall to meet Hettie or wait at the front, Marianne was relieved to see her friend hurrying around from the side of the house towards her, a big smile on her face.

'I heard it went very well,' the older woman said as they set off down the drive together.

'How did you hear that? I've only just come out!'

'There's not much stays private in a place like that, especially not with Stokes as butler – he likes to know what's going on at all times . . . But according to him, Her Ladyship is very pleased, and is taking you with her to Norwich to advise her on the best fabrics to buy.'

'We're going in the chauffeur-driven car! No going by train for her,' Marianne said.

'I told you she's an even bigger fish to catch and where she goes to have her clothes made, others will follow.'

Marianne laughed. 'Just like Rosalind, the poor woman's got some clothes in her wardrobe that really don't do her any favours.'

'Well, not everybody's got an eye for what fits and suits people like you have. You being evacuated to Great Plumstead is going to revolutionise the way some women dress around here. Just look at me, for instance.' Hettie smoothed down the skirt of her dress, which to Marianne's delight the older woman had worn at every opportunity to show it off. 'You've got a talent that benefits others when you use it and provides you with an income, too. It benefits us all!'

Chapter 32

Marianne moved the pattern piece slightly so that it was exactly lined up with the grain of the silk and then carefully pinned it into place. She was working on the first of the two dresses for Rosalind, having already made her two silk blouses with the material that they'd bought on their trip to Norwich last week. She was glad to have the large table in the dining room to work at, which enabled her to spread out the material at a height that was easier for her to work at – her ever-growing belly made it harder to bend forwards to work if she knelt on the floor.

She ran her fingertips over the fine silk, marvelling at the softness and the way it caught the light – it was such a pleasure to work with such beautiful fabrics as this – before pinning on the next pattern piece. The fabrics that she'd helped Lady Campbell-Gryce choose for her dress and coat on their shopping trip into Norwich yesterday were even better – no expense had been spared – and they now lay on the shelf in her sewing room upstairs waiting for her attention. With such fine working materials and the chance to create her own designs, Marianne was loving her work more than ever and it was earning her a good income as well.

A sharp, insistent rapping on the front door made her stop – it was unusual for anyone to knock there as most visitors to Rookery House came and went through the kitchen door at the back. Leaving her work, she went to answer it, knowing that Thea was in the back garden planning her 'Dig for Victory' and Hettie was busy baking in the kitchen.

Opening the front door, she was surprised to see Iris Stokes, the seamstress from Wykeham, standing there looking smart in a dark green wool coat and matching hat.

'Miss Stokes.' Marianne smiled at the woman, wondering why she'd come; had she changed her mind about offering her a job? Well, if she had, it was too late now – Marianne had found plenty of work of her own.

'Good afternoon, Mrs Archer,' Iris said.

'Would you like to come in?' Marianne felt obliged to ask.

The older woman shook her head. 'No, thank you, I've a bus to catch. I just called to offer you a job.'

'That's very good of you, thank you, but I'm not looking for one any more.'

Iris narrowed her brown eyes, her mouth pinching into a thin line before she spoke. 'And why is that?'

'Because I have enough work already.'

'Well, you can bring that with you and work on it from my workshop. Of course, I'd have to charge you a commission for use of the sewing machine and space. And any further commissions from those customers would come to me but I'd put you to work on them, they wouldn't lose your talent and skill just because you'd be working for me.'

And no doubt she'd be getting less money for doing the same work, Marianne thought, and losing control of her working life. 'I'm happy working the way I am, so thank you for the offer, but I really am going to have to decline it. Thank you for calling.' Marianne went to close the door but like a well-rehearsed salesman, Iris Stokes rammed her foot in the doorway to stop it closing.

Leaning in closer she hissed, 'I wrote to your former employer, Dorothy Abrahams, to enquire about you and received the most *interesting* reply ...' Her eyes were on Marianne's face, watching her reaction.

Fighting hard not to show the feeling of icy dread that the woman's words had stirred in her, Marianne tried to brazen it out. 'So, you'll know that I'm a fully qualified seamstress, then?'

Iris laughed, sneeringly. 'Oh yes, and then some ...' She paused before delivering what she'd found out. 'Such as how she had to sack you for *immoral* behaviour.' Her eyes slid down to Marianne's swollen belly, which was pushing out the front of her maternity dress. 'She couldn't have an *unmarried* mother working in such a prestigious establishment, her customers wouldn't have liked it and neither would she. She'd thought you were a respectable young girl when she took you on ... but you let her down.'

Marianne felt sick. Her past had suddenly leapfrogged

right into the present and threatened to knock down everything that she'd achieved here. She opened her mouth to speak but before she could say anything Iris pressed home her advantage.

'Of course, if you come and work for me, no one around here need know that you were sacked from your previous job for being an unmarried mother.'

Before she could defend herself, Marianne suddenly felt the door being pulled from her grasp and flung wide open.

'What on earth are you thinking about, Iris Stokes?' Hettie roared. The small woman had pulled herself up to her full height and was puffed up like an indignant hen. 'All right, Marianne might have been dismissed for getting in the family way before she was married, but she's not the only one to have it happen to her and at least she's a respectable married woman now, with a husband serving his country.' Hettie paused for breath for a moment. 'You're very quick to forget your own sister's hasty marriage with her eldest born just six months after the wedding . . . and there's plenty more around here that have done the same over the years.' Hettie pointed her finger at Iris. 'Shame on you for trying to blackmail a young woman into working for you. You're only jealous that she's doing well now and all through her own hard work and talent . . . and now you want to sponge off that.'

Iris stepped backwards on to the front doorstep. 'I didn't mean . . . ' she blustered.

'I suggest you go before you dig yourself into a deeper hole than you're in already.' Hettie's voice was now dangerously quiet. 'And if I hear of you spreading malicious and untrue rumours about Marianne, then I'll make it my business to tell everyone what you did here today. Blackmailing someone is a low-down, disgusting trick, even for you ... The constable might be interested to know about it.'

Iris's face paled. 'I won't say anything to anyone, I promise.' She turned and scuttled off towards the gate.

'I'll be listening out for any rumours,' Hettie shouted after her. 'I won't forget about this!'

They watched Iris leave and then Hettie closed the door quietly. 'Good riddance to her.' She turned to Marianne. 'She must have heard how well you're doing with your dressmaking commissions.'

'But how?'

'Her brother, of course – he's the butler up at the Hall. He will have told her you're doing some work for Lady Campbell-Gryce and Iris wanted a slice of that for her own business.'

'Of course, he saw me there.'

'And he's a right busybody as well. Right, come on, we'll have a cup of tea and you can tell me what's going on and I want the *whole* truth, mind.'

Marianne sat quietly at the kitchen table while Hettie bustled about making a pot of tea. Was this the end of her time here at Rookery House? Where would she go if she was thrown out? She put her head in her hands, not wanting to think about it.

'Here, eat this up.' Hettie put a plate with a warm scone topped with melting butter in front of her. 'You look a bit peaky, and I don't want you passing out on me.'

'Thank you.' Marianne took a small bite and although she knew the scone and butter would be delicious, it tasted like ashes on her tongue.

Hettie poured them both a cup of tea and sat down at the table opposite her. 'I wasn't intending to spy on you, but I heard the knock on the front door while I was getting the scones out of the oven, and by the time I went to see who it was, you were talking to Iris. I wouldn't have stayed only I heard her threaten you and I wasn't having that – she always could be spiteful, that one, right from school days.'

Clutching her hands tightly in her lap, Marianne met Hettie's blue gaze behind her round glasses. She sighed. 'What she said is true: my boss did sack me. I hid my pregnancy for as long as I could but when it became obvious because I was being so sick, she found out and was furious. I lost my job there and then.' Tears welled up in her eyes as she recalled the humiliating day when the boss she'd respected and admired had turned on her, calling her horrible names and almost literally throwing her out the back door of the workshop. Being an unmarried mother was a crime in many people's eyes and now she'd added to it by lying about her marriage as well.

'You're not the first and you certainly won't be the last young woman to fall for a baby outside marriage,' Hettie said gently.

'I'm not really married either!' The words were out before Marianne had time to think about it. She bit down on her bottom lip, fat tears rolling down her face. 'I'm sorry I lied to you.'

Hettie didn't say anything but got up and came around to the side of the table. She wrapped her arms around Marianne and let her sob. 'You cry and get it out of you.' She fished a neatly ironed handkerchief out of her apron pocket and pressed it into Marianne's hands. 'Dry your eyes and drink that tea, it'll make you feel better.'

Marianne took a small sip of tea but had trouble swallowing it as her throat was so tight with emotion. 'I'll go and pack my suitcase.'

'Whatever for?'

'I lied to you and Thea, and everyone here, and you won't want someone like me living here after what I've done.'

Hettie squeezed her hand. 'Says who? I judge a person by how they are now, not by what mistakes they've made in the past. And as I said, you aren't the first and won't be the last. Did you say you were married to protect yourself?'

Marianne shook her head. 'Not for me, but for my baby.' She laid her hand on her belly, feeling a squiggling movement inside as the baby shifted in its watery world. 'I didn't want it to grow up being called a bastard like I was; people said such unkind things because my mother and father never had the chance to marry. My father was killed in the Great War after he went back from his last leave, he'd asked my mother to marry him and they had plans to do that when he next came home ... only he didn't and then my mother found out she was having me. I wanted to protect my baby even if it meant I had to live a lie.'

Hettie nodded. 'I can understand that. What about the baby's father?'

'Alex. That picture beside my bed *is* him. But he's not in the Navy – at least, not as far as I know. I thought that if I said my husband was, then it would explain why I didn't hear from him very much.' Tears filled Marianne's eyes again. 'I loved him very much, I still do.'

'So, what happened? Did he run out on you when he found out he was going to be a father?'

Marianne shook her head. 'He doesn't know about the baby. I never told him.'

'Why ever not?' Hettie frowned.

Marianne wiped the tears away from her eyes with the handkerchief, which was now crumpled and creased from being squeezed in her hands. 'Because I found out he was going to be engaged to someone else, someone far more suitable for him than I was. I heard his sister telling one of her friends while they were having a fitting for another new dress. That's how I met him: his sister was having an evening gown made where I worked and he came along to wait for her, only the fitting took longer than usual and my boss told me to make him a cup of tea while he waited. He seemed very nice and the next day he came in and asked if he could take me for a cup of tea, but I said no as it wouldn't have been right to have accepted his invitation with him being the brother of one of our customers; my boss wouldn't have approved.' She shrugged. 'But the next day he was waiting for me when I finished work, and he pleaded with me to go and have that cup of tea with him and . . . 'She smiled. 'He really was so lovely, and we talked for hours. It didn't seem to matter that we came from such different backgrounds, he wasn't at all stuffy or stuck up like his sister and we carried on seeing each other and fell in love. It felt real and I think it was for him as well as me, but his family obviously had other plans for him that he'd never told me about. It was only hearing his sister talking about it to her friend that I found out, and by then I'd realised that I was in the family way.'

'You should have at least told him, given him a chance to do the right thing,' Hettie said.

'I was going to, but he was away on business when I found out about his engagement, and before he came back my boss discovered I was expecting and sacked me that same day. She asked me who the father was and when I told her she just laughed in my face . . . ' Marianne twisted the handkerchief in her hands. 'She told me I was a fool and that people like him would *never* marry someone like me, and that I'd been nothing more than a distraction for him, a plaything.' She shrugged. 'So I left, moved to the East End, bought myself a gold ring and pretended to be married. I got a job in a garment factory and when the chance came for me to be evacuated out of London, I grabbed it.'

'Didn't he come looking for you?'

'I have no idea, my boss didn't know where I'd gone and even if she did, I doubt very much that she'd have told Alex where to find me. She had her business's reputation to think about. So, that's my story.' Marianne sighed. 'I was a fool to get involved with him and now I'm paying the price, but I'm doing my best to protect my baby – it shouldn't have to pay for my naivety.'

Hettie pulled out the chair next to her and sat down, taking both of Marianne's hands in hers. 'You can't always choose who you fall in love with, and it sounds as if he was a nice man – knowing you, I don't think you'd have fallen in love with a scoundrel. I suppose his family's expectations rather than his feelings were going to dictate his life – that happens for many people of his class. It's a pity you never got the chance to tell him about the baby, though. He might have defied them all and married you.'

'Or he might not . . . and I think being rejected would have felt worse. It was best that I walked away with my dignity intact – I would only have wanted him to marry me out of love, not out of duty, and especially if it caused problems with his family. I'm really all right like this. As long as people think I'm married, I can cope with pretending.'

'I think that Thea needs to know,' Hettie said.

Marianne nodded, it was what she expected and yet dreaded. 'I know. I hope that she's happy to have an unmarried mother living in her home.'

'Thea won't mind at all, but I'm sure she would rather know the truth. Do you want me to tell her?' Hettie asked. 'I don't mind.'

'Would you?' She'd rather not see the look of disappointment on Thea's face; she'd come to like and respect her very much. If knowing about her past and her lies was going to change Thea's opinion of her, then she'd rather

222

Thea had a chance to take it in before she spoke to her about it. 'It feels like a coward's way out but . . .'

'It isn't, and I honestly don't think she'll be bothered in the slightest. She'll be more worried about you and the baby than anything else, knowing Thea. Why don't you go up and have a nap and I'll tell her when she comes in?'

Marianne nodded and stood up. 'Thank you.'

'And don't lie there worrying, either,' Hettie said. 'You need to rest . . . it *will* be all right.'

Marianne woke up at the sound of gentle tapping on her bedroom door. She'd lain awake for some time after coming upstairs, her mind going over and over her conversation with Hettie and worrying about the future before she'd eventually managed to drift off.

Pushing herself up into a sitting position she called out, 'Come in.'

The door opened and Thea put her head round it. 'I'm sorry, did I wake you?'

'It's all right; I've been here long enough.'

'Can I come in?'

Marianne nodded and swung her legs around so that she was now sitting on the bed, her feet resting on the rag rug on the floor.

Thea came in and sat down on the bed beside her and reached out and took hold of Marianne's hand.

'Hettie told me about what happened with Iris and what you talked about afterwards, and I want you to know that it makes not a single jot of difference to you living here. I don't care if you're married or not.'

It felt as if a heavy weight had slipped off Marianne's shoulders as she turned and smiled at Thea. 'Thank you. I was so scared that you'd tell me to go. Not everyone approves of unmarried mothers or people that have lied to them as well.'

'That's true, but I'm not one of them, though I think it's best that you carry on as you have been doing as a married woman – you're right: not everyone in this village is unbiased.' Thea squeezed Marianne's hand. 'I'd love to have seen Iris Stokes' face when Hettie came wading in to do battle, she can be quite fierce when pushed.'

Marianne laughed. 'She was! I've never seen her like that before, but she sent Iris packing.'

'We'll just carry on as we have been doing then, shall we?'

Marianne nodded, thinking how lucky she was to live here at Rookery House. Had she been billeted elsewhere in the village it might have been a whole different story and she'd have either had to accept Iris Stokes' offer or start looking for somewhere else to live.

Chapter 33

Prue was sitting by the fire in the sitting room, a cup of tea by her side and the latest copy of the WI's monthly magazine, *Home and Country*, on her lap, doing her best to distract herself from what was happening today. It would change her family life for the second time in a matter of months. She was grateful to have the house to herself, needing the peace and quiet while she prepared herself for what was to come – Alice had gone to see a friend from school and Sally was out with her husband, Arthur, who'd arrived this morning on a surprise flying visit, much to the young woman's delight.

It had been lovely to see how thrilled Sally had been at her husband's arrival, the pair of them clearly very much in love. She couldn't help herself thinking what a contrast it was to her marriage: she and Victor had never been in love like that, even at the start.

She flicked through *Home and Country*, which had been

cut down in size compared with previous issues owing, it said, to difficulties due to the war. She read the stirring message encouraging all its members to do what they could to maintain the spirit of friendliness and corporate activity, which had been the distinguishing mark of the Women's Institute since it had first been formed during the Great War. And now here they were again at war, being called upon to do all they could to help on the home front and, Prue thought, leaning back into the armchair, they most certainly were. The day club was proving a great success with the evacuee mothers; the jam making – first blackberry and then damson, too – had saved many pounds of fruit from going to waste and was selling well at the weekly markets. She felt proud of what they'd achieved so far, and yet she knew there was plenty more that they could do.

She took a sip of tea and stared into the flames of the fire, letting her mind drift as she watched the embers glow and dance with an orange energy that radiated a welcome heat into the room: the weather had taken a turn for the worse over the last few days. The cold, blustery day outside somehow seemed appropriate, matching the dread in her heart as she thought about what Edwin had gone to do this afternoon and how Victor would be gloating about it later, no doubt with that smug look on his face.

She heard the front door open and slam shut, pulled by the buffeting wind; someone had come home.

'I'm in here,' she called, wondering who it was. Victor would never leave work early; perhaps it was Sally and

Arthur, she'd make them some tea and there were fresh scones that she'd baked earlier.

'Hello, Ma,' Edwin said, coming in and closing the door quietly behind him. He walked over to the fire and held out his hands to warm them.

'Hello, darling, how did it go?' She did her best to keep her voice upbeat.

Edwin didn't say anything for a few moments and then turned to look at her, his face reminding her of when he was a young boy and he'd done something that he shouldn't have and was worried that he'd be told off. Her heart picked up its pace and seemed to lodge itself in her throat. 'Did you go to register?'

He nodded.

'Did they let you choose which service you'd like to go in?'

'I don't know.' He ran his hand through his hair and then looked her in the eye. 'You see the thing is . . . ' He hesitated. 'I've registered as a conscientious objector . . . I *can't* and *won't* kill another person.'

Prue stared back at him, a mixture of emotions swirling inside her: relief, worry, happiness and fear. Out of all the ways she'd imagined his call-up to serve going, this hadn't been one of them, but she realised now that it perhaps should have been. She'd been so wrapped up in worrying how he would cope with being forced into the Army, Air Force or Navy that she hadn't considered he might choose another path. 'That's . . . ' She stood up and put her arms around him and as she hugged him tightly to her, she could feel the relief in his body. Even though he towered above her these days, it felt like he was that young boy again being comforted when he was hurt or upset.

Stepping back, with her hands clasping hold of his, she said, 'I think that's the right thing for you, Edwin. I really do.'

He nodded at her, his blue eyes glittering with tears. 'Thank you.'

'What will happen now?'

He pulled a form out of his jacket pocket. 'I've got to fill this in with my personal statement explaining my reasons for registering as a conscientious objector and return it within fourteen days. After that I'll have to go to a tribunal where they'll decide if I can have an exemption or not.' He shrugged. 'I'm not against doing *anything* for the war effort like some COs are, it's just the killing part I object to and if I went in the Army or other services that's what I'd be expected to do to defend the country ... And I can't ... I honestly can't.'

Prue squeezed his hand gently. 'I understand and I'll stand by you.'

'But Father won't.' Edwin's shoulders slumped. 'He'll be furious when I tell him.'

Prue couldn't deny it. 'Perhaps when you explain how you feel about killing another person, he'll understand.'

Edwin pulled his hand out of hers and started to pace around the room. 'He won't! You know what he's like as well as I do; being a conscientious objector will be like a red rag to a bull. He's not going to like having a son refusing to do his bit to defend the country. He'll be bothered about what people will say, him being a councillor and businessman.'

'I could try to talk to him,' Prue offered. 'Make him see it from your point of view.' But even as she said the words, she knew that what Edwin had said was true. Victor would never look on this in any other way apart from how it affected *him*. He wouldn't be interested in the reasons his son felt the need to go against the flow of other men answering the call to join up; he wouldn't understand that it was because of Edwin's strong convictions. Her husband would never think that it took a braver man to stand up for what he believed in rather than following like a sheep.

'At least let me tell him for you.'

Edwin shook his head. 'Thank you, but no, this is something I must do myself, I don't expect any sympathy or understanding and once I've told him I don't expect to be welcomed here by him any longer either.'

Tears filled Prue's eyes. 'But this is your home! It will be your home for as long as you want it.'

Edwin smiled at her. 'With you it is, but not with him. I'll be all right, don't worry.' He came over and kissed her cheek and then left the room and she could hear him going up the stairs.

Prue slumped down in the armchair and put her head in her hands. She didn't want either of her boys to have to fight and face the danger of being injured or killed themselves. With Jack there had been no option, he'd wanted to go and she'd had to accept that, but Edwin had the chance to do something else, something still worthwhile that would help the country, but which wouldn't demand him to kill another. She admired him for making that decision and taking a stand, but it would come at a cost and she dreaded what would happen when he told Victor. She took a deep breath to try to calm her racing heart, knowing that there was only one place that she must be in this, and that was right by Edwin's side, supporting him.

'What!' Victor roared, his bad temper accelerating like a rocket.

Prue, who was standing next to Edwin, her hand firmly pressing on the middle of his lower back in support, felt her son quake at his father's reaction. It was just as they'd feared.

Victor slammed his fist down on the kitchen table, making the cutlery laid out for their tea jump.

'Let's get this straight: no son of mine is going to be one of those bloody namby-pamby conchies.' His face was scarlet, his piggy eyes bulging, and flecks of spit gathered in the corner of his mouth. He jabbed his finger towards Edwin. 'You can go right back to the recruitment office and tell them you've made a mistake.'

'No! It wasn't a mistake.' Edwin stood firm. 'I can't and won't kill another person.'

'He's brave to stand up for what he believes in,' Prue said. 'It's not—'

'You keep out of this, Prudence!' Victor snapped, glaring at her. 'He's *my* son, not yours!'

Prue felt the blood surge around her body, thrumming in her ears. 'I *am* his mother, perhaps not by birth, but very much by the care and love I have given him over the years.'

Victor laughed in her face, sneering nastily at her. 'You were no better than a nanny; I should have stuck to having one of them for my sons, it would have been a whole lot less hassle.'

His words stung her as if he'd slapped her in the face. Was that really how he thought of her? She'd never pretended to herself that they were a great love match, but she thought they were a partnership, parents to their children, together. Obviously Victor had never seen it the same way.

'You don't talk to Ma like that.' Edwin stepped nearer to Victor, pulling himself up to his full height and standing a good head taller than his father.

'Get out!' Victor roared.' You're no son of mine if you're a cowardly conchie, and you're no longer welcome in this house. Don't bother coming into work on Monday either: you're sacked and don't expect anyone else around here to employ you once they find out what you are.' Victor stalked towards the door. 'I want you gone by the time I get back.'

'No! Let him stay,' Prue shouted. How could he do that to his son? Didn't he care for him at all? 'He's your son, you shouldn't do this.'

Victor halted, his hand paused on the kitchen door-knob, then he turned and looked Prue straight in the eye. 'It's *my* house and I say who lives here, and I'll not have a conchie under my roof . . . ' He jabbed his finger towards her. 'And if you want to stay here you accept what I say or you and your little Cockney tramp will be out on the street as well, and you won't see Alice again either.' Not waiting for her reply, he opened the door and went out, slamming it loudly behind him. Seconds later they heard the front door slam too.

Prue slumped down in one of the chairs, the strength suddenly draining from her legs, which were shaking and felt as if they were made of jelly.

'It's all right.' Edwin put his hand on her shoulder. 'I'm prepared to go.'

'But you shouldn't have to, this is your home.'

'I know, but I don't want to stay here with him. I'll be fine, Ma, honestly.' He did his best to smile, but she could see he was shaken by Victor's reaction. 'I won't be sleeping in a ditch.'

'I'm so sorry it's come to this.' Prue grabbed hold of his hand. 'Where will you go?'

'To Aunt Thea's and Uncle Reuben's, they've offered me a bed.'

'Have you told them about you being a conscientious objector?'

'Yes, and they don't mind.'

Prue sighed, grateful that her brother and sister could offer Edwin refuge. They weren't the sort of people to hold it against him; they both knew the reality of war having been in France, unlike Victor. 'When are you going?'

'In a minute or two, my cases are already packed. I knew Father would react like this and probably sack me as well.' His eyes met hers. 'But I'm worried about you staying here with him.'

'I'll be fine, and there's Alice and Sally to think of – I need to be here for them.'

Edwin nodded. 'All right, but if you need me, I'll be here, I'll come back.'

Prue pasted a smile on her face. 'I know you would, but I think it's best if you steer well away from here for the moment – give him time to calm down and get used to the idea.' She stood up and hugged Edwin tightly. 'Go before he comes back. But if you need any money tell me, because he's right about there being a lot of people around here who won't employ a CO and especially you, because they'll be scared about falling out with your father, what with his business and connections. Promise me you'll ask if you need money?'

'I promise, thank you.' He hugged her swiftly. 'I'll see you soon, look after yourself.'

Prue nodded, biting on her bottom lip to stop herself from crying as she watched him leave, taking his suitcases from the cupboard under the stairs where he'd stowed them earlier, then grabbing his coat from the hall stand and going out of the front door for what might be the last time. As the door closed behind him, she let the sobs that had been building up inside her spill out and it was only when she felt the soft touch of a hand on her arm that she realised Sally had come downstairs and was leading her into the sitting room.

'Come and sit down,' Sally urged her. 'I couldn't help 'earing what happened. Are you all right?'

Prue shrugged. 'I'm glad Alice wasn't here to see that.'

'Perhaps Victor will change 'is mind once he gets used to the idea,' Sally suggested.

Prue shook her head. 'He won't, his pride and stubborn,

233

narrow-minded ideals won't alter, even if it means he's disowned his own son.'

Sally patted her arm. 'At least Edwin's got you, Thea and Reuben on his side; he's not on his own.'

No, he wasn't, and he never would be, Prue thought, not while she had breath in her body. She'd do everything in her power to support him and she didn't care whether Victor liked it or not, not now, not after what he'd said and done. She knew he'd be angry, but to throw out his own son was cold-hearted and cruel, and his words that she was 'no better than a nanny' had pierced her like knives. She felt betrayed, the man she'd stood by all these years – putting up with his difficult ways, his lack of affection – simply regarded her as someone to look after his children, no better than if he'd paid for someone to do it. In fact, she'd been cheaper than a nanny as he'd never had to pay her wages. Knowing Victor, that was probably something that he'd factored in to marrying her in the first place.

She closed her eyes and took some deep, steadying breaths, feeling as though her world had suddenly tipped off its axis. It wasn't pleasant but at least now she had a sudden clarity of what her marriage was really like: it was a hollow shell, looking whole on the outside, but in reality quite empty inside. The only good things to come out of it were her children.

Chapter 34

Looking at the paper plan spread out on the kitchen table before her in the soft glow of the light from the paraffin lamp, Thea couldn't help smiling at the thought of her and Reuben's many discussions and walks around Rookery House's land over the past couple of weeks, which had led to this. Together, they'd worked out what needed to be done and when. She'd already made a start by clearing out the old greenhouse, turfing out smashed pots and broken glass to get it ready to be mended, and had ordered the replacement glass panes to go in.

'What are you going to start with?' Hettie asked, moving some of the many pieces of paper that covered the table to the side and putting cups of tea down for each of them.

'With the chicken coop first, aren't we?' Thea directed her question at her brother who sat opposite her, chewing on the stem of his pipe. He nodded in response. 'Then the greenhouse as soon as the new glass has arrived. I'm going to order some blackcurrant bushes to plant, here.' Thea pointed to an area marked on the plan. 'They are good for vitamin C and if oranges get in short supply, we'll be glad of them. We'll plant them this wintertime. And we'll be sowing lots of seeds, I've marked in the catalogues the ones we want to start with.' She handed one of the seed catalogues that she'd sent for to Hettie, who flicked through its pages.

'You're going to be busy,' Hettie said.

'It won't all be done at once,' Thea said. 'We've worked out a plan of action.'

'What about the chickens? When are they coming?' Hettie asked, pointing on the plan to where Thea had drawn the chicken coop in the orchard.

'I'm going to make the coop tomorrow,' Reuben said. 'We'll get the pullets and a cockerel later in the week.'

'They'll be able to run about in the orchard, picking up plenty of grubs and worms in there so they'll lay rich eggs,' Thea said. She was looking forward to having chickens, they used to have some at home when she was young, and it had been her job to look after them.

Hettie nodded. 'They'll be good for cooking with.'

Bess, who'd been lying on the rag rug in front of the stove, suddenly stood up and went over to the back door, her tail wagging as she whimpered to be let out.

'What's the matter with you, Bess?' Reuben asked, getting up from his chair and going over to her. Bess scrabbled at the door with her front paws and as soon as Reuben opened it the dog dashed out and returned a few moments later trotting along beside Edwin, her tail wagging joyously.

'Can I come in?' Edwin hesitated in the doorway, and Thea noticed the two suitcases in his hands.

'Of course, you don't have to ask.'

Edwin came in and Reuben shut the door behind him. 'I hope you don't mind me turning up like this, only you said if I needed somewhere to stay ...' His face looked drawn, his eyes shadowed and nervous.

Thea went over to him and touched his arm. 'I meant what I said: you are welcome to come and live here any time you want and for as long as you want.'

A look of relief washed over Edwin's face, and he put his suitcases down on the floor. 'Thank you ...' He swallowed hard. 'Father threw me out.' He shrugged. 'I expected he would, but it was still ... unpleasant.' He sighed. 'And he's sacked me as well.'

Thea and Reuben exchanged glances.

'Well, it just so happens that I'm looking for someone to come and help me here. I want to grow as much food for ourselves as we can because they'll be bringing in rationing sooner or later and we've been told to "Dig for Victory". I couldn't pay you as much as you get working at the shop, but you'd get your bed and board included if you're interested.'

Edwin's face broke into a wide smile. 'I'd love to, thank you. I really appreciate the offer and I'd much rather be outside than stuck in a shop like I have been. I didn't get a lot for working for Father anyway, probably less than most of the men who work there. I'd much rather help you here.'

'That's settled, then.' Hettie poured another cup of tea and put it on the table. 'There, get that down you and have a look at the plans, see what you're letting yourself in for.' She chuckled. 'There's going to be a pig as well and a cow, too.'

Edwin sat down at the table next to Reuben, and Thea stood back and watched as her brother explained their plans to her nephew, grateful that she'd been able to offer him not only a home but a job as well. It was no suprise that Victor had thrown Edwin out, but it was still terrible to see that he wouldn't support his own son who was being so brave in standing up for what he believed.

Chapter 35

Prue was in no mood for going to church this morning. How could she sit there next to Victor pretending that nothing had changed? She couldn't bear to watch him shaking hands with people afterwards like an upright member of the community rather than someone who had treated his son so unkindly with no attempt to try to understand or support him. Not to mention how he really regarded her.

She hadn't seen Victor since he'd stormed out of the house yesterday evening. She'd been in bed when he'd returned home, and she'd stayed in her room this morning until he'd left for church, which was quite unlike her as usually she'd be up making breakfast for him. She'd heard him go out a short while ago and had peeped out of her bedroom window to see him walking down the road towards the church, dressed in his best Sunday suit. He'd gone alone, Alice making the most of not having been woken up on a Sunday morning and probably still sleeping, and Sally wisely keeping a low profile.

Now, washed and dressed, Prue tapped on Sally's bedroom door. 'Sally?'

The young woman opened the door and smiled at her. 'I've been keeping out of the way.'

Prue returned her smile. 'So have I, but the coast is clear now – he's gone to church. I'm going to cook some breakfast, can you tell Alice?'

'Of course. Aren't you going to church this morning, then?'

'No! It would have felt hypocritical to sit there with Victor this morning after what he said and did yesterday. He might go to church on a Sunday but there's not much Christian blood flowing through his veins. I think there's only one thing he worships and that's himself. And money, of course!' Prue sighed. 'So downstairs in five minutes, then?'

Sally nodded. 'I'll be there and so will Alice.'

While she put some eggs on to boil and cut slices from the loaf of bread to make soldiers, Prue thought through what she was going to do this morning. Normally, she'd have had a roast dinner prepared, with the meat going in the oven before they went to church, but that wasn't going to happen today either. Her priority was to go and see Edwin and check that he was all right and she'd take Sally and Alice with her, keep them out of Victor's way when he returned from church. With any luck he'd be going off to one of his meetings in Norwich this afternoon. He hadn't said as much, but they'd become a regular occurrence and one that she'd grown increasingly grateful for.

'I can't believe that Father threw Edwin out,' Alice said a short while later, dipping a soldier into her boiled egg. 'I know Father can be . . . ' She pulled a face. 'But to kick him out and sack him because he registered as a conscientious objector . . . Can't you persuade him to change his mind, Ma?'

'I tried but he won't hear anything of the sort.' Prue poured some milk into her tea and stirred it. 'I'm going over to see Edwin this morning. I think you should come with me, both of you.'

'All right,' Sally said. 'I'll be able to see Marianne as well.'

Alice nodded her agreement as she took a bite of a toast soldier glistening with orange egg yolk. 'I don't want to be around here when father comes home if he's in a bad mood.'

'Good, that's settled then.' Prue smiled at them both.

Prue could hear the thunderous notes of the church organ and some distinctly lacklustre singing from the congregation as they walked past St Andrew's Church on their way to Rookery House. Huddled in their coats, they leaned into the blustery wind, which was blowing leaves off the trees and sending them bowling along the road in scurries of orange and rust.

She suspected her absence in church would have been noted but she really didn't care, her main concern was Edwin – how he was feeling and what his future held. She knew from what happened during the Great War that just because someone registered as a conscientious objector, it

241

didn't mean their plea to be exempt from military service would be accepted. It depended on the tribunal and how strong a CO's conviction was in the eyes of those who were judging him. If Edwin failed to get the exemption he wanted, she dreaded to think how he'd cope if forced into the armed services. *Stop right there*, she told herself, *you need to take this one step at a time, it's no good worrying about the what-ifs and the maybes.*

'Do you think Edwin's gone to church this morning?' Alice asked, walking alongside Prue.

'I'm not sure. He likes going to church but whether he could face seeing Victor there or not I don't know.' She sighed. 'I certainly didn't want to be with your father, and I haven't been thrown out of the house or disowned for my beliefs. Edwin must be feeling a lot worse than me.'

'Where's he going to work now Father's sacked him?' Alice asked.

'I'm not sure about that either; hopefully he can find something soon.' Prue tucked her arm through her daughter's. 'Try not to worry.'

'He'll be all right staying with Thea and Reuben,' Sally said. 'Marianne loves it there, it's a nice place to live and they're all good, kind people, not angry and shouty like Victor . . . ' She clamped a hand over her mouth.

'It's all right, Sally, you only spoke the truth. And I quite agree with you.' Prue hooked her free arm into Sally's elbow, smiling at the young woman. 'I'm grateful that I've got my family here to help; I think Thea came back to live in Great Plumstead just at the right time.'

*

The kitchen at Rookery House was filled with the delicious smell of roasting meat – lamb with rosemary, by the smell of it, Prue thought, sniffing appreciatively.

'Sit yourself down and I'll make a fresh pot of tea,' Thea said, pushing the kettle on to the middle of the range's hot plate to bring it to boil again while she added fresh tea leaves to the large brown, earthenware teapot. 'No doubt Reuben and Edwin will be glad of a cup to warm themselves up.'

Prue did as her sister asked, glad that she had a chance to talk to her on her own as Alice and Sally had gone to find Reuben and Edwin and tell them to come in for a tea break as they were working outside in one of the sheds building a coop for the chickens. 'Thank you for taking Edwin in. I dread to think where he'd have gone if he didn't have you and Reuben to come to.'

Thea nodded. 'We're happy to help him and he can stay here for as long as he wants.'

'Thank you.' Prue clasped her hands tightly in her lap. 'I'm ashamed and disgusted with the way Victor reacted and treated his son. I can't forgive him for that. He said some cruel things—' Her voice cracked.

Thea's eyes held hers. 'There's room here for you too, and Alice and Sally, any time you want.'

Prue nodded, unable to speak for a few moments for fear of starting to cry – if she did, she might not be able to stop, and she couldn't let that happen with the others coming inside at any moment. 'Thank you, I'll remember that,' she eventually managed. 'Edwin's my priority at the moment.' She pasted a smile on her face. 'I'm worried about what he'll do for a job now. I'll give you money for his keep – I don't expect you to have him here for nothing.'

Thea smiled at her. 'You don't need to worry about that, Edwin's already got himself a new job. In fact, he's already started, insisted on getting going today.'

Prue frowned. 'What do you mean?'

Thea fetched the boiling kettle from the range, poured some water into the teapot and covered it with the brightly coloured tea cosy. 'I'm employing him to help me.'

'With what?'

'Getting this place ready to "Dig for Victory" and growing or raising our own food. I've got the land to do it, so I am. Edwin's helping me get started.'

Prue felt a huge sense of relief; that was one worry that she could cross out in her mind, because it *would* have been difficult for Edwin to find a job around here with people who either knew Victor or were against conscientious objectors, or both. It was wonderfully and deliciously apt that Edwin had found not only a home but a job with Thea, his own aunt. Her sister had no biases against people following their beliefs, she would take no notice whatsoever if she upset Victor or anyone else by her actions. In fact, knowing her, Thea would probably have enjoyed being able to give Edwin the job precisely because his father had sacked him!

The teapot had been drunk dry when Reuben, Edwin, Sally and Alice had joined them in the kitchen, and everyone was in a good mood, full of chatter and laughter, when Hettie and Marianne arrived home from church.

'There you are, Prue,' Hettie said, taking off her coat. 'I thought you were ill.'

Prue frowned. 'Why would you think that?'

'I heard Victor telling someone who was enquiring why you weren't there this morning,' Hettie explained.

'Well, he *lied*.' Prue shook her head. 'Obviously didn't want to tell them the truth: that I couldn't face being there with him.'

'Me neither,' Edwin said.

'There's a world of difference between going to church and being a so-called Sunday Christian and acting like a Christian the rest of the time,' Prue said. 'Victor's only worried about how it looks for him, so he lied.'

'Well, you leave him to stew on his own while you all stay here and have your dinner with us. Roast lamb and all the trimmings suit you?' Thea asked.

Prue looked at her daughter, who smiled and nodded back at her, as did Sally. 'Thank you, that would be lovely.'

Chapter 36

'I couldn't believe it when Arthur turned up out of the blue yesterday morning. I was helping Alice wash up the breakfast things when Prue went to answer the door and I'll never forget the sight of 'im walking in the kitchen behind her.' Sally sighed. 'Seeing 'im standing there so smart in his uniform . . . it was a sight for sore eyes. I flew across the kitchen and flung my arms around him.'

Marianne squeezed her friend's arm as they walked along arm in arm, well wrapped up in coats, scarves, gloves and hats, the pair of them coming out for a walk after the delicious meal. 'You're glowing from it today. Him visiting you was better than any dose of medicine.'

Sally laughed. 'It was! And such a wonderful surprise, I thought I was dreamin' to start with, but it was real, and he was there looking so 'andsome in his uniform.'

'What did you do?'

'I gave him a tour of the village, showed 'im all the

places I'd written about in my letters, we just wanted to be on our own for a bit. I wish he could have stayed longer than a few hours but he had to get back. With only a twenty-four-hour pass most of it was spent travelling, but I'm so grateful he came.' Sally stopped walking and looked at Marianne. 'I wish your 'usband could come and see you too, but I suppose they can't do the same when they're on a ship.'

'It's all right, I'm used to it.' Marianne smiled at her friend. 'What did Arthur think of it here, did he like it?'

They started to walk again. 'Yes, he did, and he thought Prue was really nice. He didn't meet Edwin or Alice because they were out and thankfully Victor was at work. He wants me to stay 'ere, nothin' might be happening to London yet, but he reckons it's only a matter of time before Hitler turns his attention on our capital, only he's a bit busy takin' over other countries at the minute to bother about us.'

'I think he's right, London might not have been bombed yet, but I think it will be, it's an obvious target.' She glanced at Sally. 'I'm glad you're staying – it wouldn't be the same here without you.'

Sally laughed. 'Hark you. We ain't known each other very long but it feels as if we've been friends all our lives. I don't think I'd 'ave settled here so quickly if I hadn't met you on the train. And we've been lucky who we've been billeted with as well. Except for Victor, of course! But Prue's lovely and Edwin and Alice ... ' She paused. 'Only Edwin's left now. I could 'ear it goin' on from my room with it being above the kitchen, I was just 'aving a lie-down after I got back from seeing Arthur off at the station. Victor came home from work and Edwin told him about registering as a conscientious objector and he went berserk, shouting and laying down the law. He's an 'orrible man, Marianne, I don't know what Prue's doing married to him, she's so kind but he's . . . he's like a mini Hitler: what he wants and says *must* happen as far as he's concerned. He ain't willing to see anythin' from other people's points of view.' She sighed. 'You should have seen poor Prue's face when I went down after Victor had stormed out and Edwin had left, the poor woman looked heartbroken.'

'At least she knows Edwin's got somewhere to live and work at Rookery House and that he's safe. It would be a lot worse if he'd just taken off and she had no idea where he was.'

'I know,' Sally agreed.

'Thea's no fan of Victor. I'm sure she's delighted to be able to give Edwin a home *and* a job. Victor may have thrown his son out, but Edwin's got other people that love and support him no matter what he believes in,' Marianne said as they stopped in the gateway of a field and looked over at the cows grazing in there. 'Families are funny things; growing up with just my grandmother was a lot different to bigger families. The more there are, the bigger the chance of people falling out, I suppose. Luckily my grandmother and I got on really well, but now she's gone and I don't have her any more . . . I really miss her . . . '

'But you've got your 'usband, and the baby,' Sally said, nodding towards Marianne's protruding stomach. 'They're your family now.'

For a moment, Marianne was tempted to tell Sally that she had no husband, that she'd been lying, but she stopped herself. Although she rarely talked about her so-called husband, even pretending he was there in the background didn't sit easily with her, she hated it. But she reminded herself just why she was having to do this and simply nodded and smiled. 'And I have a good friend in you, and live with good people, Thea, Hettie and Reuben. They might not be blood relatives, but I know they care about what happens to me and I do about them too. It might only be a matter of weeks since we first came to live here, Sally, but it feels like home to me now.'

Chapter 37

On Wednesday afternoon, a few days after Edwin had moved in, Thea was on her way back from the wood just down the lane from Rookery House, walking along the road swinging the basketful of plump chestnuts that she'd gathered there, when a car came towards her going far too fast. Leaping on to the bank, she caught a fleeting glimpse of the driver – it was Victor.

Spotting her, Victor braked hard and brought his car to a stop further down the road, then he reversed back fast to where she stood and opened his window.

'Dorothea . . . I've been hoping to see you.'

'Really?' Thea raised her eyebrows. The same certainly couldn't be said about him. 'What do you want, Victor?'

He put his elbow on the open window frame and leaned towards her, narrowing his cold blue eyes. 'To talk to you about *you* harbouring my son.'

'Well, *you* threw him out! I wasn't going to see him

sleeping in a ditch and I'm *glad* to have him living at Rookery House and working for me.' Edwin had thrown himself wholeheartedly into life with her, Hettie, Marianne and Reuben, and this very afternoon was fencing in the orchard to stop the hens from straying when they got them later in the week.

Red blotches bloomed on Victor's cheeks. 'You need to tell him to leave. The boy needs to forget this ridiculous conchie business and accept his responsibilities. Going in the forces will make a man of him; he needs to serve his country like I did, like any decent young man is doing. It's his duty to fight for our freedom and he's acting like a coward.'

Thea put one hand on her hip. 'Like you did?'

'When the call came, I answered it.'

'And served your time safely behind the counter of the army stores and nowhere near a battlefield. You didn't even leave the country, Victor! You're hardly in any position to go spouting off about people going to fight when you didn't do any of it yourself.'

'I wasn't asked to go to France,' Victor blustered, drumming his fingers on the steering wheel.

'But you didn't volunteer to go either, did you?' Victor wouldn't meet her eye. 'Edwin is actually a very brave young man to make a stand for what he believes in, you should be proud of him for doing that. And just to make it clear to you – I *won't* be telling him to leave now, or *ever*.' With that she turned and started walking in the direction of home.

Victor clearly hadn't finished, he put his car into reverse

and went past her a few yards, stopping and waiting for her to reach him, a look of fury building on his face. He hated being thwarted by her.

'He's *my* son and not even a blood relation of yours, so who are you to say what he should or shouldn't be doing, or giving him a bolthole to run to like some cowardly animal?'

Thea paused for a moment and then turned and glared at him. 'Being a blood relation to you, Victor, seems to bring no loyalty or kindness, so actually I'm delighted I'm not! It makes no difference to me whether I am to Edwin or not, because I care for him and will support him through thick and thin. And let me make it clear – you *cannot* tell me who I can have living in my home, is that understood?' She approached his car and leaned in towards him, her eyes trained on his. 'You might be a little king in your own home, but you certainly aren't in mine!'

Victor's face was almost purple with rage. 'It's only a matter of time before he'll come crawling back, you'll see.'

She laughed, shaking her head. 'Oh, I doubt that very much, not now he's had a dose of freedom and lived in a home away from you, Victor.'

He opened his mouth to speak, but Thea turned and walked off before he could. She'd had quite enough of him spouting his rubbish.

Chapter 38

'What shall we call him?' Thea watched her new cockerel strutting, chest out and with his red crowned head erect and proud, around the large run that Edwin and Reuben had built joining the chicken coop where the newly arrived chickens were exploring their home.

'He's a fine-looking fellow,' Marianne said. 'Look at the way his tail feathers catch the light.'

Thea nodded, admiring the cockerel's pattern of chestnut-brown feathers on his body and the splendid curl of greenish and bronze tail feathers that caught in the breeze. He was clucking pompously around his hens who weren't taking much notice of him, their beady eyes focused, instead, on the grass as they scratched in it with their sharp claws looking for tasty worms or grubs to eat.

'Let's call him Caesar: he's in charge of his own little empire, although I'm not so sure the hens would agree!' Thea laughed. 'We'll keep them in the run for a few days until they are settled and then they can come out into the orchard during the daytime, there's plenty of grubs and bugs they can eat in here.'

'When do you think you'll get a pig or a cow?' Marianne asked.

'Next year sometime. Reuben's going to organise it, but we'll need to get the sty and byre ready first, of course. There's no rush; things will come together gradually. Having Edwin working here is a big help. I want to get more beehives as well next year, which will help when they start rationing sugar.'

Thea glanced to the far end of the orchard where two hives were set up; she'd taken them on from Reuben who used to have them in the garden of his old cottage before he'd moved to the railway-carriage home here at Rookery House. It was something of a tradition in their family to keep bees – their father had done so and Thea had helped him to look after them as a child. One of the pleasures of coming back to live here was being able to keep bees again.

'We're lucky to have them,' Marianne said.

'I know, rationing will hit people in the towns and cities far harder than it will us, but it's necessary when so much of our food has been imported and that can't go on, especially if the Nazis' submarines keep picking off the cargo ships and sending them to the bottom of the sea.' She glanced at Marianne. 'That's why it's so important that we provide as much food as we can for ourselves. At least it's easy enough for us to do here because we have the land, and anything we have that's surplus we can sell.'

'At the WI market stall?'

Thea shook her head. 'No, I'm not a member, am I? I'll sell it to the village shop and I can send some to the shops in Wykeham – it will help bring in an income for me. I have a bit of savings after buying the house but it won't last for ever; I need to earn a living, too.'

'You could take in more lodgers, as well,' Marianne suggested.

Thea smiled at her. 'I've already thought of that! And yes I probably will. This war is certainly changing things and we've all got to move with it to survive.'

Chapter 39

Edwin had been living and working at Rookery House for a week now and Reuben was impressed by the way the young man had settled in and applied himself to hard work, putting Thea's 'Dig for Victory' plan into action. While Reuben had been working at his own job on the estate, Edwin had made a start on clearing out areas that were going to be used for growing food.

Now, on Saturday afternoon, the pair of them were working together on the old greenhouse, as he'd finished his work on the estate at noon.

Scooping some putty out of the tin, Reuben kneaded it into a smooth consistency, the smell of the linseed oil filling the air, and then he carefully began to work it into the replacement wooden frame that he'd made and around the new pane of glass that Edwin was holding in place.

'Have you heard anything from your father?' Reuben asked.

'Nothing.' Edwin shrugged. 'I don't expect to, the only way he's likely to want to talk to me is if I go crawling back and admit that I was wrong, but I'm not doing that. I haven't changed my mind and if he can't accept that then so be it. I need to concentrate on getting the tribunal to understand my reasons so they don't force me to join up. I've been working on my statement but it's hard to get it right. Thea's going to have a look at it for me.'

'She's good at that sort of thing. Do you know anyone else who's registered as a conscientious objector?'

'I met a chap when I registered who told me he's a Quaker and goes to the Quaker Meeting house in Norwich. I thought I might go along tomorrow now I can't go to St Andrew's without running into Father. I don't know what he's said to anyone or how they'd take it, or if they even know. Not everyone's as accepting of it as you and Aunt Thea, and Ma of course.'

'If I know Victor, he'll have kept quiet about it. He's against it and in his narrow view will think others are too – he won't want it to be known and associated with him.'

'But people will find out eventually. No doubt they'll write about the tribunals in the newspaper and then it'll be out,' Edwin said. 'I don't care if people know; I'm not ashamed of what I believe.'

Reuben smiled at him. 'And nor should you be. I—' He stopped, listening to the sound of a plane's engines stuttering and growing louder and louder. 'I don't like the sound of that.' He turned and looked up, searching the sky for a plane and then he spotted it heading towards them – it was coming in far too low and heading their way. It was in trouble!

'Bloody hell!' Reuben's heart leapt in his chest.

'It's coming down!' Edwin shouted as the plane roared towards them and then over their heads, making the ground shake and their insides judder. It skimmed over the chimney pots of Rookery House by a matter of yards and dropped down out of sight. They didn't see it hit the ground but heard an almighty thwump as it ploughed into the ground.

Before Reuben could say anything or move, Edwin was off, running towards where the plane had come down.

'Wait!' But his nephew didn't stop and quickly disappeared from sight around the side of the house. 'Stay there, Bess!' Reuben ordered his dog, who'd been lying there watching them work on the greenhouse and was now whining in distress.

Reuben followed Edwin as fast as he could, desperately hoping that the lad wouldn't do anything foolish. Planes that came down could blow up – he could be heading into a death trap. Reaching the road in front of Rookery House, he could see that the plane – an Avro Anson – was halfway across the field opposite. It lay squat on its belly, its pathway across the field evident from the scarred earth where a channel had been gouged out of the stubble left after the harvest. The scar ran from where it had hit the ground to where it came to rest, after ploughing its way along for a good hundred yards or more.

Reuben kept following, running across the stubble, which snagged at his boots and threatened to turn his ankles over if he wasn't careful.

'Wait!' he shouted to Edwin, who'd reached the plane, but again the young man either ignored him or didn't hear, as he climbed up on to the plane's wing and was trying to get inside. The plane could go up at any moment, explode into a fireball. The yards between him and the plane hardly seemed to get any fewer and his legs, though he knew they were moving, felt as if they were made of jelly, his bones dissolved away.

'Edwin!' he called again and this time his nephew looked back and gave a quick wave before helping a figure who'd just emerged out of the plane, putting his arm around him and supporting him as they hopped away from the plane to a safe distance. Leaving him there, Edwin ran back and helped a second figure who was emerging from the body of the Avro Anson.

It was all over quickly, and by the time Reuben reached the plane, both crew members were safely out and, thankfully, there was no sign of fire. They'd been extremely lucky.

'Are you all right?' Reuben asked the pilots, leaning his hands on his knees while he caught his breath.

'Smashed up my ankle, I think,' the young airman who was sitting on the ground said, undoing his sheepskin flying jacket. 'Hurts like billy-o if I try to put any weight on it.'

'Just banged my nose,' said the other man, who was older and had a fine moustache. He pressed a handkerchief to his bleeding nose, his lower face smeared with blood. 'Apart from that I'd say we've been bloody lucky – something went wrong with the old kite and we needed to land, didn't help that the undercarriage wouldn't come down properly either, so we had to belly-flop on here. Must have given you an awful fright.' He grinned and took off his leather flying helmet to reveal his dark hair cut to regulation RAF shortness.

Reuben nodded. 'Thought you were going to take the chimneys off.'

'We were avoiding the village, didn't realise there would be a house out here,' the younger pilot said. 'Some training flight this turned out to be.' He shrugged.

'Look on the bright side, young man, you've just learned how to crash-land!' the older pilot remarked. 'And walk away ... well, sort of – hop away more like!'

'Come on, let's get you to the house. We'll carry you in.' Reuben and Edwin linked themselves together, putting a hand on each other's shoulder and grabbing each other's wrist at the front to form a chair. Then the older airman helped his colleague up and settled him in their arms and they slowly made their way across the field, meeting Marianne, who was making her way towards them, her face pale.

'I heard the plane come down,' she said. 'How can I help?'

'Go on ahead and put the kettle on and get out the first-aid box,' Reuben said.

Marianne nodded and hurried back to the house, going far quicker than they were.

Reaching the field gate, they crossed the road and went along a few yards to the entrance to Rookery House and were just about to go in when they spotted the village constable pedalling fast towards them on his bicycle.

He waved when he saw them, which made him wobble across the road.

'Is anyone hurt?' he panted, braking hard and bringing his bicycle to a halt near them.

'Minor wounds, thankfully,' the older pilot said. 'We'll need to inform our aerodrome so they can send out someone to guard the Avro.'

'That's no problem. We can telephone from the house,' Reuben said.

'I'll stay on guard until they get here, don't want no one messing with the plane.' The policeman looked behind him: villagers were already coming along the road to see what had happened. There were several boys there who looked only too keen to explore a downed aeroplane and help themselves to a few souvenirs. 'Leave it to me, no one will get anywhere near it.'

'Thank you,' the older pilot said.

Leaving the policeman to set up guard in the field gateway, they carried on to the house and were met by Bess, who'd crept around to the side of the house to wait for Reuben. She wagged her tail at her master's return but kept a respectful distance as he and Edwin carried the injured airman.

'Hello, there,' the older pilot greeted Bess, who happily accepted him stroking her ears. 'I've got a dog at home and miss him terribly.'

Reaching the kitchen, Reuben and Edwin carefully lowered the younger airman on to a chair.

'I've just poured hot water into the teapot, so the tea won't be long,' Marianne said, setting out some cups on the table. 'There's a cake in the tin, I'll cut some slices.'

'Thank you.' Reuben smiled at the young woman. 'The telephone's this way if you'd like to follow me.' He led the older pilot into the hall and left him there to contact the aerodrome. He'd just returned to the kitchen when the door burst open and a breathless Thea, who'd been shopping in the village, came in and halted, looking at the airman in surprise.

Quickly recovering herself, Thea said, 'I heard the plane ... and saw it in the field ... Is anyone hurt?'

'Think I might've broken my ankle,' the young airman said. 'I can't put any weight on it.'

'I'll take a look.' Thea knelt down on the floor beside him. 'Don't worry, I used to drive ambulances in the Great War, learned how to do first aid then.' She gently examined him, feeling through the thick sheepskin flying boot. 'It's hard to tell through that and I daren't pull it off because if it is broken, I could make it worse. The boot will probably need cutting off but I think I'd better leave that to the doctor to do. I'll just check in case there's any bleeding.' She carefully eased her fingers down inside the boot to check. 'No, it's fine, so we'll leave the boot on for now as it's supporting your ankle and they can cut it off later.' She looked over at Reuben. 'Have you sent for an ambulance?'

'The other pilot's telephoning the aerodrome, so no doubt they'll send someone out to fetch them,' Reuben explained.

As if on cue the older pilot came back into the kitchen. 'They're sending out a car to collect us and guards to watch over the plane, shouldn't be long.' He smiled at Thea. 'Sorry to barge in on your home like this. We had to make an emergency landing. We really should introduce ourselves: I'm Rex Collins and my trainee pilot here is Charlie Greenwood.'

'You're very welcome.' Thea quickly introduced herself, Reuben, Edwin and Marianne. 'I'm glad that nobody's badly hurt, or worse . . . ' She frowned, looking at Rex's blood-stained nose, which had finally stopped bleeding although traces of blood were smeared around his face. 'You look like you need cleaning up. I'll sort you out, it won't take long. If you follow me, the bathroom's through here.' She picked up the first-aid box that Marianne had put out on the table.

'Thank you.' Rex followed her into the bathroom.

'It's very kind of you to help us like this,' Charlie said. 'It must have been a heck of a shock us dropping out of the sky like we did. Everything was going fine until we turned to head back to the aerodrome. This was my last training flight in the Anson – didn't expect it to end up with a crash-landing!'

'You did well to bring it down in one piece, I reckon.' Reuben sat down at the table opposite him.

Charlie nodded. 'I had to avoid the village and there wasn't much time to look for an open field to land in . . . and then the undercarriage failed . . . ' He sighed. 'We're lucky to have walked,' he grinned, 'or rather hopped, away from the plane with nothing more than a broken ankle and a banged nose.'

'Here.' Marianne passed him a large slice of Victoria sponge and a cup of tea into which she had spooned a generous helping of sugar. 'Get this down you, it'll help.'

The young pilot smiled at her. 'Thank you. That's just the ticket, and even better for it to be made by a beautiful woman!'

When it was time for the two airmen to leave, the car having arrived from their aerodrome to collect them, along with a lorry of RAF guards to stand watch over the downed plane until it could be removed, quite a crowd of villagers had gathered near the field entrance and were being kept from approaching the plane by the constable, who looked like he was rather enjoying himself.

'You've caused quite a stir in Great Plumstead,' Reuben said as he and Edwin helped the young airman out to the car.

'Thank you very much for all your help,' Rex said. 'We really appreciate your bravery getting us out of the plane.' He shook Edwin's hand and then Reuben's. 'And for all of you for your assistance and care, and the tea and delicious cake, we needed that.' He smiled at Thea and Marianne, who'd come out to see them off.

'So did we, it's not every day planes and airmen drop out of the sky,' Marianne said. 'You be careful next time you're up there.'

'We will be.' Rex smiled at her and got into the car and with a final wave they were driven away.

'You all right?' Thea asked, slipping her arm through Reuben's as they made their way back to the house.

He nodded. 'It could have been a whole lot worse: I thought the plane was going to take the chimneys off at the very least.' He looked up at the roof of Rookery

House. 'They were lucky to come down in one piece and that the plane didn't catch fire.' The image of Edwin running towards the downed plane flashed through his mind. 'It was Edwin who got there first – ran like the wind to get them out with no concern for himself, though the whole thing could have blown up. He's a brave man. Pity his father wasn't there to see it, that would shut him up saying his son's a coward.'

Chapter 40

'What do you think?' Edwin's eyes were anxious. 'That's the ninth version I've written and I have to send it off in a few days' time.'

Thea laid her hand on her nephew's arm. Edwin was sitting beside her at the table in the kitchen and had been patiently waiting while she read through the latest draft of the personal statement needed to support his registration as a conscientious objector.

'I think you come across as a very genuine, caring young man who knows his own mind and is not afraid to stand up for what he believes, and you've explained it very clearly and openly. The one thing that strikes me they'll want to know, and which I think is essential if you're going to stand a chance of getting an exemption from enlisting into the army or whatever, is what could be a good workable alternative that still fits in with your beliefs.'

He nodded. 'There is something – I'm not sure that I'd get in, though, but I think it might suit me very well. I heard about it when I went to the Quaker meeting on Sunday. It's the Friends' Ambulance Unit. I'd like to join it and work helping people.'

'I met COs working in the FAU during the Great War. They were on the ambulance convoys and ambulance trains, they made a big difference.' She smiled at him. 'I think that's an excellent job for you to do. How do you go about joining it?'

'I'd have to apply and if I get in, then I'd go to a training camp. One of the Quakers told me it's near Birmingham and they're already training recruits for the FAU.'

'Then you should apply too.' She squeezed his arm. 'I must warn you, though, if it's anything like in the last war it won't be an easy option. You'd see things that aren't pleasant and be in the thick of things, but I'm sure you'd do a good job because you care. Make sure you write that in your statement, too. Explain why you'd like to do it and that you know it could take you into tricky and dangerous situations, and that you might be sent abroad with soldiers even. It'll show that you're serious and have thought about what you can do to contribute even though you don't want to fight.'

Edwin smiled at her. 'Thank you for believing in me.'

'Of course I do!' She returned his smile. 'It's not easy to do the opposite of what's expected of you, and especially if it means going against some of your family, not to mention losing your job and your home.' Her eyes met his. 'Even right here when that plane came down, you showed great bravery thinking of others rather than yourself. Reuben says he's going to write to the tribunal telling them about it.'

'And the vicar of St Andrew's is going to write a letter of support for me, too. I didn't ask him to, but I saw him in the village a few days ago and he told me he'd heard about me registering as a conscientious objector and he appreciated my values and said he'd like to help.'

'That's excellent. Clearly he doesn't follow the same values as your father, thankfully. I wonder what he thinks of Victor throwing you out.' Thea was aware that word had got around the village that Edwin had left home under a cloud and was now living at Rookery House and working for her rather than at his father's business in Wykeham.

'I'm glad he's not judging me badly for what I believe in.'

'Well, he shouldn't really, should he? Not if he's living by the Ten Commandments he teaches. "Thou shalt not kill", remember, and that's what you're objecting to.'

Edwin frowned. 'You don't like going to church much, do you?'

'No. I used to go, right from when I was a child, and more than once on a Sunday too, but then I went to France and saw so much suffering and death that I lost any belief I had. I'm not the only one, either.' Thea shrugged. 'I live by the principle of being kind to people, and you don't have to go to church to do that, and to be honest some that do go don't live by its teachings anyway.'

She stood up. 'Write another draft and tell them what you want to do and why, and then I think it will be ready.'

'Will you read it again?'

'Of course. I'll do anything I can to help you, Edwin, and I always will.'

Chapter 41

Marianne guided the soft silk with her fingers, watching the needle bob up and down, up and down, while she kept a steady rhythm pushing her feet on the treadle underneath the sewing machine to power it along. She loved this whole process, it was both creative and calming. Finishing the French seam that ran along the side of the blouse that she was making for Rosalind, she lifted the sewing machine's foot, raising the needle out of the way, and carefully removed the material, taking care that it didn't snag and pucker on anything, which would have ruined it.

Cutting off the threads to sew in later, she held it up to inspect her work, checking that the French seam was perfect, and it was. There was just the other side seam to finish and then she'd be able to start work on setting in the sleeves, hopefully getting them both finished before the others returned, as she was here on her own this afternoon: Hettie was doing a shift at the day club in the village and Thea had gone into Wykeham.

She'd just pinned the second side seam into place to create another French seam and was about to start sewing when she heard a loud knocking at the front door. Putting her sewing to the side, she headed down the stairs from where she could see the shadowy outline of a figure through the stained glass of the front door.

Opening the door, she was surprised to see who it was. 'Charlie! How are you?' The airman who'd almost crashed into Rookery House last week took off his RAF cap and beamed at her, all the while keeping his balance on crutches.

'Hello there, I'm off my foot for a few weeks – turned out that my ankle was broken.' He waggled his lower leg, which was encased in plaster. 'But apart from that I'm fine; it takes more than a crash-landing to dent my spirit. I've come to thank you all for your help that day. With the assistance of my friend here, I've brought along a few tokens of mine and Rex's appreciation for you to enjoy.' He nodded his head at his companion, who like him was dressed in the blue RAF uniform, but who'd held back behind him until now. He stepped alongside Charlie, took off his cap and looked directly at Marianne.

The air left Marianne's lungs and she grabbed hold of the door frame to steady herself. She knew the man standing before her holding a bottle of whisky and two boxes of chocolates in his hands. It was Alex.

'This is Alex, he volunteered to drive me over,' Charlie explained.

271

'Hello,' Marianne managed to say, forcing the words out and doing her best to look as if she didn't feel like a pail of icy water had been thrown in her face.

'Hello.' Alex nodded at her, his face pleasant and neutral, giving nothing away.

'I'm afraid I'm the only one at home ... ' What should she do? If Thea were here, she'd ask them to come in, give them tea and some of the biscuits that Hettie had baked yesterday, but to do that would mean spending time with Alex, risking questions. The other option – to send them away – would be rude, especially when Charlie had brought them gifts. She had no choice but to do the hospitable thing. 'Would you like some tea?'

Charlie grinned at her. 'I'd love a cup, thank you.'

Marianne stood back and ushered them in. 'This way.' She led them through the hall and opened the door of the sitting room, thinking it would be better for them to go in there, that way she could escape to the kitchen to make the tea and give herself time to recover before having to play hostess.

'Make yourself comfortable in here and I'll go and make the tea.' She smiled, waiting for them to go in and then closed the door behind her and fled into the kitchen, her legs shaking. She grabbed hold of the back of one of the kitchen chairs and told herself to breathe steadily and slowly, focusing her mind on drawing air into her lungs and then releasing it. Just because Alex had turned up here, it didn't change anything, all she had to do was get through the next half an hour or so and then they'd be gone. She just needed to keep calm.

Pulling herself together, she went over to the range and

put the kettle on to the hotplate to boil and busied herself with making up a tray of tea things, putting out the cups and plates, taking some of Hettie's biscuits from the tin and arranging them on a plate. She was just spooning fresh tea leaves into the brown teapot when the kitchen door opened and Alex walked in.

'I came to carry the tray in for you.'

'No need,' Marianne said, over brightly. 'I can manage.'

'I'm sure you can.' Alex's eyes met hers. They looked at each other for several long moments. 'When Charlie told me about the young woman called Marianne who'd made him tea after his crash, and described what she looked like, I had to come and see for myself. Marianne's an unusual name and his description . . . ' He shrugged. 'It fitted you exactly, apart from the wedding ring and . . .' His eyes fell briefly on her swollen belly. He took a step closer to her, then stopped, frowning. 'You'd gone when I got back from my trip, vanished . . . and no one could tell me where you were. What happened?'

The sound of the kettle coming to the boil gave Marianne an excuse to think for a moment before she replied. Seeing Alex again was a shock but really it didn't change a thing. He was still a man who was engaged to someone else, he might even be married by now. That hadn't altered, she reminded herself as she picked up the thick, padded potholder and carried the hot kettle over to the table to pour water into the teapot, before refilling it at the sink and returning it to the back of the range.

Then she looked at Alex again. 'I lost my job and had to move.'

Alex frowned. 'But why didn't you get in touch, tell me what had happened? It was only a job, it shouldn't have made any difference to us.'

It wouldn't have if she hadn't found out about his engagement plans; she'd have done anything to stay with him. Thankfully she'd discovered the truth before she'd made even more of a fool of herself and told him about the baby, hoping for a marriage that could never be because he was promised elsewhere, but she wasn't going to tell him that. She needed to keep her dignity and not expose herself as someone pretending to be married.

'It was too far away ...' She shrugged. 'We just had a bit of fun while I was in London.'

Alex raised his eyebrows. 'I didn't know *you* saw it that way ...' He shook his head. 'But clearly you must have if you married so soon after. Who is he?'

'Oh, someone I've known for years, he's in the Navy.' The lie slipped off her tongue, and even though she knew it was necessary to protect herself, it didn't feel right. She wanted to ask him why he'd played her for a fool when he was promised elsewhere, but it was better that she didn't.

She went to pick up the tray, but Alex moved forward. 'Let me.'

She stepped back. 'Does Charlie know about ... that you knew me before the war?'

'No. He's an excellent chap, but doesn't know when to stop talking sometimes, so it's best not to tell him anything that you don't want spread around the mess. Don't worry, I won't say a word.' His eyes held hers again. 'I just had to come and see if it was you and find out what happened, I hope you understand.' She nodded. 'And I wish you nothing but joy in your life, Marianne.'

He picked up the tray and carried it into the sitting room, leaving Marianne staring after him, sudden tears filling her eyes.

Closing the front door behind them some forty-five minutes later, Marianne leaned back against the wall and sighed with relief. It was over, and she was so grateful that she'd been here alone this afternoon. She would tell the others about Charlie's visit when she gave them the gifts he'd brought, but there was no need to mention the name of the airman who'd driven him here. No one need know that Alex had been here. She dreaded to think what might have happened had Thea been at home, she'd probably have recognised Alex from the photograph beside her bed. All things considered, she'd got off lightly, although the shock of seeing him again had rattled her deeply.

She started to cry as she finally allowed herself to acknowledge the spark of delight that had flared inside her at seeing him. There was no doubt that she still loved him though it was in vain. Thankfully she'd managed to suppress it while he was here, because how foolish she'd have looked showing that to a man who belonged to someone else, a man who'd never really been hers at all.

Their meeting today had been the last they were ever likely to have. He now believed her to be married and expecting another man's child and there was nothing left for them. It truly was the end of their relationship.

Chapter 42

Prue spooned some loose tea leaves into the large, brown teapot, listening to the gentle hum of chatter interspersed with laughter and the sound of young children playing together that drifted in from the main room of the village hall, where the day club was in full flow. She smiled to herself, delighted at the way the evacuee mothers had taken the club to their hearts and attended it regularly, many of them coming every day of the week. It had made a real difference to their lives and thankfully no more had opted to return to London, each friendship connecting with others and forming a close-knit group.

Pouring boiling water from the kettle into the teapot, she let her mind drift to Jack's latest letter, which she'd received this morning and had read quickly before leaving to come here. As usual, he hadn't written more than one sheet of paper, but there was no denying that he was loving every moment of his training – even the long marches in freezing rain with a full pack of kit on his back hadn't dampened his enthusiasm. She was glad that he was enjoying himself, and that made her happy for him too, and the same could be said for Edwin. His decision to register as a conscientious objector might have riled his father, but she was inordinately proud of him for being brave enough to go against the flow and stand up for his beliefs – it wasn't easy for him and he'd paid for it with Victor throwing him out and sacking him. She knew that there were some people in the village who shared Victor's opinion and weren't afraid to voice it in gossip in the shops and streets. Thankfully with him now living at Rookery House and working there for Thea, Edwin was spared most of the looks and mutterings that he might have received if he'd still been living at home in the heart of the village. She'd been to visit him yesterday and seen how happy he was, and she was grateful for that.

Prue was putting teacups on to the tray ready to take out into the hall when Sally came into the kitchen, tears streaming down her face, which had turned very pale.

'I think me waters 'ave just broke ... I've had stomach cramps since I got up this mornin' and just went to the lavvy and whoosh ... I know it weren't a pee because I'd just been ... I think the baby's comin'... but it's too early ... It ain't due for another month yet.' Sally began to cry, great sobs that heaved her thin shoulders.

Prue hurried over and put her arm around her. 'It's all right, I'll get you to the maternity hospital, they'll know what to do. Try not to worry, babies sometimes come before they should and they're fine, maybe a little bit smaller than if they'd gone full term but quite perfect in every other way.'

She pulled out a chair from the table and gently guided Sally into it. 'You sit down here, and I'll go and get my car, I won't be long. I'll send Vera in to keep an eye on you.'

Sally grabbed her arm. 'It will be all right, won't it?'

Prue took hold of her hand and squeezed it gently. 'I'm sure it will be. As soon as we get you to the maternity hospital the midwives will be able to look after you, they've done it hundreds of times before – you'll be in safe hands. I'll be back as soon as I can, I promise.'

She dashed into the hall and over to Vera, who was pulling out an old jumper, winding the wool into balls ready to be re-knitted into something new. Leaning close, she whispered in her ear: 'It looks like Sally's baby is on its way, can you go into the kitchen and keep an eye on her while I nip home and get my car, please? I won't be long.'

'Course I will, I'll take this and she can wind the wool up for me as I pull it out, it'll give her something to do while we wait.' Vera got up and headed off to the kitchen.

The drive to the maternity hospital that had been set up to deal with the increased number of expectant mothers in the area because of the evacuation seemed to take ages, far longer than it usually would to drive the five miles from Great Plumstead. It wasn't that she was going any slower than usual, it was simply because she was aware that Sally was most definitely in labour now – her pains were stronger and coming more rapidly, making her groan and clutch at her belly.

Prue was glad that she'd saved her rationed petrol for such emergencies, walking or bicycling everywhere rather than using her car, so that when she really did need to use it, like now, she had enough fuel. She urged her little Austin 7 on, wishing that it had wings so that she could go directly as the crow flies rather than having to take the winding lanes that led to the hospital.

'It won't be long, we're nearly there,' Prue said, as she turned the car in through the gate posts and down the long drive leading to Langdon Hall, a large house that had been requisitioned for the duration to serve as a maternity hospital. She took one hand off the wheel and patted Sally's arm. 'You're doing so well. I know it's painful, but it will soon be over and then you'll have a lovely little baby.'

'I didn't expect it to 'urt this much!' Sally groaned as another pain began to grip her in its vicelike claws. 'Oh, Gawd!'

Prue pushed hard on the accelerator, soon covering the final few hundred yards and coming to a halt outside the front doors with a spattering of gravel. She flung open her door and ran around to the passenger side to help Sally out. Putting her arm around her, she guided her up the front steps between the porticoed pillars and in through the front door to the entrance hall. 'Hello! We need some help here!' A nurse came out of the room leading off the hallway, took one look at them and, to Prue's relief, immediately took command.

'This way, we'll soon have you sorted.' The nurse smiled at Sally then turned to Prue. 'I'll take her from here, thank you; if you'd like to take a seat, I'll be back to take some details down in a moment.'

Sally had no time but to glance briefly at Prue before she was whisked away down a corridor leading off from the hall.

Prue sighed as she sat down on a chair and did her best to calm her racing heart. She'd never expected the day to pan out like this. Sally hadn't shown any signs of going into labour at breakfast and it had all happened so quickly, no doubt a shock to her evacuee as well as to her. She hoped Sally's labour would be over soon for her and that the reward of the beautiful baby would help her forget the pains that had racked her body, just as had happened after she'd given birth to Alice. She smiled to herself as she remembered holding her daughter for the first time and how all the agony of the preceding hours had slipped away when she looked into her daughter's face, her tiny hand curling around her finger.

Her memories were interrupted by the return of the nurse. 'My colleagues are looking after Sally now and she'll be fine. If you'd like to come with me into the office you can perhaps give me Sally's details – her address, et cetera – so that we can get her booked in properly.' She smiled. 'I don't think she wants to be bothered with the formalities herself right now.'

Prue stood up and followed the nurse into the office.

'Take a seat.' The nurse indicated the chair in front of her desk and went around to sit behind it, taking a form out from one of the drawers. 'Is Sally your daughter?'

'No, my evacuee, from London. Her baby wasn't due until next month.'

'Well, babies come when *they* decide and rarely by due date.' The nurse smiled at her. 'Don't worry, we'll look after her.'

Prue nodded. 'Thank you. It was quite a shock when she said her waters had broken. She was so scared.'

'Naturally, going into labour for the first time is going into the unknown, but she's young and strong and there's no reason why she shouldn't give birth perfectly well, but if she should need assistance we have doctors on standby.' The nurse picked up a pen. 'Now, let's get this form done.'

Prue was relieved that by the time she got back to Great Plumstead her time on duty at the day club was over, so she could go straight home where it wouldn't matter if she couldn't concentrate on much except worrying about how Sally was getting on.

Going into the kitchen she put on her wraparound apron having decided it was best to apply her nervous energy to some mundane household tasks. Sweeping floors and bashing rugs slung across the washing line in the garden were ideal jobs, along with scrubbing the kitchen floor – anything to busy her hands and yet leave her mind free, while still being within range to hear if the telephone rang as the hospital had promised to call with any news.

Several times as she passed the telephone on its table in the hall, Prue picked it up to check for the buzzing sound. She had conjured up different scenarios, one of them being that the hospital had tried to ring her and had been unable to get through, but the reassuring hum was still there and she replaced it quickly before the telephone operator could ask her which number she wanted.

It was a little after half past three that afternoon, when Prue was sitting at the kitchen table having a slice of toast and some tea, the house having been swept, scrubbed and polished in the hours since she'd arrived home, when the telephone jangled into life in the hallway. She leapt out of her chair, knocking it backwards where it fell with a clatter on the tiled kitchen floor and dashed through to the hallway, snatching up the receiver.

'Hello.'

'Is that Mrs Wilson?' a woman's voice asked.

'Yes, that's me.'

'I'm Matron Hollis from the Langdon Hall maternity hospital. You brought your evacuee, Sally Parker, into us this morning . . .' Matron paused. 'She gave birth a short while ago but I'm sorry to tell you that her baby was stillborn. It was a little girl.'

Prue gasped and slumped down on to the chair beside the table where the telephone stood, her legs having turned to jelly. 'But how . . . ?'

'We don't know. Sometimes these things happen, I'm afraid.' The matron's voice was sympathetic.

Prue bit on her bottom lip, fighting to keep her voice even despite the hot tears stinging her eyes. 'And Sally, is she all right?'

'Yes, physically she's absolutely fine and will make a full recovery. Of course, she's understandably very distressed at what's happened but we are taking great care of her.'

'Can I come and see her?' Prue asked.

'Yes, but I think it best for you to wait until tomorrow afternoon, give her a chance to come to terms with losing her baby and get some rest.'

'I'll be there, thank you.'

'I'm sorry it wasn't better news, I really am.' Matron's voice was kind. 'She's a healthy young woman and there's no reason why she shouldn't go on to have more babies in the future. I'll tell her you'll be in to see her tomorrow, then. Goodbye.'

'Goodbye.' Prue put the receiver down and leaned forwards, elbows on her knees and her head in her hands. Stillborn. She had never expected that, no one did. Poor Sally, she must be devastated. Prue began to cry. Crying for Sally and her loss, and for the tiny baby who never had a chance to draw breath and who would have been so dearly loved by her mother. The matron was right in saying that these things happened, but it didn't help when it happened to someone whom one had grown to care for and who would suffer such pain and grief.

Fishing a clean handkerchief out of her pocket she dabbed at her eyes. She had to pull herself together and be strong for Sally, the young woman would need her to be there for her to help her through this. And the other expectant mothers, too: news like this was bound to shake those who had yet to give birth, they'd be worrying that something might happen to their own babies. It would rock everyone in this close-knit group of women. She hoped that none of the rest would have to go through what Sally was experiencing, one lost baby was more than enough.

Chapter 43

'Stillborn!' The colour drained from Marianne's face and her hands went to her protruding belly as if to cradle her own unborn child.

Hettie gasped, putting a hand to her mouth, her eyes brimming with tears as she pulled a neatly ironed hand-kerchief out of her pocket.

Prue nodded. 'Yes, I'm sorry. Sally's waters broke when she was at the day club this morning and I took her into the maternity hospital and her little girl was born there this afternoon.'

She'd come around to Rookery House to tell them, and especially Marianne, not wanting her to hear rumours of Sally having to leave the day club and not knowing what had happened to her friend. Thankfully she hadn't been there this morning herself as she'd been busy with her dressmaking. She and Sally had formed a close bond and Prue knew that Marianne would be upset.

'Is Sally all right?' Thea asked, taking hold of Marianne's hand as the young woman began to cry, tears sliding down her cheeks and dripping on to the front of her pale blue maternity smock, leaving dark marks where they soaked into the fabric.

'The matron said she's fine physically but obviously very upset by what's happened, and she needs to rest today but can have visitors tomorrow. I'll go in the afternoon.'

'I'll go and see her, too.' Marianne's voice was croaky.

Prue smiled at her. 'I think she'd like that. It might be a good idea for us to spread our visits out so that she has some most days. I expect they'll keep her in for the usual two weeks after someone gives birth.'

'And we can get there by train – the maternity hospital's not far from the station at Langdon, is it?' Hettie asked.

'No, just a short walk. I'll be going there by train: I need to save what petrol I've got in case of other emergencies like this one.' Prue sighed. 'I haven't told any of the other expectant mothers yet. I'll go to the day club tomorrow and let them know what's happened. Sally was in the kitchen before she left for the hospital, so I suspect they don't know she went in. Naturally they'll be upset about what's happened as well.'

'What will Sally do now – I mean, when she comes out of hospital?' Marianne asked.

Prue shrugged. 'I'm not sure, the main thing is for her to recover from the birth. We'll have to wait and see what she decides to do after that.'

'Do you think she'll go back to London?' Thea asked.

'I don't know. Let's just get through the next few days

286

and weeks and then we can see. I'd be very sad to see her leave, though, if she did decide to go back.' Prue stood up to go. 'I'm sorry to have brought this news. I'll telephone and let you know how she is tomorrow after I've been to see her.'

Marianne nodded. 'Thank you.'

Thea got up and followed Prue outside and the two sisters walked around the outside of the house to where Prue had left her bicycle propped against the wall.

'It must have been one heck of a shock.' Thea laid a hand on Prue's arm. 'Are you all right?'

'Yes, but I wish this hadn't happened, Sally was so looking forward to having her baby . . . She'd have made a smashing mother, she really would. It doesn't seem fair.'

'I know. We'll all do everything we can to help her, you know that.'

'Thank you. Just a couple of months ago we knew nothing about these evacuee mothers and here they are having wriggled their way into our hearts.' Prue sniffed back the tears that threatened to spill out.

'But that's good, Prue: it means that they're cared for here, which is what we wanted for our evacuees, wasn't it?'

Prue nodded and managed to smile, then she took hold of her bicycle and climbed on to the saddle. 'I'll be in touch tomorrow. Goodbye.' She pushed off and started pedalling, heading out of the gate and back towards the village feeling like the telegram boy probably did after he'd delivered one of those dreaded envelopes with the news of a loved one's death.

Chapter 44

Thea was coming down the stairs when the front door's letterbox rattled and letters fell on to the mat – today's first post had just arrived. She picked up the envelopes and glanced through them to see who they were for; there were two for her, one of them from Jack, she thought. The other was from Violet Steele, whose handwriting she instantly recognised. The two women had been writing to each other for years, ever since they'd met and become friends during the Great War when they'd worked together in France. She was now running an ambulance station in London and Thea would enjoy reading her letter later to hear her latest news. The other letter was for Edwin and looked official. Was it to do with his registration as a conscientious objector? She'd better take it out to him as he might need to respond to it as soon as possible.

Outside, dressed in her coat, scarf, hat and woolly

gloves – the cold November weather made it necessary to dress up warmly whenever you went outside now – Thea headed to where Edwin was planting out the blackcurrant bushes that she'd ordered and which would hopefully grow well and produce some rich, tangy fruit in the coming years.

Despite the cold weather, Edwin had discarded his coat, leaving it hanging on the branch of a nearby tree, the digging clearly making him quite warm enough.

'How are you getting on?' Thea surveyed what he'd done; a row of six bushes were neatly planted already.

'Fine.' Edwin thrust his spade into the soil and looked at the wooden crate of bushes still to be planted. 'I'll be done before I stop for dinner.'

'Good, but if you need to do something about this first, they can wait till later.' She held out the envelope. 'This came for you. It looks official.'

Edwin bit his bottom lip as he took it from her. 'Thank you.'

'I'll leave you to read it.' Thea turned to go.

'Wait!' Edwin ripped the envelope open. 'There's no need to go.' He pulled the sheet of paper out and read it through.

From where she stood, Thea could see that it was type-written and had an official mark at the top of the page.

Edwin blew out a breath. 'It's the date for my tribunal.' His eyes met hers. 'It's on the first of December – that's . . . four weeks' time. At the court in Norwich.' He looked worried.

Thea stepped forward and put her arm around him.

'You won't be going alone: I'll be there, and Reuben and your mother, of course.'

'Thank you.'

'It will be all right, you've told them you want to work for the Friends' Ambulance Unit, haven't you? That must stand for something. You want to do your bit, but just in a way that your conscience will allow. Helping others is just as important as fighting and if, or more like *when*, Hitler decides to start bombing us, then FAU will be desperately needed. I've just had a letter from my friend Violet in the post, she's now running an Auxiliary Ambulance Service station not far from the Tower of London, so London is definitely preparing itself for what might come. And it probably won't be just in London, other cities will be targeted too. There'll be no shortage of work for ambulance crews.'

Edwin shrugged. 'I'm sure you're right about that, but will the people on the tribunal see fit to give me an exemption so I can join the FAU? I hope they will, but there's no guarantee.'

'I know, but we've got to be positive, prepare as much as you can and hope that on the day, it works out well for you.'

'I hope so.' Edwin eased the spade out of the soil. 'Better get back to work. Will you take this back inside for me?' He held out the letter to her.

Thea took it. 'I'll put it on the dresser in the kitchen for you.'

Leaving her nephew to get on with his work, she headed back to the house, hoping that the tribunal would have the sense to listen to Edwin's plea and allow him to do a job that he would be excellent at, and which would be desperately needed when the war escalated here in England as it was bound to do sooner or later. So far very little had happened on these shores apart from the build-up of the military – the Army were a common sight these days and the sky never seemed to be free of the RAF's planes – but it wouldn't last. Hitler would send his fighting force to attack at some point. It was just a question of when.

Chapter 45

'She's this way.' The nurse led Marianne towards a doorway at the end of the corridor. 'We put mothers who've lost their babies in a room on their own so they don't have to watch other mothers with their babies. That would be too hard for them.'

'How is she?' Marianne asked. She'd been worrying about her friend ever since Prue had brought the news that Sally's baby girl had been stillborn two days ago.

'She'll be fine, she just needs to rest and gather her strength.' Her voice was brisk and no-nonsense, although her eyes were kind and Marianne could see that she had sympathy for her friend. She stopped outside the closed door. 'You go in then, and I'll bring you both a cup of tea in a little while.' She touched Marianne's elbow and turned and went back the way they'd come.

Now she was here, Marianne wasn't sure if she'd done the right thing coming here today. Would Sally want to see her? Wouldn't she be a reminder, with her own baby still to be born, of what Sally had lost? How would she feel if the situation were reversed, she considered, would she rather be alone or see her friend? The answer came to her immediately: she'd want to see her friend, no matter what.

Taking a deep breath, she tapped on the door and went in. The figure lying in the bed, propped up against a pile of white pillows, looked far smaller than Sally usually did. Of course her swollen belly was smaller, but the loss of her baby seemed to have shrunk her all over; her face was pale and wan, and even her auburn hair didn't seem to be as vibrant as usual.

'Hello, Sally.' Marianne went over and sat on the edge of the bed and took hold of her friend's hands, and as she did so, Sally's blue eyes filled with tears that spilled over and trickled down her cheeks.

Marianne gathered her into her arms and held her as she sobbed, Sally's whole body shaking with the strength of her grief. Tears were soon streaming down Marianne's own face and she had no idea how long they clung to each other, their sadness spilling out.

'Here, take this.' Marianne handed Sally one of the several neatly ironed handkerchiefs that Hettie had pressed into her hands as she was leaving Rookery House to come and visit. Using another handkerchief to mop up her own tears she said, 'I'm so, so sorry about what happened.'

Sally nodded, sniffing as she blotted her blotchy face. 'She never even 'ad the chance to take a breath . . . ' She swallowed hard, more tears filling her eyes and spilling over. 'I just never thought this would 'appen. I know it can, there ain't no guarantees in life ... but she was always so lively, kickin' me, keeping me awake at night.' She shrugged. 'They don't know why she was stillborn, just said these things happen.' She paused for a moment, wiping away her tears. 'What am I going to do now?'

'Does Arthur know?'

'Prue sent him a telegram. I don't know if he'll be able to get leave to come and see me. Probably not, knowing the Army. He's in their control now.'

Marianne squeezed Sally's hand gently. 'Try not to worry about anything more than getting your strength back. That's the first thing you need to do and after that you can see.'

'They said I 'ave to stay here for ten days before they'll let me go back to Prue's, though I wish I could go sooner, it ain't nice hearing the babies crying when mine's dead.'

Marianne nodded. 'Is there anything I can do? Is there anything you need?'

'No, there ain't nothing, thanks. Prue brought some things in yesterday.' Sally bit her bottom lip. 'There is one thing I'd like to know, though – can you find out what they did with her? They wouldn't let me hold her, just bustled her away, said it was for the best that I didn't see her, but I want to know where she is.'

The thought of not knowing what had happened to her baby, even if it had been stillborn, would have eaten away at Marianne too. It was bad enough that Sally hadn't been able to hold her daughter or even see her properly, and her mind must be churning over what had happened to her child.

'I'll go and find out for you now, all right?' She stood up. 'I'll be back as soon as I can.'

Closing the door of Sally's room behind her, she stood still for a moment, shutting her eyes and willing herself to keep calm and dampen down her own tears, which were threatening again at the thought of how her friend was suffering and the fate of her baby daughter. If she could find out where she was, it might go some way to helping Sally accept what had happened.

She'd noticed the door marked 'Matron' on the way in and headed back down the stairs to it. She knocked gently on the door.

'Come,' a voice called from inside.

Marianne went in. 'Good afternoon, I'm a friend of Sally Parker, and I wondered if you could tell me what happened to her stillborn baby. Where was she taken?'

'Sit down, dear.' The matron indicated that she should sit in the chair opposite her desk with a bob of her head. 'A sad business, but alas one that happens sometimes. She was a perfect little girl, nothing outward to show why she died, just one of those things.' She sighed and shook her head. 'She's been taken to the local undertaker's and will be placed in the coffin of a deceased woman. She won't be alone and will be buried in a proper Christian burial.'

Marianne nodded, grateful that the baby would be afforded a proper burial. 'Thank you. Knowing that will help Sally, I hope.'

'She's still in shock, understandably, and we're keeping

a close eye on her. Plenty of rest, good food and time will help her get her strength back. She was all for returning to her billet this morning, but thankfully her host ...' She paused for a moment before going on. 'Mrs Wilson?' Marianne nodded. 'Well, Mrs Wilson persuaded her that she should stay here for ten days and then she can go home.' Matron's eyes strayed to Marianne's own swollen belly. 'When are you due, dear?'

'January.'

'Well, we'll expect to see you in here as a patient yourself, then.' Matron stood up. 'Go and tell your friend that her baby is being treated with the greatest respect and dignity and if there's anything else she wants to know she just has to ask me.'

She smiled at Marianne and came around from behind her desk to open the door for her. 'Some women find it best to try to forget what happened while others will want to talk about it; having a good friend to do that with will help if Sally needs to.'

'I'll be there for her.'

'Good.' Matron laid her hand briefly on Marianne's arm. 'It's at times such as these that good friends are priceless.'

Back in Sally's room, Marianne explained to Sally what Matron had told her.

'I'm glad she won't be alone.' Sally sniffed and dabbed at the tears brimming over her eyes. 'It 'elps, it really does. She might not have been born alive, but she was once, kicking away inside me, and she deserves to have a proper burial same as anyone else.'

'Perhaps we can find out where she's being buried and visit the woman's grave?' Marianne suggested.

Sally shrugged. 'Maybe.'

The door opened and a nurse came in with a tray of tea.

'I thought you could do with a drink.' She put the tray down on the table beside the bed and looked at Sally. 'I think you're looking a bit brighter.' She smiled. 'I think it's done you good having your friend visit.'

Sally nodded and smiled at Marianne. 'We've only known each other since the day we was evacuated, but it feels like we've been friends for life.'

'That's the best sort of friend to have,' the nurse said. 'I'll leave you to enjoy your tea.'

After the nurse had gone Marianne passed Sally her cup of tea. 'I wasn't sure if you'd want to see me ... that it might be too upsetting with me still expecting and all that.'

'Of course I did. My little girl being stillborn ain't going to stop other women 'aving babies, is it? And I 'ope with all my 'eart that all the women who were evacuated with us have 'ealthy babies when their time comes.' Sally leaned her head on Marianne's shoulder. 'I'm glad you came to see me and I 'ope you'll come again while they make me stay 'ere, will you?'

'You try and stop me! I need to keep you up to date with all the goings-on back in Great Plumstead, don't I?'

'Yes, I don't want to miss out on anythin'. I've only been in here two days but it feels like an age since I arrived and left real life out there. So, tell me what's been 'appening? What've you been doing?'

By the time Marianne hugged Sally goodbye, her friend was looking much better than when she'd arrived. Together they had cried and laughed this afternoon and their friendship had become even stronger.

Chapter 46

Prue tucked the woollen blanket around Sally, checking that it was snugly fitted to stop any draughts getting in.

'I'll be all right, honestly, I don't need tucking in.' Sally laughed. 'I ain't an invalid.'

Prue smiled at the young woman who was sitting in the passenger seat of her Austin 7. 'I know you're not, but you've been in the hospital for the past ten days and it's much colder out here than in there; I don't want you to get a chill.' Her breath misted in the cold air. 'Right, let's get you home.' She closed the passenger door and went around to the driver's side and climbed in, glad to finally be allowed to take Sally home: the house hadn't seemed the same without her cheerful presence.

'Marianne's going to pop in to see you this afternoon, if that's all right.' She started the engine, put the car into gear and smoothly pulled away.

'Course it is, I'll be glad to see her. I really appreciated all of you coming to see me, I'd have gone mad cooped up in there without visitors. I suppose I could 'ave gone down to talk to the women on the ward but . . . ' Sally shrugged. 'Couldn't bring myself to do it, not with their babies there. It would have been too 'ard.'

Prue reached over and patted Sally's arm. 'That's quite understandable, and we were happy to come and visit you. I worked out a rota so you had someone to see you every day.'

'I 'eard!' Sally laughed. 'You're so good at organising things, Prue, the Government ought to recruit you to help run the war effort.'

Prue glanced at Sally. 'I'm not sure they'd want me, I'm more likely to stop the war . . . stop mothers and wives having to send off their men to who knows what. I can't help thinking that if women were the ones in charge, wars would be less likely to come about. Any problems would be solved by talking rather than fighting because they appreciate the terrible cost of it in lives and injuries.' She paused, concentrating as she drove slowly past a farm worker leading a horse and cart filled with fodder beet along the road. 'It's Edwin's tribunal on the first of December. I just hope they don't make him join the Army.'

'Me too,' Sally said. 'Your Edwin's a lovely, kind person; he's much more suited to workin' on the ambulances than in the Army.'

'I quite agree, but whether the tribunal will, remains to be seen.'

They drove along in silence for a little while, Prue

aware that Sally was watching the passing countryside where the land had donned its winter drabness, the trees bare of leaves under a glowering grey sky.

'I've decided to go back to London,' Sally suddenly announced. 'I'll stay for a few days, if that's all right, and then I'll go home.'

Prue brought the car to a halt, parking it in a field gateway, and turned to look at her. 'But why? Please don't think that just because you're not . . . expecting any more, that you have to leave. You can stay with me for as long as you want. I like having you with us.' She reached out and touched Sally's arm.

Tears filled Sally's eyes and she nodded. 'Thank you, but I think it's for the best. I'll need to get a job now I ain't got a baby to look after.'

'You could get a job around here.'

'It ain't just that, though.' Sally sighed. 'I associate being 'ere with being pregnant and lookin' forward to having my baby, and now that's gone . . . I think it's best to leave. It'll be 'ard to see the other mothers having theirs when their time comes . . . I don't grudge any of them that, honestly I don't, but it would just be a reminder of what I've lost. Bit like rubbing salt in the wound, I suppose.'

Prue nodded, she completely understood the young woman's reasoning and appreciated how hard it would be for her. 'At least have a week here before you go back, help build up your strength. Are you sure there's nothing I can do to change your mind?'

Sally shook her head. 'I've been thinking about it for days and it's the right thing to do. I only came 'ere because

I was expecting and it's been lovely, really it has, I've loved stayin' with you and getting to know the village, making friends . . . but 'onestly I think it's for the best that I go home.'

'I hope you'll come back and see us, stay with us sometimes.' Prue's voice came out in a croak.

'I'd like that, thank you.' Sally smiled at her. 'I was lucky to get billeted with you, Prue. Thank you for everything you've done for me.'

'It's been my pleasure, and I'm so sorry that it hasn't worked out for you as you'd hoped.' Prue blinked back tears as she started the engine again. 'Let's go home.'

As she pulled away, Prue thought that she wasn't completely surprised at what Sally had just told her. In a way it made perfect sense for the young woman to return to where she'd grown up, with everything familiar and where she could pick up her life again, although she hoped that when she did return to London, it wouldn't be for good and that she might come back and stay with them sometimes.

Chapter 47

'I wish you'd stay.' Marianne and Sally were walking arm in arm towards the station. The week since her friend had returned home from the hospital had passed by so quickly and now her planned day of departure had arrived.

'I know you do, but 'onestly I think it's the best thing for me to do. I'll feel better in my old surroundings and it will 'elp me to accept what's 'appened.' Sally smiled at her. 'Let's not waste what time we've got left together, eh? It's 'ard enough saying goodbye to people without going over what we've talked about already. I'm not changin' my mind, so let's be 'appy together while we can.'

'I'm sorry, it's only because we like you so much that we want you to stay!' Marianne, like everyone else, had been shocked when she heard about Sally's decision to return to London. They'd all understood the reasoning behind it and had talked to her about it, but no one had managed to convince her to stay. And so this morning she'd gone to Prue's house to meet Sally and go with her to the station, her friend not wanting anyone else to see her off, not even Prue. Sally had said a tearful farewell to Prue at the house and now she was on her way to the station where she would get the train into Norwich and then on to London, reversing the trip that she'd made with Marianne back at the beginning of September. It was only a few months ago and yet it felt like a lifetime as they'd both settled well into life in the countryside with their host families and become firm friends.

'I've been wonderin' if I'll get my old job back in the shop,' Sally said as they walked past the church and turned into the road that led out of the village. 'Or I might want to try somethin' else – my Arthur's mother says they're makin' uniforms in the garment factories now, and that's maybe something I could do. If I did you could give me some tips about sewing, eh?'

'I could give you the name of the factory where I used to work if you like.'

Marianne hadn't thought about the place where she'd worked before they'd been evacuated for some time, but now memories of the few months that she'd spent there came tumbling into her mind. She hadn't disliked the job, even though the sewing was more rough and ready than the made-to-measure garments that she'd been used to designing and making in the West End, but needs must, as they say, and at the time she'd needed to earn a living and keep a low profile.

'I need to tell you something before you go, Sally . . . I'm not really married.' The words were out of Marianne's mouth before her brain could clamp her lips shut. Why on earth had she blurted it out?

Sally stopped walking and stared at her. 'Not married? But what about Alex? Who's he? Did you make him up? Only you've got a photo of 'im by your bed.'

'No, he's real.' Marianne looked down at the ground before returning her gaze to her friend's face, meeting her square in the eye. 'Alex *is* the father of my baby, but we're *not* married. He doesn't even know I'm expecting his child.' She placed a hand on her swollen belly which pushed out the front of her coat. 'I'm sorry I lied to you, but I did it to protect my baby.' So why had she told Sally the secret that she'd been so careful to keep over the past few months now, just as she was leaving? *Because she's your friend*, she thought, *and she deserves to know the truth.* 'I grew up the child of an unmarried mother. I know what it's like to be taunted over something that isn't your fault. My parents were engaged and would have been married if my father hadn't been killed in the Great War.'

'Oh, Marianne!' Sally's eyes were sympathetic. 'I ain't blaming you for doing it to protect your child. Believe me when I say I'd never have 'eld it against you.'

Marianne nodded. 'Thank you. But unfortunately not everybody thinks as you do.'

'Then they ain't worth bothering about!'

Sally and Marianne started to walk again. 'I loved Alex very much and I thought he loved me as well.'

'So, what happened?' Sally asked.

'I found out he was getting engaged to someone else, someone of his own class and far more suitable than someone like me.' Marianne quickly explained how she'd discovered this, lost her job and moved to work in the East End. 'I made up a story based on the truth but embroidered it to include a husband away in the Navy to explain his long absences and lack of letters.'

Sally shook her head. 'And there was me asking questions about him all the time, you must have been fed up with me wanting to know.'

'It was only natural to ask questions.'

'What are you going to do?' Sally asked as they walked in through the gates of the station yard and headed for the booking office so she could buy a ticket.

'Carry on as I have been so my baby isn't tainted by my mistake.' Marianne put a hand on Sally's arm, bringing her to a halt. 'I didn't like not being honest with you; it's not how I like to do things.'

'I'm glad you told me, and I'm sorry that he messed you around when he was promised elsewhere, that ain't nice. If there's anything I can do to 'elp, you will ask, won't you?'

Marianne nodded, threw her arms around her friend and hugged her tightly. 'I'm going to miss you so much.'

'And me you.' Sally's voice was muffled. 'But we'll write often, won't we?'

'Definitely.'

'And I'll be back to see you when I can, I promise. If I don't, Prue will be after me and you know how bossy she can be!' Sally laughed. 'Come on, I need to get my ticket. The train will soon be here and I don't want to miss it.'

Waving Sally off, Marianne stayed on the station platform until the train had disappeared from sight around the bend further down the track. Already the place seemed quieter without Sally's friendly chatter; Marianne was going to miss her very much. She'd made friends with some of the other evacuees, but it was with Sally that she'd developed a strong bond and it had helped both of them to settle in here. Now, with her friend on her way back to London, Marianne was going to feel her absence deeply. She'd once pictured them both with their babies, living in the village for some time to come until it was safe to return to London or the war was over, but that dream had dissolved like early-morning mist when the sun climbs higher in the sky. She was going to have to learn to live here without her friend and was grateful that she still had the support of Thea and Hettie, as well as her work to keep her occupied. She would be all right, she *had* to be all right, because her unborn baby was depending on her – it had no other parent to rely on. It was up to her to look after it and she would.

Chapter 48

Prue felt sick as they walked into the courthouse, the heavy wooden door making a resounding clunk as it closed behind them – a sound that must have resonated with so many people who'd crossed this threshold over the years as they went inside to face judges and juries who'd determine their future. She was grateful that Edwin wasn't here to face the possibility of a prison sentence, but whatever the outcome here today, it would be life changing and would determine the path that his future took.

At least Edwin had plenty of support today: Thea, Reuben, Hettie and Marianne had all made the journey into Norwich on the train, each one dressed in their best clothes. Alice had wanted to come too, but Prue and Edwin had managed to persuade her that she should go to school: with it being her School Certificate year, it was important not to miss her lessons. The only other notable absence was Victor, but he didn't know about today: everyone had been sworn to secrecy for fear that he might try to influence the result, perhaps even turn up and demand to have his say. It would be hard enough for Edwin without having his overbearing father present. Victor didn't need to know anything about it till afterwards when Edwin would have a decision one way or another.

She looked at her son, dressed smartly in a jacket, shirt and tie, his blond hair neatly brushed, but his face pale and strained; he'd been so quiet on the journey here. He must have sensed her gaze as he turned to look at her, his blue eyes meeting hers.

She touched his arm. 'Are you all right?' she asked quietly.

Edwin smiled at her, but it didn't reach his eyes. Knowing him so well, Prue could read him: he was scared. 'I want to get it over with and yet I don't.' He shrugged.

'I know.' She nodded sympathetically, squeezing his arm. 'We're all behind you and if the tribunal has any sense, they'll let you do what you want and do your bit for the war effort *your* way.'

Prue smiled, forcing herself to look optimistic when all the while her stomach felt leaden. What would happen if they didn't see sense and grant Edwin exemption from military service?

'Looks like there's one case to be heard before you,' Thea said, nodding towards the far end of the corridor where another young man stood waiting for his turn. He had some friends with him of his own age, but no one who looked like his parents.

Edwin glanced at his watch. 'They must be running a bit late; I'm supposed to go in at two o'clock and it's almost five to now.' He ran his hand through his hair.

The door of the court at the far end of the room suddenly opened and several people came out, the young man whose tribunal it must have been looked upset.

'But you can appeal,' one of the others accompanying him said as they hurried past, heading for the door.

'I'm not joining the Army Medical Corps because they carry guns and I'm *not* doing that,' the young man said.

Prue didn't hear any more of their conversation as they went out and the door clunked solidly behind them. She looked at Edwin: from the look on his face he had clearly heard everything. She knew that he'd feel exactly the same way as that young man if the tribunal reached the same decision, because carrying a gun meant you had to be prepared to use it, to kill, and that was against all that her son believed in.

The door of the court opened again, and a court usher called out the name of the young man standing waiting with his friends and they filed in behind him.

'I need to sit down,' Hettie said, heading towards the row of seats set out along the corridor nearer the courtroom. 'Come on, Marianne, come and take the weight off your feet, too.'

At that moment the outside door opened and Prue's sister Lizzie came rushing in with a clicking of high heels and her trademark pillar-box-red lipstick. Prue felt her hackles rise: what was Lizzie doing here? This was a serious business and no time for any of her frivolity? But seeing the look of surprise and delight on Edwin's face, her sister's arrival momentarily distracting him from what lay ahead, Prue bit back the retort that was hovering on her tongue. Perhaps Lizzie's arrival was a breath of fresh air when they needed it, she thought, and it was good of her to come to support Edwin. 'Hello, Lizzie.'

Lizzie looked at her and smiled warmly. 'Hello, Prue, everyone, thank goodness you're still out here, I was worried you'd have gone in.' She looked around at them all, beaming her wide smile. 'My, don't you all look smart?' Her eyes settled on Reuben. 'It's not often we see you in a suit, but you look very spruce indeed.'

Reuben ran a finger around the inside of his shirt collar. 'Just as well,' he muttered. 'This isn't the most comfortable outfit.'

Lizzie laughed and then turned her attention to Edwin, laying a hand on his arm. 'I hope they'll see sense and let you go and work with the Friends' Ambulance Unit, otherwise we might have to protest. I'll put them right if they suggest anything else.'

Edwin opened his mouth to say something but before he could Prue stepped in.

'You mustn't do anything of the sort, Lizzie! If it doesn't go the way we want today then the proper thing to do is appeal; arguing with them will only put their backs up.'

Lizzie raised her eyebrows and laughed. 'It's all right,

Edwin, I promise I won't do anything to jeopardise you.' She winked at Prue before going over to sit down on an empty seat next to Hettie, putting her arm through the older woman's and starting to chatter to her about something or other.

Prue turned away. It was kind of Lizzie to come – she must have taken the afternoon off work to be here – but there were times when she just wished her sister would go about things the right way and not cause a fuss. If it came to it, protesting against the tribunal wouldn't help Edwin one little bit.

'Ma.' She felt a hand on her arm and looked up to see Edwin. 'Are you all right?'

She nodded. 'A bit nervous but apart from that I'm fine. It won't be long and then it'll be over and done with. Sometimes the waiting is the worst bit.'

Edwin bit his bottom lip. 'What if they tell me to go in the RAMC like the other man? I honestly couldn't because of the gun thing.'

Prue reached up and touched his cheek. 'I wouldn't expect you to. If that's their verdict, then you'll have to appeal against it. I—' She stopped as the door of the court opened and the young man who'd been called in, came out, his face looking like thunder as he strode past them and stormed outside at the end of the corridor, his friends following a little way behind.

Thea called out to them. 'How did your friend get on?'

One of them stopped and shook his head. 'He was refused and will be removed from the conscientious objector register.'

'I'm sorry,' Thea said.

The young man nodded. 'So am I.' He nodded towards the door. 'I'd better go.'

Prue's stomach dropped down into her shoes as she met her sister's eyes and could see that they were both thinking the same thing: if the last two young men to go up before the tribunal had been given a verdict that they didn't want, would the same thing happen to Edwin? Was the tribunal a harsh one? But before she could say anything the door of the court opened once again, and the court usher came out.

'Edwin Wilson,' he called.

Edwin glanced at Prue, his eyes were full of fear. She nodded at him and smiled, doing her best to instil a sense of hope into that brief look before he turned and followed the court usher into the courtroom.

Thea touched Prue's elbow. 'Come on, chin up.'

Prue nodded and they filed in behind Edwin and were directed where to sit at the back of the courtroom, which smelt of polish, overlaid with the scent of dusty books and ages-old wood. Sitting down on the hard, wooden bench in the boxed-off seats, Prue breathed in slowly to steady her thudding heart. She fixed her eyes on Edwin, who stood in the witness box with his back to them as he faced the front of the court. He was holding on to the front of the box tightly and she could see he was shaking. Her heart ached to go to him and put her arms around him. She squeezed her hands into tight fists in a bid to stop herself from crying at the sight of Edwin standing in the dock like some criminal,

313

facing the line of grey-faced, dour-looking men who looked down at him from their elevated position while talking in hushed tones among themselves, referring to the sheets of paper they shuffled in front of them. A judge sat in the middle, with two other men on each side – they were the men in whose hands her son's future lay.

'They don't look very friendly,' Hettie whispered, leaning close to her ear.

Prue glanced at her and nodded. 'I—' she began but halted as the judge began to speak.

'Edwin James Wilson?' the judge asked, peering at Edwin over his half-moon glasses.

'Yes, sir.' Edwin's voice sounded very strained.

Prue tried hard to concentrate as the judge introduced each member of the tribunal; she was vaguely aware that he mentioned one was a trade union member, another a military representative, another a clergyman and others from the local community – had any of them got a son who was brave enough to stand up for what he believed in and go against the flow, she wondered?

'We have read your statement,' said the judge, 'and the letters in support of your application.' He picked up some letters from the bench in front of him. 'Your uncle, Mr Reuben Thornton, writes of your bravery rescuing two airmen from their crashed aircraft whilst showing no concern for your own safety.' He raised his eyebrows. 'And that, indeed, is to be commended.'

Prue glanced at her brother who sat ramrod straight, his eyes locked on the judge, a look of worry on his face. She knew he'd written and rewritten that letter many times to get it as perfect as he could to support Edwin.

'And the vicar of your local church, the Reverend Balding,' the judge went on, pointing at another letter, 'informs us that you have been a regular attendee of his church since you were a small child and take the Christian teachings seriously. He believes that your objection to conscription – in that you are unable to kill anyone – is a genuine one and comes from your strong belief in the teachings of the Church, as you indeed have explained in your own statement. It is our duty here today to assess the sincerity of your beliefs and your application for exemption from military service.'

He nodded to the man sitting on his far left, who cleared his throat and fired the first question at Edwin. 'Do you eat meat?'

Prue saw Edwin's shoulders rise, he was clearly as surprised at this question as she was; she'd expected something more complicated.

'Yes,' Edwin answered.

'And so you believe that it is all right to kill animals, then?' the man fired back at him.

'I . . . I've never personally killed an animal for eating or otherwise on purpose . . . and don't think I could.'

'So, if a wasp stung you, would you kill it?' The man leaned forwards to peer down at him.

'No, I wouldn't. Wasps only sting if they think they are being threatened, in which case I must have done something that it sensed as threatening.'

The man nodded and sat back in his chair and it was

315

the turn of the man next to him. 'I see here that you're working as a gardener, is that right?'

'Yes. For my aunt, to increase food production. I was sacked from my previous job when I registered as a conscientious objector.'

Lizzie tutted loudly and Prue glanced at her, but her sister was oblivious to it, sitting forward in her seat, her elbows on the high wooden side of the barrier that separated them from the rest of the court, her chin in her hands as she stared at the members of the tribunal.

The man who'd asked the question frowned. 'And you want to work for the Friends' Ambulance Unit?'

'That's right. I want to help but not be expected to kill another person.'

'You would be prepared to go into a battle zone with a FAU ambulance, then?'

Edwin nodded. 'Yes, I would go wherever I was needed.'

Satisfied with that, the man nodded and glanced at the judge, who sat next to him.

'You say in your statement,' the judge said, referring to a piece of paper, 'that you believe it is wrong to kill another person, therefore do you think *every* man should believe that and stick to it as you want to?'

Prue bit her bottom lip. The first two questions had been relatively easy – were they to lull Edwin into a false sense of security, to trick him? This was an important question and the court was silent as everyone waited for Edwin's answer – it seemed an age before he spoke but could only have been a matter of ten or twenty seconds as he gathered his thoughts.

'It is not my place to judge what others do; every person should make their own decision,' Edwin said, his voice starting off wobbly but growing stronger as he explained himself. 'My personal belief is that I know I couldn't, if asked, or ordered, kill another person and knowing that, I believe that to help with the war effort I would be better placed somewhere other than in military service, somewhere where my conscience would allow me to do something useful and worthwhile, like in the FAU.' He paused for a moment. 'I'm not afraid to do my bit, but simply ask that I be allowed to do it in a way that I believe in and will do well, and with my whole heart.'

'Indeed.' The judge nodded and passed on the questioning to the next man.

More questions were fired at Edwin, some easier, some more difficult, and it was obvious to Prue that the tribunal was working as a team, attempting to test his sincerity. She wasn't sure how long it went on, it felt like hours, but it couldn't have been more than ten minutes before they finally stopped questioning him and then began a whispered conversation.

Edwin turned around to look at his supporters and Prue smiled back at him encouragingly, while Hettie waved at him.

'Edwin James Wilson.' The judge's voice drew Prue's attention back to the front. 'The tribunal are satisfied that your application of conscientious objection to military service is genuine, and we are therefore giving you a category-B exemption from military service conditional on your doing alternative service by joining the FAU. You will receive the documentation in due course.'

Prue sighed, tears of relief blurring her eyes as the weight of worry slid from her shoulders, while Hettie gasped and Lizzie clapped, earning her a stern look from the judge.

'Thank you very much,' Edwin said. He glanced back at Prue and smiled, the first genuine smile she had seen from him all day.

The judge nodded. 'Good luck.'

The court usher gestured for Edwin to leave and they all got to their feet and hurried out after him.

Outside in the corridor there were other worried-looking young men waiting their turn, their faces pinched with concern as Edwin's had been just a short while before, Prue thought. But now . . .

'You did it!' She flung her arms around Edwin and hugged him tightly. 'I'm so happy for you.' She took a step back and looked up at him, her eyes bright with unshed tears.

'Thank you, I can't quite believe it!' Edwin smiled happily.

'Well done, lad.' Reuben held out his hand to shake.

'Thank you for your letter of support.' Edwin shook his uncle's hand.

Prue watched as her son was congratulated by all of them, it really was the best outcome: he would be able to do his bit the way he wanted to, and she knew he would pour his heart into it and do an excellent job. She was so proud of him.

'Come on, we need to celebrate this!' Lizzie grabbed hold of Edwin's arm and led the way to the outside door.

'Some tea and cake before you get the train home, and it's on me.'

Prue looked at Thea, who raised her eyebrows and smiled back at her. 'This is something worth celebrating.' She linked her arm through her sister's and together they followed their youngest sister outside.

They'd not gone far, following Lizzie and Edwin along the pavement, her sister leading them to a teashop that she loved, when Lizzie halted just ahead of them, and Prue and Thea almost barrelled into the back of her.

'What's going on?' Prue asked.

'Just look who it is!' Lizzie hissed, nodding to the other side of the narrow street where a familiar figure was walking along the pavement going the opposite way.

It was Victor. Prue's heart lurched. What was he doing in Norwich? He hadn't said anything about coming here today.

'Victor!' Lizzie called out to him before Prue could stop her, making him glance across the street to see who'd called him, and the look on his face when he saw them all looking at him was extraordinary. He looked shocked, guilty, caught out, emotions that Prue had rarely seen him express in all the years she'd known him, but he quickly recovered his composure and with a swift check to see that the road was safe to cross, came over to them.

'What are you doing here, Prudence?' He directed his question to Prue, ignoring the others.

'I was just wondering what *you* were doing here?' Prue parried back, emboldened by having her family around her. 'You didn't say you were coming to Norwich today.'

'An emergency meeting was called, on my way there now.' Victor narrowed his eyes. 'And why are you all here?'

'For Edwin's tribunal,' Reuben said.

'And he's been granted exemption from military service,' Lizzie said, with a broad smile on her face.

Edwin said nothing, he looked very uncomfortable as this was the first time that he'd come face to face with his father since he'd thrown him out.

A muscle in Victor's cheek twitched but he didn't react to the news. Not surprising as he was outnumbered by her family, Prue thought; like all bullies he preferred to pick his battles when he was going to win. In a contest between Victor and her siblings, she had no doubt who'd come out victorious.

Instead, he made a show of taking out his pocket watch to check. 'I must go or I'll be late to the meeting.' Without saying any more, he hurried off.

'Now there's a shifty-looking man if I ever saw one,' Lizzie said. 'He's up to something, and if he really is going to an emergency meeting I'll forgo my afternoon tea!' Her eyes met Prue's and she winked at her. 'Come on, let's not worry about him, we have something wonderful to celebrate today.'

'Absolutely.' Thea pulled at Prue's arm. 'Come on, forget about Victor, let's go and have some fun.'

Prue glanced back in the direction Victor had gone but there was no sign of him, he must have gone down a side street. What was he really doing here? She hadn't believed what he'd said, the look on his face had definitely been shifty ... She sighed; she wasn't going to let his sudden appearance spoil things for her, not on this momentous afternoon when Edwin's wish had been granted. He didn't have to go and fight, and that deserved celebrating.

She smiled at Thea. 'Lead the way!'

Chapter 49

Marianne stitched along the hem of the baby gown which she'd almost finished making, smiling to herself as she looked forward to hopefully being able to dress her child in it in six to eight weeks' time, depending on when it decided to make an appearance. Although, after what had happened to poor Sally, she knew that there were no guarantees and just hoped that nothing bad would happen. As it was, Hettie had been adamant about not having a pram in the house until the baby was actually born, saying it was bad luck to bring it in and after what had happened to her friend, Marianne wasn't going to tempt fate even if she didn't fully agree with it. Hettie had been kind enough to find her a pram from an old friend of hers whose daughter no longer needed it but was willing to hang on to it until Marianne's baby had arrived.

Out in the hallway the telephone began to ring.

'I'll get it.' Hettie got up from her chair near the range where she was knitting.

'It's for you,' she said, returning to the kitchen a few moments later. 'It's Stokes, the butler from the Hall, he wants to ask you something.' She pulled a face. 'Wouldn't tell me what it is – needs to speak to you directly, apparently!'

Marianne frowned. 'Wonder what he wants?' She got up, left her sewing on her chair and went through to the hall where she picked up the telephone receiver. 'Hello.'

'Good afternoon, Mrs Archer. Lady Campbell-Gryce has asked if you would be able to come over and help her daughter with some alterations on a gown that she needs for a party this weekend? It's short notice, but Her Ladyship would send a car to pick you up and return you home again if you are willing to help. She'd be very much obliged.'

Marianne smiled to herself; she could imagine Stokes standing there in his immaculate uniform, happily being the one to pass on the message since he liked to be in on everything that was going on at the Hall.

'When would you need me?'

'This afternoon. If you say yes, I can dispatch the chauffeur immediately and he can pick you up in the next ten minutes or so, would that be convenient?'

Marianne thought for a moment, her silence prompting him to add, 'You will be paid, of course, your usual hourly fee.'

And be picked up and returned home in a chauffeur-driven car, Marianne thought, which would be most welcome on a cold December day. 'Yes, of course I'll come. I'll get myself ready straightaway.'

'Excellent, I will pass that information on to Her Ladyship and her daughter.' And without saying anything else he finished the call.

Returning to the kitchen, Marianne started to pack away her own sewing. 'I've been called out to a job doing alterations for Lady Campbell-Gryce's daughter,' she explained to Hettie. 'They're sending a car to pick me up and will bring me back as well.'

'Oh, Miss Cecilia must be home, she's always been a right one for her clothes,' Hettie said.

'Hopefully it will be an easy job to do what alterations she wants.'

Hettie smiled at her. 'Well, Her Ladyship obviously thinks a lot of your dressmaking skills, after you made her that dress and coat; you might even get some more work making something for Miss Cecilia as well.'

Settled on the back seat of the car that had been sent to fetch her, Marianne stroked her hand over the soft leather surface, enjoying riding in such a grand vehicle. Lady Campbell-Gryce certainly lived a very different lifestyle to most people and was lucky to still have a car on the road. Most people had abandoned the use of their car, if they had one, saving their petrol rations for emergencies.

Pulling up at the front of Great Plumstead Hall, the chauffeur got out and hurried around to open the door to let Marianne out, offering his hand for her to take as she heaved herself out. Her swollen belly didn't make for a particularly easy exit from the car and she was glad of his assistance.

'Thank you.' She smiled at him and he nodded back.

'You're welcome, Mrs Archer. I'll be waiting to take you home when you're ready. If you just tell Mr Stokes he'll let me know and I'll have the car around the front to meet you here.'

'I will, thank you.'

Carrying her bag for her, the chauffeur led Marianne up the steps and through the porticoed pillared entrance, but before he could pull on the doorbell, the door was opened and Stokes stood there, looking down his straight nose at them.

'Good afternoon.' He held out his hand to take Marianne's bag from the chauffeur. 'If you'd like to follow me, I'll take you up to Miss Cecilia.'

The chauffeur turned his back on the butler and winked at Marianne before going back to his car.

'Miss Cecilia is in her room,' Stokes explained, as he led Marianne up the grand staircase, the walls lined with portraits of the family's ancestors, and then along a corridor on the next floor. He stopped outside a door halfway along and tapped gently on it, waiting for an answer.

'Come in,' a voice called.

He opened the door but didn't go in. 'Mrs Archer to see you, miss.' Stokes held out Marianne's bag to her and indicated with a subtle nod of his head for her to go in.

'Thank you.' Marianne took her bag and stepped into the room and the door was closed quietly behind her.

A tall, slim, young woman stood facing the window and as she turned around Marianne thought for an awful moment that she was going to pass out, the bones in her legs seeming to dissolve as she instantly recognised the young woman before her. Her name hadn't rung a bell when she'd been told it by Stokes when he'd telephoned, but that was because she'd always been called Cissy when she'd seen her before – she was a friend of Alex's sister, Marguerite, and had also had a dress made by Marianne when she'd worked in London's West End. By answering Her Ladyship's request for help, Marianne's old life had suddenly slammed right into her new one.

'Oh, it's you, Marianne!' Cissy's face broke into a wide smile as she rushed across the room towards her. 'When Mummy said this most marvellous dressmaker, Mrs Archer, had been evacuated into the village I had no idea it was *you*! I can't believe you're here. The dress you made for me has been so much admired. I went back to Dorothy Abrahams to see if you'd make me another and she said you'd left . . .' She paused, her eyes drawn to Marianne's swollen belly. 'Of course you're married now! But how lucky that you're here . . . So how are you?'

'Fine, thank you.' Marianne liked Cissy, she was one of the very few upper-class women who'd come to get clothes made at Dorothy Abrahams who actually looked at her, called her by her name and spoke to her as if she was a person with feelings and not just a servant. 'I'm enjoying living here. And I'm doing the work I love, which is wonderful.'

'And creating quite a stir among the ladies of the village with your skills, by all accounts.' Cissy waggled her eyebrows and laughed. 'Mummy talks about how Mrs Archer's going to make me this and that . . . Anyway, I hope you can help me, my new dress is too loose, I knew it was when I bought it, but I thought I could get away with it . . .' Cissy shrugged. 'I was planning to wear it to a party tomorrow night.' She strode across the room and picked up the dress that lay on the bed. 'Look, it's too loose here.' She pointed to the seams at the waist and the bust. 'Do you think you can fix it?'

'Of course, but you'll need to put it on for me, then I can see what needs to be done.'

'Yes, of course.' Cissy quickly undressed down to her silk underwear, completely unfazed by Marianne being in the room. This complete lack of self-consciousness in upper-class young women was something that Marianne had been shocked by when she'd started work at the dress-makers, but she'd quickly become accustomed to it, her boss explaining that many of them had been to boarding school where it was quite the norm to undress in front of others.

'Can you do it up for me?' Cissy turned her back to Marianne and pulled her long hair to the side while Marianne fastened the small buttons.

'Right, if you can just stand still for me, I'll see what needs to be done.' Marianne quickly saw that it wouldn't be a difficult or long job to alter the dress. She opened her bag and took out some pins and set to work, carefully tucking in the fabric at the waist and pinning it to make a better fit. 'Right, how does that feel? Have a look in the mirror to see what you think.'

Cissy went over to the large cheval mirror and looked at her reflection, turning this way and that, running her hands down the front of the dress and then putting her hands on her hips. She smiled widely at Marianne's reflection. 'Yes, that's so much better, thank you. Will you be able to get it done in time for me to wear it to the party?'

'Yes. Now you'll need to be careful of the pins as you take it off.' Marianne undid the buttons it to the back of the dress for her. 'I'll take it home with me and it will be ready in the morning.'

'Excellent.' Cissy stepped out of the dress and handed it to Marianne, who carefully folded it up and placed it in her bag.

'I'll have it ready by ten o'clock, if you can send someone to collect it.'

'Thank you, I appreciate it. Now I know where you are, I'll be asking you to make some more dresses for me. Though I may have to join the queue!' Cissy laughed.

'Let me know if you do want me to make something for you, I'd be delighted to.'

'You'll be hearing from me!' Cissy said. 'I'll ring the bell for someone to see you out.'

'No need, I know the way.' Marianne smiled. 'Good to see you again; I hope you enjoy your party tomorrow night.'

'I'd rather not go, to be honest. Mummy's hoping that I might meet someone suitable . . . ' Cissy rolled her eyes. 'Someone she considers to be from the right sort of family.'

Just like Alex's family, Marianne thought, who'd wanted him to marry the right sort of girl. 'Well, good luck.' She smiled at Cissy and slipped out of the door.

'Mrs Archer, is everything all right?'

The voice made her jump. She turned and saw that Stokes was standing a little way along the corridor and had clearly been waiting for her to come out.

Plastering a smile on her face she nodded. 'Absolutely, I just get a little tired, you know, with the baby.' She laid her hand on her belly and did her best not to smile at the uncomfortable look on the butler's face.

He held out his hand. 'May I take your bag, then?'

'Thank you.' She handed it over and followed him down the grand staircase and out of the front door where the chauffeur was already waiting, ready to take her home. Cissy was nice, far nicer than many of the young women of her class that Marianne had made clothes for, but her going to a party with what her mother considered the 'right sort of person' reminded Marianne of the gap between them. She had mistakenly thought her and Alex's love could bridge that divide, but sadly she'd been very much mistaken.

Chapter 50

Prue hung a red glass bauble on to the Christmas tree, feeling less festive than she ever had before in her life. She'd always loved Christmas but this year all joy in it seemed to have drained away. She was having to force herself to appear cheerful for Alice's sake, while inside she was desperately missing Jack and Edwin being here and just wanted to cry. There was nothing she could do about Jack's absence, the Army was in charge of his life now, but that wasn't the case for Edwin. He could be here ... he *should* be here and there was only one person stopping that happening. Victor.

As she helped Alice decorate the Christmas tree that they'd set up in the sitting room, Prue kept an ear out for her husband. As usual, he was going to one of his regular Sunday meetings in Norwich, even though it was Christmas Eve. She heard him coming down the stairs – this was her chance.

'You carry on, I'll be back in a minute,' she told Alice and slipped out of the room, closing the door quietly behind her. 'I want to ask you something before you go.'

Victor, who was shrugging himself into his thick winter coat near the front door, turned to look at her. 'Can't it wait? I don't want to be late.'

'I won't keep you long; I just want a simple answer.' Prue clasped her hands tightly behind her back, balling her fingers into fists. 'I'd like Edwin to come here tomorrow, on Christmas Day; it won't be the same without him.'

'Absolutely not!' Victor's rocket-like temper exploded, his cheeks flushing and his eyes glaring at her. 'I'll not have that blasted conchie in my house again, and that's final.' He opened the door and went out, slamming it behind him.

Prue let out the breath that she'd been holding, tears stinging her eyes. The season of good will to all men had clearly passed Victor by. She'd expected as much, but she'd had to ask. It wouldn't have been fair to tell Edwin to come anyway, because it would be asking him into a lion's den, Victor would throw him out again, perhaps even physically this time. No, she had to accept it was as it was, even though it would probably be the last time for who knew how long that her son would be here in the village for Christmas now that he'd been accepted to join the Friends' Ambulance Service and was waiting to be called to the training camp. This time next year he could be working with them anywhere. She took out her hand-kerchief and blotted her eyes, then, taking a deep breath, she pasted a smile on her face and went back to the sitting room to finish decorating the tree, pretending that her heart wasn't crying inside her.

At Rookery House, Thea was singing along with Hettie and Marianne as they joyfully blasted out 'We Three Kings of Orient Are'. They'd spent the afternoon decorating the sitting room ready for Christmas and now the mantelpiece was draped with holly and ivy brought in from the garden and the Christmas tree was festooned with glass baubles that caught the light of the fire. There was just the final touch to add to the tree. She gently took out the angel from the box of Christmas decorations that she'd brought with her from London; she'd made it for her first Christmas there and it was a bit shabby-looking now but she wasn't going to replace it.

'There, she always goes on last.' Thea reached up and carefully placed the angel on the top of the Christmas tree, fanning out the paper skirt so that it fell nicely around the tip, then stood back to admire the whole thing. 'What do you think?'

'It's lovely,' Marianne said. 'I love the smell of Christmas trees, it's so fresh.'

Hettie sniffed. 'I think the warmth from the fire is bringing it out more, it's a beautiful tree.'

'First one we've had here,' Thea said. 'It's going to be a lovely Christmas, war or not. The tree looks wonderful.' She smiled at Marianne and Hettie; it had been a delight to decorate the tree with them. Reuben had been given it as a perk of his job at the Hall's estate, but he didn't want to put it up in his own little home and since he'd be spending Christmas Day here anyway, Thea had gratefully received it.

Everything was almost ready for tomorrow: a plump cockerel hung in the scullery, plucked and gutted and ready to roast, and Hettie had made a rich Christmas pudding and fruit cake, too.

The door opened and Edwin came in with a basket of logs for the fire, which danced brightly in the fireplace.

'This should keep us going for a while.' He put the heavy basket down to one side of the fireplace. 'Reuben said to tell you he's going to the station to meet Lizzie.'

'I'd better go and get the mince pies in the oven then, so they'll be ready by the time they get back.' Hettie bustled off to the kitchen, her cheeks rosy from the warmth and her eyes bright with enjoyment.

'It'll be nice to have her staying for a few days,' Thea said, who'd made a bed up for her in the dining room as they always ate in the kitchen as it was easier and cosier. 'We'll have a full house tomorrow.' She put her hand on Edwin's arm. 'Do you mind not being at home?'

He shook his head. 'Not really, I'll miss being with Ma and Alice, of course, but I have no desire to spend the day with my father, and the feeling's probably mutual.'

'I've told Prue that she and Alice are welcome to come here tomorrow.'

'Thank you.' Edwin smiled at her. 'I hope they'll come; I bet it will be a lot more cheerful here than there.'

Chapter 51

'It was a really lovely meal.' Marianne took another clean plate from the wooden drainer and started to dry it. She was feeling full of Christmas dinner, which had been delicious: the cockerel cooked to perfection, light batter puddings, roast potatoes and parsnips, carrots and sprouts, combined with a rich gravy, followed by a fruity Christmas pudding and custard, the whole meal combined with much chatter and laughter around the table. Now with their two cooks, Hettie and Thea, shooed through to the sitting room to relax by the fire, and Reuben and Edwin gone outside to take Bess for a walk and bring in more wood for the fires, she was helping Lizzie do the clearing-up.

'Hettie's a wonderful cook, and so she should be with all her years of experience cooking fancy meals for them up at the Hall.' Lizzie said, her hands busy washing up another plate. 'It's lovely to come and stay here for a few days. I'm so glad Thea bought this place, I always liked it as well.'

'Why don't you come back and live here too?' Marianne asked.

'Thea asked me to, but I don't think that would be a good idea, I like my independence too much. Plus there's my job, I don't want to be too far from it, though I've been thinking I need to be doing something more interesting, perhaps tied in with the war effort. Working in the office of Curls department store isn't the most exciting job. I'm looking around to see what's on offer.'

'You could always go in by train from here.'

Lizzie shook her head. 'Much as I love my sisters, I like my distance from them too, especially Prue. We'd only fall out if we saw too much of each other.' She put another clean plate on the drainer. 'Living in Norwich suits me better than here; in a village too many people know each other's business, whereas a city's more anonymous.'

'You three sisters are all very different.' Marianne added the plate she'd just dried to the pile of clean ones on the table.

Lizzie laughed. 'We certainly are, but there's a strong bond between us.' She looked thoughtful for a moment. 'So it's hard to see someone you love do something you know is the wrong thing for them ... You know both Thea and I tried to persuade Prue not to marry Victor, we could see what he was like but she wouldn't listen and it ...' She sighed. 'It makes me mad to see her putting up with him. Look at what happened with Edwin! I really don't trust him. I'm sure there was something odd going on when we saw him in Norwich after Edwin's tribunal.

He looked downright shifty.' She pulled a face. 'I feel sorry for Prue, I really do, but somehow we often rub each other up the wrong way.'

'She did stand up for Edwin, I know that, but I suppose Victor's in charge,' Marianne said.

'Indeed he is, like a mini Hitler.'

Marianne giggled. 'My friend Sally, who was billeted with them, said he always reminded her of Hitler.'

Lizzie joined in laughing. 'He's the ruler of his own little kingdom. Enough talk of him, tell me about your sewing business, Marianne. How are you getting on?'

'Very well.' Marianne dried a bowl. 'I've got more customers wanting clothes made – more than I can manage, so there's a waiting list. Having Lady Campbell-Gryce ask me to make her a dress has really helped.'

'That's good, if you're deemed good enough to match Her Ladyship's high standards then you must be good! And where she goes others will follow. Well done, you!'

Prue could hear laughter coming from the sitting room as she and Alice let themselves into the kitchen at Rookery House, the joyful sound making her realise it was the first she'd heard all day. There certainly hadn't been any laughter at home.

Bess got up from where she'd been sleeping in front of the range and padded over to her, her tail wagging from side to side and her eyes bright and welcoming, and to Prue's surprise, this simple gesture brought a lump to her throat.

'You go through to the others and I'll join you in a

minute,' she said to Alice, putting the tin of mince pies that she'd brought down on the table, and stroking the dog's butter-soft ears. She waited until Alice had disappeared and sighed. The joyful feeling in this house was such a marked contrast from the one she'd just left, where Victor had been snoring in his chair by the fire having stuffed himself with food. This Christmas Day was the worst she'd ever had: she'd cooked the same Christmas dinner as she always did, the tree had been decorated with the same decorations, but it felt as if the heart of the day was missing. Jack and Edwin weren't there, and she'd missed them terribly, but even more than that, her husband's vile rejection of Edwin and his refusal to let him come home, even for today, had soured the day for her. She'd tried hard to keep things normal for Alice's sake, but having to share the same table with a man who could so wholeheartedly and vehemently reject his own son, showing no respect for his beliefs, saddened her to her core. Her home was not a happy one. Christmas Day had brought no joy to it and she'd been relieved to slip out, leaving Victor to his miserable self because she wanted to spend part of the day with their son even if his father didn't.

'Ma!' Edwin had come into the kitchen and strode across to her, a broad welcoming smile on his face. 'Merry Christmas.' He threw his arms around her, hugging her tightly. 'I'm glad you came.'

'Me too.' She stepped back, still holding on to his arms, and looked up at his face. 'Merry Christmas, son.'

'Come on, come and join everyone.' Edwin put his

arm round her shoulders and led her through to the sitting room.

'Prue! Merry Christmas,' everyone called out to her.

She smiled, fighting hard not to show the tears that threatened at the genuine warmth of their greeting and the picture of contentment and happiness shown by everyone in the room. No one here was dominating anyone else, each accepting of the other, supporting and caring. 'Thank you. Merry Christmas to you all.'

'Come on, come and sit here.' Thea budged along on the settee to make room for Prue between her and Lizzie. 'We were thinking of having a sing-song. Edwin's going to play for us.'

'What would you like first?' Edwin asked, going over to the piano.

'Some carols, of course!' Hettie said from her armchair by the fire. 'You choose.'

'All right.' Edwin ran his fingers up and down some scales to limber them up.

Prue instantly recognised the introduction to the first carol – he'd played it often at home, going over and over it until he'd learned it by heart – 'Oh Little Town of Bethlehem'. She joined in the singing with everyone around her, Reuben's fine voice complementing Hettie's, the two of them leading them all as they sang together, some with better voices than others, but it didn't matter because they were all enjoying themselves.

Prue caught Thea's eye and her sister smiled at her, giving her arm a gentle squeeze, and to Prue's surprise, Lizzie did the same on the other side. Her singing almost faltered, and she had to focus hard on Edwin's playing to keep going. Her family might be crumbling at home, but it was very much alive here at Rookery House.

Chapter 52

January 1940 arrived with a blast of freezing weather, the coldest for some forty-five years, and this morning the mothers at the day club were huddled around the stove, everyone dressed in several layers to keep warm.

'You need to pick up this stitch here.' Prue was teaching one of the mothers how to turn the heel of a sock. 'Then turn your knitting around and purl back to here, then pick up another stitch at the other end.' She handed the knitting over to the young woman with a smile. 'Just take your time and if you're not sure about anything ask.'

'Thanks, I ain't ever managed to get this far with a sock before.'

'You're doing very well.' Prue smiled at her, patting her shoulder before moving on to help someone else.

'I've gone wrong somewhere!' another of the women said, handing her sock to Prue. 'It's a bit of a mess and I don't think any soldier would want to wear this.'

Prue looked at what was supposed to be a sock and laughed. 'I think you're right about that, but don't worry, I'll pull it out and you can try again. Rome wasn't built in a day.'

She sat down beside the woman and was engrossed with pulling out the mess of stitches and winding the untangled yarn on to the ball of wool, when a blast of freezing-cold air made her look around to see who had come in. She almost dropped the knitting in surprise when she saw who it was: Jack.

'Hello, Ma!' He grinned his delightful smile, crossing the hall in what seemed a few strides, helped her to her feet and flung his arms around her, getting the attention of everyone in the room.

His arrival was met by much cheering and clapping from the women who knew that Prue's eldest son was in the Army.

'You never told us he was such an 'andsome fella,' Gloria called out, comically batting her eyelashes in Jack's direction.

'You'll be making 'im blush,' another woman said.

'It's the uniform that does it!' Jack sparred back at them, clearly not put out by their comments.

'I didn't know you were coming,' Prue said, recovering her power of speech after the shock. 'I would've come to meet you at the station.'

'I didn't know myself until yesterday.' Jack's eyes met hers. 'I've got seventy-two hours' leave.' He smiled at her, not needing to say what that meant.

Prue felt sick. He was home on embarkation leave. Her son was being sent to war.

'Tea's up!' Hettie came bustling in from the kitchen pushing a trolley with the large brown teapots and cups and saucers on it. She halted at the sight of Jack and a beaming smile lit up her face. 'Oh, it's good to see you, lad.' She glanced at Prue, their eyes meeting, and she, too, instantly understood what Jack's appearance meant. 'Come on, let's get you a hot cup of tea, you must be perished.'

Prue was glad of the distraction, grateful for Hettie stepping in and giving her a few moments to calm herself. This wasn't totally unexpected, she'd known that it was highly likely that Jack would be sent to join the British Expeditionary Force in France, who were standing against the tide of Nazi troops sweeping across Europe, but now that it was imminent, she was terrified what would happen to him, only she couldn't − she mustn't − show what she was feeling. She had to keep up a strong front for his sake, not crumble and spoil what time they had together.

'Here you go.' Hettie handed her a cup of tea. 'I've added a bit of sugar in for the shock,' she added in a low voice. 'You all right?'

Prue nodded, not trusting herself to speak. She took a sip of sweet tea, the warm liquid soothing her.

Hettie looked at her watch. 'There's only half an hour left of our shift here, so why don't you take Jack home after you've finished your tea, I can manage here till the ladies on the next shift take over.' She patted Prue's arm. 'Go and spend time with your son.'

Prue swallowed hard against the lump in her throat. 'Thank you.'

*

Prue opened the oven door to check on the shepherd's pie; the meat mixture was bubbling gently, and the tips of the potato topping were starting to turn a golden brown, while the delicious smell wafted around the kitchen. Below it, on the next shelf down, an apple pie was cooking nicely, too. Both dishes were Jack's favourite, which she'd been glad to make for tea while he had a nap to catch up on some sleep he'd lost getting an overnight train to come home. Cooking them had also given her time to compose herself. Five more minutes and she'd take them out, she thought, closing the oven door.

'That smells wonderful, Ma.'

Jack's voice made her spin around and there he was, standing in the kitchen doorway, his hair all ruffled from sleep, reminding her of how he'd looked as a young boy. She smiled at him. 'Thought you might like some home cooking.'

'I'm desperate for it; the army cooks aren't renowned for producing tasty grub. It isn't a patch on what you make. I've been dreaming about your cooking.'

'Then I'll have to fill you up on it while I can. Any special requests apart from shepherd's pie and apple pie?'

'I'd love a steamed syrup pudding and . . . ' He paused at the sound of the front door opening. Prue glanced at the clock, it was twenty past five, the time that Victor always came home and somehow the atmosphere in the house instantly changed like the flick of a switch. Her husband hadn't even come into the room yet, but knowing that he was now in the house and would head straight for the kitchen expecting his tea as he always did, his volatile moods potentially spoiling what had been a precious time with Jack, made her heart sink.

Jack must have sensed this as he came over to her and touched her hand, his eyes meeting hers; he understood. She nodded and smiled at him, bracing herself for what was to come.

The door of the kitchen burst open and she immediately saw that Victor was not in a good mood, but then to her surprise, the moment his eyes fell on Jack standing in the kitchen in his army uniform, Victor's expression changed and he smiled at his son.

'Jack! I didn't know you were coming home. We weren't expecting you, were we, Prudence?'

She shook her head.

'No, I didn't know myself until yesterday,' Jack said. 'I'm on embarkation leave.'

'Embarkation leave!' Victor spoke the words as if he were savouring them. He came over and slapped Jack on the back. 'So, you're off, then. Off to sort Hitler out.'

Prue turned away, pretending to check on the carrots that were simmering in a saucepan on top of the range, biting her bottom lip to stop sudden tears from spilling out, frustrated and angry at the way Victor was revelling in the fact that their son was about to go to war against an enemy who wasn't afraid to sweep away all who stood in its way, and who would have no hesitation in doing the same to Jack.

Sitting at the table a short while later, just the three of them as Alice had arranged to go to a friend's straight from school today, not knowing that Jack would be coming home, Prue did her best to eat the meal that she'd so lovingly cooked for Jack, but her appetite was gone. Jack, on the other hand, was clearly enjoying the shepherd's pie, already on to his second helping.

'What do you think of all this nonsense of your brother's?' Victor asked. 'Never thought a son of mine would be a blasted conchie.'

Prue stopped moving the food around on her plate and stared at her husband, watching him digging his fork into the pile of food on his plate and shovelling it into his mouth.

Jack glanced at her, his eyes full of concern, before turning to answer his father. 'I think he's doing the right thing for him.'

Victor snorted, frown lines creasing his forehead. 'So, you'd agree with him standing by and letting a Nazi paratrooper attack your mother and sister because he isn't prepared to kill anyone. I'm ashamed and disgusted with him.'

Jack shook his head. 'One thing I've learned in my training is that a team is only as strong as its weakest link. If you had a soldier in your unit who couldn't bring himself to kill then that could have terrible consequences. Edwin's brave enough to know that and joining the Friends' Ambulance Unit is the perfect thing for him. It won't be easy – he'll have to deal with difficult things and probably be put in dangerous situations.'

'Being in the Army would have made a *man* of him,' Victor said, spearing a piece of carrot with his fork. 'He's always been too soft.'

Jack put his knife and fork down and sighed, looking directly at Victor. 'Everybody's different, Father. I'm proud of how Edwin has stood up for what he believes in.'

Prue watched as Victor's cold, pale-blue eyes narrowed as he stared at his son, but Jack continued to look him straight back in the eye, something that he wouldn't have dared to do before he'd left to join the Army.

'Humph.' Victor dropped his knife and fork with a clatter on to his empty plate. 'You can think what you want, Jack, but I won't have that conchie in this house again while there's still breath in my body. I've disowned him.'

Jack shrugged. 'Well, that's your choice.' He turned to face Prue and smiled warmly at her. 'Any chance of some more shepherd's pie, please, Ma?'

'Of course.' Prue reached out to take his plate to serve him another helping from the dish, smiling warmly at her son. She was so proud of him for standing up for his brother against their father. Victor stood quite alone in his belief and treatment of Edwin.

Chapter 53

Thea felt as though she was flying. The freezing air stung her warm cheeks, her breath pluming behind her like smoke from a steam train, as she glided across the surface of the frozen lake. She hadn't felt like this for a long time, not since she'd last skated here with her brothers and sisters, the five of them spending all day on the ice with their friends enjoying the winter sport, laughing and joking with each other, showing off and trying to do tricks, having races to see who could go the fastest and the furthest. They'd been such joyous times and today she was recapturing some of that, only this time with some of her family missing and gone for ever, others not here today to take part, but instead with new family members.

Bringing herself to a halt she caught her breath, turning to look back at the others who were a little way behind her although Jack was coming in fast, his cheeks glowing like hers must be, his woollen scarf streaming out behind.

Reuben and Edwin were following on behind at a slower pace, though both of them were smiling and clearly enjoying themselves.

'I never knew you could skate like that!' Jack caught hold of her as he reached her, spinning her around and pulling her along with him until he came to a halt. 'You went off like a rocket.'

Thea laughed. 'I surprised myself! It's years since I last ice skated, although we used to do it as often as we could when we were children; as soon as this lake froze over enough, we'd be on here.'

The lake in the grounds of Great Plumstead Hall always drew a crowd of people from the village in winter when it froze thick enough to be safe to skate on, and now, with the weather being so cold, its surface had become a perfect ice-skating playground.

'Ma used to bring us when we were children,' Jack said. 'You were living in London then, but I remember her telling us about how you all used to come here when you were younger.'

Thea nodded. 'It's a shame she couldn't come today because of that Women's Institute committee meeting.'

Jack grinned. 'You know Ma, she's always got something on the go.'

She laughed. 'I know, but a lot less would get done in this village without her.'

Reuben and Edwin caught up with them. 'Have you got the hang of it again?' Thea addressed her brother, who'd been reluctant to come skating this afternoon, saying he hadn't done it for years and wasn't sure he remembered how to. 'It looks like you've remembered how to do it after all.'

Reuben nodded. 'I think it's come back to me. How about a relay race? Me and Edwin against you and Jack. Out to the island and back for each team member.'

Thea looked at Jack and Edwin, who both nodded their agreement. 'All right then, if you're sure. Jack, you skate against Edwin and I'll skate against Reuben.' She turned her gaze on her brother. 'But I won't be slowing down so you can keep up, it will be a race.'

'Of course.' Reuben laughed.

Edwin and Jack lined up ready to go.

'Go around the island clockwise,' Thea instructed. 'On your marks, get set, go!'

The two young men shot off, keeping almost together, although Jack had edged slightly ahead by the time they disappeared around the back of the small island that stood in the middle of the lake.

'Do you remember the last time we did this?' Reuben asked.

Thea nodded, her eyes meeting his. 'It was the winter before you and William joined up and were sent to France, we were all out skating every spare moment we had: you, me, William, Prue and Lizzie.' She smiled at the memories of how much fun they'd had with their friends from the village, what happy times. So many of the young men that had been skating that last winter had not come home from the war. And some of those who did would never skate again because of injuries. Would the same be true of the young men now out skating on the lake – not just

349

Jack and Edwin, but all the others from the village who were out here enjoying themselves this Sunday afternoon?

Thea felt a touch on her arm through her thick wool coat and looked down to see Reuben's gloved hand resting on it.

'Best just to enjoy the moment,' he said. 'Don't taint this lovely time by worrying about what might or might not happen.'

'You're right. I—' she began but stopped at the shouts coming from Jack and Edwin who were steaming towards them, neck and neck again; the yards of ice left between them and her and Reuben were getting fewer by the moment.

Thea glanced at her brother and could see he was preparing to launch himself across the ice, a look of determination on his face, one that she'd seen plenty of times before when they'd done things like this as children. There was no doubt that he was taking this race seriously, but after his earlier reluctance and slow progress across the lake, he couldn't really think he would out-skate her, could he?

Before she had time to consider the wisdom of Reuben's challenge, Jack and Edwin returned, their gloved hands held out to tag them to start the next leg of the relay race.

'Go!' Jack cried breathlessly, slapping her hand as he whizzed past.

Aware that Edwin had just done the same to Reuben, Thea pushed off hard and quickly got into her stride, smoothly kicking back her skates against the ice in a satisfying rhythm, loving the sensation of flying along, the cold air making her eyes water. To her delight she was in the lead, having got off to a better start, now all she had to do was maintain it.

The island was fast approaching and as she prepared to go around it, she became aware of the sound of skates on the ice behind her getting closer and closer. She dared a quick glance over her shoulder and saw that Reuben was bearing down on her. *Focus*, she told herself, knowing that if she took too broad a path behind the island she could lose time, but if she took a route that hugged the shore of the island more closely, she'd need to lose speed or risk falling. Either way, the lead that she'd felt so confident about only moments ago could be lost as, clearly, Reuben hadn't lost his prowess at skating as his earlier efforts had suggested. Was it all part of his tactics? Thea couldn't help herself from smiling, it was just the sort of game that her brothers had always played, either together as a team or individually, but she wasn't going to let him win without a fight.

With little time to think which was the best strategy, she decided to abandon a fast but much wider and longer sweep around the back of the island in favour of a shorter one, and as she adjusted her stride and upright posture to take her close by the shore of the island she was aware that Reuben was doing the opposite, seeing him out of the corner of her eye taking a wider arc but going faster. Coming around the side of the island, to where she could see Jack and Edwin waiting near the far shore, she glanced across as Reuben drew level and went past her, a look of joy on his face that she recognised so well. He might have grey in his hair and lines around his eyes, but she could see the face of her brother as a boy in the man.

A spark of determination fuelled her to push herself on – she wasn't going to give up now, there was still a chance that she could catch him and overtake him. She skated as fast as she could, sucking the cold air into her lungs, the work of her muscles making her glow warmly. Inch by inch she crept nearer Reuben but couldn't manage to close the last yard or two to reach him. Rushing towards Edwin and Jack who were shouting and cheering them on, calling out their names, her lungs felt fit to burst and her legs were starting to protest. It looked, in spite of her efforts, that the race was lost. Reuben was the faster skater, having come from behind and overtaken her, but then to her surprise he slowed slightly and reached his gloved hand out behind him for her to take, looking over his shoulder at her. Thea grabbed hold of it and together, hand in hand, they glided past their nephews and came to a halt a few yards from the shore.

'You didn't need to do that,' Thea said breathlessly, leaning her hands on her knees. 'But thank you.'

'It could have been either of us,' Reuben said. 'I went wide and you went close in.' He shrugged, and then started to laugh. 'You should have seen the look on your face when I went past.'

Thea stood upright, narrowing her eyes as she looked at him. 'Says the man who thought he couldn't remember how to skate any more. Clearly you were very much mistaken.'

'That was close!' Jack said, skating over to them. 'I'd have had Aunt Thea as the fastest, but the pair of you are good.'

Thea looked at Reuben and grinned. It was a great feeling to be out here doing something like this, something fun and unrelated to what else they had going on in their lives. For a short time they were able to forget their responsibilities and worries about what lay ahead.

'We'll be ready for that hot soup Hettie's making for us,' she said. 'But I'm not ready to go back just yet, let's carry on skating for a while longer – enjoy it while we can.' She smiled at them before pushing off and heading out across the ice once more to lose herself again in the steady rhythm of her skates on the ice and the rush of air on her face, under the cool blue winter sky overhead. This was a time to enjoy, and store away in her memory for the future, for when times weren't as much fun as this.

The sun was low in the sky and the air was growing colder by the time they set off to make their way back to Rookery House, their energy spent but their internal wells of happiness and joy overflowing.

Thea linked her arms through each of her nephews. 'I thoroughly enjoyed myself, thank you all for making it such a fun afternoon.' She glanced over at Reuben. 'I think we should come out and do this again while we still can, don't you?'

'You might not think that in the morning when it's painful to walk, but if you can manage it then I'm up for another skate, only I warn you I might not be so generous next time we have a race,' he teased.

'A rematch,' Jack said. 'I wish I could be here to see that, I wouldn't know who to cheer for. Perhaps you could get Ma to come out with you, she might be faster than either of you.'

Thea laughed. 'She always was a good skater.'

Jack looked at her, his face suddenly serious. 'You will keep an eye on her for me, won't you? She's not happy, she pretends to be, but I can see that deep down she isn't. I didn't really notice it before I went away but . . .' He sighed. 'Coming back now, it's like looking at her and Father with fresh eyes. I can see he's more pompous than ever with his narrow views and dictating what goes on in his home and his business, it's his way or no way – and I'm glad to be out of it. You must be, too, Edwin.'

His brother nodded.

'Of course I will, we *all* will.' Thea squeezed his arm. 'We always keep an eye on Prue and nothing you've said surprises us, we all know that deep down she's not happy with Victor. I've tried talking to her about it many times but she's adamant that she's fine.'

'I miss Ma, but I certainly don't miss Father,' Edwin said.

They'd reached the gate leading out through the wall that encircled the estate and went through it on to the road and headed in the direction of Rookery House, still walking four abreast as there was no traffic around.

'Father hasn't changed his mind about you being a conscientious objector.' Jack sighed. 'He didn't like it when I said I thought it was the right thing for you to

354

do. I thought he was going to blow up when I said it, but he didn't because I stared him down.' Jack glanced at his brother. 'You're definitely doing the right thing, you know. I'm proud of you for standing up for what you believe in. It takes a brave man to swim against the tide and going to war is no joke, you've got to be prepared to fight . . . to kill, if necessary . . . and I'm not too proud to admit that part of me is scared of what I'm going into.'

Without saying anything they all instinctively stopped walking at Jack's confession and looked at him.

'You're right to be scared,' Reuben said, after a few moments of silence. 'Any fool can go into a war zone full of bravado and being cocksure of themselves, it's the ones that feel the fear that understand and are more likely to come out of it in one piece. I saw it many times in France, believe me; feeling scared is good, it can make all the difference to you surviving, so don't ever be ashamed of feeling that.'

Thea looked from her brother to her oldest nephew, tears smarting her eyes as the wisdom and experience from one generation at war was passed to the next, to a young man who was on the cusp of experiencing it for himself.

Jack nodded. 'Thank you, I'll remember that.'

'Good.' Reuben put his hand on Jack's shoulder. 'Now I don't know about you, but I'm hungry and Hettie's promised us soup, so let's get home.'

The kitchen at Rookery House was warm and filled with the delicious aroma of freshly baked, yeasty bread, combined with a hearty vegetable and bean soup.

Quickly peeling off their layers of clothes they were soon seated around the kitchen table tucking in and retelling the tales of their ice-skating exploits to Hettie and Marianne, both of whom hadn't gone as they didn't want to risk falling over – Hettie as she hadn't skated for a long time and Marianne as she was in the late stages of her pregnancy.

'I remember you lot as children always skating whenever you could,' Hettie said, ladling another helping of soup into Jack's empty bowl. 'Lizzie was a demon on skates; she used to fly along, her pigtails streaming out behind her. She never seemed to get tired.'

'Perhaps we can get her to come here while the lake's still frozen,' Edwin suggested. 'Get Ma on the ice as well.'

'I'll ask her when I get home.' Jack spread some more butter on a slice of bread. 'You'll have to write and tell me about it if you do get her and Aunt Lizzie to skate, I want to hear all about it.'

Thea smiled at him from across the table. 'Of course we'll write and tell you what's going on; letters from home are important when you're away.'

Reuben nodded. 'I remember the arrival of the post was one of the highlights of the day in France. Letters from home kept us going.'

Hettie squeezed Jack's arm. 'Don't worry, lad, you'll be hearing plenty from us.'

'And you'd better write back to us, when you can,' Edwin said.

Jack nodded. 'I will.'

When the time came for Jack to go, Thea felt like

356

crying. She was frightened of what the future held for him. She'd known Jack since he was a small boy, and now as a man he was off to war and in spite of his training and advice from Reuben, he wouldn't fully understand the nature and horrible, sickening seriousness of it until he was in it. All she could hope for was that he wouldn't be injured or worse, and would come out of it in the end, but she knew that he would undoubtedly be utterly changed by his experiences. What he saw and did would change him, just as it had changed those who had gone to the Great War and come home again.

She watched as Jack went around everybody, hugging and kissing them goodbye, and when it was her turn she held him tight, squeezing him.

'Look after yourself, and be careful,' she whispered to him. 'I want the chance to ice skate with you again.'

He released his hold of her, his eyes meeting hers. 'I'll be back, and we'll skate again, I promise you that.'

She smiled at him. 'I'll be waiting.'

Chapter 54

Coming to the station to see her son off didn't get any easier, Prue thought. In fact, this time was even worse because Jack wasn't just going to do his basic training, he was leaving to go to war! All she wanted to do was grab hold of him and never let him go to keep him safe.

They'd come alone, just the two of them. Jack had said goodbye to his father before he'd left for work this morning and Alice before she'd gone to school. He hadn't wanted anyone else to come to see him off, not even Edwin this time, and Prue knew that for all his apparent cheerfulness and eagerness to put his training into action, Jack was feeling nervous about what he was heading into.

'Do you know when you're leaving?' Prue asked the question that she'd promised herself she wouldn't, but now on the verge of his departure she couldn't help herself.

Jack threw his arm around her shoulders. 'You know I can't tell you that, Ma, and even if I could, it's probably best that you don't know, you'd only be worrying and there's nothing you can do about it. I'll write and let you know how I'm getting on, I promise.' He smiled sheepishly. 'I'll try to be a better correspondent than I have been so far because I know you'll be worrying if you don't hear from me from time to time.'

Prue nodded. 'Thank you. You're right: I do worry.' She shrugged. 'I can't help it – it comes with the job of being a mother.' She looked up at him, drinking in his face, committing it to memory, so she could picture him in her mind when she needed to see him. 'You will be careful, won't you?'

He laughed, his breath clouding in the cold air. 'Of course I will, I have every intention of coming home again.'

Prue's stomach knotted even tighter, as the memory of the last time someone had said those words to her flagged up in her mind – her brother William, home on his last leave during the Great War. He'd said just the same thing but he *hadn't* returned and now lay in a cemetery in France, and all that was left of her once-vibrant, funny and charming brother was a headstone marking his final resting place – they'd been sent a photograph of it. The last war had robbed him of his life, of his future, and the thought of it happening to Jack was utterly terrifying.

Prue felt tears welling up as the sound of the train approaching the station made her composure slip. Time was running out – she really didn't want to cry, but the tears slid hotly down her cold cheeks regardless of her best efforts to be brave and stoic.

Jack wrapped his arms around her and hugged her tightly, crushing her against the wool of his army great-coat, as the train came to a halt along the platform. 'Look after yourself, Ma,' he said, his voice muffled. Then he quickly released her, picked up his kitbag, and with a final glance at her, his eyes over-bright, he opened the nearest train door and climbed on board, slamming the door shut behind him.

Panic rushed through Prue's veins, she had to see him for every last moment she could. She hurried along the platform, looking to see where he'd gone, and then spotted him going into an empty compartment further along the carriage, where he stowed his kitbag, in the overhead luggage rack and then came and stood by the window, opening up the sliding section at the top and reaching out his hand. She grabbed hold of it and smiled at him, her throat aching painfully at his imminent departure.

'Take care, Jack,' she managed to say, her voice sounding strained.

'And you.' Jack squeezed her hand as the guard's whistle blasted its long note further down the platform, and the train jolted forwards, the steam engine at the front chuffing out puffs of smoke that billowed up into the winter air.

'Goodbye.' Prue held on as long as she could but as the train picked up speed, she was forced to let go. She ground to a halt, tears running down her face and her eyes fixed on Jack's outstretched hand that waved back to her until the train rounded the bend and it was lost from sight.

'Ma.'

360

Prue felt a hand on her arm and turned to see Edwin standing beside her looking worried.

'Jack wanted me to come to meet you so that you didn't leave alone. I was waiting by the booking office.' He handed her a neatly pressed clean handkerchief and linked his arm through hers. 'Come on, come back to Rookery House for a bit. You shouldn't be alone.'

She nodded, wiping the tears from her face, grateful for Jack's thoughtfulness. He'd known how hard it would be for her to see him go. With a final glance down the track, she went with Edwin, knowing that he was right. It was far better to go to Thea's for a bit where the company would do her good, than return to the empty echoing rooms of her own home.

Chapter 55

'It's coming down thicker than ever,' Hettie said, staring out of the kitchen window.

Marianne heaved herself out of the chair by the range where she'd been sitting sewing after their midday meal and went over to stand beside Hettie. Out in the back garden the snowflakes were floating down thickly like soft feathers, blotting out the horizon and adding generously to the covering of snow that already cloaked the muted winter colours of Rookery House's garden, transforming it into a dazzling white world. The flakes were drifting gently down, falling so thickly that the air was full of them, it was a mesmerising sight.

'It's so beautiful,' Marianne said.

Hettie glanced at her, her eyebrows raised behind her round glasses. 'Snow like this is all well and fine if you haven't got to travel far in it, but if it carries on like this, I'm worried about getting you safely to the maternity hospital on Thursday. We might have to pull you there on a sledge.'

Marianne was booked to go in to stay a week ahead of her baby's due date, as was the practice with most of the evacuee mothers to save the problem of having to rush them there while they were in labour as had happened with Sally whose baby had come too early.

'I'm not keen on having to go in, to be honest,' she admitted. 'I'll be there for at least a week beforehand and then ten days after it's born, and if he or she,' she placed a hand on her large belly, which had grown so much in the past couple of months that she could no longer see her feet when she looked down, 'is late, then I could be away from here for over a month.'

Hettie reached out and gently squeezed Marianne's hand. 'I know, and we'll miss you dearly, but it's the safest place to be. You'll have the midwives there to help you and you can rest after your baby's born and focus on getting your strength back.' She smiled. 'And we'll be along to see you often. It will be fine, Marianne. You'll be in there with some of the other evacuee mothers as well. Prue took Lily in the other day ready for her baby to be born, so you'll have a familiar face there.'

Marianne nodded and did her best to return Hettie's smile. She knew it was for the best, though the thought of being away from Rookery House, Hettie, Thea, Reuben and Edwin, who'd become like family to her, was hard to be cheerful about, but she had to put the welfare of her baby first. Hadn't she been doing that ever since she'd found out that she was expecting and been thrown out of her job and forced to carve a new life for herself? Going to stay in the maternity hospital was just the next stage of that and it wouldn't be for ever, she just needed to accept it and make the best of it.

A figure, with a generous coating of snow on its hat and coat, emerged out of the swirling snow and came hurrying towards the back door carrying a basket – it was Thea who'd been out tending to the hens. Rather than coming in the kitchen door as usual, she went into the scullery.

'Push the kettle on to boil, Marianne,' Hettie instructed. 'Thea will be needing a hot drink. I'll go and help her get out of her things; we don't want snow trampled indoors.'

Marianne did as she was asked and then set about making a fresh pot of tea, stopping to rub her lower back, which had been aching on and off ever since she'd got up this morning.

'It's cold out there, but so beautiful with the snow coming down,' Thea said when she came into the kitchen a few minutes later, her cheeks red from the cold. 'The hens aren't so keen on it, though, but they're tucked up inside the run and the tarpaulin that Edwin and I put over the top is keeping the worst of the snow off so they can still scrap around.' She put some letters on the table. 'I met the postman out in the lane, there's a letter for you from Sally, I think – looks like her handwriting.'

'Thank you, I'll read that in a minute.' Marianne poured boiling water into the brown, earthenware teapot. 'Her letters are always so funny, it's a bit like having her here again.'

Hettie came bustling in with the eggs Thea had collected, four of them, ready to put in the pantry. 'I'll be glad when the weather warms up and the hens start laying better.'

'You can't blame them at this time of year,' Thea said, warming her hands over the range. 'They're more interested in keeping themselves warm and fed than laying eggs. Come springtime we'll have more eggs than we can eat.'

'Then we'll sell them, and the hens can earn their keep.' Hettie took the lid off the teapot and, satisfied that the tea had brewed for long enough, poured out three cups and handed one to Thea. 'That will warm you up.'

Settled at the table with Thea and Hettie, Marianne opened Sally's letter and read it, smiling to herself as she could hear her friend's cheerful voice in the words on the page.

Dear Marianne,

I hope you're well and looking after yourself, it won't be long now until your baby's on its way. I hope this reaches you before you leave for the maternity hospital, if not I know Thea or Hettie will bring it in to you.

You'd be so proud of me, I've been promoted to sewing the hems on the bottom of sailors' trousers — imagine that — they trust me enough to let me do a good job on those wide, bell bottoms. I was that nervous the first time, my heart was pounding in my chest and I could feel the supervisor's eyes boring into my back. I told myself that I could do it, remembered what you'd told me about

going steady, not rushing it, and I did it. I did it! Just
think, somewhere out there on the high seas there'll be
sailors wearing trousers I hemmed. It's a good feeling
doing my bit.

I heard from my Arthur yesterday. I'm glad he's still
posted guarding the Norfolk coast, he ain't happy about it
but I'd rather he was there than in France.

Anyway, cheerio for now. Write back soon.
Love from your friend,
Sally

'Is Sally all right?' Thea asked, warming her hands
around her cup.

'Yes, she's in fine spirits, just been promoted to sewing
the hems of sailors' trousers. Here, you and Hettie can
read it for yourselves.' She passed the letter across to Thea,
imagining her friend working in the same sort of garment
factory that she'd worked in herself before being evacuated to Great Plumstead. Since Sally had returned to the
East End she seemed to have settled down and was happy
in her new job, although no doubt she was still mourning
the loss of her baby.

A sudden uncomfortable cramp low in her pelvis made
her wince and shift in her chair.

'Are you all right, Marianne?' Hettie's face was full
of concern.

She nodded. 'I'm fine, it's just my heavy belly makes it
awkward to sit comfortably now.' She rubbed her lower
back, which was protesting more now than it had been
when she'd got up this morning. 'I might go and lie down

366

for bit, that will help.' Hettie and Thea glanced at each other. 'I'm fine, honestly. It's just I'm carrying a lot of weight here.' She rubbed the front of her belly. 'It's putting me off balance.'

'You get some rest then and hopefully you'll feel better in a bit. If you want, I could light the fire in your bedroom for you?' Thea offered.

'No, it's fine, but thank you.' Marianne smiled gratefully at Thea as she hauled herself out of her chair. 'I'll be all right, I'll be snug and warm once I'm under the eiderdown.'

Marianne must have drifted off to sleep as when she woke up the light outside her bedroom window was fading and not just because of the snow, which was still falling thickly. Taking a moment first to fully wake up, she swung her legs out of the bed and sat up, then levered herself up to standing, but as she did so a sharp cramp gripped her low down in her pelvis making her gasp. Grabbing hold of the post of the iron bedstead, she caught her breath as the pain eased, and the horrifying thought that something might be wrong with the baby hit her. Was she going to lose her child as Sally had done? But the pain passed, she was fine again. It was probably just indigestion, perhaps she needed to visit the lavatory, Marianne told herself. She would feel better downstairs.

In the kitchen, met by the warmth from the range, the comforting soft glow from the lit lamp on the table and the delicious smell of a stew cooking, Marianne felt cheered. She was fine, she told herself, but as Thea and Hettie turned to look at her from where they were setting the table for tea, a gushing sensation of warm, wet liquid rushed out between her legs and pooled on the tiled floor. She stared down at it and began to shake, tears filling her eyes and spilling over to run unchecked down her cheeks. And then another cramping pain hit, making her gasp.

Thea and Hettie were by her side in an instant.

'Take my hand.' Thea pulled out a chair and guided her into it. She crouched down in front of her. 'How long have you been having pains?'

'My back's been aching all day ... but the first pain came when I woke up.'

'Your waters have just gone, dear.' Hettie put a gentle hand on her shoulder. 'Looks like your baby's decided it's time to be born.'

'But it can't ... not here ... not yet ... That's supposed to happen at the maternity hospital!'

'It's all right. We'll get the midwife to come here, there's one in Wykeham; she often delivers babies at home.'

'But the snow ...' Marianne said.

'Midwives come out in snow, too, you know.' Thea stood up. 'I'll go and telephone her now.'

Edwin came in while Thea was telephoning, his cheeks red from the cold. Taking one look at Marianne, his face was full of concern. 'What's happened?'

'Marianne's baby is on the way. Thea's telephoning for the midwife,' Hettie explained. 'We need to get ready. Can you go and light a fire in Marianne's bedroom, we'll need to get it warm in there.'

Edwin nodded. 'Of course.' He quickly gathered what he needed from the store of kindling and coal that was kept by the range and went upstairs.

Thea came back in the kitchen looking concerned. 'The midwife's out at another delivery; they're going to get a message to her but don't know how long it will be before she can get here.'

A wave of panic hit Marianne. 'Can't we go to the maternity hospital then?'

Thea shook her head. 'It's five miles there and the way the snow's coming down there'll no doubt be drifts in places, I doubt my car could get through. It would be foolish to try.' She bit her bottom lip. 'We'll have to manage until the midwife can get here.'

'But we've never delivered—' Hettie began but stopped at a look from Thea. 'Or even had a baby ourselves, we wouldn't know what to do.'

'But Prue has, she'll be on duty at the day club. I'll ask Edwin to go and fetch her.'

Marianne started to cry again. She was scared; it wasn't supposed to happen like this – now wasn't the time to have her baby.

Marianne had changed into her nightgown and was up in her warmed bedroom where a fire burned brightly in the hearth, the blackout blinds fitted and curtains drawn against the winter dusk. The pains were coming more frequently now.

'You're doing really well, Marianne.' Thea gently rubbed her back, which helped to relax her between the cramps – they were growing in intensity now. 'Looks like this baby wants to be born soon.'

Marianne could feel another pain coming and leaned forward over the iron bedstead at the foot of the bed, groaning as it reached its peak and then subsided.

'Do you want to lie down?' Thea asked.

Marianne shook her head. 'Feels better standing and moving.' She started to pace around the room, wanting it to be over and yet scared of what the outcome might be in case what happened to Sally's baby happened to hers too.

The bedroom door opened quietly and Hettie came in. 'Prue's just arrived, she's brought Gloria with her, they're just warming up downstairs – they had to walk here because the roads are too deep in snow to drive. They'll be up in a minute or two.'

'Why Gloria?' Thea asked.

'She's had five babies of her own and helped deliver others, she's got more experience than any of us,' Hettie explained. 'She was still at the day club helping Prue pack up when Edwin got there and she offered to come and help.'

The arrival of Prue and the effervescent Gloria, wearing a scarlet dress that strained over her pregnant belly, was like the sun coming out after the rain. As kind and caring as Thea and Hettie were, they didn't have the experience and were as new to this as she was; but now having someone here who'd helped deliver babies Marianne felt better – or as good as she could with pains racking her body at ever-decreasing intervals.

''Ello, ducks,' Gloria said, quickly taking in the situation and coming over to put her arm around Marianne's shoulders. 'You ain't half picked a fine time to 'ave a baby. I 'ad to put some old gum boots on to walk 'ere through the snow, my 'igh heels wouldn't cope with it. So, the pains are coming quicker, are they?'

Marianne nodded. 'Not sure how often – too often for my liking . . . ' She smiled.

Gloria nodded her head, her peroxide-blonde hairstyle looking a bit more tussled than usual. 'That's what they do, ducks.'

Another pain started to build, making Marianne groan and bend forward over the bedstead again.

'That's it; you breathe through it nice and steady.' Gloria rubbed her lower back, knowing just where it would help.

'Would Marianne be better lying on the bed?' Prue suggested.

'Not necessarily,' Gloria said. 'Do you want to lie down, Marianne?'

She shook her head as the wave of pain subsided.

'You do what feels right. You can give birth standin' if you want, or on all fours, I've done it all ways.' Gloria laughed. 'Can someone be getting some 'ot water and warm towels sorted? And sterilise a knife to cut the cord and some pegs to clamp it.'

'I'll do that.' Hettie bustled off to find what was needed.

Marianne had no idea how much time passed as her world became one of waves of pain and relief. It seemed as if her body was taking over as it worked to push the baby out.

'It won't be long now.' Gloria looked up at her and

smiled from where she knelt on the floor in front of her, ready to catch the baby.

Marianne was standing, supported on each side by Thea and Prue, her legs apart, and she could feel the baby moving downwards inside her and then a burning sensation burst between her legs.

'Don't push, pant, like this.' Gloria demonstrated what to do. 'The head's crowning.'

Marianne did as she was told and then another pain gripped her.

'Push gently,' Gloria said, her hands ready to guide the baby. 'That's it, the 'ead's out. You're doin' really well, ducks, you're nearly there. One more push when the next pain comes and it'll be born.'

It was over quickly: another pain came, she pushed, and the baby slithered out and Gloria caught it in a warm towel.

'You've done it!' Thea said, her voice thick with emotion.

Gloria rubbed the baby with the towel, and it started to cry. 'You've got a little girl, Marianne. She's a cracker. Look.' She held her up for them all to see.

A rush of euphoria that it was all over flooded through Marianne – the pain had gone in an instant and she had a daughter, a beautiful, live daughter.

Tucked up in bed a short while later, with her daughter cradled in her arms, Marianne couldn't quite believe what had just happened, but the evidence was there to see.

'What are you going to call her?' Thea asked, sitting on the edge of the bed and gently stroking the sleeping baby's downy cheek with one finger.

'Emily Rose, after my grandmother,' Marianne said.

'That's a beautiful name.' Gloria smiled down at her from where she stood next to Prue and Hettie. 'She's a little darlin', all right.'

Marianne nodded, looking down at Emily Rose; her daughter may have been less than an hour old, but the strength of her love for her had hit with such force, she felt like a lioness and knew she would do anything to protect her child.

Chapter 56

Prue added the final item to her list and read it back through to herself, mentally ticking things off: peas, broad beans, beetroot, Brussels sprouts, broccoli, cabbage, carrots, leeks, lettuce, spinach, parsnips, onions, potatoes, tomatoes and turnips. There were also soft fruits that could be added – strawberries, raspberries, blackcurrants, redcurrants, gooseberries – and the orchard fruits like apples, pears and plums, but all of those depended on how much room members had in their gardens. The important thing was that members should grow as much food as possible.

She tapped her pencil against the side of her cheek for a moment, her eyes falling on the letter that had been passed over to her by the chairman: the Government had written to each WI branch in the country, inviting them to contribute to food supplies by providing two hundredweight of onions and three hundredweight of tomatoes for sale on their market stalls – and that amount was in addition to what members would grow for themselves. It was quite a challenge, but nothing that Prue didn't think the members were capable of if they worked together. Look what a great success the blackberry harvest and jam making had been, and then the damson jam after that. They'd already done their bit to stop fruit being wasted and were making a good contribution to the war effort on the home front. Not forgetting the day club, which was turning out to be a great success and very popular with the evacuee mothers. She was proud of the way the village's Institute had risen to the challenge of life in wartime, they were making a very visible difference, but there was always more to be done and she would be doing her utmost to help them do it.

At the next meeting she'd be announcing the Institute's latest initiative – to do as the Minister of Agriculture encouraged and 'Dig for Victory', growing more food than ever before, which was vital now that rationing had come into force.

The National Federation of the WI was arranging distribution of bags of seed potatoes and tomato seeds, and had arranged for members to be able to buy packets of Suttons seeds at special rates with enough in them to grow many different types of vegetables in a large garden or allotment, providing enough to feed a family as well as surplus to sell at WI markets.

Then, of course, there was the possibility of growing food in communal gardens or allotments in places that weren't already in production around the village, Prue thought; a few sites came to mind with land that lay idle. With some work from members they could be turned into productive plots to grow food.

Prue added that to her agenda. She smiled, enjoying having a new project to immerse herself in because it was not only enjoyable but would also help to keep her busy and give her some respite from worrying about where Jack was and what was happening to him.

'Ma?'

She looked up and to her astonishment and delight saw Edwin standing in the kitchen doorway. 'Is it safe? His car's not here.'

Prue got up from the kitchen table and went around to Edwin. 'Don't worry, he's at work, the place he loves best.' She put her arms around her son and hugged him warmly – this was the first time he'd dared to come home since Victor had thrown him out, and it was lovely to have him here, no matter how fleeting his visit might be.

'Come and sit down and I'll make some tea, and there's a cake I made yesterday. I'm sure you'd like a piece.' She smiled at him.

Edwin sat down at the kitchen table. 'Of course I would, thank you.' He looked at the papers scattered on the table. 'What are you doing?'

'Getting organised for the WI's new initiative.' She pushed the kettle on to the hotplate of the range to boil before getting out two clean teacups and putting them on the table. 'I'm going to announce it at tomorrow's meeting so we can start to get things in place ready for spring and the start of the growing season. In fact, you might want to help us, what with the experience you've gained working for Thea – we're going to be growing more food. "Digging for Victory" like you and Thea already are at Rookery House. Here, have a look at what's planned.' She pushed her notes over for him to look at and then spooned tea leaves into the china teapot.

'Two hundredweight of onions and three hundredweight of tomatoes – that's a lot to grow on top of what members need for their families!' Edwin said.

The kettle had come to the boil and Prue poured the boiling water into the teapot and placed the tea cosy on top. 'I know, but if we all work together then I'm sure we can achieve it. I was just thinking that there are plenty of areas of land around the village that are lying idle and could be used for food production.' She cut a generous slice of cake for Edwin and passed it to him. 'I have every faith in our members; look what we've already done with the jam making and setting up the day club. And as I said, it would be lovely if you could help too.'

Edwin waited to answer as his mouth was full of cake. 'I will help while I'm still here, but that might not be for much longer.' He reached into his jacket pocket and pulled out an envelope. 'This came in the afternoon post: I've got a place on the next FAU training camp. I'll be leaving in April to take up my place there.' He beamed at her, his delight at this news plain to see.

Prue reached out across the table and grabbed hold of his hand for a moment. 'That's marvellous news, just what you've been waiting for.' *Not you!* a little voice whispered in her head. Stop it! she told herself.

Edwin was a grown man and it was only right that he should leave and do what he wanted to. She needed to remind herself that it was better that he was joining the Friends' Ambulance Unit than the Army or one of the other services and be sent to fight; at least this way he would be doing something that he was happy with. Like mothers all over the country, she just had to get used to her children going off to do their bit and get on with her own life here at home in the meantime. Thank goodness she had the WI and the evacuee mothers to keep her busy.

'I'll be going to Manor Farm near Birmingham,' Edwin explained, taking the letter out of the envelope. 'It's a six-week training course to teach me to do "ambulance and relief work in areas under civilian and military control". It's an unpaid job but I'll get board and lodging, and some pocket money from the special assistance fund if I need some.'

Prue frowned. 'Doesn't seem right that you won't get paid; Jack gets paid in the army.'

Her son shrugged. 'I don't need much beyond bed and board, and perhaps a little bit of money to buy books or stamps to send letters. I really don't mind. The important thing is that I'll be doing my bit in a way that I feel comfortable with.'

Prue poured them both a cup of tea. 'Fair enough, but if you do find you need some money, let me know and I'll send you something.' She added some milk to the tea and handed Edwin his cup.

'Thank you, I appreciate that, but I'm sure I'll be fine.'

He smiled at her, his blue eyes meeting hers. 'They sent a kit list of things I need to take with me.'

He handed her one of the sheets of paper and Prue scanned it, noting the things he was required to take: blankets, stout shoes, gym shoes, one tidy suit (not new), knife, fork, spoon . . . The list went on. 'I'll help you get this lot organised, there's nothing there that's difficult to sort out, most of it you've already got.'

Helping Edwin organise his kit list was something else she could busy herself with, at least she'd know that he'd be well prepared for the training camp and that would be of some comfort when he left.

She picked up a pencil and opened a new page in her notebook, doing what she did best – organising. 'Right, let's make a list of all the things on the kit list that you've already got, or that I have in the house that you could take, and we'll see what's left that we need to get.'

Chapter 57

Thea stood back to check for smears on the glass, but the scrunched-up newspaper, vinegar and water, combined with a good dose of elbow grease, had done the trick. The window was sparkling clean and she could see her reflection in it. She'd enjoyed cleaning the bay windows at the front of the house, it being a beautiful late February afternoon, the sky a crisp clear blue overhead; it was a pleasure to be outside.

She caught movement behind her in her reflection and turned to see a young man dressed in blue RAF uniform walking in through the gates.

'Good afternoon. Is Marianne at home?' he asked.

Thea recognised him from somewhere and then it hit her – Marianne had a photograph of him in her bedroom. He was Alex, the father of Emily Rose. Instantly, she felt defensive of Marianne and her baby. What was he doing here? What did he want?

'And who might you be?' she said, as though she didn't already know.

'Alex Fordham.' He came forwards, took off his RAF cap and held out his hand.

Thea shook it, taking in his handsome face, noticing that his brown eyes were the colour of conkers. 'I'm Thea Thornton.'

'I'd like to see Marianne, please, if she's here.'

Thea folded her arms. How did he know Marianne lived here? 'What do you want with Marianne?'

'I just want to talk to her, ask her something. We knew each other in London ... I don't mean her any harm, I can assure you, I just want to find out something that's been puzzling me ...' He ran a hand through his thick, dark brown hair.

Thea looked at him, judging from his manner and body language that he seemed genuine. This could be a chance for the young woman to sort things out at last, get straight what had happened and put the past behind her. 'I'm afraid she's not here.' Alex's face fell. 'But she'll be back soon; she's gone into the village.' She narrowed her eyes, looking at him. 'Does your fiancé know you're here?'

He frowned. 'I don't have a fiancé.'

'Wife, then?'

'No wife either. I don't understand why you would ask that.'

Thea stared at him. If he wasn't married or even engaged to be married, then had his proposed engagement broken off? Was there a chance for him and Marianne to be together?

'It's not for me to say. Why don't you come in and wait and Marianne can explain what I mean.'

'All right, thank you.'

Thea led the way around to the back door, hoping that she was doing the right thing.

Chapter 58

Marianne was enjoying walking in the sunshine on her way back from the village having been to the shops for Hettie. Baby Emily, now just over a month old, was fast asleep, tucked up cosily in her pram, with just her face peeping out from under the covers, a white knitted bonnet on her head, her rosebud lips sucking as she dreamed.

All was right with her world, Marianne thought, and with any luck, Emily would sleep for a while longer when she got home and she could do some more work on the dress she was making for one of Rosalind's friends. Her dressmaking business was still very much going although at a slower pace than before. Luckily her customers were understanding of her situation with a small baby to care for and were willing to be patient in order to have her design and make clothes for them.

Turning in through the gates of Rookery House, Marianne's attention was caught by Hettie waving frantically to her from the bay window of the dining room. It looked like the older woman had been watching out for her to come home, but before Marianne had a chance to return her wave, Hettie disappeared from the window, which was odd. Was something wrong?

Pushing the pram quickly around the house to the back door leading into the scullery, she saw that Hettie was waiting for her, a worried look on her face.

'What's wrong?' Marianne asked as the older woman opened the scullery door wide open, standing to the side as she pushed the pram through.

'You've got a visitor.' Hettie spoke in a hushed voice. 'He's been here for half an hour. Thea's with him in the sitting room.'

'Who is it?'

Hettie reached out and gently touched Marianne's arm. 'It's Alex.'

Her stomach plummeted into her shoes. 'Alex! What's he doing here?'

Why had he come back? She thought she'd never see him again after he'd come here with Charlie last autumn. So why had he returned? She'd never told Thea and Hettie about his first visit.

'I don't know, but he wants to see you.' Hettie's eyes met hers, full of sympathy behind her round glasses. 'I know this is difficult, but perhaps it might be better for you to speak to him and you can finally put what happened to rest.'

Marianne glanced down at Emily, who was still sound asleep. 'Will you keep an eye on her for me?'

'Of course I will.'

Marianne gently took off Emily's bonnet so she wouldn't overheat now she was inside the house and peeled back one layer of covers, then she leant over and softly kissed her daughter's downy cheek.

'She'll be fine.' Hettie smiled at her reassuringly. 'Now, go and find out what he wants, and remember I'm here if you need me – just shout.'

She nodded. 'Thank you. I remember how you saw off Iris Stokes, but I need to deal with this myself.'

Her heart was thumping hard as she stood outside the sitting-room door, bracing herself for what was to come. She wished she could turn and run but that wouldn't achieve anything and the only way to know why he'd come back here was to go in and face him. She took a deep breath, opened the door and stepped inside, her eyes immediately drawn to Alex, who leapt to his feet from where he'd been sitting in the armchair opposite Thea, each of them either side of the fire that burned brightly in the fireplace.

'Marianne!'

His brown eyes met hers and for several moments she was lost for words, feeling like she'd been pulled back to the times she used to meet him in London, when he'd been his usual caring and loving self with no indication of his forthcoming engagement to someone else. That reminder of where his future lay, how he'd hidden it from her, hardened her heart. Whatever he'd come here

385

for today, she wasn't the naive and foolish girl that she'd been back then; life had taught her that she had to look after herself, and her daughter.

'Alex.'

'I'll go and fetch you a cup of tea, Marianne.' Thea got up. 'It will give you a chance to talk to each other in private.'

Marianne nodded, and was grateful for Thea's gentle touch on her elbow as she left the room, closing the door quietly behind her. She went over and sat down in the chair Thea had vacated, very aware that Alex's eyes were on her.

She paused for a moment, looking at her hands, and then raised her head to look at him, standing with his back to the fire. 'Why have you come back?'

'Marianne, I . . .' He ran a hand through his brown hair. 'I need to ask you something because ever since I found out about it, it's been gnawing away at me and I need to know for sure.' He paused for a moment. 'Why are you called Mrs *Archer*? Why don't you use your husband's surname?'

'Why do you think that's what I call myself?' She knew there'd been no mention of her surname when she'd been introduced to Charlie, he only knew her as Marianne. No one else had been here when Alex had turned up that day with Charlie to tell him then. How could he know that she still went by Archer, just adding the Mrs bit in her pretence of being married.

'Because a great admirer of your dressmaking skills was singing your praises when I saw her a couple of weeks ago when I was on leave in London. My sister dragged me along to tea with her friend Cissy and they were talking about clothes, and Cissy was full of finding the magnificent Mrs Archer again, the one who used to work at Dorothy Abrahams, and was now living in Great Plumstead and making clothes for Lady Campbell-Gryce.'

Marianne felt cornered. What could she say, that she happened to marry someone else with the same surname? Before she could reply, Alex sat down opposite her and leaned forward, his eyes searching her face.

'Are you really married, Marianne? You're wearing a wedding ring but you haven't changed your name. Please tell me the truth. After what we had together you owe it to me.'

A spark of fury ignited in her. 'Truth? What do you know about telling the truth? I trusted you, I believed in you, and all the while you were just stringing me along like a fool!' She glared at him. 'And I don't owe you anything!'

She leapt to her feet and made for the door, but Alex caught her arm. 'Please, wait! I don't understand what you mean. I wasn't stringing you along, I loved you very much, Marianne ... I still do.'

She spun around to face him, her eyes meeting his. 'But you were promised to someone else, you've probably married her by now. I was only a distraction, and like a fool I let myself fall in love with you.'

Alex shook his head. 'I'm not married to anyone or engaged either.' He frowned. 'Why do you think I am?'

'Because I heard your sister talking about your fiancé-to-be when she came in for a dress fitting.' She swallowed hard, doing her best to keep her voice steady and not betray the emotion that was building up inside her.

'I don't have a fiancé, I never have, I promise you.'

'Your sister said that it was all arranged, your family wanted it, too ... I thought you were just playing me for a fool, and I'd been gullible enough to believe you.'

Alex sighed and shook his head. 'My parents might have wanted me to marry their friends' daughter, who they consider most suitable, but it's not what *I* want, and believe me when I tell you it's *never, ever* going to happen, no matter what they say. *I'll* be choosing who I marry.'

'It wasn't true?' Marianne slumped down in an armchair, glad to be off her wobbly legs. He wasn't engaged or married. He was free. Her doubting him had been for nothing ... but would he still have married her when he'd found out she was having his baby?

Alex shook his head. 'No.' He sat down opposite her. 'Is that why you disappeared? Was it just because of what you'd heard? If you'd just asked me then I'd have told you the truth.'

'I did lose my job – that was true.'

'You still should have asked me about what you heard, not just believed my sister and her gossip.' He leaned forwards and went to take her hand, but she pulled it away. 'What we had together was real, Marianne. My feelings were honest and true, there was nothing false about the way I felt ... still feel about you.'

Marianne looked away, staring at the orange flames flickering in the fire. She needed a moment to take in what he'd said. He *wasn't* engaged, he wasn't going to do what his family wanted. She'd believed what his sister had said and doubted him because of it, she'd questioned both her own ability to judge someone's character and what she and Alex had had together. She hadn't tried to find him to tell him about their unborn baby. What a mess had been created by those overheard words.

'I believed what your sister said, but it wasn't just that, I was sacked because ... because I was expecting, and after hearing that you were going to be engaged I thought you'd never want to have anything to do with me. Mrs Abrahams threw me out and I was on my own and had to look after myself. I couldn't bring myself to come begging to you because I was having your child when I thought you'd be marrying someone else and would turn me away. I had my pride.'

'We have a child?' Alex's face had gone pale.

'Yes, a daughter, Emily Rose, she's just over a month old now.'

'I can't quite believe I'm a father.' Alex shook his head. 'So are you married? Did you marry someone else to give my child a father?' Alex looked down at the gold ring on her left hand. 'You still haven't answered my question.'

Marianne shook her head, looking at the ring, which she'd been twisting round and round on her finger. 'I'm not married, it's a lie.' She sighed. 'I did it to protect my child, our child. I didn't want her growing up like I did, being called names and seen as something bad just because her parents weren't married. I went to live and work in the East End so that nobody could question my story, it was safer there.'

'You're really not married?'

She looked up and saw Alex's eyes were bright with tears.

'No, I'm not.'

He sighed. 'When I heard that you were a married women, it ...' He shook his head, swallowing hard as his voice cracked with emotion. 'Marry me, Marianne. Please, marry *me*. I tried to find you when you disappeared, but no one knew where you'd gone. Now I've found you again and we both know the truth, I want you to be my wife. I've never stopped thinking about you and loving you.'

Marianne's eyes met his and they looked at each other for several long moments and then she smiled at him. 'If you really mean what you said, and you really want it, then yes, yes please, I would love to marry you.'

Alex got to his feet and pulled her up and kissed her tenderly before drawing her into his arms and hugging her tightly. 'I love you, Marianne, and that's all that matters to me. You're the woman I want to spend the rest of my life with.'

Marianne rested her head on his chest, not quite believing what had just happened. Knowing that he'd had no intention of doing what his family had wanted and that he intended to marry her because he loved her was wonderful, completely and utterly marvellous.

The sound of a baby crying made them loosen their hold slightly, but still with their arms around each other they turned to look as somebody tapped on the door and then opened it. Thea came in carrying a crying Emily. She took one look at the pair of them and smiled broadly. 'I think this young lady's in need of a feed.'

She came over and gently placed Emily in Marianne's arms and then retreated, leaving the three of them alone.

'This is Emily Rose, your daughter.' Marianne held her out for Alex to take in his arms.

He quickly sat down in a chair and she placed their daughter in his arms then knelt down in front of him.

'She's beautiful, like her mother.' As Alex gently stroked Emily's cheek, the little girl stopped crying and looked at him, her blue eyes focusing intently on his face.

'Emily, this is your daddy,' Marianne said, tears filling her eyes as her family came together for the first time.

'Next week!' Hettie had been about to pour a cup of tea but lowered the teapot on to the table with a loud clunk instead and stared at Marianne. 'You're pulling my leg.'

Marianne glanced at Alex, who sat beside her at the kitchen table holding on to her hand. He winked at her and she smiled back at him before returning her attention to Hettie.

'No, we're quite serious. Alex is going to be posted again and will be leaving for training in two weeks' time and we want to marry before he goes, and have some time together as a family. I know it's short notice, but we don't want anything fancy. The main thing is to get married, that's all that matters after everything that's happened.'

'Where are you thinking of marrying, at St Andrew's Church here in the village?' Thea asked.

Marianne shook her head. 'No, at the registry office in Norwich.'

'You don't need to do that, I'm sure the vicar can fit you in at St Andrew's, even if you do want to do it next week; you'd just have to get a special licence instead of having the banns read,' Hettie said, finally managing to pour out the cups of tea.

'I don't think that would be a good idea.' Marianne passed a cup to Alex and then took one herself. 'I'm supposed to be a married woman already and there are people in the village who'd look upon my . . . fabricated marriage very poorly, and one of those is one of my best customers. I don't want to lose business because of that.'

'You wouldn't need to work,' Alex said. 'I'll be sending you money each week.'

Marianne squeezed his hand. 'I know but I like working, I enjoy designing and making clothes, it's what I'm good at and I don't want to stop, even if I don't do as much as I needed to do before.'

'Well, I think you're wise to avoid stirring up gossip in the village unnecessarily.' Thea poured some milk into her cup of tea and stirred it. 'There are plenty around here who love to judge others, best not to give them any ammunition.' She smiled at them. 'I think the idea of getting married in Norwich is different and rather lovely.'

'Won't people notice when you suddenly change your surname?' Hettie asked.

Marianne hadn't thought of that. Their plans to marry in Norwich would be for nothing if she suddenly went from being Mrs Archer to Mrs Fordham.

'Why not do as the Americans sometimes do?' Alex suggested. 'Tag my surname on the end of yours and then just carry on going by Mrs Archer while you live here, no one need know about the other bit.'

'Good idea,' Thea said.

Marianne nodded. 'Yes, that's what we'll do.'

'What about your wedding dress?' Hettie asked.

'I'll make my own, of course.' Marianne already had ideas of what she'd like, she'd thought about it often over the years when she'd worked in London making dresses for well-heeled young women. She knew what would suit her and didn't want anything fussy or complicated; it would be a rush to get what she wanted done in time, but it was possible. 'We're going to go to Norwich tomorrow to make the arrangements and I'll pay a visit to Gordon Thoday's to buy the fabric.'

Alex put his arm around Marianne's shoulder and she leaned into him, still pinching herself at how events had panned out this afternoon. Little over an hour ago she hadn't considered that she would see Alex again, but her world had suddenly flipped on its axis and here he was back in her life and the pair of them engaged to be married. Their daughter, who was now sleeping happily in the pram again after her feed, would grow up as part of a proper family with parents who were truly married, not with just a mother who had to pretend that she was to protect her daughter.

Chapter 59

'Say something.' Thea urged her sister. She'd just told her about Marianne and Alex getting married next week, the pair of them having gone into Norwich the day before to put the arrangements in place.

'I don't know what to say.' Prue fiddled with the corner of one of the magazines she'd just laid out on the table in preparation for the day club session where she and Thea were on duty. 'I'm shocked.' Her eyes met Thea's. 'I never imagined Marianne would be capable of such a thing, pretending she was married and lying about having a husband off in the Navy.'

'Now don't go getting on your high horse, Prue! Marianne hardly ever spoke about her husband, she wasn't spinning complicated yarns about him and she only did it to protect her unborn child. She'd experienced taunts from others and the stigma of being born illegitimate herself and didn't want her child to suffer the same fate.

People, and especially other children, can be cruel about it, ignoring the fact that having unmarried parents is no fault of the child's. We saw it ourselves when we were at school, remember?'

'But times have changed since then,' Prue said.

Thea sighed. 'In many ways they have, but there are still plenty of people around who are all too happy to judge others harshly and especially in this village. I think Marianne did the right thing, and it wasn't easy for her because she's an honest and genuine young woman.' Thea added some books to the table they were setting out. 'Anyway, Marianne's story will be coming true shortly, so it won't matter any more that she pretended she was married – in a few days' time she will be, and to the father of her child and the man that she loves dearly, and who loves her back.'

'That's all very well.' Prue added some more books to the table. 'But questions will be asked, people will gossip when they see them getting married at the church, because how could someone who's apparently already married get married again? Marianne's secret will be out.'

'They're not getting married here, they've arranged to marry at the registry office in Norwich, and Hettie, Reuben, Edwin and I will be going along to cheer them on. It would be lovely if you would come too?'

Prue suddenly smiled. 'Of course I will, I love weddings. I'm glad that things are working out for Marianne and the baby. Why didn't she marry Alex in the first place?'

'It's complicated.' Thea explained what had happened

to Marianne and how she'd ended up living and working in the East End before being evacuated to Norfolk.

'Poor girl,' Prue said. 'Other people's wants and opinions well and truly got in the way for her. Thank goodness fate brought them back together again. What would have happened to her if it hadn't?'

'She'd have been perfectly fine. Marianne's a very strong and capable young woman,' Thea said. 'She would have provided for them both with her dressmaking and brought up her daughter single-handedly, so now to be reunited with Alex and for them to marry is a bonus.' She smiled warmly. 'Just looking at them together it's clear how much they love each other, despite what's happened, and I'm sure they'll be very happy.' Thea glanced at her watch. 'We'd better get a move on with setting up or the mothers will be here and we won't be ready. I'm glad you're coming with us to see them married, Prue. It wouldn't be the same without you.'

Chapter 60

'There.' Thea adjusted Marianne's short veil and smiled at her. 'You look beautiful, a stunning bride.'

She really was. The dress Marianne had designed and made for herself fitted her exactly. Made from a gorgeous dusky-rose pink silk, it had a scooped neck, long sleeves, a fitted waist and ballerina-length skirt held out with net petticoats. It was simple, but striking, and it suited Marianne perfectly.

'Thank you.' Marianne smiled. 'I'm nervous, but so happy.'

Thea handed her the posy of snowdrops grown in Rookery House's garden. 'You'll be fine.' She touched Marianne's arm and then turned to her brother. 'Are you ready, Reuben?'

He nodded. 'Absolutely.' Marianne had asked him to give her away and he'd been delighted.

'I'd better go and find my seat. I'll see you in there.'

She left them in the foyer and slipped through the heavy wooden doors into the room where the ceremony was to take place, taking a seat beside Hettie who was holding a sleeping Emily Rose in her arms.

'Ready?' Reuben offered Marianne his arm.

She nodded and put her hand on it, she was ready to go and marry the man she loved. Unbelievable as it seemed, after all that had happened to keep them apart, Alex was waiting for her beyond those doors – she was so thankful that they'd found each other again.

She smiled at Reuben. 'Let's go.'

Walking down the short aisle between the rows of chairs towards where Alex waited for her, it didn't matter at all to Marianne how few people there were to see them marry compared with most other weddings. The guests may have been few in number – Hettie, Thea, Edwin, Prue and Lizzie – but each person here was important to her. They sat on the front rows of chairs on each side of the aisle, ignoring the usual tradition of bride's family to the left and groom's to the right, because apart from Charlie, Alex's friend who'd crash-landed near Rookery House, and who was his best man, none of his family were here.

Nearing the front, she smiled at Hettie, who cradled Emily Rose in her arms, and the older woman beamed back at her.

She'd almost drawn level with Alex, who looked so handsome in his RAF uniform, when he turned around to her, and the look he gave her was filled with such love that it took her breath away. There was no doubting how much he loved her, and it filled her with happiness as she stepped forwards to become his wife.

'They make a beautiful couple, don't they?' Thea said, watching the best man taking a photo of Marianne and Alex on the steps of the registry office.

'Yes, and they're clearly very much in love.' Prue linked her arm through Thea's. 'It's a delight to see. Are they off on honeymoon?'

'Of sorts. They're coming back to Rookery House but are going to be staying in Reuben's railway-carriage for the rest of the week before Alex has to return to the RAF. Reuben offered it to them and he's moving into the house for a week,' Thea explained. 'They can have some time together as a family and Alex can get to know where his wife and daughter will be living.'

'That's good of Reuben.'

Thea nodded. 'He's very fond of Marianne and Emily and he likes Alex, too. He wanted to do it as a wedding gift to them and I think it's a perfect one.'

She laughed as Hettie and Edwin threw handfuls of confetti over the bride and groom and the best man caught it on camera. Emily Rose was starting to stir from her sleep, so Thea jiggled the pram to keep her slumbering for just a while longer.

'I didn't expect something like this to happen when I signed up to have an evacuee, you know. I thought I was going to have some little boy or girl to look after.' She caught Prue's eye and smiled at her sister. 'What a stir these expectant mothers have brought to our lives, they've certainly shaken up life in Great Plumstead. Mind you, the village needed it.'

'What do you mean?' Prue asked.

'They've brought fresh views and ways and it's been a delight to see it. You can't say you haven't enjoyed having them, Prue.'

Her sister tried to look serious for a moment and then smiled at her. 'Of course I have. After the initial shock of their arrival it's been, on the whole, a pleasure to have them and get to know them. Life wouldn't be the same without them, and I rather like the changes they've brought and what we've done because of them.'

'Come on, you two,' Hettie called. 'We need you in the photo and then we can go to Lizzie's house. There's wedding cake waiting there for us.'

Thea scooped the stirring Emily out of the pram and she and Prue joined the rest of the wedding party on the steps and smiled for the camera as the moment was captured on film.

She'd meant what she'd said to Prue: the coming of the evacuee expectant mothers because of the war had been like a breath of fresh air in their lives, and she wouldn't have missed it for the world. What changes to their lives would the war bring next? she wondered.

Dear Reader,

I hope you've enjoyed reading Marianne's story and getting to know the new characters and setting. The idea for this book was sparked by a document I found in the archives of London's Imperial War Museum several years ago when I was researching for another novel. It was an account of what happened to an evacuee expectant mother on 3 September 1939, who heard that war had been declared as she was walking to a station with other evacuees. Moments later the air-raid siren had sounded, and despite fearing they were about to be bombed they kept on going. This was such a powerful image I knew I wanted to write a story inspired by it and finally, several years later, here it is!

Before I came across this account, I had no idea that expectant mothers were evacuated as we mainly tend to hear about the thousands of children who were moved to the safety of the countryside. I hope that by writing this book these expectant mothers will not be forgotten.

Great Plumstead is actually entirely fictitious, although I have borrowed the name from a parish in Norfolk because I love the sound of it, and my village is sited in a different part of the county. It's set north of Norwich, halfway between the city and the coast, and not far from my imaginary market town of Wykeham, which is similar to the many market towns of the area such as Reepham and Aylsham.

Rookery House is partly inspired by the Victorian house in which I grew up, and other similar ones in the village. I merged them in my imagination to make Thea's house. For quite a while I didn't know what to call it, but when I was walking home from the beach one day I looked out across the field to watch the rooks that feed there and the words 'Rookery House' popped into my mind and I knew it was the perfect name.

I love hearing from readers — it's one of the greatest joys of being a writer — so please do get in touch via:

Facebook: Rosie Hendry Books

Twitter @hendry_rosie

www.rosiehendry.com (where you can sign up to get my newsletter delivered straight to your Inbox, with all the latest on my writing life and exclusive looks behind the scenes of my work and competitions).

If you have the time, and would like to share your thoughts about The Mother's Day Club, *do please leave a review. I read and appreciate each one as it's wonderful to hear what you think and it helps inform other readers who might be interested in Marianne's story.*

Watch out for Thea, Prue, Hettie and co returning in the next book, The Mother's Day Victory, *where our old friends from the East End Angels will be back for a brief visit, too.*

With warmest wishes,

Rosie

Acknowledgements

This book is a complete change from the London streets of the East End Angel series, and I've headed back to my home turf in Norfolk. It has been a joy to set my story in a place I love and know so well.

Many people have helped me with my research into wartime Norfolk – a big thank you to the volunteers at Reepham Archive and Aylsham Heritage Centre and Archives for their support, Norfolk Library Service for supplying many research books, and the Imperial War Museum in London for access to recorded oral histories and documents.

My mum patiently answered my many questions about life in rural Norfolk in the Second World War – thank you.

The team at Sphere have done a magnificent job in bringing the book together. Thank you to my editor Maddie West, and also to Tamsyn Berryman, Alison

Tulett, Rachel Cross, Bekki Guyatt, Francesca Banks and Brionee Fenlon.

Thank you to my fabulous agent, Felicity Trew, who listens so well and supports me through the ups and downs.

My fellow writers are a great support and I appreciate their friendship, company, wise words and listening ears. Thank you especially to Pam Brooks, Victoria Connelly, Elaine Everest, Fiona Ford, Jean Fullerton, Jenni Keer, Lizzie Lamb, Clare Marchant, Heidi-Jo Swain, Claire Wade and Ian Wilfred. Belonging to the RNA's Norfolk and Suffolk chapter and the Strictly Saga Group is a great joy – thank you all.

Finally, thank you to David, who listens and supports me with all I do.